ALICE BELL

Displeasure Island

Alice Bell grew up in South West England, in the sort of middle-of-nowhere where teenagers spend their weekends drinking Smirnoff Ice in a field that also has at least one horse in it. In 2018 she became the deputy editor of Rock Paper Shotgun, a popular PC gaming website. In 2019 she was named one of the one hundred most influential women in the UK games industry. After spending several years in London, Bell now lives in Cork, Ireland, where she watches giant ships, makes crochet animals, and plays video games where you can set things on fire and make elves kiss. She has probably read more detective fiction and watched more episodes of *Midsomer Murders* than you. Her debut cozy crime novel, *Grave Expectations*, came out in 2023.

ALSO BY ALICE BELL

Grave Expectations

Displeasure Island

Displeasure Island

ALICE BELL

VINTAGE BOOKS

A DIVISION OF PENGUIN RANDOM HOUSE LLC

NEW YORK

Library of Congress Cataloging-in-Publication Data
Names: Bell, Alice (Gaming website editor), author.
Title: Displeasure island / Alice Bell.
Description: First edition. | New York : Vintage Books,
a division of Penguin Random House LLC, 2024.
Identifiers: LCCN 2023054429 (print) | LCCN 2023054430 (ebook)
Subjects: LCGFT: Cozy mysteries. | Ghost stories. | Novels.
Classification: LCC PR6102.E435125 D57 2024 (print) |
LCC PR6102.E435125 (ebook) | DDC 823/.92—dc23
LC record available at https://lccn.loc.gov/2023054429
LC ebook record available at https://lccn.loc.gov/2023054430

Vintage Books Trade Paperback ISBN: 978-0-593-47065-7
eBook ISBN: 978-0-593-47066-4

Map by Jeff Edwards
Book design by Nicholas Alguire

vintagebooks.com

Printed in the United States of America
10 9 8 7 6 5 4 3 2 1

To the Word Appreciation Pals:

Harry, Rules, Deano, and No Relation
"It's better to light a candle than curse the Peter."

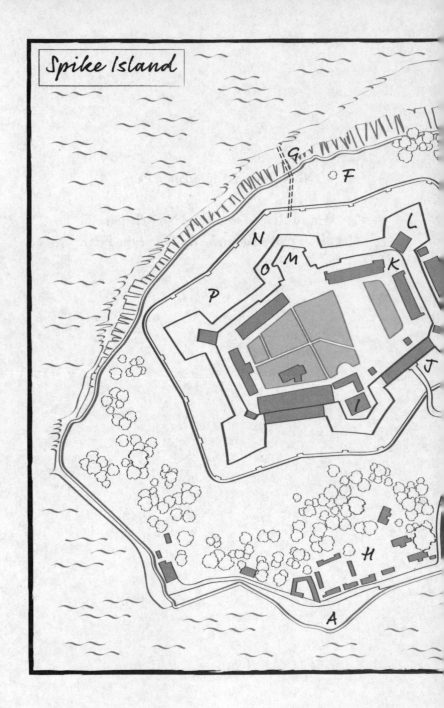

Ferry Point Pier

Key

A. Beach where dead bodies are not supposed to show up and ruin your holiday
B. Schoolmaster's house with tree in chimney
C. Pillbox and small beach
D. Sports ground that is actually big field
E. Convict cemetery (avoid)
F. Bones's tree
G. Grim smuggling tunnel under walls
H. Abandoned village and hotel
I. Punishment block
J. Fort's main gates
K. Burned-out prison blocks
L. Opportunists' lookout
M. Lookout with creepy room underneath it
N. Outer wall
O. Inner wall
P. Dry moat (dangerous)

Displeasure Island

I

A Crime Scene

The exhaust fan whirred with gentle insistence. Claire peered into the bathroom from the doorway, leaning a bit awkwardly to avoid stepping over the threshold. It was a shocking sight. The bathroom was tiled in white over all four walls, the ceiling, and the floor. Claire had always hated the claustrophobic design: it made her feel like she was inside a giant tooth.

But today every shining white surface was spattered with red. There were small dots, smeary streaks, little bits of spray that looked like they came from an aerosol can. There were even long, elegant, looping lines that dripped down, like you'd see on the more lurid kind of police procedural show (which was obviously Claire's favorite kind). There were red spots on the bottles of shampoo and conditioner, on the white shower curtain pulled halfway around the bath, and on the narrow mirror reflecting the scene back double. Everywhere you looked you saw more. The taps, the hand towel, the soap. Like noticing an ant on a paving slab, and, as you relax your eyes, suddenly becoming aware of dozens of them over the entire pavement. All the spatter in a bright, deep arterial red.

A body was lying half in and half out of the bath. Legs and a skinny bum in similarly skinny—and offensively lime green— jeans were hanging out over the side and partially splayed over the fluffy white bath mat, while the head, wedged against the bottom of the bath, and torso were slumped on the inside.

There was a rush of cool air as Sophie, Claire's closest friend and constant companion for more than fifteen years, stepped past Claire and into the room. She whistled.

"I'm impressed," she said. "This mess is, like, comprehensive. LOL." Sophie pronounced it *el-oh-el*. She looked around the bathroom with interest, the action setting the chestnut curls of her hair dancing in their tight, high ponytail. She wore a turquoise velour tracksuit of the kind that was popular among teenage girls in the early-to-mid noughties, and the acid brightness of the color against the white walls, the green legs, and the red splatter made Claire wince. She'd finished off a bottle of white wine the night before, plowing on despite the fact that it had started to go a bit vinegary. It wasn't really an ideal morning to confront . . . *this*.

"You need some of those little crime scene booties. Come and have a look, weirdo," said Soph, beckoning her in.

Claire stepped gingerly around the sticky marks on the floor. It was a small room and there was barely enough space for them both to fit around the legs that cut across most of it. Claire looked into the tub and saw that the inside was almost completely red, turning rosy at the sides as it faded out against the white of the bath. A bottle of vodka was turned over next to a lifeless, pale pink hand.

Basher was still standing in the doorway. He had been a fairly seasoned police officer, a detective and everything, before quitting a couple of years ago. Now he held his hand over his mouth.

"It is . . . just . . . barbaric," he murmured in his peculiarly deep, soft voice. "I cannot even conceive of how this happened. The white will never be properly white again."

"Yes," agreed Sophie. "It's going to leave some stubborn stains, for sure."

"Yeah, this tooth . . . has got some serious gum disease," said Claire.

The other two stared at her.

"Because . . . because the room is like . . . Er. Never mind."

"Ohmigod. Every day I question the decision to let you out in public, weirdo," said Sophie.

"Well. Um. Anyway," said Claire. "Why did you call, Bash?"

"Because," said Basher. He paused to sigh and rub his eyes in frustration. This was a habitual gesture, Claire had noted, as he spent much of his life frustrated in one way or another. "Because I tried a couple of times, but it seems I am not up to moving a dead weight by myself. Being completely honest, I found them slumped on the floor. They are only in the bath because I dropped them. You are the only person I could think of to call for help who would not be . . ."

"Judgey?" suggested Soph.

"Too sensible to say no?" said Claire.

"You have to admit that this is not the strangest thing that we have dealt with together," Basher said. Claire noted that there were dark hollows under his gray eyes. He looked more tired than usual.

"Can't we just leave them there?" she asked. She was not a fan of physical activity, and this sounded suspiciously like it would require a lot of effort. Plus, she didn't want to get red on her clothes. She was wearing the first new jumper she'd bought in ages and it was a pale sage color that wouldn't do well, given the circumstances.

"We cannot. Because that would be incredibly irresponsible. If you help me you can have a cup of tea and a custard cream."

"Ugh. Two cups of tea and at least four custard creams."

"*One* cup of tea and two chocolate digestives."

". . . Yeah, all right. But I'm taking the legs."

"That seems fair."

Claire and Basher maneuvered around one another, so he could grab the body in the bath under the armpits and she could hoist up the ankles. In this way they managed to roll the body over and out of the bath, and then carry it down the hall, where Basher nudged a door open with his foot to reveal a room that was possibly a bedroom and possibly an explosion at a charity shop.

They alley-ooped the body onto the heap of clothes that was covering the bed. The body rolled over onto its side and started snoring.

Basher, quite tenderly, smoothed away the damp strings of newly red hair, revealing the pale, delicate features of Alex. Basher was Alex's uncle, but had been in theoretical loco parentis since Alex had moved in with him in lieu of going to university. The position had been recently solidified, owing to the fact that almost all of the rest of their family, the Wellington-Forges, had been arrested on suspicion of murder about six months before. Basher and Alex had started going by the last name Forge to disassociate themselves from the whole thing, which was understandable.

Alex was only nineteen but had inherited the fine, high-cheeked bone structure that ran in their family, and the soft gray eyes their maternal great-grandmother had also given to Basher. Alex, who still had a bit of growing to do, was already cultivating the kind of good looks that could be described by modeling agents as "ethereal." The good looks were only partially diminished by open-mouthed hangover drooling. Owing to Alex's teenage propensity to get blackout drunk and dye their hair whatever color they wanted sometime around 3:00 a.m., they could also easily be pigeonholed as "alternative."

Claire eyed Alex with a little concern. "Er. Do we need to put them in the recovery position or something?"

"I don't think so," said Basher. He leaned over and jabbed Alex in the side a couple of times. They made a noise that sounded like "geafucffzs" and rolled onto their other side. "I think it would be all right to leave them be. I will check on them later."

"Okay. You owe me some biscuits."

Basher raised his hands in a gesture of defeat, then stuffed them into the front pocket of his faded blue hoodie and sauntered off to the kitchen. Alex loved color and unusual combinations in their clothes, but Basher dressed to disappear into the background, all sun-faded hoodies and tattered jeans. Claire's own vibe was, she self-assessed, sort of scene kid in '06 trying to fit in at the office: badly maintained bottle-black hair with about two inches of roots at all times, old boots, skinny jeans ripped at the knees, but amorphous sensible jumpers on top. She had a lot of warm jumpers.

Claire followed Basher, after beckoning Sophie away from peering at the new odds and ends on Alex's desk. Their room was like a tidal pool for general art *stuff*, with new things appearing and disappearing all the time—although they stuck most faithfully to embroidery and altering clothes.

The three currently conscious occupants of the flat waited for

the kettle to subside, an ancient and, Claire suspected, demoni-
cally possessed machine, which spat and roared but which
Basher insisted was very well made and would last for years yet
if he descaled it regularly.

"Aw look," said Sophie. She was watching Basher pour out
two mugs of tea. "He's using the one you got him. See, maybe
he doesn't actually think you're the worst person in the world!"

Claire had found the mug in a charity shop. It said:

IF IT BE THUS TO DREAM, STILL LET ME SLEEP!!!

There was a picture of a mug of coffee underneath the quote.
The little mug of coffee was smiling and blushing, and though it
was clearly coffee, there was also a tea bag label hanging out of
it. The label had a heart on it. The quote was from the character
Sebastian, from *Twelfth Night*. Basher—whose actual first name
was Sebastian also—loved Shakespeare, which was why Claire
had bought it (and it was a very confusing mug, which was the
other reason she had bought it).

"So. Er. How is the sale on the Cloisters going?" Claire asked,
referring to what was technically Basher and Alex's ancestral
home, which had been left to Basher by his grandmother, skipping his parents. Because of the aforementioned murder issue,
the Cloisters had become a crime scene, and Basher was not
enjoying being the owner. He'd also found out that the family was property rich but cash poor, and was trying to reverse
this.

"Not too terribly, I have to admit, although it was always going
to take quite a long time," said Basher. He pulled the sleeves of
his hoodie down to cover most of his hands, and wrapped them
around the mug. "I thought Mum might try and block a final

sale, but I think they all have other things on their minds at present, so I'm clear to accept the hotel's offer."

"The lower one, is it?" said Claire. Basher nodded. Owing to the aforementioned crime scene status, the hotel that had initially offered to buy the estate had lowered their offer on the basis that murder goes in the column marked *CONS* rather than *PROS*. The back-and-forth had been all he'd talked about for weeks.

"So you're having to decide whether to make a quick buck now and get it over with, or hold out for more in the long term," summed up Sophie.

"Yes. I am a toddler with a marshmallow. I can eat it now, or wait around for the possibility of two marshmallows from someone else. But in this instance, it is a marshmallow that causes significant psychological distress the longer I go without eating it."

"What does Alex say?" asked Claire.

"They just keep laughing and suggesting I 'kick that sour-faced old git in the balls,' the sour-faced old git in question being the representative of the hotel chain. I have explained that assaulting the other negotiating party is not the way to resolve a financial conflict. Or indeed any conflict."

Claire wasn't sure about this. She had always wondered why people didn't do this more in movies or on TV. Many times in *Murder Profile* (her favorite TV show, in which a team of universally perky and quirky FBI agents tracked down wizened gnomes who committed weird murders, which they insisted weren't about sex but were definitely quite a lot about sex) had an agent been locked in a life-and-death struggle with a perp over a gun. It always seemed to her that the situation would be very easily resolved by one party punching the other in the dick. Nobody cared about realism in cinema anymore.

"History is written by the victors, Basher," she suggested. "Nobody need know you kicked him in the balls."

"I fear it would easily be found out. And in any case, I would know. Either way, I am leaning toward taking the low offer, just to be done with it all."

The only things Basher had rescued from the Cloisters were some Royal Doulton porcelain figurines, and a rose plant dug up from the garden. It now lived in a big pot in the corner of the living room, where it was constantly in bloom with large, preternaturally beautiful flowers.

Basher watched Claire stuff a biscuit into her mouth, sighed, and got a small plate out of a cupboard. He held it under her chin like she was a child, until eventually she rolled her eyes and took it.

Basher, much to his growing and often loudly stated chagrin, and despite the fact that Claire was a couple of years older than him, was sloping into the role of being their little group's dad. He was just sort of naturally a middle-aged librarian: he was clean, read a lot of books, watched documentaries about art theft, had opinions about biscuits, went to great lengths to crowbar Shakespeare quotes into conversation in a way that made you want to drive a thin blade into his kidneys, and was basically a decent person. Thinking about it, there probably *were* a bunch of librarians who shaved their heads and dressed like nineties skaters with depression—and Basher took pills for that, from a weekly organizer Alex had made him. It was covered with diverse and lovingly sculpted penises made from polymer clay.

They went into the living room, where Basher put a coaster under Claire's cup as she set it down. Sophie, already bored again, went to look out of the windows. They were almost floor to ceiling, and since every other flat on the street had similar ones, Sophie could easily gawp into other people's front rooms.

"While you're here anyway, Strange . . ." said Basher, watching with a slightly alarmed expression as Claire forced another digestive into her mouth like an anaconda swallowing a piglet. "There is something else I have to ask you. Or possibly tell you."

"Those are very different verbs," said Claire with some difficulty.

"Yes, true." Basher sighed. "Hmm. Where to start. So, as you know, Alex and I were left some money by our grandmother. No, wait. Let me back up further. As you are aware, almost all of mine and Alex's family are out on bail pending a murder trial."

"Yes."

"Big LOLs," added Sophie.

"You might not be aware that if pretrial is dragging on, you sometimes have to have repeat bail hearings every few months."

"Right. And?"

"And the next bail hearing for most of them is coming up. And Alex has decided they don't want to be anywhere near the proceedings, and that they need some time away."

"Probably wise," said Claire, nodding.

"Oooh, maybe he wants us to house-sit!" said Sophie.

"What? Why would he want us to house-sit?"

"Alex is nineteen years old and dealing with an ongoing, fraught emotional situation. Benders at home are fine, but I am not currently sanctioning remote benders with other nineteen-year-olds," Basher went on, unperturbed.

"Really? I mean, Alex is technically an adult," said Claire, aware that even if she did want to accidentally co-parent, she wouldn't even know where to start.

"Yes, and you also just had to help me move them from my absolutely ruined bathroom and hoy them onto their bed," replied Basher. His tone was very even. Maddeningly reasonable, in fact. "They have had weekends away before and will again. I just prefer to be with them right now. Which is where the compromise comes in." Basher had spread his hands in supplication.

"Ohmigod," said Sophie, who was beginning to grin. She had always been quicker on the uptake than Claire.

"So, er . . . What is the compromise?" Claire asked.

"The compromise is that, if Alex has to go on a trip with me, instead of four days in Greece with their friends, then they would like to invite you as well. On the basis that I am not fun, whereas you are much *more* fun."

Basher looked embarrassed. Claire maintained eye contact until he looked away.

"Um. They didn't say I was fun, did they?"

Basher sighed. "I confess that no, they did not."

"No, they didn't!" echoed Sophie, hopping from one foot to the other. She started to giggle.

"They said Sophie was fun, didn't they?"

"Yes. Sorry."

"People used to say that at school too," said Sophie. She was outright laughing now.

"Ugh. Well I'm not saying yes," Claire started to say.

"You bloody are! I'm bored off my tits!" shouted Sophie.

"Oh shut up," Claire snapped back. "You don't get a say."

"Yeah technically, but you know I'll make your life a misery if you don't say yes."

Basher watched Claire with one eyebrow raised, and waited patiently.

"*Anyway*," she said, turning back to Basher, "I'm not saying yes, but where would we be going? I'm not up for day-long flights out of the country." And also, she added to herself, could not afford one.

"How would you feel about hour-long flights out of the country?" asked Basher. "I assume you've heard of Ireland."

Claire had. It was one of those countries that she said "oh, I've always wanted to go there!" about, but when it came down to it that was a lie because Ireland was right *there*, and the flights were so cheap and short that the plane barely had time to get in the air before it was time to land again, and yet she still hadn't been.

Basher sorted through the mess of the coffee table, which was always a mixture of piles of books (which he was either reading, had just finished reading, or was thinking about reading, rotated in and out on an hourly to weekly basis) and small drifts of Alex-ephemera that had escaped from their room. Eventually he located a foldy-outy brochure. On the front was a glossy drone-shot of an island in a jewel-blue sea—a largely grassy place but with some trees near the bottom shoreline, and what looked like a flat, star-shaped castle in the middle. On top of this picture was printed *SPIKE ISLAND WELLNESS RETREAT* in a font that was sort of going for "modern" and sort of going for "rustic and/or Celtic," and landing, as a result of this collision of influences, on "confused." It seemed likely the graphic designer had given up on the brief after getting increasingly conflicting feedback from the client, because this was all the front of the leaflet said, though there was an inset photograph of what looked like some very small whitewashed terraced cottages. Claire flipped it open, in the spirit of inquiry. So the front had, she supposed, sort of worked.

Inside were photos of people laughing in a hot tub and people laughing while doing yoga at sunset and people laughing while standing in the doorway of one of the aforementioned cottages. Some more text further explained that Spike Island was a famous and very historical prison-slash-fort, now home to a newly updated and refurbished wellness retreat.

"It is a small island, just off the coast," said Basher. "The prison bit is a tourist attraction, and had an attached quaint village where the workers used to live with their families, which was falling into picturesque ruin. Whoever owns it sold some of those buildings, which have been refitted and rebranded as a lovely getaway, with many added relaxing activities and luxurious catering and so on."

"Oh, cool," said Claire, brightening up. She was currently living in a tiny flat near Brighton station that was incredibly cheap and had bills included, because it was a windowless basement underneath a newsagent and even during a housing crisis including bills was the only way the landlord could get anyone to live there. Everyone leaving the newsagent's used her stairwell as a bin, so she had to walk through a drift of Twix wrappers and empty Fanta cans. A spa break didn't sound the worst.

"Yes. Of course, we would be going in a couple of weeks, in the off season, when it is a small island hotel with most of the facilities shut down, for much cheaper."

"Oh. Right," said Claire, returning to normal luminosity. She folded out the last page in the leaflet. "An island with a dark history!" she read aloud.

"Yes, it is actually quite interesting. It has a storied past, because Cork harbor would be a very good way to invade Ireland, and Spike Island is right in the middle of it, making it an attractive strategic property. Hence: fort. Then it was a prison. Before all of that it was some species of monastery. I believe what has most interested Alex is a story that the Spanish Armada sailed all the way around Scotland and Ireland and lost a lot of ships along the way, and"—here he waved his hand vaguely—"there are rumors that maybe one was sunk near this island. Or possibly a pirate ship. Lost treasure, et cetera. They have been looking online."

"Not sure I believe all of that," murmured Claire, reading a story about how lamps were tied to donkeys' arses to trick ships during storms. She squinted at a small map printed farther down the page. "I mean, I knew about the Armada but I'm not sure wherever this island is would be the right area at all for that. And most people doubt wreckers actually ever existed, anyway. There's no contemporaneous evidence of people doing it. It's a cool story, though."

"I always forget you studied history," said Basher. "Whatever the case, Alex thinks it sounds very exciting."

"Oh right, I see," said Soph. "I bet you a million pounds the island is still haunted by lads searching for their lost treasure, or whatever, and Alex wants us all to go on a treasure hunt without thinking that it would in fact end in us sitting about getting rained on, on an island we can't leave. I'm in. That sounds mega fun. Or at least, more fun than moping around Brighton with you."

"There *are* apparently a lot of ghosts," said Basher. "So perhaps one more can't hurt?"

Claire sighed and looked at Sophie. She was standing in the sunlight beaming through the windows, so she was washed out and almost see-through—but still very clearly sticking her tongue out at Claire.

"Oh," said Claire, "I think you'd be surprised."

2

Have Ghost, Will Travel

They took off from Gatwick at 9:25 a.m. on Tuesday morning and landed at Cork Airport a scant hour and a bit later, a short flight that was still long enough to demonstrate they were all very different fliers. Claire had only been on an airplane a couple of times in her life, and found the whole thing very exciting; Alex was the type of relaxed flier who would get to the gate a minute before it closed; and Basher was extremely nervous and sat bolt upright, fists clenched in his lap, for the entire flight. Similarly, Claire had a black-and-white checkerboard Vans rucksack, which Alex had got her as a present, and a scruffy holdall for anything that wouldn't fit in the rucksack; Alex was lugging a suitcase with broken wheels and a zip held closed by safety pins, and which was so full it was seriously in danger of triggering an extra weight payment; while Bash had a compact, gray case that conformed exactly to flight regulations.

Sophie, of course, traveled very light, and had to sit in the aisle.

Claire was the only person who could see or hear Sophie,

which was inconvenient, because it meant she had to relay everything Sophie said. Unless she decided she wanted to edit her, Claire spent a lot of time repeating Sophie so she could be involved in, for example, discussions of islands and buried treasure. Claire did not edit Sophie that often because each instance was followed by between twelve and thirty seconds of Sophie complaining about being edited, which tended to drag conversations out.

Historically, Sophie had been something of a barrier to Claire forming long-term relationships of any kind, but luckily Basher and Alex had actually caught a glimpse of Soph once. It had been during a storm and at night, though, and would have been very easy to put down to a trick of the light, so while Alex enthusiastically believed, Claire sometimes thought that Basher was humoring her when he talked to or about Soph.

Claire, however, was in no doubt that Sophie existed. She had been haunting Claire for a long time, ever since she'd disappeared when they were both seventeen, and then reappeared as a ghost only Claire could see, right in the middle of a candlelit vigil for . . . herself. Claire and Sophie were still the only two people who knew that she'd been murdered—well, three, including whoever had done it—but Sophie couldn't remember any of what had happened to her. Neither of them particularly liked to think about the circumstances. (The murderer, if Claire's favorite TV shows were any indication, probably did like to think about it, and kept Sophie's head in a jar in the fridge, but she thought it would be in bad taste to mention this to Soph.)

Fortunately, or very unfortunately, depending on what mood Claire was in, Sophie's return meant that Claire was suddenly able to see and hear all the ghosts hanging around everywhere. This meant she was able to become a medium. She was a mostly unpopular one, who didn't have a slot on talk radio or a twenty-four-hour TV channel, because she was a bit too matter of fact about the whole thing and didn't even have a crystal ball, but she did make enough to pay for rent, pasta, and cigarettes. Slightly more pasta than usual, now that Alex had persuaded Claire to move out of London and down to Brighton.

The downside, of course, was the actual seeing of ghosts. It was probably more accurate to say that Claire had to become a medium, because being able to see ghosts rendered her too weird and distracted to do anything else.

Initially her new enforced psychic status had come with all the therapy and angst that you'd expect. When it had first started happening, Claire had told her parents, and they naturally assumed she was having some kind of grief-related breakdown. But now, after so many years, the seeing-ghosts thing was mostly very annoying. Claire found the majority of ghosts to be morose, but desperate to tell her why because they didn't have many people to talk to; there are also more ghosts in general than people would be comfortable knowing about, so Claire was very good at avoiding eye contact. She had specific issues with Sophie just always being around, but these were different and complex and did not bear talking about. It is very hard to, for example, successfully close a date if a dead seventeen-year-old is watching you, let alone any furtive and even more private nocturnal activities. Sophie's response would, no doubt, be that she never even got the chance, and wasn't that a terrible thing for someone who was perpetually seventeen but also thirty-two?

Making and keeping friends was something of an unknown quantity to Claire. As soon as she said she was a medium, the people who tried to self-select into Claire's life were quite intense. Many of them were people who claimed to be mediums as well, but the fact that they couldn't see or hear Sophie when she was sticking the Vs up right in front of their faces meant Claire realized that they were actually liars. The people who tried to self-select out of Claire's life assumed she was one, too.

But also, she just didn't make great company. Claire was prone to: binge drinking cheap cider; binge drinking cheap spirits; binge watching the same police procedurals and true crime documentaries, repeatedly, in cycles; chain smoking; biting her nails; eating different kinds of instant noodles for all meals; not washing up her bowls of instant noodles; general antisocial hermitry; suppressing all intense emotion, be that negative or positive, and therefore coming across as completely detached; anxiety; and not changing her pillowcases often enough. She also talked to thin air and always had very cold hands.

Claire said that all these things and more were because of Sophie haunting her. The last two definitely were, at any rate.

Now, though, Claire was dealing with having the sort of friendship where you got invited on a holiday. She was unsure how you were supposed to behave in this situation.

"Ohmigod," said Sophie, as they wheeled and/or hauled their way out to the airport bus stop. "Remember when we went on that school trip to France, and they'd just brought the rules in, and that utter bastard threw away my new liquid eyeliner?" Claire did. It was a grievance Sophie had brought up for weeks afterward, and every eighteen months or so in the years since. You don't collect that many new grievances when you're dead.

"Don't look now," she added, "but our designated grown-up looks like he's going to be sick."

Basher did indeed look green around the proverbials. Claire hesitated, then squeezed his shoulder. "Um. You all right?"

Basher nodded, thin-lipped, in reply.

Alex looked up from their phone. "Poor Uncle B is like the soft fruit of your choice. Doesn't travel well. He's a little stress ball basically the whole day of a flight. I should be more sympathetic, but he woke me up at five a.m. to check I knew where my passport was."

"Did you?" said Claire.

"Not at all!" replied Alex cheerfully. "Found it in the end, though. Anyway, he won't be happy again until he's had a shower and a biscuit at the other end, which won't be for a while 'cause according to his terrifically anal schedule we have to get a bus and a train and a boat first."

"What, really?" asked Sophie.

"How did you think we were getting to an island? Did he not email Claire his whole itinerary? He even printed one out for me. I'm being dramatic, it's only an hour from here."

They fished a bit of paper out from their pocket. They were wrapped in their favorite black faux-fur coat, and it fairly crackled with static. The disastrous dye session from a few weeks before had taken well, and the bright blood red of their messily tied-back hair contrasted with the coat to great effect. They also appeared to have a five-o'clock shadow, and Claire couldn't tell if it was by accident or design, but either way it was adding to the elegant-yet-distressed vibe of someone who had just crawled out of a coffin after a hundred years and wanted to join a rock band. Alex held out the paper so Soph could read it, too, which was the sort of thing they regularly did that made them Sophie's favorite.

"Jesus, all this to get there?" Claire said.

They did indeed have to get the bus, then transfer onto a train for a half-hour journey somewhere else, and then wait to meet someone called E. McGrath in a town right on the mouth of the wide estuary. The Mystery McGrath would take them on a boat out to Spike Island, which was off the coast, but still inside the harbor enough to not count as being properly in the sea.

"You're crossing the fucking Rubicon," Soph went on. "Has anyone ever come back from that place alive? How do you know you're not going to be turned into some kind of human-pig hybrid by a reclusive scientist?"

"Would make no never mind to you," murmured Claire, hoping nobody noticed her talking to herself.

"It would be very boring. At least—" Soph paused to consider, and tipped her head on one side, sending the shining curls of her high ponytail falling over one shoulder. "Huh. Can't decide if you'd be more or less dull as a little piglet."

Claire stuck her tongue out in lieu of a ruder response.

It would not be ideal to be hybridized, because when Sophie got bored she had a habit of shouting in Claire's ear or loudly singing poorly remembered song lyrics (out of tune) until Claire paid her attention.

Fortunately, the bus and train journeys were short enough that she didn't completely go off on one, and after another couple of hours they decanted from a train onto a single-platform red-brick station that looked directly out onto the water. It was very sunny, with fluffy white clouds scudding across a blue sky. Following the directions on Basher's phone took them down the road into a ridiculously picturesque seaside town, with houses along a broad, curved street each painted in a different color. There were cobblestones, and a park with a bandstand right on the water's edge—and the top of a tall spire looming over everything, which gave Claire a bit of the Fear, as if she had a hangover.

Alex insisted they were starving to death, but Basher was keen to finish the journey and said they could eat at the hotel.

They followed him to the end of a T-shaped pier that formed one wall of a little square harbor.

"He's going to be sick," said Soph.

Claire glanced sideways at Bash. He was paler than usual and there appeared to be a cold sweat on his forehead. She hesitated, but then patted his forearm in what she hoped was a reassuring way. This was not as fraught an action as it would have been even six months before, when Claire had been nursing a crush on Basher and touching him would have made her twitchy and excited. He was, it was fair to say, a good-looking man, even if it was by accident; he constantly had, for example, a kind of catwalk-ready stubble highlighting his cut jaw, but this was because he was blond and didn't shave much, not because he thought it looked good. But whatever else he was, Basher was also gay, which Claire had discovered through the surprisingly expedient method of trying to kiss him. Rerouting her feelings toward friendship had been quite easy for Claire, as it turned out, and left only a lingering feeling of catastrophic embarrassment.

"This town is fascinating you know. It's a shame we can't stay here longer. I thought you would have heard of it already, C. It's right up your street, all history and that," said Alex.

"Um. It's not like I know all of recorded human history," said Claire.

"Well, whatever, I looked it up as part of my research into the area," they went on. "This was the last port of call for the *Titanic*. Next stop: bottom of the Atlantic. Isn't that bananas? And there's loads of other wrecks and stuff around this coast. *Lusitania* sank sort of around the corner, and all the bodies were brought here."

"Oh. Yikes. It sounds like we actually are lucky there aren't loads of depressed deados hanging around. Apart from the one I bring with me."

"I'm not depressed," protested Soph. "I'm, like, totally affable. I'm affable as fuck."

Basher snorted when Claire repeated this. "If Claire's reportage of your comments is accurate, I would say you have a tendency to be quite . . . barbed."

"See, Basher has only known you a matter of months and he can already tell you're a terrible bitch."

"You need me and you know it, weirdo," said Soph, her voice even. "Ask Alex about the treasure. Nobody has explained the pirate treasure aspect yet."

"Oh lord, don't ask them about that," said Basher. He ran a hand over his face. "They won't shut up about it."

"Well actually I am *so* glad you asked, because—"

Alex suddenly fell silent, because a man had arrived. The arrival was so silent, it was as if he had stepped out of thin air, in defiance of all known physics. Previously there had been no man. Now, here was man. He had a big, fulsome but tidy chestnut beard, correspondingly bushy brows over dark brown eyes, and, as if in deliberate contrast, a close-cropped haircut. His nose prevailed right, from about halfway up the bridge, in a way that suggested it had been soundly broken at some point. In general, he projected an aura of gruffness; it said that here is a fella—definitely fella as opposed to man, and definitely not boy—who does not have time for your shit, no matter what it might be. He looked down at Basher, standing a head taller than him and Claire.

"How's it going? Forge, is it?" Claire realized he'd said, after about a second and a half of processing.

Like many, or indeed all English people, Claire's experience of Irish accents was limited to—

CATEGORY: Northern Ireland;

CATEGORY: Dublin comma Bob Geldof shouting;

CATEGORY: Dublin comma Andrew Scott shouting;

CATEGORY: Dublin comma Colin Farrell frowning;

and SUBCATEGORY: Americans doing accents in film and television.

The Cork accent presented a new and unfamiliar option. It was very sing-song, the sounds rising and falling around the central thread of the words like a chirruping nursery rhyme, and always hooking up at the end of the sentence. It was the Australian accent of Irish accents. The bigger issue was that everyone they'd spoken to in Cork so far also spoke very quickly indeed. It took time for Claire's brain to catch up, and she felt like she was on a satellite delay.

The man seemed content to wait, though, and pulled a rollup from behind his ear. He tried to light it with a fitzing lighter. Basher looked nonplussed.

"Er . . ." Claire tried. "Hello . . . Mr. McGrath . . . ?"

This turned out to be the wrong and right answer simultaneously, because he nodded but also grimaced.

"Jesus. Just call me Eidy, would you?"

Claire thought she'd also seen the minute eyebrow raise and seamless transition to talking slightly more slowly that she'd noticed in other locals the instant they registered her own accent. It seemed they all came with a separate setting for talking to English people.

Alex held their own lighter up, deployed with their most winning smile and the practiced ease of someone who definitely pulled this move on people outside nightclubs. The man took it, but exchanged it for what Claire assessed to be a quite ungrateful "Thanks a mill" as he lit up.

"Christ," said Soph, regarding him critically. "What a barrel of fucking laughs. Odds on him drowning us all in the bay?"

Claire did not repeat this. Even if they hadn't been in public, she did not repeat Sophie's assessments of most people, because, as Basher had noted, even if they were insightful, they were also often cruel, especially about people she liked.

"Right, er, Eidy. I'm Claire, that's Alex. And Basher." She pointed, for clarity.

Eidy looked at her. He took a drag on his cigarette, shot the smoke out of one side of his mouth.

"It's, um. It's short for Sebastian."

"Okay."

Claire realized that both Sophie and Alex were snickering, and, in a rare turn of events, it was Basher who rolled his eyes. He extended a hand toward Eidy, who shook it.

"Nice day for it," said Basher. "I was afraid we'd be rained on for the whole week out there."

"Mmph. Maybe stay afraid," said Eidy. He squinted into the sky, which was presently still bright. "If you don't like the weather here, you've only to wait ten minutes and it'll change." He looked at the four of them—or the three that he could actually look at, anyway—and his eyebrow twitched as if he was only now taking them in properly.

"Well, I wouldn't have pegged ye as parents," he said, motioning at Claire and Basher. He then seemed surprised at his own frankness.

"Rude!" said Alex with a grin. They went to punch Eidy on the shoulder and he flinched away a little. "Basher's my uncle."

"Yeah, um. Basher and I aren't together. We're friends," said Claire. She immediately regretted this, because she knew it would open up room for Alex and/or Soph to make fun of her for trying to kiss Basher that one time a few months ago.

"Not for want of trying, eh, C?" said Alex, entirely on cue.

"We will never let it die, weirdo," added Soph. "Like me, it will haunt you forever."

Basher rolled his eyes, and said, "Let's just go, shall we?"

Eidy nodded, once, and stomped off to a metal marine bridge that led to a pontoon. He walked as if he had a grudge against the planet, the heavy sound of his footsteps exacerbated by the big waterproof wellies he was wearing. If it weren't for those he would have fit in favorably in any craft beer pub in London: heavy-duty cargo pants and a blue, thick-knit jumper with the sleeves pushed up his forearms. In other circumstances Claire wouldn't have been surprised to hear this man espousing strong opinions around the Campaign for Real Ale. He would wear one of those little beanies that barely covered his whole head and be loudly feminist and say things like "Guys, the change has to start with us, yeah?," except a few years later, it would turn out that he was basically a sexual predator and the fallout would cause a schism in the group because his friends, although they said they hashtag believed women, would be able to find enough reasons that either it was all a misunderstanding or it was a crazy ex lying to trash his relationship, but enough people took against him that the local scene was irreversibly affected because he was a big name in—

"Oi!"

Claire looked up as Sophie shouted, and realized she'd nearly walked off the side of the pontoon. Soph tutted at her. "I dunno where you disappear to these days," she said. "It's ghosts that are supposed to forget who and where they are as time goes by, right? What's your excuse?"

"Frustration with my present circumstances," Claire said, under her breath.

"Huh?" said Eidy.

"Er . . . What?"

"What?"

"Nothing."

Soph watched this exchange. "Yes, in fairness I can see why you would be frustrated being you," she said. Claire ignored her.

Eidy had progressed down the metal bridge and was presently doing some nautical fussing around a medium-size green-and-white boat, joining two other men who were also doing presumably critical things with ropes. They were, Claire surmised with her well-honed detective skills, probably supposed to follow him and get on the boat, but they stalled at the top gate of the bridge because a couple were trying to go down it ahead of them, each with their own luggage. The man nodded at them in exaggerated delight.

He was tall of height, square of jaw, and cowboy of hat. An honest-to-God cowboy hat. Claire looked down and, yep, blue jeans, a prohibitively large belt buckle, and proper cowboy boots. He was wearing a red-and-black-checked shirt, the collar of which was held closed by a bolo tie. He was very tanned. He was a cowboy.

"Hoo-eee, that there wind is really kicking it up a notch, and no mistake!" said the cowboy. He talked like . . . well, like a cowboy. Like, if someone said "Do an impression of a cowboy," his was the voice you would do. Claire was only surprised he didn't crack a whip or click spurred heels together to punctuate his speech.

"Say, you fine folks ain't heading on over there (*thar*) to Spike Island (*Spahk Ay-land*), are you?" he went on. "Only, well, my Tiffany here and her mates have the place for a private function." Here he paused to swipe off his cowboy hat and thwack his own forehead.

"You must think I'm about as mannerly as the last whippet in whelping season!" he exclaimed, a metaphor that made Sophie stare at him in disbelief so hard she nearly went cross-eyed. "I must introduce my princess, my angel on earth Miss Tiffany Thomas. She's a blogger and an advocate and I'm just so proud of her every day. She makes me a better man."

"Tiffany posts long Instagram stories about the climate, sure," said Sophie, distinctly unimpressed.

The indicated Tiffany was a sort of honey-blond Rosie the Riveter cosplayer, in denim overalls and with her hair tied up in a scarf, and both overalls and scarf were clearly very expensive rather than from Primark's current seasonal stock. Claire was unsure how blogging and advocating paid for visible Louis Vuitton logos, but her boyfriend and his absurdly chiseled face provided the likely answer.

"And me? I'm Ritchie Walker and, well, I'm just a simple Texas oil (*ohl*) man, and that's seen me right."

"There's no way that's his name," said Sophie. "Might as well be called Tex McShortrib."

"That's your real name?" said Alex, equally fascinated. Ritchie blinked at them in the polite way some Americans have when confronted with certain kinds of English sarcasm.

Tiffany stepped in. "Yes, yes, nominative determinism. But he's right, there aren't supposed to be any other guests this week." As Tiffany moved closer, Claire caught a whiff of strong floral perfume, and noticed that Tiffany had a round, cute face that she camouflaged as snatched and glamorous with impressive makeup techniques. "You lot are going to have to find somewhere else to stay," she added. Tiffany had the arch, confident voice of someone who had been the most popular girl at school.

"If I could just *advocate* for us," said Alex, wiggling their eyebrows, "I will say that we've paid and have a confirmation and everything."

"We shall ask Eidy," said Basher calmly.

"Yes, let's," said Tiffany, and marched ahead, as Ritchie tipped his hat at them. But Tiffany was to be disappointed, as Eidy insisted that the boat was taking all of them, and if she didn't like it, she and her boyfriend could stay where they were. In this he was as immovable as an angry, bearded little bollard, and his case was strengthened when one of the other men whistled and said something about the tide. At this Eidy stepped into the boat with practiced ease, and gestured impatiently for them all to follow in a way that suggested there would be no more argument about it.

"Mind yer back, C," said Alex. They swung their large case around Claire and heaved it into the boat with a thud, then jumped in after it with no hesitation. Alex was very good at being at ease anywhere. They helped Claire by pulling her holdall in, because Claire was not confident enough to throw anything, including herself, into a boat. She crouched and sort of crabwalked into it, because she had not been on a boat before and was suddenly very aware of that fact. Basher got in like a normal person, followed by Tiffany and her tame cowboy, Ritchie, who also got in normally but were not, Claire suspected, entirely normal people.

Most of the boat was taken up by a large covered section with bench seating, and would fit quite a few people. Basher said he thought it was probably the boat that took weekend tourists out to visit the prison on the island. Because it was a nice day, the six guests all sat at the back of the boat, which was open to the elements. Eidy was there, too, leaning against a tall roll cage like Claire had seen staff pulling around Sainsbury's full of yogurts and packs of sliced ham.

To Claire's surprise, even though the boat was small compared to, say, a massive cruise liner, there wasn't a lot of movement once they got out onto the water. The bay was as flat as a pane of glass, one huge broad sweep of mirror reflecting the sky and sun back at them. No wonder Eidy had a ruddy, raw outdoorsman tan over his nose and cheeks.

This did not, of course, stop Claire from feeling nauseous almost immediately, and she began to yawn and hiccup to try to clear the feeling. Basher nudged her and gave a questioning thumbs-up, a reversal of the situation just minutes before.

"How long does the boat trip take?" asked Alex. They were attempting to peer around Eidy's shoulder, with some interest, to look at the contents of the roll cage.

"It's only fifteen minutes, like," said Eidy. And then, as sort of a consolation: "'Tis a good view of the town and the mainland once we get a bit farther out."

"*Ohmigod*," said Soph, in tones approaching genuine awe. "He's not wrong."

As they got farther and farther away, they could indeed look back at the town they'd been standing in minutes before and see all the colorful painted houses at once. It was the sort of image that would decorate the front of boxes of novelty flavored fudge. This far out you could see that most of the town was crawling up a steep hill moving back away from the water. It was all crowned by an incongruously huge cathedral: massive, gray, and built on top of a sheer wall that seemed to be holding the hill together, so the building looked at least half as tall again. It looked like someone had made a living collage by sticking an absurdly gothic cathedral from a horror film right on top of a picturesque holiday postcard.

"A town fit for Dracula to land in," said Basher.

Claire shivered, even though the sun was still out. It did look impressive, and she knew she should think it was breathtaking and beautiful—the sort of sight you'd take a picture of and send to your family WhatsApp group, where your aunts would respond with a confusing series of emojis. Claire didn't have a family WhatsApp group, because, while they weren't exactly estranged, she and her parents were in a period of prolonged uncertainty, owing to Claire's continued insistence that she could see ghosts and was a medium. Unfortunately, Claire's reality was operating on a parallel line to everyone else's, as she couldn't *not* see Sophie, which ultimately resulted in her parents operating on parallel lines to each other and getting a divorce.

But this association wasn't actually what unsettled Claire about the cathedral. As she looked at it, she couldn't stop imagining it falling on the town. This didn't help the nausea.

She turned away and poked her head into the cabin next to Alex. Sophie was right. She was spending a lot of time . . . not in the present. She'd always been prone to daydreaming, but since the time last year when she'd been chased through the night by Basher and Alex's family, dug up a half-skeletonized corpse, and pushed herself to exhaustion and fainting in the process, her imaginings were becoming more intrusive.

"Here, weirdo," Sophie said. "Ask him where Spike is. Like, how far away is it?"

Claire put Soph's question to Eidy, and he snorted. "I said the trip is fifteen minutes, didn't I? Lucky ye arrived when ye did, or it'd take longer. Spike is in front of us. Past that you go out to Roches Point."

"Oh! Oh!" said Alex, like a child in class. "That's where the *Titanic* anchored!"

Eidy didn't respond. The town continued to shrink behind them. There was an uneasy half-silence, as Tiffany and Ritchie talked quietly with their heads close together, not wanting to be overheard.

"Er. Why would it take longer?" Claire asked.

"What?" said Eidy.

"You said it would take longer if we'd arrived at a different time."

"Sandbar," said Eidy. "Right across here. Tide gets too low, you've to go the long way around the estuary. Right now we can go straight over, more as the crow flies, like. The currents are dangerous, though, 'specially when the tide turns, so no pissing about sea swimming once you're ashore."

This lengthy speech seemed to exhaust Eidy, because he asked them to move away from the edge of the boat as if he were a bus driver reminding them to stay behind the line.

As they moved farther out from the port, the boat began to rock in the swell of waves. Alex pointed out a huge, green cargo ship coming in, loaded with a Jenga tower of shipping crates. Claire wondered what was in them. Coffee? Wool? Wellington boots? Novelty Minion-shaped dog toys? What if the crate full of dog toys fell off? Then it would be like that town where the river was full of rubber ducks. Or was it a beach full of Garfield phones? Or alarm clocks? It probably wasn't alarm clocks. Garfield was a terrible alarm clock character, because he famously did not like Mondays, so would not be convincing at waking you up on a Monday. She remembered Sophie had had a Wallace and Gromit talking alarm clock, which was pretty good because Wallace had many ingenious ways for getting up and at 'em—except the alarm clock was just an alarm clock, and did not provide you with mechanical robot hands that got you dressed and made you toast. Also, it only took AAA batteries, and when they'd run out Soph's mum kept forgetting to get more, so then it was just a big lump of plastic.

She blinked. The cargo ship was past them and heading farther up the river. Tiffany got up and stretched theatrically, and came over to her.

"Well, I suppose this is happening," she said. "You coming to the island, I mean."

"She's the brains of the outfit, you can tell," remarked Sophie, who was leaning over the side of the boat in what was technically a dangerous way—for a living person.

"Er, yeah. Sorry," said Claire. "I didn't really have anything to do with booking it, so I don't know what any of this is, really."

"It's a very exclusive resort—or at least, it will be. It's not finished yet, but I'm old friends with the owner, Minnie. A few of us were going to have a private mini-break here, the first people to ever use the place," said Tiffany. Claire had not asked for this explanation, but Tiffany seemed to want to show off about it. She raised an eyebrow at Claire and waited for a response. Claire had only recently started to hang out with people who weren't a dead teenager, so she was a bit rusty at how conversation worked.

"Oh, right. Very cool, yeah. How do you all know each other?" she asked.

"We were all in the same society at university—Edinburgh, actually—and we all meet up for trips still. Or at least, we did. It's been a while. Look, here—"

Tiffany got out her phone and brandished it at Claire. Sophie came to lean over and look at the photo on the screen with her. It was a group of half a dozen, mostly women, standing on a beach doing the smiles people do when someone behind the camera says "Smile!" about three seconds before they actually take the picture.

"That's a few of us at the last one, but it was ages ago now," said Tiffany. "We got scuba certifications, isn't that fun? It was George's idea—that's him there in the middle, and of course it was before I met Ritchie, and Dan and Ashley couldn't make it. But that's Minnie, on the left."

She pulled the phone back and swiped busily for a few more seconds, before it was thrust under Claire's nose again. It was a bunch of students smiling in a bar, slightly washed out by a too-bright flash. Claire could date the picture because she herself had studied history, and short-sleeve tees over long-sleeve ones, or V-necks over lace-strap tops on the girls, were artifacts from the noughties with which she was personally, regretfully familiar. Sophie had been delighted when Juicy Couture velveteen tracksuits like her own became old enough that they were beginning to be in style again.

"That's us in the SU bar," said Tiffany.

Sophie looked closer. "Why is one of them scribbled out?" She pointed: there was a man—boy, really, given their ages at the time—on the far left of the picture, standing by a girl who

looked like a younger, less perfect version of Tiffany. His face
and torso had been scribbled over in the photo app.

"Who's that?" Claire asked.

Tiffany frowned. "That's Andy. He was a big nerd, bit of a loser,
and he had a thing for me. He's not one of the gang anymore."

Tiffany whipped the phone away before Claire had time to
properly internalize this. "I wonder what's going to happen with
you lot here. It really wasn't planned for, you know . . ." She trailed
off, and wandered over to Alex and Basher, possibly to do a similar smug showing-offing.

"Strange couple," said Sophie. "There's something weird about
a woman who'd willingly get on top of an actual cartoon character."

"Oh stop. We probably won't see them again after this anyway," muttered Claire.

The boat was approaching another pier, concrete and utilitarian, with another pontoon and marine bridge. The shoreline
was weirdly flat, and so graduated that it seemed the island was
melting back into the sea. It was a forbidding place, and Claire
wondered what feelings of wellness it would engender.

Soph whistled. "I was joking before, but you may die here. I
mean, who would know?"

Soph was evidently not the only person to whom the thought
had occurred, because Alex clapped a hand on Claire's shoulder.

"Don't worry, C," they said with a lopsided grin. "If anything
happens to you, I'll make sure to arrange the scene in as suspicious and bizarre a way as possible, so one of the podcasts you
like will spend three episodes discussing what kind of sex criminal killed you."

"You always make out like I'm the only person who listens to
them," said Claire. "It's not weird to like true crime stuff."

"Yeah, but it's, like, totally immoral."

"Have any last-minute regrets, Nibling?" asked Basher. He had stepped up to stand next to them.

"Not on your very sad life, Uncle B," Alex replied. "I make my own fun, wherever I go."

"God," said Sophie with a frosty sigh, "you have no idea how much I wish you were more like Alex."

"I do," said Claire. This neatly provided a response to both Basher and Sophie.

The engine cut down to a slower throb that vibrated in Claire's legs, and the boat sidled gently up to the pontoon, and parked?—Claire didn't know what the nautical equivalent of parking was—against it. They waited while Eidy and the small crew of the boat secured it and opened the little door in the side to let them off, and then stood around for a few moments saying variations on phrases like "Not a bother, boy!"

"C'mon then," said Eidy eventually, as if they had kept him waiting. He pulled the roll cage off the boat without any apparent effort.

"Impressive place!" said Basher.

"Shows well in the sun," said Eidy. Claire detected a note of pride at that. Eidy could probably trace his family back through countless generations of living here. Probably there'd been a miserable ginger-bearded bastard stomping around the forest here in 8 BC, making people feel bad for not knowing what sort of flint was the best flint.

Claire noticed him looking at Basher out of the corner of his eye. Sophie did, too, and muttered that if Eidy did anything even approaching a homophobic hate crime she would find a way to push him off the nearest cliff—which would probably be handily close, given the location.

"Can you help us get up to the hotel?" asked Basher, once Eidy appeared to be finished.

"I will, *yeah*," said Eidy. He powered up the marine bridge without looking back at them.

"I think from context he was being sarcastic," said Soph. "Look, there's really only one way to go, anyway." She pointed down the long pier.

They made their way up the marine bridge, following Eidy like ducklings—except Alex who, in typical Alex style, put their head down and powered along past him, whooping and jumping.

"*Please* be careful, Alex!" called Basher.

As soon as they were on the pier proper, they were rocked by a gust of sudden freezing wind, which appeared to be localized entirely on the island. Possibly it was itself a very naughty weather pattern, and had been imprisoned here in penal servitude by the other weathers, honorable Judge Thunderstorm presiding.

"Bs cwbs, dnt?" said Alex, who had stopped to wait for them. Claire couldn't hear anything they said above the wind.

"You what?" she yelled back.

"I said: It blows! The cobwebs! Out!" shouted Alex. They still looked quite happy about the whole situation. Eidy rattled past them with the roll cage, still going at the same speed. He was quietly very strong, Claire noted.

"I wt," said Basher, grumbling.

"He said he wants tea," said Sophie. She didn't need to shout, because when ghosts talked to Claire their voices landed directly in her brain, without any apparent need to navigate the air in between. "I want to look around as well. It's boring when you can't repeat me to the others."

They moved into a concrete shelter, slightly out of the wind.

Freed from the presence of Tiffany and Ritchie, who were well out of earshot behind them, Claire told the others that Sophie was bored. This was not a remarkable state of affairs. Basher swung his rucksack off his shoulder and pulled out a palm-size bag that disgorged some sort of huge hooded cape that he pulled over his clothes. It was roughly the same color as Irn Bru, or non-EU compliant Tango.

"What—sorry, Uncle B, but what on God's tropical earth do you think you're wearing?"

"It is a portable rain poncho," said Basher quite calmly.

"It's . . ." Claire wondered how best to put it. "I mean, I'm sure it's very, er, practical, but it's pretty fucking orange, Basher." It was, in fact, so luminously orange that he looked more like a school trip chaperone than a man on holiday. Claire realized that this might actually have been a deliberate choice on his part.

"Yes. I think it is probably orange on purpose," said Bash. He straightened the sleeves. "If I got lost hiking it would be quite easy to see me."

"If he got lost hiking on this island, he'd have to have done it on purpose," commented Sophie.

"You're clashing with my hair," Alex complained.

"Well, that may be, but this is very wind resistant."

"I refuse to be seen with you while you're wearing it," said Alex. "People might think we're related." Alex blazed ahead again, hopping and skipping with the enviable energy of the young. Basher ran after them, powered by the loaned energy of anxiety, which would demand interest later. It took Claire longer to follow them as she was both a trying-to-quit smoker and very unfit in general, because watching American police procedurals, listening to true crime podcasts, and eating noodles are not athletic pursuits. By the time Claire reached the end of the pier she was convinced one of her lungs was about to collapse, which was not a good state of affairs after a very short walk on flat concrete. Basher and Alex were already halfway down the path along the front of the island, still a little behind Eidy. To add insult to injury, Claire had to get out of the way for Ritchie and Tiffany, who actually tutted as she went past. Soph snorted.

"I know I keep joking about it, but if you do actually die here it would be quite funny."

"If I . . . die . . . here," panted Claire, "you'll be . . . stuck . . . here too . . ."

"LOL. Yeah, fair point. Just hanging around a freezing fuckin' rock that had no significance to either of us, forever."

Claire contemplated asking if a fucking rock was a rock for fucking or a rock you did fucking on, but Spike Island was so clearly suited to neither that she couldn't even be bothered. At the end of the pier the path became a tarmacked road, and there was a large map board that she stopped to examine. The island was much bigger than she'd expected, and vaguely oval in shape, but with a few angular man-made bits. One of these was the pier that she'd just walked up, rendered on the map as a little stick poking out of the bottom-right corner of the oval. Taking up most of the island was a massive building in the shape of a flat, six-pointed star. It was labeled *Fort*, so Claire intuited it was a fort of some description. Claire was, according to the map, presently standing in front of a road that led up a suddenly steep hill to it, but it seemed unlikely this was the hotel. Around the sides of the fort the map showed green space dotted with trees, and occasional buildings.

"Here." Sophie reached out with a ghostly finger and tapped the point of interest on the map labeled *H*, which was at the water's edge, down a path to Claire's left. Claire looked at the key

and saw that *H—Abandoned village and hotel* had an addendum
in the form of a sticker reading *Spike Island Wellness Retreat.*

"Could have worked that out myself," she muttered. She was
a good enough detective to at least read signs. If given enough
time. Other points of interest, she noted, included *D—Sports
ground* and *E—Convict cemetery*, both of which were in the
top-right area of the island. She made a mental note to avoid
those if possible, because at school she'd taken to PE like a duck
to concrete, and because ghosts in cemeteries were boring and
annoying.

Sophie huffed at her taking too long, so she turned and looked
down the path everyone else had taken. On her left was the
water, now fussing like a toddler. On the right was a brick wall,
corralling in a surprisingly dense growth of trees. A lot of them
were still bare, but there was ivy crawling up so many trunks that
they gave the impression that they were green.

Claire was keen to get inside because she was fairly sure that
it wasn't windy in a "you're on a sea island" way, but windy in a "it
is now windy" way. The air was full of salt. She hauled her bags
along as Sophie watched with the dispassionate expression of a
cat watching a dog try to walk, making what she considered to
be decent progress when, out of nowhere, she found her path
was barred.

"Avast, landlubber!" cried the apparition. It brandished a
short, slightly curved but noticeably see-through sword at her.
Claire was shocked into gasping into the wind, which precipi-
tated a fit of deep, hacking coughs until she spat up some black
phlegm.

"Oh for Christ's sake," she moaned. "A fucking pirate!"

"A fucking pirate!" said Sophie, her eyes bright with excitement.

3

Cowboys, Pirates, and Wreckers—O My!

The pirate lowered his cutlass and looked somewhat alarmed himself.

"Oh lass," he said. He had a very broad Bristol accent, which was befitting a pirate, but slightly contextually confusing. "That's a churchyard-cough you have there, no mistake. I'm truly sorry. I try that on everyone, but it has never worked before."

Claire narrowed her eyes. "I get that a lot. I'm Claire. This is Sophie. We're here for the week with our friends."

He goggle-eyed at them, and clapped his hands to the sides of his head. "Oh thank the good Lord! You're my saviors! My ladies, I am in sore need of your help. Only you have the power to deliver us!" He almost jumped for joy, and then started. "Ah, but forgive me. I've lost my manners. What must you think of me?"

Without any further ado—and Claire got the sense this man held the potential for a lot of ado-ing—the pirate swept a floppy maroon cap off his head and effected a low bow at Sophie that

Claire judged to be over-the-top. She looked across to share an eye roll with Sophie. To her surprise, Soph *giggled*.

"A pleasure. Cole Tovey, late captain of the *Fancy Fortune*, and your most humble servant," he said, almost nose-to-toe in his obeisance. He flung himself upright again.

Cole Tovey was what you'd get if you asked a freelance illustrator, who was most used to drawing porn for furries, to turn in a cartoon of a pirate. He had long black hair tied back in a loose, low ponytail, a ludicrously thick black beard, sparkling blue eyes, and a very straight, proud nose. His smile could credibly be described as roguish, most especially because he appeared to have a full set of gold teeth. Claire briefly wondered if finding the good captain's skull would itself count as treasure, and made a mental note to point out to Sophie that this technically meant Cole had dentures. This would probably not be enough to wipe out the impression made by the open-necked white linen shirt, which was struggling to contain a barrel chest and a prodigious amount of dark chest hair. A beautician would need a weed-whacker. Cole even had the kind of loose knee-length trousers you'd describe as pantaloons, although he was bare from the knees down, exposing hairy calves. His feet were bare, too. And once she noticed this, Claire looked closer and realized that once you got past the initial impression, Cole was, like most pirates, basically just a grubby sailor. His trousers were patched, his hair was slicked back in its own grease, and his shirt could have been used as the before example in a Persil advert.

"Fallen on hard times, have we, Captain?" she asked.

Cole raised an eyebrow. "The hardest, madam," he said. He spread his hands. "I'm still being rude, of course. 'Tis a great pleasure to meet you as well, sweet Claire."

He took her hand and bent as if to kiss it, but Claire snatched it back because she felt the electric *zip* that meant a ghost had physically connected to her and was able to draw off her energy, as if she were a big Duracell battery. She allowed it with Sophie for séances, because it enabled Soph to become solid enough to pick up objects and create a spooky atmosphere. Doing it with another ghost felt wrong. Intimate.

"Don't bother, Captain," said Soph. "That sort of thing is wasted on her, anyway."

"Oh please, call me Cole. Let us not stand on ceremony. And since you're to save us, I shall have to introduce you to my crew! They didn't serve on the *Fortune* with me, but are other sailors that washed up here since and gave me the honor of leading them."

"There's more of you?" asked Claire.

"Why, yes! A merry company of antiquated rogues such as myself. And of course," he said, his brows suddenly knotting together with an effect not unlike the gathering clouds in the sky, "I shall warn you off that arseworm Finny and his gang of scoundrels. Wreckers to a man. It's because of him you find me in this wretched circumstance!"

"What? *Another* gang? Fucksake."

The news that Spike Island was crawling with ghosts would delight Alex, but was anathema to Claire. Ghosts spend years, sometimes hundreds of them, with a very limited conversation pool. The second that pool got a millimeter deeper they were all in, and now that Cole knew Claire could talk to him, so would all the others. The next few days stretched ahead of her with more annoyance in them than had been previously agreed.

Plus, there was a good chance the other ghosts would be more off-putting to look at than Cole. Though all ghosts—especially Sophie—wanted attention, they varied in form, ranging from exactly what they looked like when they died (complete with drippy wounds), to what they looked like on their best day living, to insubstantial mists or mindless skeletons. Claire was pretty used to gruesome spooks after so many years of them popping up, but a drippy, bloated, see-through corpse hanging around and demanding to know who was king of England or who won the Hundred Years' War wasn't going to improve her focus.

"Look, fucking—ugh—I'm not going to ask who Finny is, because right now we are going to check in to the lovely hotel and start our break and *not be bothered*." Ultimatum thus delivered, Claire swung her holdall onto her shoulder and stomped off toward the house. But Cole was quick to follow her.

"Ah, but, madam, 'tis to my point and purpose," he said, jogging a little to keep up. "We may be of great use to one another. I have grave concerns that Finny and his troop of filthy dogs are up to much mischief on this island, mayhap even in cahoots with a living mortal! You must help us thwart the bastards. You're the only one who can!"

Claire stopped. "Cahoots? With someone who can see ghosts? What are you talking about?"

"Ah, it is a sad story, but, to be brief: our ship foundered in a storm, a night as black as the heart of—"

Claire paddled her hands, indicating he speed up.

"Finny and his brothers stole some of the cargo from my ship, and stashed it here on the island. They themselves drowned shortly after, and so it has lain here for centuries, as we guard it with our lives . . ." Here he paused as Claire raised an eyebrow. ". . . A mere figure of speech, you understand. But this morning we found some of that self-same cargo missing," Cole said. He seemed slightly put out that he'd had to edit his theatrics down.

"But this Finny guy and his gang couldn't have moved it themselves, so you think someone is helping," reasoned Sophie.

"Exactly! Sharp as a blade, Miss Sophie. Some visitors to that infernal retreat of wellness arrived last night. I think 'tis mostlike one of them."

Claire heard a snatch of laughter behind her, to where Basher had paused along the path to look back at her. Alex was still going farther along, whooping and shouting into the wind. Bash gave an exaggerated shrug and Claire flapped her arm at him, so he kept moving. She dragged her bag off the path and stood against the wall to try to get out of the wind, but it did not work.

She turned back to the captain. "So what is it? You want us to spy on the people here in case they're in league with some other ghosts?" said Claire, her tone flat.

"Indeed, for even if we identified the thief working with Finny, t'would take another living soul to bring them to justice! It would be no challenge at all. I'm sure Finny will be as eager to speak to you both as I was, and you, Miss Claire, are most well fitted to speak to living folk. Say, how is it you're able to move from place to place, Miss Sophie? We unhappy few can't slip the bounds of this island."

Claire narrowed her eyes, and ignored this. "If you're a pirate," she said, slowly, reasoning it out, "didn't you steal whatever the stuff is in the first place?"

"We liberated it, ma'am, from the wrecked ships of a fleet of Spaniards we'd been shadowing at a distance. Not improper behavior from a privateer."

"Right, but I mean, like, can it be stolen from you?"

"Yes," said Cole. There was evidently little room for argument.

"Hm. But why do you fucking *care*? You'll never get your hands on it again."

Cole spread said hands in appeal and made a face like an unhappy Muppet. Claire wasn't entirely unsympathetic. Ghosts had to get fixations on *something*, or they turned into a blurry, indistinct clump of mist, and forgot who they were entirely. "Surely," he said, "for the purposes of our agreement, 'tis enough that I say it's real and that I do care?"

"We've not actually made an agreement," Claire reminded him. "What's in it for me?"

"If you agree to help us, I can make sure that no other ghosts bother you this week. I and my crew shall be your personal guard," he said, having accurately assessed Claire's personal hierarchy of needs within the space of three minutes.

"Oh, come on, it'll be fun," said Sophie. "Even if we don't believe him, we're going to meet all the other losers here this week anyway. We can always check where the supposed treasure is tomorrow, or something."

Cole kept quiet, but nodded encouragingly.

"So . . . to be clear, you're saying if we try to find out who stole your—heavy air quotes on 'your,' by the way—treasure or whatever, I won't be bothered by any depressing ghosts this week? Doesn't sound like a great deal."

This was in fact a lie. Though Claire would not admit it out loud, because she had a vague feeling you weren't supposed to show your hand to other players at the table, ghosts leaving her alone was an attractive proposition. Having to speak to whoever this Finny was, as well as Cole, to facilitate whatever theatrical and clandestine exchanges of information he felt needed to happen, did still mean there wouldn't be *none* talking to ghosts, but it was a significant improvement on being followed by an unknown number of deados from now until they went home on Friday. At the same time, finding a thief hidden among whatever other living guests were here was a great chance to cosplay as a member of the *Murder Profile* team, but without the high stakes of actual murder—which, she had discovered, wasn't as enjoyable as TV made it seem.

"Don't look at me," said Sophie at the exact moment Claire was about to look at her. "I'll be bored anyway. I always thought I'd be a great spy, LOL."

"I'm promising nothing," said Claire with an air of much begrudgery, but Cole took this and ran with it well into the opposing team's half.

"Huzzah!" he shouted. He clapped his hands together, like a devil who'd just been promised all the firstborn of the town.

"Christ. 'Huzzah.' I'm going to live to regret meeting you."

"I won't," said Sophie. "Best to act first and deal with consequences later. That's what Alex would do."

"Yes, that's what I'm afraid of. Anyway, *Cap-i-tan*, you can fuck off for the rest of the day, all right? Come and see us tomorrow."

"With pleasure, gracious gentlewomen! I shall return anon, to discuss our bargain! But stay away from the fort, for the piliferous Irishmen hold it now, and we've not yet taken it back from them."

Claire, not particularly wishing to find out what he meant by this, turned and continued her stomp. It was interesting that Cole had apparently looted the lost Armada ships, only to have his own ship wrecked here, much farther along the Irish coast than where the Spaniards had run into trouble, as he was on the way home. It explained where the treasure rumors came from, anyhow. After a bit more stomping, she realized Sophie wasn't with her. She turned and saw that Sophie had lingered behind and was still chatting to Cole. This was, Claire decided, probably fine. Right? She took a few more steps until she felt the tether between her and Sophie, invisible but taut like stretched elastic. Another slow step and she began to tug Sophie along, like she was towing a bright blue balloon. Cole kept pace with her, talking quietly.

Claire rounded the corner and saw what she presumed was the hotel, a large boxy sort of building with a red-brick frame and white rectangular windows that spoke of a utilitarian design ethic, and gray concrete extensions that felt hurried. More modern embellishments made of glass and metal grew from the sides, and the roof looked brand spanking new, the timber supports suspiciously bright compared to the dull building beneath it. But the whole thing looked far too close to the water for Claire's liking. The door was right in the center, and it was the kind with a big handle in the middle, rather than at the side where it was most useful for normal people.

She felt the little tug on the tether again, enforcing the limit on Sophie's maximum distance from her. As Cole had observed, ghosts normally haunted where they'd died, or somewhere important to them. Sophie haunted Claire, and when they got too far apart—about fifty meters in any direction—they both experienced a vague discomfort, like a sort of annoying hangnail snag, but with the whole body.

The hotel's door was slightly open, so Claire shouldered her way inside, then pushed it closed against the wind, though it still made the unsettling tearing, whipping noise that wind does when screaming around the wall of a building.

Claire looked around. The bones of the house were old— thick walls with boxy windows—but the flesh was new. New plaster, new carpets. She was standing at one end of a pristine cream hallway, with sterile spotlights dotted in the ceiling, and she could see it intersected with another identical hallway to make a cross shape dividing the main building into four. On her right was a tan wooden staircase, going up and turning a sharp corner. It had a runner carpet in a soft slate color. On her left was a door in the same tan wood, with a little frosted glass sign on the wall next to it reading RECEPTION. Claire knocked, and the door swung open noiselessly, revealing an entirely empty little office.

She padded back down the hallway, fighting the urge to flop down into one of the sage green velvety chairs, with similarly velvety saffron yellow cushions, placed at an artfully skewed angle at the intersection. She saw more doors and more signs: Treatment Room A, Treatment Room B, Indoor Studio, Kitchen, Living Area. She plumped for this last, which was opposite the front door, and kitty-corner to the kitchen door on her left. She could hear the murmur of voices, and put her most confident face on as she walked in, relieved that she was cocooned from all the weather starting to happen outside.

Ah, no. Her mistake. It was an extension stuck on the back and side of the house, with exposed metal framework and a floor-to-ceiling window taking up most of the back wall, offering a disconcerting view of the darkening trees and bushes outside. Claire wondered what kind of damn fool built a house here in the first place.

The floor of the extension was split level, so on one side was a living room with a firepit and some bookshelves, and on the other, separated by a rustic-looking breakfast bar, was a raised area with some round tables covered in white cloth. It created the illusion of a sunken living area, even though that part was at ground level. The whole room smelled quite savory, and Claire saw a door on the wall to her left that was also marked KITCHEN. There were an alarming number of people in the extension, although Claire knew two of them, at least, and could recognize some others.

"Wotcher, C!" called Alex. They were sitting at one of the tables with Basher. "Got given a cup of tea, didn't I?"

"I also have tea," said Basher. He spoke lazily, but looked tense. Dealing with everything that had happened to his family was clearly taking more of a toll on Basher than Claire had realized. He seemed so jittery and uncomfortable that she feared he was in danger of doing something out of character, like taking off his hoodie. She'd never actually seen him without one on, and imagined that underneath was either a robot body or some kind of black hole. Or a little mutant face with stubby arms like off *Total Recall.*

Claire risked a little wave at Tiffany, who definitely saw her do it, but did not respond. She was sitting at a table that the other strangers had all huddled around, like a group of meerkats who'd been disturbed in their foraging by the arrival of unscheduled predators. They seemed as alarmed to see other guests as Tiffany had been, and Ritchie, who was standing behind her with his arms on the back of her chair like they were posing for a portrait, was loudly explaining what had happened when they got the boat together. Claire went over to Basher and Alex and drew a chair out. Basher pushed a mug toward her.

"Milk, no sugar." He grunted.

"Thanks. Er. Who are—"

"Don't worry," said Alex. Their eyes twinkled. "He's about to—"

Ritchie, who, like a T. rex, seemed to have vision based on movement, noticed Claire at last and leaped into action. He bounded across the distance between the two tables and grabbed her forearm.

"Woo-ee! Some more introductions are in order, I reckon!" he said—or rather, yelled. He didn't wait for Claire to respond, but launched into an, ahem, roundup of everyone else around the table that she didn't know, pointing out each person in turn. Claire realized that she recognized most of them from the picture Tiffany had shown her on the boat. Sophie, who had been loitering at the very extent of her tether outside, walked back in just in time to add her own commentary.

"Now over here we got Ashley and her hotshot husband Dan Merlin. I don't rightly understand their line of work, but they tell me they're figuring out how to save the environment with Bitcoin, and that sounds just mighty fine to me."

This couple looked healthier than Ritchie and Tiffany with their glow-in-the-dark fake tans, but less outwardly harmonious. Dan was sprawled in the chair next to Tiffany, and was wearing jeans and a suit jacket over a T-shirt. He had a naturally smug expression and a long thin nose above an honest to God goatee, which was a combination that made him look distinctly *goaty*. His wife was several seats away from him, and was sitting up very tall. She was evidently a big fan of Marilyn Monroe, because she was in danger of appearing in one of those magazine stories with a headline starting "The Woman Who Paid £150k to Look Like . . ." Ashley Merlin had perfectly coiffed hair and a perfectly beautiful face, and neither of them looked as if they would move in a hurricane-force wind.

"Standard-issue tech dickheads, okay," said Soph.

Claire felt herself leaning back as Ritchie continued his performance, as if she was in a car hitting sudden acceleration. The cowboy wheeled around the table dramatically, taking his hat off and putting it back on and continuing to gesture to each new person he introduced. Basher and Alex leaned toward her.

"He did the same with us," murmured Basher.

"Next we have the MacInallys, Susan and Flick, with their beautiful little Caity, almost four years old. Why, darling, you're almost a debutante!"

"It's Mac," said apparently Mac, who was a British Chinese woman with an Edinburgh accent and impressively long hair. She was wearing almost the same outfit as Ritchie was, really, but she looked a lot better in it than he did. "Not Susan. I told you before."

"Susan is a wonderful vet, a friend to the animals—and couldn't we have done with that back on the farm!" said Ritchie.

"I thought you were an oil ma—" Claire started.

"And Flick just bakes the sweetest cakes you ever did eat in your life," Ritchie continued. "Why, one bite of her cinnamon apple cake and you're right back as a kid, getting under your mama's feet and begging for peel for dipping."

Claire did not know what this meant. Flick was far too busy dandling what appeared to be a small bear cub to participate in the conversation. This was, Claire realized, most likely to be a child in a bear onesie.

"So we've got our self-conscious friendship group's diversity lesbians, check and check," Soph put in.

"With them is George Lyons, and he ain't a family man just yet, but gosh, he's a doctor, so I'm sure the ladies are chasing after him."

George Lyons was large, redheaded with sandy beard stubble, and so handsome that Claire had to immediately look away, as one does when one accidentally looks directly at the sun. She started to compulsively chew on the pad of her thumb, realized she was doing it, and began to blush instead.

"A strapping but ultimately uninteresting man who takes hearty walks," said Soph.

"And of course, we've got our gracious host Minnie, although where she is just now I don't rightly know," said Ritchie, deflating a little as he realized he couldn't reach a proper crescendo with his intros. "'Course, though she owns the place, her real passion is genealogy (*gee-knee-al-o-gee*), which is a fancy five-dollar word meaning that if you sit still long enough she can tell you what your great-great-grandaddy had for breakfast."

There was a pause. Claire realized Ritchie was looking at her.

"Er . . . Oh wow. Amazing. Thank you."

"And you're a friend of Alex and Sebastian?" asked Ritchie.

"Yes. Correct. Yeah."

The silence continued. Evidently more was required.

"Oh! Right, yeah. Um, I'm Claire." She was aware Alex was fighting a laugh.

"I'm going to watch him and Tiffany when they're alone, I bet they have sex in literal missionary position—like, he keeps one hand on the Bible at all times," said Sophie.

"The owner-slash-manager is going to explain what the plan is," said Basher. "Since there was a mistake in the system and we were not expected. She is presently in discussion with the stoic Mr. McGrath." He pinched the bridge of his nose.

"So . . . no one is talking," said Soph. "These people clearly all know each other but they're just sitting. Not talking. Watching you drink tea. Fucking hell."

Somewhere in the house a door slammed. Someone shouted.

A big gust of wind made the glass wall rattle and whine. The shouting got louder as whoever was doing it came down the hallway toward them. But when the dining room door opened, the woman on the other side was perfectly composed.

"Right. Hi. Hello. Gosh. I'm Minnie."

She spoke staccato, incomplete thoughts rattling out past large teeth. Minnie was rake thin and was dressed in black leggings and a black long-sleeve shirt, with dyed black hair and waxy, unhealthy-looking skin. A machine gun of a person. She was English, like most of the others. In fact, Claire realized, Eidy was the only Irish person they'd yet encountered on this small Irish island. He had come through after Minnie and was leaning against the wall by the door.

"So. There's been a mix-up. Bit of a mix-up. Yes. The hotel isn't strictly open yet. This week was supposed to be a private party. For my friends. You see. So. And Eidy put your booking through. He didn't realize. I didn't spot it. But he says he can't take you back."

"Look at him," said Soph. She got up close to Eidy and started leaning into his face like the bad cop in a suspect interrogation. Claire was familiar with the tactic from many episodes of *Murder Profile*. It was usually effective, so it was a shame Eidy couldn't actually see Sophie. "He did it on purpose."

Eidy's beard was, indeed, twitching almost imperceptibly. Claire wouldn't have noticed if Sophie hadn't pointed it out, but Sophie was the one who was good at reading people, and always had been. Claire had the imagination to spin what Sophie told her into stories people wanted to hear. She was, as she had told Basher several times, an ideas woman more than a facts woman.

"We can't go back to the mainland?" Basher clarified.

Eidy sniffed. "Storm," he said. He appeared to consider this sufficient explanation. Claire glanced out the large window again to check she hadn't imagined the absence of a storm beyond it being quite windy. "Boat isn't coming back until Friday, anyway."

"Wait, *what?*" said Claire. "That boat, the one we came on, that's gone? What if there's an emergency or something?"

Eidy shrugged. "Flares. Radio. There's a dinghy with an outboard, if it comes to it." He advanced no further information.

"That's okay! We wouldn't want to go anyway, right?" said Alex. They grinned.

"Well. Yes. Quite. I have a work-around," said Minnie. "You see, the rooms aren't all furnished yet. So there isn't room for everyone in the main house as it is. But we have some luxury units in the renovated village just next door to us here. They're all en suite and heated. Mod cons, you know. I daresay we'll have enough portions at dinner. But other meals you'd have to. You know. Sort things out. You can use the kitchen and supplies here."

"What about the Jacuzzi in the photos?" asked Claire, clinging to the final plank of hope on a rapidly increasing sea of boring holiday.

"We've not put that in yet," said Minnie. "Next year, maybe."

"Hotel's run out of money before it's even opened," sniffed Sophie, as Claire stifled a groan. "Not a great sign, is it?"

"Sorry—you said we'll have to cook for ourselves?" asked Basher.

"No staff, I'm afraid. But I'll discount you more. On your rate, I mean. Of course."

Claire and Basher both opened their mouths to say something but Alex got there first.

"Right!" they said, slapping both hands on the table. "Sounds well good. An adventure." They stood up, with an air of great and terrible purpose.

"Oh, one last thing," said Minnie. She opened a cupboard in a sideboard—which had a guestbook on top and, presumably in lieu of seasonal flowers, a vase of ivy trimmings and aesthetically pleasing sticks—and produced a lockbox. "Since you're here, you might as well. Do the whole thing, you know?"

She unlocked it and held it out. Claire had a growing sense of unease.

"Er. What are we supposed to do, sorry?" she said.

"Phones off and locked in here, please. For the duration."

Alex blinked. "I'm sorry, what the fuck did you just say?"

4

Best Frenemies Forever

"Interesting pool of suspects for treasure seekers, aren't they?" said Sophie.

She and Claire were sitting alone at a table watching everyone moving around the room, navigating one another cautiously, like teenagers at a school disco (to anyone else, of course, it looked like Claire was sitting by herself staring at people).

"Did you find anything interesting upstairs?" Claire asked quietly. She had seen Sophie slip away for a few minutes while everyone was arguing, to do her customary nose around people's stuff—something she did whenever they arrived somewhere new. She could read any scandalous receipts for purchases of vibrating anal beads that they may have left out on the side, or poke her head into the wardrobe and see it was full of secret, hidden jars of pickled eggs. It was a perk of being dead that played into a natural gossipy impulse she'd had as a living teenager. It helped when they did séances, too, because Sophie was able to feed Claire extremely accurate information for cold reads.

"Negative, although I think I can tell whose rooms are whose by, e.g., number of spare cowboy hats in them," said Soph. "But no maps left open on the table with a note saying 'my fucking genius plan to steal treasure from a dead pirate.' They're weird. Very chirpy and friendly on the face of it, but it doesn't seem like they actually have anything in common. Different styles, different vibes."

"I think pretending your life is blessed and amazing and that you eat avocado toast every morning, but secretly being miserable and hating your friends, is an increasing trend in our generation," said Claire.

"LOL. What does avocado taste like? I died before it became a big thing."

"What, really? You never had avocado? Did you never even go to that Mexican place in—"

"No! I didn't."

"Oh. Sorry." Claire thought about it. "Sort of like . . . if you chewed a hazelnut and spat it out, and then had a spoonful of double cream."

"Doesn't sound like it'd be good on toast."

"If people were honest they'd say it's not, really. Not compared to, like, Nutella, or spaghetti hoops. It's nice with other stuff, just not toast. Unless you put a load of other stuff on it. And at that point you might as well have saved time and had beans."

Claire noticed that Mac, the Scottish one, was looking at her, so she'd clearly been talking too loudly. She zipped her lip and looked at the group as a whole, rather than individuals, and realized Sophie was right. They were different enough that they could form the cast of a wacky sitcom: the hot one, the rich bitch one, the sub–Silicon Valley tech bro, the skinny uptight one. Frankly, Claire couldn't imagine any of them bothering their arses to haul antique junk around—but then again, people's habits weren't limited by imagination. She'd once had a flatmate who, when it was his turn to do the washing up, had done it in the bath at the same time as washing himself. You can never tell with people.

They heard George McDreamy, the doctor, volunteer to move into the separate part of the retreat as well. He seemed quite eager, because the original plan was that he'd be on a camp bed in the same room as Mac, Flick, and Caity; not an ideal situation for anyone involved. Ashley opined that she was fine with this, because she was a light sleeper and last night George's snoring had kept her awake through the bloody walls, so Claire was a bit worried she'd be next door to him.

"Honestly, Min, I'd prefer it," he said.

"Oh! Well! If you're sure!" said Minnie. "You need bedding. And towels. So let me just . . ."

Minnie disappeared again, presumably to source the aforementioned bedding. The other guests began talking among themselves again. Alex and Basher came back over, Basher having found some of his favorite custard creams in the kitchen with the unerring ability of a homing pigeon.

"Come on then, C," said Alex. They flapped their hands around as if to gin up enthusiasm and energy. "Here we, here we, here we fuckin' go and all that."

"I believe Claire is less than enthused about the prospect of several days on a haunted island without any electronic distractions," said Basher. He smiled at Claire and gave her a little nudge. "Come on, Strange. Chin up."

"Er, okay. And since when were you so chilled out about things like this?"

"Everything else has gone wrong. Why not this as well? 'It

boots not to resist both wind and tide.' Especially if wind and tide are allied with Alex."

The Wellness Retreat part of the name of her new hotel meant, Minnie had explained, a technology detox, so guests surrendered their phones on arrival and didn't even get to enjoy a TV in their rooms. This lack of amenity seemed to be something you paid extra for. Alex, who was never knowingly offline, was initially explosively resistant, and asked if Minnie thought they were Jared fucking Leto, or what? But then they had paused, as if in thought, and had turned on a dime to being suspiciously on board with the idea, and had insisted Bash and Claire hand their own phones over as well.

"Well, I thought it's more fun if we go undercover while we look for the treasure, you know," said Alex, who was already very excited at the mere rumor of treasure from local legends. At some point when they were alone, Claire would tell them a ghost insisted the treasure was real, at which point Alex would probably start levitating. "Do all the weird yoga and meditation stuff that they've got planned, blend in, and then: BAM! Make off with the goods right under their noses."

Claire looked at Bash, and he shrugged. "I thought this was a real holiday, I didn't realize we were undercover as people pretending we're on holiday."

"We are and we aren't. We're on holiday, but it's going to be a fun escapist holiday where you let me act like I'm Indiana Jones. He didn't have a mobile phone and he managed to steal *loads* of stuff."

"If this conversation is heading in the direction of you buying a whip, then so help me, I will turn this island around and take you home," said Basher.

"Har-de-har. Honestly, there's still a chance I'll go postal and kill you all myself—" Claire spotted that Tiffany overheard this and looked slightly alarmed.

"But," Alex went on, "at what point must we not take responsibility for our own happiness? We're here to treasure hunt, and if a storm arrives as I uncover the treasure, it will just make the denouement of the secret project more dramatic."

Claire was unsure about this. She exchanged a glance with Sophie, who had also been looking hard at Basher, her head to one side like a mum watching a baby that is being suspiciously quiet, despite not having had a nap.

"Secret project, eh?" said George McDreamy the doctor. "This week sounds like it just got more interesting."

"I concur," said Sophie, looking him up and down. "Keep yer knickers on, weirdo." Claire looked away and started to chew her thumb again.

He had walked over in a long stride. A lope, Claire thought. That's your classic lope. When he'd been sitting down it was obvious George was a big boy, but standing up he had what seemed like a clear foot and a half on Claire. He could, she felt, crack her back like a glowstick with very minimal effort. She tried not to feel this more than once but it was quite difficult. George also had his strawberry blond hair tied back in a bun, and Claire decided it was of paramount importance to see how long it was when he let it down. This could be a diversionary case to the main case of Who Stole a Possibly Imaginary Thing from a Ghost (Who Himself Stole It in the First Place).

McDreamy made eye contact with her. "Hope you won't be disturbed by having a stranger bunking nearby," he said. "This place is supposed to be haunted, you know."

"Um. That's good to know," said Claire. "I have a bad track record in hotels with ghosts."

He smiled, tipped his head, and raised an eyebrow, as if asking the question he didn't say out loud. "George Lyons," he said. He stuck his hand out for handshakes. He was wearing a Henley shirt with the sleeves pushed up toward the elbow, which made his forearms look well fit. "I thought we could have a more normal introduction, since we're going to be neighbors."

Claire, terrified of touching him, waited too long.

"Not a handshake person, okay," said George, tipping his head again.

Alex rolled their eyes and grabbed George's hand themself. "Alex. Pleased to meet you. This is Uncle B aka Basher to everyone else, and apparently Sebastian to Texans he's never met before."

"I didn't even tell him I'm a Sebastian," said Basher, almost to himself. He shook hands with George in his turn. "This is Claire."

"Aka C, aka weirdo, aka Strange, or Strange Ghost Talking Girl if Uncle B is feeling fancy," added Alex, with the air of a helpful prefect.

George grinned more widely than before, pricking dimples into his cheeks. "I have so many questions," he said.

"You will not like the answers," replied Claire, sinking down into her seat and wishing she could melt into the cloudy carpet. She wanted very much to have a shower. And possibly an extremely shameful wank she would regret almost as soon as it was over.

"You seem like a proactive man, George," Alex went on. "We might let you in on our secret plans later, if you do seem sound. Right now, it's a need-to-know thing." They wiggled their eyebrows.

"I see," said George very seriously. "I hope to be worthy."

"Would you like a custard cream?" asked Basher.

"Thank you, but no—I should go and help Minnie. Nice to meet you all!" He headed in the direction Minnie had taken. Claire decided to make an effort to not mentally think of him as McDreamy, because that was just admitting defeat before she even started. In any case, George the Viking was a much more apt descriptor.

Soon, Minnie returned to bring them around to where they'd be staying. Claire wasn't sure what she'd expected, but it wasn't what they found: a miniature town square, with grass in the middle and everything. The entrance faced the water, and Claire could hazily see the town they'd just left, almost directly opposite them. The cathedral tower would be out there, too, and she looked for the light flashing on top of it.

Sophie ran into the square and tried to do a cartwheel. On either side of the entrance were two low one-story buildings, which Minnie said were the old schoolhouse and church, the latter now being a little flat that Eidy lived in. Opposite the entrance was a small tower, like a mini-castle, with crenelations and everything, and on the left side of the square was a tiny terrace of four cottages, evidently split into upper- and lower-level suites, each with their own outdoor steps leading to the second story. The rest of the buildings around the square were still all empty shells with collapsing roofs, empty window frames, and some wire construction fences placed at random intervals around them.

George the Viking was sitting in the doorway of one of the renovated cottages, on the top floor at the end farthest from them, and he waved.

"I thought I'd leave you enough space," he said.

Alex nodded. "Like leaving a free urinal as a buffer," they called back, making George laugh.

Basher gently slapped their shoulder with the back of his hand. "Be normal, please," he said.

Alex took the top-floor room on the other end, so they had the best view of the sea, and Basher took the room underneath, presumably to keep an ear out for any foolishness Alex might get up to. Claire took the room next to Alex, leaving one house as a kind of social DMZ between her and George. She struggled up the steps with her bag collection.

"Wow, this is nice," said Sophie. She whistled. "Bet you're the first person to ever use this room."

She wasn't wrong. The main feature was a giant white bed with sea-green sheets and an embroidered gray runner, in front of a feature wall of leaf-print wallpaper. In one corner was a cupboard and worktop unit, with a half-size fridge, sink, built-in hot plate, and a kettle. There was also an electric fireplace. Claire sat on the bed and saw that the wall above the fireplace had, where you'd expect a massive TV, a framed print of a wide-lens photo of the sea, light on one side and dark clouds in the sky on the other. Everything smelled too new, like a car straight after being cleaned. It made Claire feel a bit nauseous.

"It's all plumbed and wired in. To the hotel generator, I mean," said Minnie, suddenly standing in the doorway. Claire jumped.

"Sorry, knock knock," Minnie said. "Bathroom is just through there, all the light switches here. And there's underfloor heating. The remote for the fire is by your bed there. Here's your key. Yale is for the main hotel door, if it's ever locked."

"Tightly wound, this one," observed Soph. "Ready to fuckin' snap. Like the elastic on a nun's knickers."

Claire could not disagree. Even she could tell that Minnie was stressed, and, even more evidently, the type of person who preferred to keep a lid on things like being stressed.

"You can use whatever you want. From the kitchen, of course— Whenever you like—not three a.m. or anything, though. We're a bit low on milk. George spilled a carton yesterday. So. Easy on the cereal."

"Sure, of course. Not a night owl," said Claire. "This must all be brand-new, then?"

"Actually, I bought the place about three years ago. A friend convinced me. Saw these buildings were for sale, very cheap but a fixer-upper, you know. Basically just shells. Spent a lot of time on it. Doing it up. Getting permits and approval. We were going to try a pool, but. You know. The logistics."

"Um. Well, it all seems lovely. Thank you so much. Sorry for the mix-up."

"Not your fault. Eidy sort of came with the place. Package deal. Anyway. We thought it'd be best to include you. In the activities and so on. We're going to have stew for lunch in a couple of mins, and then go up to the fort in about half an hour. Do let me know if you need anything before then."

Claire had never met anyone who actually said "mins" instead of minutes. She had a quick shower to wash away the unreal feeling of having been in an airport, and was dithering about whether to knock on Alex's or Basher's door when the question was settled by Alex knocking on *her* door and asking why she was arsing about, then dragging her out so they could go and get something to eat.

Upon arrival back at the main building, they discovered that when Minnie had said "we're having stew" she had meant "we" as in literally her and her friends. Claire could tell this was the case, because when they walked in and Basher said, very politely, "That smells delicious," Minnie froze like a deer in headlights that did not have enough crockery. But Flick, the progenitor of the stew, immediately broke any awkwardness by opining that, as to her stew, the more the merrier. Claire thus moved Flick into a mental column marked *PROBABLY ALL RIGHT*. Claire and her friends instinctively sat at an entirely separate table, creating a buffer between those who were sort of not supposed to be there and the big table of people who were. So, they had stew, and Alex even got an extra bowl for Sophie, as was their habit, which, Claire was relieved, nobody commented on.

Claire was returning their bowls to the kitchen when someone said "hello" unexpectedly, and she nearly dropped them all in the sink. She shot a look at Sophie, who was nominally supposed to stop people sneaking up on her by shouting "Someone's trying to sneak up on you!" but Soph merely picked at her sleeves. Claire made a note to ask what she was in a strop about.

"Oh, sorry, I didn't mean to startle you," said the voice, which turned out to belong to gorgeous George the Viking. Claire froze. And continued to freeze.

"Please, just say something," said Sophie.

"Oh, I just . . . um. I'm fine. Probably just paranoid," said Claire. She regretted it immediately.

"Do you have a reason to be paranoid?" George asked with a little chuckle. "Is it something to do with your many nicknames? Are they your secret identities for criminal ventures?"

Claire snorted. "I wish. No, that's . . . something else."

"I see. And are you going to tell me what?"

"Ohmigod. Weirdo, I think he's flirting with you."

Claire tried to ignore Sophie. "No," she replied to George, after doing a quick cost-benefit analysis on the idea of telling him she could see ghosts. Although it was inevitable he'd find out at some point.

To her surprise, George laughed, like she had said something winning and flirtatious. "Interesting. I enjoy a mystery," he said. "I'm sure I can convince you to tell me before the week is over. I can be very persuasive."

Claire opened her mouth to say, "Oh fuck off, mate," and was inordinately surprised when a girlish little laugh escaped instead.

"What is happening?" said Sophie, in undisguised astonishment. "It's not as if stew is a sexy food! Look, honestly, this is uncharted territory now. I have no psychological insight into a man who gets horny around dirty dishes."

"Are you coming to the fort?" George asked.

"Oh, erm. Yeah, I guess so. Let me get Bash and Alex . . ."

George followed her out of the kitchen and back into the main living space, where she found Alex. They were sitting with Mac and Flick and prodding Caity the baby bear.

"Hullo, C," they said. "I'm going to make olive bread. Isn't that exciting?"

Claire didn't even know Alex liked olives. "Are you not coming to the fort thing?" she said, bereft. "Where's Basher?"

"He said he was going for a walk, which is not normal for him, but then he is on holiday." Alex seemed to have, in the space of about forty-five minutes, entirely forgotten that they were supposed to be undercover treasure hunting. But then they did move from interest to interest at speed, like a hurricane that wanted to learn every craft it could, as quickly as possible.

"I dunno if I want to go without someone else," said Claire.

George coughed theatrically. "I'm going," he said.

Flick looked at him and raised an eyebrow. "I can confirm George is a person and counts as 'someone,'" she said, and half smiled.

"See? And—oh quick, let's make a run for it. Dan is coming over." George started walking toward the main door, and Soph chivvied Claire to follow him.

They were headed off by Crypto Dan pretty quickly. He greeted George with the loud, boneless sort of wail of greeting peculiar to a lad who considers himself possessed of, as they say, top bants. Up close, Claire could see that his T-shirt read EAT SLEEP **CODE** REPEAT.

"LOL. I hate him. We hate him, right?" said Sophie.

"Do you?" Claire asked, on impulse. "Know how to code, I mean?"

"What? Oh. No, it's just, like, a *vibe*, yeah?" said Dan. He was very loud. He talked like a man who wanted people to pay attention to him, even if they weren't in a conversation with him. It was an odd contrast with George, who spoke low and slow, so you leaned in and actually had to pay attention to him.

"Pog, bruh. Have you got time to talk portfolio today, yeah?" Dan went on, turning to George. "You've got to diversify."

"I don't have a portfolio, Dan. I don't even have a ring binder."

"Mate," said Dan in a tone that somehow managed to convey he was saying *m8*, "you've got to get on my level, yeah?"

George grinned. "Well according to Tiff, you've been looking up Korean plastic surgeons who do jaw sculpting, so your level is apparently 'midlife crisis.'"

Dan blanched, although he recovered quickly. "Investment opportunities, bruh. I'm telling you, if you keep all your money tied up in trad banking you're going to get absolutely dicked in the next crash—and a crash is coming, my friend, no doubt about it."

Claire got the strong impression that whatever idea Dan had, he instantly believed he was the first person to have ever had it.

He had eyes the color of the bottom of a puddle, but she kept looking at his goatee, dark brown against pale skin. It was like getting the mirror universe version of a man without knowing if the prime universe version even existed.

"Yes, totally will find time this week—but actually, I can't just now," said George. He gave Dan an easy-going smile.

"Oh come on, man, what are you doing instead? No time like the present to secure your future," said Dan, who was starting to sound like a life insurance salesman. Claire realized that George was looking at her. He widened his eyes.

"Your line," prompted Sophie. "Help him out."

"Er. Actually. George and I were . . . just leaving?" suggested Claire.

George nodded gratefully. "Yeah, we're going on the visit to the fort," he said.

"Oh, me too! But we have to wait for Minners to come back and take us 'round."

"It's . . . I . . ."

"No is a complete sentence. Just say you're going now to enjoy the walk or whatever," said Sophie. Soph was always extremely annoyed that Claire approached every conversation as an apology she already had to make. Claire's shoulders slumped.

"We're going to leave now to enjoy the walk," she said.

"Right! Yes, so let's go," said George. "Talk later, dude."

They had left the hotel and walked some way down the path in silence when Claire thought she heard Basher's laugh. She looked around, and thought she saw a glimpse of his orange cape thing disappearing behind one of the derelict buildings set back from the path—but they were all among the trees, behind tumbledown walls and construction fencing, and Bash wasn't the sort of person to disobey the order implied by a fence . . .

She was going to look more closely, but George suddenly burst out laughing.

"Sorry about that," he said. He staggered forward a little, then leaned an arm on Claire's shoulder, rocked by his laughter. "He's been on me to dump all my savings into whatever crypto currency thing he's into. Haven't had five minutes to myself since we arrived. I don't even have much to dump, is the thing."

"Oh yeah?" said Claire, who was interested, and aware that George had now twice breached the wall of physical contact. "You all know each other from uni, right?"

"Some of us. Me, Flick, Tiffany, Dan, and Minnie. The others married in. We're sort of a club, you see," George said, in the tone of someone gearing up for a backstory.

Oh God, maybe it was going to be that kind of week. Claire remembered a program—probably Louis Theroux or someone—where there was a weird, erotic blindfolded-people-feeding-each-other-bits-of-kumquat group. Putting strawberries in people's mouths. Claire wondered if you could get out of putting car keys in a bowl if you didn't have a car, or if they just had lender keys, like how posh country clubs supposedly had blazers you could borrow if you were the sort of pleb who only had a hoodie.

"See, there would be the place I'd expect someone to say, 'What sort of club?' You're really making me work hard, Claire," said George. He still didn't sound cross. Possibly he thought this was some sort of deliberate technique to attract men.

"Yeah, g'wan, ask him," said Soph. "These so-called friends seem to all fucking hate each other. I want to know what's up."

"Oh. Er. Sorry. What sort of club, George?"

"Better. I joined a weekly campus yoga class midway through my second term, because I felt awful all the time and I thought it might be, you know, spiritual or healthy or something. I did not, before you ask, drink less. The girls and Dan had all joined it too. It turned out to be a lot of fun. If anything, we drank even more heavily than we had before . . ." He looked into the middle distance, smiling at a memory. "Dan and Minnie got quite big into the whole lifestyle—Minnie especially. She's a proper yoga teacher and everything."

"Oh, right. I can see that," said Claire. Minnie did indeed seem like the sort of person who drank a lot of green smoothies instead of having meals.

"We sort of formed a club, unofficially, and kept doing it after graduation. We try new health innovations together. Minnie is the driving force, but it keeps us in touch, so even those of us who are a bit, er . . ."

"Skeptical?"

"Yes, exactly—well, we don't mind. And a lot of the stuff we've done over the years is quite wellness adjacent, you know. A few of us got quite into hiking and climbing for a while."

"Nah, I don't buy it," said Sophie. "There's something else. These people should have ghosted each other years ago."

They were almost at the end of the pier where they'd landed, but George pointed left and up a hill, past some colorful and largely intact cottages. Claire slowed down on the incline and tried to make it look casual. Sophie was exploring the abandoned cottages with some interest, and Claire paused to watch her as if she was looking at the houses themselves. A plaque indicated a significant child had lived in one of them.

"Well, I suppose really what's kept us together is . . . I mean it seems silly to say, but we all owe bloody Dan money. Quite a bit, actually. He's the rich one, you see. He *was* anyway, before Ritchie turned up with his oil money. A few years ago, Dan got into the Web3 stuff early. I don't really understand how, but he became really rich—something to do with lizards? Pictures of iguanas, I think that's it. He started investing the money in us lot. He backed Flick's bakery, helped with my mortgage, he's Minnie's money for this place. So there's a sense of obligation to keep meeting up but . . . Over the last few years, to be honest, I think some of us are feeling a bit resentful. When Minnie invited us here it half felt like getting our noses rubbed in it again, but also half felt like . . . I dunno, a last gasp. To be actual friends again." He was silent for a moment, and scratched his beard. "I probably shouldn't have told you that, should I? But you leave such big pauses in the conversation . . ."

Claire was quite pleased with this. It suggested she had a natural aptitude for interviewing perps, like some of the team members on *Murder Profile*, who were all not only expert criminal psychologists but also sexy and confident, and were very good at making people not ask for lawyers and confess to murders (these being reasons Alex did not like *Murder Profile*, also because the show portrayed asking for, or indeed having, a lawyer as things only guilty people did anyway). Staying silent was a risky interviewing tactic, but really she only did it to try to think of what to say next—or out of habit, because she was often listening to something Sophie was saying in the gap.

"Like that," went on George, laughing again.

"Um. Sorry. I think about things."

"Still waters run deep. What sort of things?"

"Well, like . . . what's this fort thing?"

George grimaced. "Oh yeah. The fort on the top of the island. At least, it used to be a fort. I think it was mostly a prison. It only closed in 2004."

"This island doesn't seem like a natural fit for a wellness retreat, to be honest," observed Sophie. Claire agreed, and repeated it to George.

"No, true. I'm not sure what possessed Minnie. We've all grown apart a bit, and a wellness retreat isn't Dan's speed at all these days. Or, well, he is, but it's that weird kind of tech wellness lifestyle stuff. He says stuff like 'the internet of things' a lot. Wants to optimize yogurt with an algorithm, all that weird shit."

They rounded a corner and Claire was horrified to see that their route continued up yet more hill, though it was less steep. The road was surrounded by what now appeared to be well-maintained green lawn, but, she supposed, had originally been a defensive measure. At the end of the road was a big gate in a very big wall.

"I don't know if I'd be into that," said Claire. "I wouldn't want my kettle telling Mark Zuckerberg what I get up to. I say 'thank you' to AI things, so they'll be nice to me when the Skynet Judgment Day happens."

George laughed, as if she had made a joke. Out of the corner of her eye Claire saw Sophie do a sausage roll down the slope and run back up again.

"I'll keep that in mind," George said. "You know, I feel like I need my own nickname for you, to go with your list of them."

Claire reminded herself that a dead pirate was convinced one of this lot could be some sort of paranormal thief. But George hadn't given any indication he could see or hear Sophie. And as far as Claire could tell, you didn't selectively see ghosts. It was all or nothing. Granted she only had herself as a test case, but still . . . In fact, nobody so far had reacted to Sophie's presence even a tiny bit. She didn't know if the group she was already earmarking as "The Others" would be good enough actors for that.

"You've gone quiet again," he said, and smiled at her very

nicely. "Sorry you've ended up stuck here. Although it's good to meet new people."

"Yeah, I s'pose so," said Claire.

"Ouch!" said George. He mimed being struck in the heart with an arrow. "Best foot forward, we're nearly at the top. Come on . . . Claire-Bear?"

"Absolutely not."

Sophie caught up with them, and they went through two giant gates that represented the inner and outer walls of the fort. There was also a photo op featuring a life-size model of a teenager talking to his girlfriend through one of those prison visit screens, which Sophie found hilarious. George explained that yes, it was indeed a tourist attraction, but in the off season the boats only came over Friday to Sunday, so Minnie had keys and had worked out some sort of deal for her guests to be allowed to visit it. "She goes for a run around the island first thing every morning, and unlocks the doors here as she goes past," he said.

They walked past the forever-imprisoned teenage dummy and out into a huge rectangular central yard. Improbably huge, really; it seemed like far too big a flat space to fit on the weird scraggly island Claire had seen so far. The center of it was grass, with paths around the outside, and crisscrossing the middle. There were what looked like some burned-out blocks of flats in the corner opposite where they stood, a big, white columned building down the far end, and some flat gray block structures on their left.

Sophie whistled. "Bleeding fuck," she said. "You could fit a whole other fort inside this one."

"Wow," said George. "I mean. It's impressive. Where should we go first? There are some secret tunnels under the fort somewhere, and you usually have to buy a VIP experience thing to see them. D'you want to try and find them ourselves?"

"Um. Shouldn't we wait for the others?" Claire asked.

Sophie rolled her eyes and called Claire a coward.

"If you like!" George said. "Give me a tick, though, I'm going to see if Minnie thought to open any toilets. I probably should have gone before we walked up here, and though I will admit I'm not above pissing on a building of historic significance, I'd rather I didn't have to . . ."

This made Claire laugh.

"At last!" cried George as he jogged away. "I knew I'd get one out of you eventually!"

He was heading to an obviously new building in the middle of the yard, shaped like a cross between a barn and a tent, and which signage suggested was probably the gift shop and res-taurant. Claire waited until he was out of earshot, and turned around.

"Right," she said, glaring at the ghost who was loitering in the shadow of the wall, leaning against it in a relaxed way. "Who the fuck are you, then?"

The ghost—a man—laughed and sauntered toward Claire and Sophie. When he was close enough, he raised his arm.

For the second time in almost as many hours, Claire found herself at the wrong end of a weapon being brandished by a ghost. Only this time, rather than a sword, it appeared to be some sort of weird hockey stick.

"I could ask ye the same thing," the ghost said.

5

Hold the Fort

Without breaking eye contact—or, Claire noticed, ceasing to smile—the man stuck the fingers of his free hand in his mouth, and let out an ear-piercing whistle.

"How's the form?" he said, in what Claire could now recognize as a strong Cork accent. "Conn's my name. Ye'll oblige me by waiting here a moment."

Conn was as lanky as he was languid, with tangled brown hair down to his shoulders in the kind of style that you got when you did not, in fact, have a hairstyle, but just let the stuff grow and to hell with the consequences, and pale green eyes that were hard to read. He was wearing a kind of knee-length tunic and had a wool cape thrown around his shoulders in a way that was honestly not too dissimilar from how girls strutting around Mayfair wore their comically oversized scarfs.

"Could you put your hockey stick down, please, Conn?" said Claire. "It's not like you can do anything to me."

"Maybe I can, maybe I can't," said Conn. "But you're not the only one here." He briefly swung the stick around and pushed Sophie's shoulder with it. She wasn't expecting it and fell back a step.

"You can fuck right off, pal," she said, glaring.

Conn grinned the grin of someone who had lived and died decades before toothpaste was a twinkle in Mr. Colgate's eye.

"And another thing," he said. "Now I'm going to be very nice, and give you some free education. This isn't a hockey stick." He lifted the object in question to brandish it. It was about as long as a field hockey stick, so Claire didn't feel the comparison was unwarranted, but the end was flattened out, about as wide as the span of one of George's big hands. "This is a hurley."

"All right, thank you for explaining. Now can we please wrap this up?" said Claire. "Only I'd rather not have anyone I know see me talking to thin air." She looked across the yard trying to see where George had gone. Plus, there was another load of people who'd be coming up the hill after them, and would presumably arrive any minute.

"Don't be getting agitated," said Conn, still very pleasant. "Sure he's on his way now."

Claire looked in the direction Conn was, and saw another ghost emerging from behind the shell of one of the large ruined buildings on the other side of the yard. He came over to them at a much slower pace than Claire would have hoped, under the circumstances.

"Look, there's another!" said Sophie, pointing to the left, where a third ghost was approaching from a path leading behind the smaller, grayer, blockier building.

This man arrived first. "How's the form, Mossie?" said Conn. Mossie did not reply. He eyed Claire and Sophie, but didn't say anything. He had the same green eyes and brown hair as Conn;

Mossie was shorter and stockier, but it was obvious seeing them next to each other that they were brothers.

The other man, who was coming from farther away, didn't see any particular need to speed up as he crossed the yard. When he finally arrived he tipped his head at Conn, which was all the latter needed to give a report.

"She can see us," he said, nodding at Claire. "Weren't with the big group who arrived last night. Reckon they came up today, like."

"How're things? I'm Fionnbharr, but ye can call me Finny," said the new man, obviously the leader. Something about the oval shape of his face and the set of his eyes suggested that he was the oldest brother, but his hair, though just as long, was tawny, and his eyes were blue.

"We've been warned about you, Finny," said Sophie, in the tone of voice she reserved for being incredibly unimpressed by historical ghosts that she deemed boring.

"I bet you have," said Finny with a grin. Claire was becoming alarmed at how much these lads were all smiling, and when she met Sophie's eyes she could tell her friend agreed.

"Look, is this going to be a long discussion? Can we go somewhere a bit out of the way?" said Claire, who was still mindful of not appearing especially abnormal in front of George.

"Will we go around the corner?" said Finny. He gestured to where Mossie had come from, and they all trooped over to the little gray building, which was labeled, quite ominously, as the punishment block. Finny led them behind it and around into a sun-trap corner up against the wall of another building. Claire had already lost all sense of direction, but getting unlost was one of the things she outsourced to Sophie.

The men stood looking at them, as if assessing a set of new and unexpected variables. All three of them were wearing similar clothes, but with slightly different colored tunics or their capes arranged differently—Mossie had his looped over his head in a little hood—so it was a bit like looking at a boy band, but an unusually historic one.

"G'wan then," said Finny.

"What do you mean? You stopped us, you have to go first," said Claire.

"Ohmigod, don't concede an advantage," said Sophie. "We're supposed to be undercover interrogating them for Cole."

"I don't think it's very advantageous to reveal you're undercover interrogating someone to their face," said Conn very mildly.

"All right, fine," snapped Sophie. "Are you and your . . . brothers . . . stealing the pirates' treasure?"

"No," said Finny promptly. "That's the end of it, so?"

"'No' is exactly what you'd say if you were actually stealing it, though," said Sophie.

"No it isn't. We're very honest," said Conn. Finny nodded to confirm this.

"How is it you can see us?" said Mossie, falling out of step with the Three Stooges act that had been developing up to that point. He was looking at Claire.

"Dunno. It started when she died," said Claire, nodding at Sophie. "I'm Claire, by the way, not that you asked. And that's Sophie. And yes, we came here on the boat just now. We're supposed to be on holiday."

"Well, Claire and Sophie, ye can tell that great hairy gowl that we've not touched his treasure," said Finny.

"Matter of fact, we'd very much like to know who took it off him, because it's been fierce fucking boring around here since it happened," said Conn.

"What do you mean?"

"'Tis a game, like," said Mossie, who Claire was earmarking as the shy, sensitive one. "We hold the fort and they try to take it off us. They have the old village and west of the island, and we try to take it off them. The prisoners' graveyard is contested territory. Nobody ever wins, but it keeps your head together."

"Big fort for three people to hold," said Claire.

"Big fort for three people to take," said Conn, grinning again. "Nobody ever wins, but one day we might, kinda thing."

"Sounds like you'd steal Cole's treasure just to piss him off," said Sophie sourly. She had evidently picked sides, and it was the one that had smiled very nicely at her and kissed her hand. This was, Claire thought, not the proper objective view that a detective should take in the course of their investigatoring.

"Hmm," said Claire. "And, to be clear, it was you who wrecked Cole's ship and stole the treasure in question in the first place, is that right? When you were alive, I mean."

"Ah, here," said Conn, "we never wrecked fuck all. He went into the cliffs near Roches Point out there." He gestured with his hurley. "It's not our fault we were living in the same general area that he was being a shite sailor."

"Okay, but you did take some of the cargo, right?" said Soph.

"We're not wreckers, but Conn didn't say we weren't *opportunists*," said Mossie with a shy smile. "We planned to stash it here to come back for it later, only, as you can see, we didn't make it. Went over in the surf and drowned."

"All right, but that means that you know exactly where it is, if you wanted to steal it," said Soph.

"Even if we could move anything—which you'll note we can't—we wouldn't want to. Cole has gone into a great decline the last two days. Hasn't charged the walls or tried to sneak in," said Finny in a deliberately reasonable tone. "Like Conn said, it's boring."

"Hasn't even come up to have a friendly shout at us, like," said Conn. "There's nothing else to do since the prison closed years ago. Thank God the tourists still come up at weekends, or we'd have gone cracked."

"We're not the only ghosts here, you know," said Mossie. "This island has a long history. But the others . . . they didn't have a reason to stay themselves. We've seen them fading away over time. So we made ourselves a reason. Even if Cole doesn't know it."

This did actually sound reasonable to Claire. If the Wreckers— the *Opportunists*, she corrected herself—were smart enough to have found a way to passively prevent themselves turning into an insubstantial chilly mist while actively having fun, it made sense that they wouldn't want to upset the balance. On the other hand, resolving unfinished business was a possible way to stop being a ghost and move on to . . . whatever else there was. After many hundreds of years, maybe they were making a new play for a resolution.

"I don't believe them," said Sophie.

"I might believe them," said Claire. Which was true—but she also thought that a detective team should be balanced, which meant someone had to be leaning more toward the Opportunists telling the truth.

"Ohmigod! Seriously? These chucklefucks?" said Sophie.

"I dunno, they honestly seem like they're not bothered," Claire replied.

"Again, I must question the tactics of discussing all this in front of us," said Conn. He still seemed more amused than anything.

"How about this," said Finny. "We'll tell ye where it is. I bet Cole didn't, did he?"

". . . No, he didn't," conceded Sophie. "But he doesn't know who he can trust!"

"Well, bollocks to it. There's a few chests in the water near the south cliffs. It's strange they weren't found before now, but I suppose nobody was looking."

"And for all we know, they're all rotted to pieces," said Mossie. "I'd not be surprised if one of them washed away and the old fool thought it was stolen."

"And you haven't seen anything out of the ordinary?"

"Nothing from the new gang," said Finny. "Cole's right if he thinks it's one of ye, because that's the only thing that's changed on the island."

"We're not really with the others," said Sophie. "They're a bunch of weird frenemies who seem about as functional as you lot."

"We came here with our two friends. They know about Sophie. The other people don't," added Claire. "Which is why I'd quite like to wrap this up."

"Grand, so," said Conn. "You're not as fun to talk to as I'd hoped."

"Yeah, you're no picnic either, mate," said Sophie. "Come on, let's leave these losers to patrol the walls, or whatever the fuck they do."

"That's exactly what we do, in fairness," said Mossie. He waved as they walked away.

The yard, when they reemerged, was still deserted. Claire thought she heard a distant laugh somewhere.

"Did you hear that? Did the others arrive? I thought we'd have heard them."

"Ohmigod, chill out," said Sophie.

"Maybe they're in here . . ." mused Claire, ignoring Sophie and turning to the front of the punishment block. "Look, there's an open door."

The punishment block was damp and gloomy, which was good for a haunted prison ambience. There were a couple of rooms set up to look like the old guards' quarters, and an upper and lower story of cells. Claire looked in through the peephole of a closed door and made out a life-size model of a man sitting on the floor, next to a little model rat.

"This is my favorite thing about museums, when they set up, like, dioramas," she said. "It even has a recording of moaning playing, listen."

"That's . . . not a recording," said Sophie.

"Oh."

Claire pressed her face against the door so she could look in at a sharper angle, and saw that the room still had a bed in it—she supposed it helped with the sense of scale. At the end of it, sitting in the gloom, was a ghost. He was half collapsed against the wall, filthy, in a ragged shirt and with no trousers. He was crying. He looked up and made sudden, clear eye contact with Claire, and she jerked back from the peephole.

They left quite quickly. The ghost did rather underscore the point Mossie had made. Claire couldn't stop thinking of the dummy. She could see it standing up and opening the door from the inside, stiff joints, unblinking eyes, wrong anatomy.

There still wasn't anyone in the yard outside, which didn't do much for Claire's grasp on reality. If she had already died, how would she and Sophie know? How did they know *when* they were? She kept compulsively reaching to check the date and time on her phone, but she didn't have it. What if she was an amnesiac dead person already?

"Hey. Earth to weirdo," said Sophie, and snapped her fingers in front of Claire's face. "Let's be proactive. What's the next step in a TV show?"

"Er. Dunno, really. If it was a police show I'd say to canvas the crime scene. This feels way more like a historical drama right now, which is out of my wheelhouse."

"Let's work with the crime scene thing. The Wreckers—"

"Opportunists."

"Oh whatever. Those guys said that the treasure was to the south, right? Let's see if we can see anything from the south side of the fort. Looking around a tourist attraction is normal behavior."

In the absence of a better plan, Claire followed Sophie as she walked around the central yard, up to the second of the two huge burned-out prison blocks in one corner of the fort. There were trees growing up through the middle of them.

"I wonder what happened," said Claire. She watched through a window as Sophie looked around inside.

"Riot," said Finny, making Claire jump. He had walked right behind her without her noticing. "In the eighties. Great bunch of lads."

He didn't pause as he talked, but hurried past and went back behind the building, from where they'd originally seen him emerge.

"Hey!" she called to Sophie, before remembering that there

might be other people here somewhere, and lowering her voice. "*Hey. This way.*"

Around the back of the building was a sandy gravel path that led up onto the inner wall. Finny was already at the top. He waved and headed off to the right, as Soph ran up and Claire followed at a much more sedate pace.

"Why is everything at a fucking fifty-degree angle of elevation," she muttered.

At the top it was suddenly windy again, because being on top of the wall meant they were outside the protection of it. They were on a flat bit of the inner wall that came to a point, facing out into the sea. In front of them was a deep dry moat carpeted in grass, and then the outer wall. Claire looked back, and saw they were almost directly opposite the squat punishment block building.

"What sort of a weird shape is this place? I can't figure it out."

Sophie looked around critically. "It's a star shape," she said. "Remember the map? We're on a point here, the punishment block bit in one there, and then there's another at each corner of the rectangle. Pretty good lookouts, I suppose. See, Finny is on that one."

Sophie pointed, and Claire, shading her eyes, could just about make out Finny sitting on the edge of another grassy star point. He seemed to be leaning back on his hands and kicking his legs quite happily, although it was hard to tell. He was a bit far away, and ghosts were harder to see in bright sunlight, so every time the wind chased a cloud away from the sun he half-disappeared, until a shadow covered him again. Sophie was fading in and out, too, like a sci-fi hologram running out of power.

"This is cool, but I think we're too far from the edge, and at the wrong angle, to see the cliff bit," she said.

"Yeah, fair," said Soph. The area they were on had been partially graveled, and had benches for tourists to stop and take in the view. Claire walked to the little wire fence that was set up to keep them from tumbling into the dry moat between the walls. She could see the unbroken line of the sea, almost merging into the sky. The water was a great mirror that changed as she looked at it: bright blue, then flashing white and slate under the clouds, and then sparkling with light when the sun came out. It was so big. There was a windsurfer out on the water. Claire focused on the tiny chip of yellow and red that was the sail and started to get dizzy.

She turned back, intending to try to find George or the others, but noticed some other steps, leading down directly under where they were standing.

"I'm going to look down here," she said. "Maybe it's a lookout or something."

"Suit yourself. I'm going back to the burned-out bits, I want to look around them more. Think it's close enough?" asked Sophie. She'd obviously been thinking about the reach of their invisible tether, too.

"I think so. Maybe it's like hamstrings."

"LOL. What the fuck does that mean?"

"Like . . . if we stretch it a little bit every day, it'll go farther."

"Worth a try, I s'pose," said Soph. "I mean, what else do I have going on? Apart from a treasure hunt. Actually, I suppose my calendar is quite full."

Claire didn't watch her go, but applied herself to her new solo adventure. The stairs led to an underground chamber with a paved floor. The paving bricks were bulged up in one part, as if there had been a slapstick cartoon explosion under the floor.

Claire looked at it with suspicion. The bricks weren't broken. It looked pregnant. Like something would burst out.

There were two open doorways on the back wall. Claire went through one: a sloping, echoing, low corridor. She walked down it, listening to the sound of her own feet. It opened into what did indeed seem to be a lookout, in the tip of the star point. She checked and found that another, identical corridor ran parallel to the one she had walked down. It was like she had walked down one arm of a hairpin and was standing at the end of the loop, looking down the full length of the other arm. She felt a twinge as Sophie pulled at the tether between them, stretching it beyond the normal length. Claire winced. How far had she gone? Seventy? Eighty meters?

It was then Claire heard footsteps. They echoed loudly.

"H-hello?" she called. Her voice cracked a bit. The footsteps stopped. There was no reply. "George?"

She went and looked down the first corridor again, but there was nobody there. She doubled back to the second. Empty. Despite herself, her heart rate leaped.

"Fuck. Fuckit, fuckit, shutup, shh," she muttered to herself.

First corridor: empty. Second corridor: empty.

She tried to get a hold of herself. She couldn't stay here indefinitely. She didn't want to yell for Sophie, in case somebody heard. But still she couldn't move. She stood, frozen in a slightly awkward position with all her weight on one leg, trying to figure out if she could hear anything over the low whistle of the wind coming through the open concrete window slits.

Rabbit in the headlights, she thought. And then, *No headlights, stupid. It's daytime. Also, no car.*

Suddenly, the footsteps started up again. They were moving

faster. Claire panicked. She didn't know which corridor to pick. But she didn't want to look, in case she saw what was coming. On impulse she jumped toward the second, and almost cried with relief when she saw it was empty. She started walking down it, her own footsteps reverberating and crossing over with the other person's. Claire breathed in and out very slowly, keeping very deliberate control—until whoever was following her sped up again.

They started running. She started running, too.

She skidded back into the first chamber with the uneven floor, nearly falling over the bulge in the paving, and then actually tripping on the stairs up, slamming her shins into the concrete. She yowled in pain, then stuffed her fist in her mouth to keep quiet, and scrambled up the steps using her free hand as much as her feet to get up. On top of the wall it was sunny and quiet, except for the wind. Claire looked around, panting, clenching and unclenching her fists, but there was no sign of Sophie.

She took off running down the gravel path, leaving skids and nearly tripping over herself again. At the bottom she took a sharp left and sprinted along the edge of the ruined cell blocks, aware she was hyperventilating and not able to stop, aware she couldn't see where she was going and not able to stop.

Someone grabbed her shoulders and Claire screamed and started flailing. She managed to claw someone's face and heard them swearing. She fell over, and kept trying to get up again. She could hear a lot of people talking and all of their voices were as loud as each other's and she didn't know who anyone was.

"Fuck! What the fuck?"

"She's freaking out!"

"Does anyone know where her friends are?"

"Claire. Claire! Weirdo! Calm down. What's going on? I'm here, you're okay."

Claire grabbed onto Sophie's voice, a life raft of familiarity. She pulled herself up onto her knees. A second later she felt an ice-cold hand on her neck and the *zip* that meant Sophie was touching her. She felt her energy draining; within a few seconds her heart rate slowed down and she became unnaturally calm and lethargic.

Claire opened her eyes, and saw that she had run into the group of The Others, led by Minnie, who had probably been mid-tour. Crypto Dan was holding a hand up to his face. Ashley had sourced an antibac wipe from somewhere, and was attempting to move his hand out of the way. Tiffany was looking at the sky, evidently trying to pretend nothing had happened.

"You're okay, weirdo," said Sophie. "I'm going to take my hand away now, okay?"

Sophie being openly caring toward her always made Claire more nervous than when she was being casually bitchy.

"Goodness. Right. Okay. Does anyone have a paper bag?" Minnie said. Claire's heart sank to the ground when she saw who was standing next to her. "Wasn't she with you, George? What happened?"

"I don't know, Minners, we got separated. I was looking for her when I ran into you," said George. He came over and bent down, taking her hand. Claire felt a hurt, scratchy feeling in the back of her throat.

"Jesus. You're freezing cold. What happened?" he said.

Claire burst into tears.

6

Night Man, Sneaky and Mean

Claire sat right on the edge of the land, dangling her feet over the side of a flat grassy triangle in front of the hotel. She picked fitfully at the knees of her jeans, which now boasted a couple of scrappy holes, ringed in dirt and blood from the matching grazes on her skin. Her shins felt the kind of damp soreness that had her checking she wasn't bleeding there, too, and the heels of her hands stung from where she'd put them out when she fell. This trip was going through more of her wardrobe than she'd anticipated.

After they came back from the fort, she had walked out here and sunk down. George had tried to talk to her, but she had pretended he wasn't there until he went away. Sophie had also tried to talk to her, but Claire was so unresponsive she got bored, until luckily—or unluckily—Cole turned up, with a young man in an old-fashioned navy uniform: the proper blue flared trousers, dancing-the-hornpipe kind of kit. His name was Seaman Spraggs, and Claire had made a very manful effort to not snigger

when he was introduced. Cole, not having any useful dead relatives around, had put together his small crew from other slightly
random sailors who'd died nearby, that being Spraggs and a third
ghost Cole called Mister Bones, with the full two-syllable *Mister*.
Mister Bones was apparently on guard over the remaining treasure, but Spraggs was standing to attention a few meters away
from her, like an actual chaperone.

"What's a good navy man like you doing falling in with a law-
less pirate, Spraggs?" she asked.

Spraggs saluted and clicked his clacketing, shiny heels together.
"Captain Tovey told me he had a commission from Her Majesty
the Queen, ma'am," he said.

"Doubtful. Anything else?"

"He's a good sailor, ma'am, and he's not Irish."

"Blimey. What an enlightened outlook, Spraggs. How old
were you, when you were alive?"

"Twenty-three, ma'am. Miss being alive, to be honest."

"I'm sure you'll get used to it. Or finish your unfinished business, or whatever. As you were, Spraggs."

He clicked his heels again. Claire found herself disappointed
he was a real sailor and not a jaunty pretend one from a Fred
Astaire dance routine.

Claire kicked her legs. Her toes just grazed the gray-brown
sand of the small beach, all studded with rocks and bits of shell.
If she'd sat in the same place at high tide, her feet would have
been wet. She was watching Sophie, who was paddling along the
edge of the water with Captain Cole. He'd even taken her arm.

This was unusual behavior for Sophie. When she was alive
she hadn't paid much attention to boys, which meant that a lot
of them paid attention to her. Dying hadn't really shifted her
priorities.

But come to that, Claire didn't really have much interest in men, either. Or, to be exact, she liked the idea of liking men, and thus could develop intense and dreamy crushes, but anything beyond that seemed too complicated and more trouble than it was worth. Maybe this week was like their version of Vegas. What happens on a tiny, rainy island stays on a tiny, rainy island. Or maybe the rocks on Spike Island contained some kind of natural biological contaminant that made people annoying horndogs. It would explain why George seemed to want to have conversations with her.

She narrowed her eyes and kept a close watch on Cole as he walked around with Sophie. Every time she'd got up to move closer, like a good chaperone should, they'd run a bit farther down the beach giggling, which made her feel like she was being bullied by mean schoolgirls, so she'd stopped trying.

"Hello."

She turned. Basher was standing on the grass behind her. "Mind if I join you?" he asked. Claire shrugged and indicated the empty space next to her; it was a free country, so on and so forth.

He awkwardly hopped down to be next to her.

"It's a lovely view, isn't it?" he said, making the reasonable assumption she was staring at the bay rather than two ghosts cavorting in the flat surf. "Tide is going out now, I think. Did you know it changes by about half an hour each time? So high tide was when we came over on the boat, the next low tide will be about dinner time, and the next high tide at one a.m."

This sort of generalist interest in useless facts was typical of Bash. Claire glared at him. "Where have you been, then?" she asked.

"I think you should go first. It sounds like you have had a much more interesting afternoon. What happened to your jeans?"

"I fell over."

"I had in fact brought all my training to bear to figure that out myself. I was hoping for more specifics."

"I fell over at the fort," said Claire.

"Yes, but again you are being quite vague, aren't you?"

"Is everyone talking about it?"

"'Fraid so. What happened? Are you all right?"

"Um. Yeah. No, but yeah. I thought someone was following me in the fort and I freaked out. How's Crypto Da— I mean, how's Dan?"

"He does like crypto . . . He's fine. He has three small scratches on his left cheek, but given that you bite your nails, I would say it compares favorably to walking into a bramble bush. Or being mauled by a small cat. Mac has used her vet expertise and explained he is probably not going to get rabies. *Were* you being followed?"

"I heard footsteps. It was probably just a ghost, there are loads of them about. Fucking annoying, actually. And I ran into Dan and panicked and just sort of flailed at his face. I'm fine now."

Basher scratched his chin and looked at her. "Claire, I know that what happened last year was, notionally, mostly something that happened to my family, but it did happen most acutely to you. You dug up a body and had to go to hospital."

"Correlation, not causation," said Claire. "What's your point? I said I'm fine."

"Yes," he said. "But it's okay if you're not, you know. I know you daydream a lot, but if you're—"

"I'm not hearing things, or whatever, if that's what you were going to say," Claire snapped. "You don't know me that well."

"I was going to say 'dwelling on unpleasant things.' I know you well enough to know when you're being defensive," he said, in his infuriatingly pleasant way. "And that you are not going to want to come to dinner in the main living area tonight because you will feel embarrassed."

"Fuck off. I'm going to want dinner."

"I was going to say that it might be good for you to avoid it, actually. Dan and Ashley are overreacting, but they're less than enthused about you and could do with an evening to calm down. Tomorrow is another day." He stood up and brushed down his jeans.

"Whatever," said Claire.

He set off again, a skinny little perambulatory pumpkin. It was only once he was out of sight that Claire realized he had completely avoided answering her question about where he had been. *Can't believe I bought that fucker a nice mug,* she thought, with some venom. *I'll tell you who the mug is: me, that's who.*

It was only a shame her inner monologue wasn't scored with a multicamera sitcom-esque laugh track. Although she didn't own enough brightly colored clothes to be in a sitcom filmed in front of a live studio audience.

She didn't turn to watch as Basher walked away. He was right that she didn't want to go for dinner with everyone, and she hated that he was right, but furthermore was upset that he had told her not to come. He was supposed to be her friend, wasn't he?

She splatted out to where Sophie and Cole were still talking. "Hey! I'm going inside," she said. "You can stay out here if you want, I don't care."

Sophie came over to her. "Oh, okay. I might, I dunno. Cole has been showing me what washes up on the beach. He says after the prison riot, the civilian types who lived in this village had to leave, and they threw a load of boxes of cutlery and crockery into the sea here."

Cole inclined his head. "My heart bled for them, truly," he said. "I know what it is to leave your home . . . never to return . . ." He put his hand to his mouth and looked away. Sophie said "Aw" and touched his arm.

Claire looked down and saw the handle of a cup in the sand. She bent down and pulled it up, but it turned out to be only a shard of the cup, just the part with the handle attached.

"It's all treasure, of a sort," said Cole beatifically.

"Might any bits of you wash up one day, Cole?" said Claire nastily.

Cole's head snapped back around, and he looked at her. "All bonemeal for the fishes now, I'm afraid."

Claire rubbed along the piece of porcelain with her thumb, without thinking, and it nicked her skin. She gasped and stuck her thumb in her mouth. Cole grinned. "You'd be welcome to my teeth if you could find them," he said. His golden smile flashed in the sun, and since the rest of him was quite faint in the light, it had a disconcertingly Cheshire cat kind of vibe.

"Miss Sophie has been regaling me with tales of your progress in our case," said Cole, still smiling.

"What, that we haven't made any?" said Claire. "Finny and his brothers say they don't know anything about it."

"Which is exactly what they would say," added Sophie. "I still think they could be involved. We know that all the other guests here owe one of their friends money, so they'd have a reason to go treasure hunting."

This latter point had not occurred to Claire, but even so it did not seem to be the sort of report that would earn someone a commendation on *Murder Profile*. Cole seemed very happy, though. "Splendid!" he said, brandishing a fist in triumph. "We shall double our watch on the southern paths of the island."

"Okay, first of all," said Claire, "there are three of you—apparently, not that we've met the third, maybe he goes to a different school in Canada or whatever—and you've got nothing to do all day, you should just be able to have a triple watch all the time."

"You forget that we must also protect our territory from the nefarious Irish!" said Cole. He put his hand on the hilt of his sword, apparently to look fearsome and dashing and like the sort of person who would stab Irishmen if given the chance. Claire wasn't sure what happened to a ghost if they got stabbed by another ghost with a ghost sword, but the answer was probably somewhere in the region of fuck all.

"Okay, well, whatever. If you manage to see anyone tonight then that's the job done, isn't it? Come on, Sophie."

"Wait, Miss Claire. I was curious about what happens when you touch a ghost like myself. Dear Sophie says that—"

"*Sophie*," said Claire, adding great emphasis, "should keep things to herself. It's none of your business what happens when I touch a ghost. I don't, anyway. I only touch Sophie. And we're leaving, right?"

Soph ignored her, so Claire contented herself with stalking back past Spraggs and hissing at him like a cat. He looked at her in distaste, which made her feel a bit better. His uniform buttons and shoes were militarily shiny, and as the sun dipped and the afternoon became gray and fuzzy, he became more solid-looking. Like Cole's teeth, the shine on Spraggs was almost obscene in the half light.

Claire walked back to the miniature town square, and felt like she was being watched through the dark windows. There was no sign of Basher. She felt the tight, violin-string whine of the tether as she dragged Sophie back from the beach—but she wouldn't come all the way back to the room. Claire stood at the top of the steps and glared at her, standing at the edge of the square with Cole still. Claire glared until Sophie turned and stuck her tongue out. It was probably a lost cause for the moment, Claire decided.

She went inside and fell face-first on the bed. She was just tired, that's all. People always got snippy with each other when they traveled. The airport had given her a case of the time dilations unlike anything she had experienced—outside of that one time she'd been in Amsterdam and smoked a joint way too quickly, and then had gone to have a lie down in the hotel, but accidentally put an episode of a true crime podcast on repeat and thought she was trapped in the same forty-five minutes (in which our hosts Flis and Roxanne made a Break in The Case) for eternity. If she'd had her phone, she could have passed time listening to a podcast now, but that kind of fun wasn't allowed here. She rolled over and hunted around the room for entertainment, but given that she was the first guest, there was no trashy paperback left behind by a previous occupant. The bedside drawer didn't even yield the traditional copy of a Bible, although that probably didn't make a laugh-a-minute read anyway.

In the other bedside cabinet was an instructional pamphlet on meditation, which recommended the practice for troubled minds. It was probably worth a shot, so Claire sat up against the bed and tried breathing and counting for a bit.

"Your face is all red and squashed," said Sophie.

Claire jerked awake from where she'd wedged herself against the box spring.

"Don't worry, you've only been asleep about an hour," said Sophie. Claire rolled her head, and saw Sophie sitting on the bed in the light of the table lamp, her expression unreadable. "Time for dinner, come on."

"I'm not invited," said Claire sulkily.

"Who gives? I'm bored. If you turn up they're not exactly going to tell you to go, are they?"

Claire got up and splashed her face with water in the bathroom and put on some mascara. Then she put on her nicest woolly lilac jumper dress, because she just felt like looking nice while they had dinner back at the hotel, for no reason whatsoever, just leave it, all right? God, can't a woman dress nice-ish for once in her life?

"Who're you trying to impress? Ohmigod. Don't be weird," said Soph, who was watching her. "He's got a fucking ponytail. Very bleurgh."

"Cole has a ponytail," said Claire.

"That's different. His is period appropriate. Not that I care, obviously."

"Obviously."

"And not that you care about sexy George."

"Obviously."

"*Obviously.*"

Claire hurried over to the hotel and saw the lights on and heard a burst of laughter. She slipped in through the front door and down the hall, Sophie sauntering along next to her, but as she reached out to open the door into the dining and living area, she found she couldn't. She could hear everyone talking and laughing, and the chink of cutlery and glasses. She heard Alex unleash a bark of laughter.

"What are you doing? Let's go, come on," said Sophie impatiently.

"I don't want to," Claire whispered, ashamed even as she said it. "They'll all look at me when I go in. Basher said not to." She felt stupid in her jumper dress. Alex would make a joke about it.

"Are you serious? Fucksake. Well, *I'm* going in," she said, and, without waiting, walked through the still-closed door. Claire retreated a little way and went into the kitchen by the side door. She turned the light on and hunted through the cupboards— silently, anxiously, hoping nobody heard her—and took a loaf of bread and a thing of vegan gummy bears, and a Pot Noodle that had survived the non-organic purge by being behind a bag of sushi rice.

Following a terrible impulse, she opened the door onto the living area just a tiny crack so she could see a little of what was happening. Someone had pulled a few of the tables together to create a more communal atmosphere. Most people had their backs to her but she could see Sophie lean over and blow in Alex's face. Alex looked around, frowned when they didn't see Claire, but shrugged and reached over to fill an extra plate. They put it in front of an empty seat without even interrupting their conversation.

Alex would talk out loud to Sophie as if they could hear her, and always set a place for her. It was why Sophie liked them so much, and even now she was sliding into the empty seat. Claire couldn't even make a bitter point about food wastage, because Alex was still riding out a growth spurt so torrential that they seemed to grow an inch every morning, so they always ate both portions. They usually even asked Soph if she was finished, and if they could have her leftovers, as if Sophie had eaten any in the first place or could object if they took the plate.

Claire scurried down the hall. It was quiet—the eerie kind of quiet you get in waiting rooms at the doctor, when you know other people are busy doing something somewhere close by, and so the quiet that you're experiencing feels forced and unnatural. Claire wasn't used to being alone. She looked up at the bend in the staircase and saw complete darkness, and the unknown around the bend. There could be anything up there. She remembered an unnatural snow falling on a ruined abbey, the deep dark as her phone torch spun away into the mud, and she shivered. She turned tail and hurried out of the door, spotted the solar garden lights that marked the entrance to the town square, and stumbled back to her room in the dark.

She felt the line between her and Sophie pulled so taut it was almost painful. Sophie was resisting so she could stay at dinner, Claire could tell. They must be more than a hundred meters apart now. Claire tried to move around slowly, as little as possible, in case something pinged like a footballer's ankle.

She experimented with turning the heating on, and soon had very toasty toes. This was an unusual luxury for Claire, who was used to being low-level cold all the time because of Sophie, who generated the same chilly area-of-effect as one would get from leaving the freezer door open. It was useful in the summer, or on the Central Line at rush hour, but it made Claire feel quite reptilian. She heard things like "cold hands, warm heart!" a lot when meeting people. Unlike Basher and Alex, Claire hadn't grown up with the kind of stretch in one's monthly budget that meant you could whack on the heating whenever you felt like it. Hence: jumpers. But she wasn't paying for the heating bill here . . .

She filled the kettle for her Pot Noodle, realized she didn't have any cutlery, and used a Biro to stir it and shovel it into her mouth. She dropped a lot of chicken-flavored juice on her nice jumper dress, and tried to sponge it off. She lay down on the bed and looked at the door. She got up and dragged the armchair in front of the knob, and then finally decided to be a proactive detective and got a notebook out of her bag, to make some proper case notes.

She wrote *GHOSTS* at the top of a page in Biro, and then divided it into two down the middle. On one side she put the heading *PIRATES*, and carefully wrote a bullet-pointed list:

- *Cole Tovey (captain)*

- *Spraggs (unsettling seaman)*

- *Bones (theoretical third pirate)*

"'Unsettling'?" commented Sophie, who was suddenly lying on the bed, chin in her hands, so she could read over Claire's shoulder.

"Shh, I'm concentrating," said Claire, almost to herself. On the other side of the page she wrote, under the heading *OPPORTUNISTS*, another list:

- *Finny (leader)*

- *Conn (fighty one)*

- *Mossie (thinky one)*

After some thought, she added a line across the bottom.

Various: sad man in cells

She turned a page and wrote down the names of The Others, including Eidy. Sophie, who was much better at remembering things, added everyone's last names, and some bitchy comments about them based on their conduct at dinner. So far this seemed to be the limit of what they could do in terms of casework. Still. You can't edit a blank page, her year-nine English teacher, Miss Roebuck, had always said.

"Is that really everything?" said Sophie. She sounded disappointed.

Claire lay down again, still fully clothed, and felt a bit silly—but also less anxious about the door, which seemed like a win.

"It's only been a day," said Claire. She turned the lamp off, and imagined all the fun that everyone was having without her.

"Seriously? Already? You're so fucking boring," Sophie whined. Claire rolled over and ignored her, and started to think of all the witty things she could say at dinner tomorrow night—except then she was tired, so tired. Tired in her bones.

And then without any time passing, she was awake. It was pitch black, but the wind had eased off. In its place she could hear tippy-taps of rain on the roof. Claire was uncomfortably hot—sweaty, slightly feverish—and she had the certainty that she had heard something. She had not woken up; she had been woken. She lay very still in bed, afraid but adrenalized, imagining all manner of horrible murderous clowns about to tear through the door.

"Soph?" she hissed. "Sophie, are you there?"

"Yup."

She turned her head. Sophie was sitting in the armchair in front of the door. She was watching Claire, unblinking. Claire sat up and rubbed her eyes. She scrabbled at the clock on the bedside table and winced when she saw it was half one in the morning.

"Was there a noise? Something woke me up." She felt confident enough to talk at a more normal volume.

"Yup," said Soph again. "A dragging noise, and then a thud."

"Someone stealing treasure!" said Claire.

"Could be. Or someone dropping their suitcase."

"Did you see anything?"

"Nope," said Sophie. "Couldn't tell where it came from either. Could be outside, could be next door. I wasn't really paying attention."

"Oh, come on, what else do you have to pay attention to?"

"Fuck off, maybe I was thinking deeply about the universe and my place within it," said Soph.

Claire snorted. "Yeah, right."

She got up and turned the heating off, then twitched the curtain aside to look out. She saw the flash of a torch.

"I'm going out to look," she said, wanting to make up for her lack of bravery, viz. eating dinner in a group situation.

"Ohmigod, are you off your entire rocker?" said Soph, sounding alarmed.

"I mean . . . contrary to our experience or the TV shows I watch, murder is actually pretty uncommon."

"What about everything up to but not including murder?"

Claire paused. "Well, you can watch my back, all right?"

She hustled Soph out of the chair and dragged it back out of the way, and then immediately regretted her decision because outside it was cold and, yes, raining, lightly but persistently. She stood breathing quietly on the top step and waited to get some night vision, watching for the flash of the torch again.

She deeply regretted that she was not organized enough to pack a raincoat, or indeed own one, and wobbled down the stairs with her arms folded high over her chest, like when you (age seven) are getting picked up from your friend's house by your mum, and she didn't put her coat on to drive over and she stands on the step looking all weird and faux jolly, but would really like you to hurry up, please. She made for the exit of the square, trying to stick to the edge so she wasn't making as much noise on the gravel path.

"You see anything?" she whispered.

"Yeah, maybe? I think someone is looking around with a torch out on the main path bit," replied Sophie, talking at a volume that sounded incongruously loud to Claire, because she had no reason to lower her voice.

Claire crept forward slowly, nearly falling over a couple of times and trying not to swear out loud. When they made it out of the square onto the path, she was hit by the sound of the water. By now she could see fairly well, although the cloud cover from the rain meant she couldn't make out any stars.

"I don't see anyone," she said. She looked around, and headed closer to the shore.

"Oh wow!" said Sophie. "Look how far out the water is!"

It must have been low tide, because the water really was low compared to when they'd arrived. Meters and meters of muddy-colored, pebble-dashed sand were visible.

"Not a very beachy beach," said Claire. She was about to climb down onto the sand, when suddenly a painfully bright light flicked on.

She spun around. A torch was shining right in her face.

"Who's that?" she asked.

The torch-wielder said nothing. They stepped closer.

"Don't fuck about, who is it?" she said, voice quavering a bit now. So much for Soph's ability as an early alarm system.

There was a long silence.

"It's Eidy," said Eidy McGrath.

Claire, still holding a hand in front of her face to try to shield her eyes, walked closer to him, until the torch was more of an ambient light than a torture device. Eidy's face, lit from below, was stony.

"What're you doing?" he said.

"Oh yikes," said Soph. "I told you you shouldn't have come out."

"Um. I heard something. It woke me up. I came out to see what it was. Er . . . Did you see anything?" It sounded unreasonable, she knew. The truth often did.

Eidy stared at her, breathing heavily.

"Go back to bed," he said eventually.

"You should go," said Sophie, keeping her voice almost, but not quite, level. "Let's go, come on."

Claire caught the tiny tremor in Sophie's voice and felt her pulse spike in response. She circled Eidy and backed away from him, checking behind her for the lights that marked the square—and some kind of safety. When she was far enough away that she couldn't see Eidy's face anymore she turned and awkwardly fast-walked away, stepped in a puddle, threw her arms out like a tightrope walker, righted herself, and flailed onward until she found a flight of stairs with her shins. The door at the top was unlocked, which meant it was probably the right one.

Claire turned on the bedside lamp and surveyed herself in the little mirror. Her mascara was not waterproof, so she was rocking a Babadook-chic look—although Alex had explained to her that the Babadook was a gay icon now, so possibly Claire was being very fashionable. She wasn't entirely sure, because Alex had not seen fit to give any more context.

She sat down in the little chair in the corner, and it took her a minute to realize what was wrong. The floor wasn't scattered with her old socks, pants, etc., and her case wasn't in the corner. The bed didn't have the pillows and duvet left haphazardly where they'd fallen when she got up; in fact, it didn't have any sheets on it at all, and was just a bare mattress still in its plastic wrap. She was in the wrong room. She jumped up, and knocked over the chair and the complimentary tea set and tiny kettle.

"Oh fucksticks," she said, and set about collecting the cups and saucers, and all the wooden stirring sticks and errant sachets of Silver Spoon that had gone all over the floor. As she was on her hands and knees, she noticed quite a bit of water staining and sand on the floor. She'd have to tell Minnie a window had been left open or something. Or at least, she would try to remember to tell Minnie that, but if she was being honest, it would probably slip her mind. The window was closed now, at any rate.

She slammed the kettle back up on the table, still on her knees, when the door suddenly opened. A huge silhouette was framed in the doorway, and Claire went "Erk!" in surprise.

It was George. He stood, one arm across his waist and his chin balanced in the hand of the other, watching her with a slight smile. He was wearing his jeans and jumper again, and his hair was wrapped in a towel.

"Thank God it's you," he said. "I heard something fall in here and thought I'd better check, in case it was a flock of murderous seagulls."

"Um. Isn't that just regular seagulls?" said Claire, clambering to her feet. Since moving to Brighton she had developed a healthy respect for, and fear of, seagulls. One had once grabbed almost an entire Greggs baguette out of her hand in an act of breathtaking flyby sneak-fuckery that had left her equal parts shaken and awestruck.

"All right, keep your Claire on," he said. He stepped inside the room properly. He shut the door behind him. Claire blinked.

"What?" she said.

"I'm still looking for a nickname, since you nixed Claire-Bear. Not a lot of things rhyme with 'Claire' to be honest. What are you doing in here?"

"Oh, right. Um. Something woke me up. Like someone moving around. And then I saw a torch so I went out, but it was only Eidy. And I must have got lost on the way back to my room, and went up the wrong stairs. Is this your room?"

"It's not, it's the empty one keeping us apart," he said. "I do use bedding, you know. I can show you. Or do you think I hang from the ceiling like Batman?"

Claire swallowed. "The Michael Keaton films are the best ones," she whispered. Her thoughts pinballed away again. "There's a load of staining on the carpet, look. You should tell Minnie."

George moved closer, close enough that Claire had to tilt her head to look up at him. He tucked some of her hair behind her ear, which Claire had hitherto thought was the kind of thing that only happened in movies. Oh God.

"Never mind about that. You're very damp. And very cute."

"But she'll have to replace it and it's brand-new—" George very gently took her wrist, spun her so she wasn't facing that patch of floor, and raised an eyebrow at her. She stared back. She wished Sophie was here, but also wished that she would stay gone, and that made her wonder where Sophie actually was.

George very gently tapped the side of her head. "What's going on in here, then?"

"I'm . . . Um . . . I was thinking of trying out yoga while we're here."

"It's good exercise," he said, nodding seriously. "But . . . there are other kinds of exercise I can recommend for tonight."

This line threatened to break the spell, and Claire recoiled slightly and frowned as if she had just avoided stepping on a dead pigeon while crossing the road. George laughed.

"No, no, sorry, you're right, that was awful. I take it back. Instantly. Can I try kissing you instead?"

Claire looked at her shoes.

"Oh, no, don't go all silent on me now," he said. "I'm out over my skis, here."

"I'm thinking about it," said Claire. She did quite like George, apart from finding him very physically attractive. There was a danger that she would then dream up an entire relationship with him, and be sad when they didn't have a deeper connection and/or ever see each other again after this week, and would then spend the better part of a year not talking about this to anyone but being quietly wistful whenever she glimpsed someone with his approximate height and hair color. On the other hand, this was the first time in a very long time that she had been alone with someone—*alone* alone, with Sophie off doing her own thing, and, furthermore, that someone was showing obvious interest in her. The last person she had tried to kiss was Basher, and he had reflexively dropped her in disgust.

Fuck it. She looked up. "Um. Yeah, g'wan then," she said.

"Are you sure? You don't sound very enthusiastic," he said—although he was still smiling, and a smile that reached his eyes.

"No, I don't," she sighed. "But I never do about anything, really."

He laughed, and he kissed her.

It was ... fine. Claire felt curiously remote from her body as it happened. She kept her eyes open. George's beard was scratchy. He pulled away.

"So?" he asked.

"Yeah, that was okay."

"You wound me. I can do better than that," he said. He pulled her closer, one of his hands drifting down to the small of her back, and she felt it there, heavy and large and warm, the ends of his fingers gripping a little.

This time he kissed her very slowly, and Claire felt her breath catch and her skin fizzing. It felt like time was slowing down, and as it did the air crackled and became hot like a thunderstorm was coming. Without thinking, she brought one hand up to the side of his face. She could feel George had twisted a finger in her hair, at the nape of her neck.

He pulled away and bit her bottom lip, which was when she felt time stop entirely. He laughed softly and pulled her into a great hug, and nestled his face in her neck.

"Come on," he said, slightly muffled. "We should get you back to bed."

He gave her another hug, verging on a cuddle, and a kiss, and called her "Claire the Wild Things Are," which made her laugh, before opening the door and ushering her into the night. In the time they'd been in there, the rain had gotten a lot heavier, and George swore in a good-natured way as it stung him. George had actually prepared and had a small torch in his pocket, and he lit Claire's way back to her own room. She turned to wave, and he turned off the torch, and she heard his door close over the wind. She assumed he'd waved back, but it was too dark to see him behind the light.

As she opened the door she thought she heard something else on the wind—maybe a sudden cry. Or was it the scream of an animal? Was it a bark? She stood frozen on the step, staring out into the dark.

Then she threw herself inside the room, slammed the door, and scrabbled for the light switch. Turning it on revealed a lack of a ghost, which was alarming. She had expected that Sophie had just gone back to the right room, and here she wasn't—and Claire could feel the tether humming again. But she wasn't going out to look for Sophie alone, and besides, it wasn't as if anything was going to happen to her.

Instead, she put on a sleep shirt and crawled into bed and, for the third time that night, and despite the tether feeling like a stretched piece of elastic, Claire fell asleep.

She was not, it was fair to say, physically or mentally prepared to be woken up to the news that someone had been murdered. But that's exactly what happened.

7

Sleep Is for the Dead

If pressed, Claire would have to admit she wasn't *exactly* woken with news that someone had been murdered, but if she was telling the story she'd edit out a lot of nonsense that preceded it.

The next day she felt like most people do when they get woken up in the small hours of the morning and then don't really get back to sleep; that is, she felt like she was hungover, but without any of the fun of going on a bit of a rager, which was deeply unfair. She could tell, without opening her eyes, that the storm had eased up, but she could also tell—also without opening her eyes—that there was a ghost in the room, because the tip of her nose had gone numb.

"Wotcher, dickhead."

Claire relaxed. It was the usual ghost.

"Hello, Sophie. Out late?" she said, not wanting to address Sophie's newfound independence directly. At some point she should establish just how far Sophie was able to go from her now. Claire suspected it was already at least double what it used to be.

"I could ask you the same," said Sophie, in a tone of voice that suggested she knew what—and indeed, who—Claire had done last night. But Claire was not willing to address that directly, either.

Claire groaned and rolled over. "What time is it?"

"About six," said a distinctly Corkonian accent. Claire sat bolt upright and opened her eyes.

"Oh yeah, these absolute pricks are here as well. Pretending to not know what football is, et cetera," said Sophie, waving an arm to encompass the three Opportunists, and her disdain thereof. "They turned up about an hour ago and refused to leave, and you wouldn't fucking wake up. Just lay there snoring. No use to me, are you?"

Mossie waved. He seemed slightly sheepish.

"Yes. I suppose this might as well happen," said Claire. She fell back against her pillows. Then a thought occurred, and she narrowed her eyes. "What are all three of you doing here? This isn't your turf, he only said so last night." She pointed an accusing finger at Mossie. "You've left the fort undefended, right? What's going on?"

"Cole and his crew have other things to worry about, they'll not be bothering with us," said Finny, in a deliberately mysterious tone that Claire chose to ignore out of spite.

"Hmm. What do you want anyway?" she said. "And how did you know I'd be here?"

"It's basic logic, girl," said Conn. "Where you sleep is where you either just were or will be again."

"And where I'd prefer you piss off from," said Claire. "Wait there. I'm going to get dressed."

She collected a mélange of acceptably clean and dry clothes, keeping her duvet awkwardly clutched around her like a cloak, and changed in the bathroom as Sophie complained loudly about being left alone with a bunch of grubby wankstains again, after enduring their company for ages. Claire ignored her all the way through making a cup of tea. She sat down to drink it, and ate a slice of bread. She had forgotten to steal any butter or jam, but was no stranger to eating dry bread. It was basically toast. But she would have to find a better meal substitute if she was going to avoid eating with the group.

"I repeat," said Claire, swallowing a knot of dough, "because it is very early in the morning and I am tired: What do you want?"

"Well, a couple of things," said Finny. "A favor for us, and a favor for you, see? First of all, we wanted to propose that you step up your efforts to find the treasure for that bastard Cole. We're very bored and we'd like the matter resolved so we can go back to how things were. Good old-fashioned territorial war games."

"Pass," said Claire. "Next?"

"Ah g'wan, you're not doing anything else," said Conn.

"I'm supposed to be on fucking holiday, actually! Or is that another thing you're going to pretend you don't understand."

"Ah, shur, but holidays are only for the Lord, and so on and so forth," said Sophie, doing a terrible and nasty impression of their accent. The Opportunists all carefully ignored her.

"This is bollocks, no matter what that weirdo eating bread says," Soph went on. Claire put down the second slice she was holding, slightly ashamed. "Claire, for fuck's sake, they probably just want to pretend they want a truce and then, I dunno, fucking ambush the pirates or stab them in the back or, or—"

"Kneecap 'em?" suggested Conn.

"Yeah! Look at this guy, he's a grinning fucking maniac, he probably ate crabs whole when he was alive." This only made Conn smile more widely, which infuriated Sophie. It was clear that Conn had the measure of her much more than she had the measure of him. "There's no evidence that you want to be helpful, and no evidence at all that you're not a bunch of dirty lying fucking pricks," Soph hissed.

"Sure what else are pricks good for?" said Mossie with a very innocent expression. It made Conn roar with laughter, and he leaned over to slap his brother on the back appreciatively. Claire had to look away so Sophie couldn't see her smiling. If Sophie hadn't nailed her colors to Captain Tovey's mast as soon as she'd seen him—jokes about masts and nailing aside, obviously—then it seemed to Claire that Soph actually had much more in common with Conn. And Mossie had, it seemed, positively burst out of his shell. He was in danger of not being the shy one anymore.

"I think," she said, once Conn had calmed down, "that we're maybe losing perspective here, Soph. We'll be gone on Friday morning. This is all incredibly low stakes from my point of view."

"Ah. Well," said Finny. "That's the other thing. The favor to you. We mainly wanted to talk about the truce thing but to be honest, we saw something on the way here." He scratched the back of his head and looked uncharacteristically guilty. So far when Claire had met him, Finny had looked guilty because he was doing something suspicious with a beatific expression on his face. This time he wasn't doing anything untoward, but he was avoiding her eyes.

"Oh no," said Claire, her stomach dropping several feet, taking the bread on an uncomfortable ride.

"Well, I wasn't going to say anything, like, but someone thought it would be only fair to mention it . . ." He glanced at Mossie.

"Finny. What is it?"

"Erm. Well. It's like this: there's a dead fella on the beach out there," he said. "And to be honest, you'll want to move fast, or the tide will have him."

"Oh my fucking God!" Sophie shouted.

For once on this trip, Claire agreed with her. "Do you not think you should have led with that?"

"Why?" said Conn. "It wasn't us."

Claire jumped up, a sudden horrible thought rolling an ice cube of fear down her back. "It's not . . . Is it one of our friends? The ones we came with, I mean?"

"Well, we've not been formally introduced, so I wouldn't like to say," said Finny, with the same infuriating lack of urgency that seemed to be his stock in trade. "Average height, dark hair."

"Not bright red hair? Or a shaved head?"

"What did I just say?"

Claire relaxed slightly. It probably wasn't Basher or Alex, in that case, which was one emergency dealt with. But still. "Fuckin-ell," she groaned. "This is all I bloody need, isn't it?" She was pulling on socks as she spoke, and bent over to find her trainers. An investigation of the insides revealed that they hadn't had enough time to dry out since the night before, but in Claire's heart she knew that nobody on the team from *Murder Profile* would wait to investigate a crime scene just because they had wet shoes. So she put them on. It felt horrible.

"Right, come on. Christ alive," she muttered.

Finny, having dispatched his brothers back to their posts at the fortress, elected to lead them to the body—although Sophie insisted it was probably a lie to trick them, and to get them out of the room so they could do something. She was nonspecific about what two ancient and incorporeal ghosts would be able to achieve when left alone in a room, but she repeated the claim for the entire time it took Finny to lead them to the body. Because there was one, and it wasn't far away.

Dawn was tea-staining the sky a little, but it was still at least half an hour away, so the world was an unhappy, static gray color. As soon as they left the square they could see many ghosts were standing in a cluster by the water's edge—more than the ones they'd met so far. It was something of an occasion. There were a few who looked more or less like the miserable prisoner they'd seen in a cell at the fort—though he himself evidently didn't get out much—some others in strange and unsettling cloth hoods, and even one who looked like an old monk. The pirates were all present and correct, though, and it was obviously this that had drawn them away from their territory and given the Opportunists an opening to come down to the village in the first place. Claire skirted the group, not wanting to engage with any of them, but they were all staring at the water anyway. Cole gave her a nod of acknowledgment.

"Finny," he said.

"Cole," said Finny with his customary smile. "Nice morning for it."

"Indeed. I'll thank you to leave our territory."

"Ah, you're grand. Just wanted to see. I'll be out of your hair soon enough."

"Ugh, is this what you meant by Cole having other things to worry about? Looking at a dead person?" Claire asked. Finny shrugged. Dead bodies were, the shrug indicated, of inescapable interest.

It was still raining, and the water was choppy. Some of the beach was exposed as the tide crept back out into the estuary. There was a darker shape, almost like a log, in the water on the tide line. Sophie stepped off the grass and hunkered down next to it. Him.

Dead bodies were, Claire considered gloomily, becoming something of a growth sector for her. In less than a year her "Number of Dead Bodies Seen" metric had increased by 200 percent. This was not ideal. Most people, unless they are a mortician or similar, are not in the habit of seeing dead bodies. Claire was very used to seeing dead people, so ghosts and mortal wounds and just the general concept of death were all things she was, if not at home with, at least not an incitement to actively turn the lights out and hide behind the door pretending to be out. Dead bodies were different, because they did things like decompose, smell, and take up space, all solid-like. Flesh was somehow a lot more disconcerting than a cold, substance-less hologram-type person who went a bit see-through in bright light.

"Fucksake," she said, with some feeling. "Who is it?"

"Ohmigod, this is so exciting!" said Sophie, for whom lasting consequences were a distant memory. "Has to be one of the hotel lot, right?"

Claire was fairly sure it wasn't George. She felt . . . relieved? Maybe relieved. Maybe nothing. Put a pin in that.

"Stick your head in the water to look," she told Soph.

"Fuck you, *you* stick your head in!"

"Flip him over," said Finny, who was also keen. It had been a long few centuries on the island, after all. "Will I help you find a stick? Ah, look, there's one just here! Gorgeous. Haunted." He grinned at her. "'Haunted' here means I'm saying you're lucky," he said, and winked.

"Oh yeah, I'm well lucky. Anyone saw me in this situation, they'd definitely think I was lucky." Claire was starting to shiver. Nevertheless, identifying the vic seemed like a sensible first step, per what she had seen on *Murder Profile*, so she stomped over to where Finny was pointing at the ground and retrieved quite a sturdy branchlet.

After some more effort, one horrible moment where she leaned over too far and almost fell in, and several ghosts starting to give competing advice in the style of middle-aged men helping a lorry round a corner in a narrow street, Claire got enough leverage under one of the man's shoulders, and flipped him.

"Oh. Er. Fuck."

He was surprisingly floppy, and sort of wallowed in the water, arms trailing. His skin was moon-pale in the predawn light and his eyes were open, which made Claire feel very uncomfortable, and she looked away.

"Who is it?" Claire asked.

"It's Crypto Dan!" said Soph. "You know what? That's fair. He'd be in my top-three most murderable of that lot. Personally, I think the cowboy is way more murderable, but that's me. No accounting for taste."

"This can't be real. I only saw him yesterday. Anyway, how d'you know it's murder? It could have been an accident," said Claire.

"Pissing heck, I swear you only actually engage your brain about fifty percent of the time," said Soph. "Yeah, I'm sure Dan was like 'kin hell, you know what I fancy in the middle of the night, during a massive storm? A ruddy bloody sea swim!'"

"He might've," said Claire. "Some people suck the chocolate off KitKats or have fetishes for being covered in worms. A midnight swim isn't that weird."

"LOL. Broad context maybe not; present context, yeah it is.

You're clutching at straws. But even if he can only get aroused if he sits in a freezing estuary for half an hour, what then? He came out here and went swimming with his clothes on, did he?"

". . . Yeah all right, good point. We still don't know for sure, though. So no jumping to conclusions. Either way, we should get someone." Claire was shivering more now, and was fairly sure she needed an adult, because she was only thirty-two and could not be expected to be one in these circumstances. Functionally, that meant going to get Basher.

She noticed Finny had gone quiet, and he and Cole were eyeing each other. But Finny was also watching her and Sophie with a faint half smile, belying a sharp attention in his eyes, half-visible as they were under his fringe. Claire refiled him under In Some Measure Suspicious, even though she had only recently put him and the Opportunists in the Probably All Right column, and despite the fact Finny couldn't have actually killed anyone. At least not in any way Claire knew about.

Currently, though, she had more pressing matters to deal with. She started off back toward the square, to wake up her friends, and Sophie chivvied her along.

"More urgency, dickhead," she said.

"Why? It's not like he's waiting for us."

"Ohmigod, pay attention to literally anything! Finny said the tide would take him, right? It's going out, remember."

"Oh yeah. Shit."

Claire started to run, and slalomed around the square and up to Basher's door. She paused, both because she was a bit out of breath, but also because—

"You're wondering what kind of knock to do, aren't you?" asked Sophie.

"Am not. Fucking . . . shut up."

She knocked, and repeated the knocking with more force and urgency because he wasn't answering.

"What are you doing?" said Basher's voice, behind her.

"Argh! What the fuck? What are you doing?" she yelled.

"Yeah, what the fuck *is* he doing?" commented Sophie. "It's just after six. He's one hundred percent up to something." After a moment's thought, she conceded: "Probably not murder, though."

"Is something the matter?" he said.

"Yes, fuck, yeah. Um. Right."

"It's honestly not complicated, weirdo, there are really only a couple of bits of information you need to deliver here," said Sophie.

"Right. Basher, Dan's dead. Dan's dead and he's in the water out there and we need to get him now because the tide is going to turn soon."

Basher's posture changed, like he was lowering his center of gravity and preparing for an attack. "You're sure?" he said.

"Pretty fucking sure, unless he can hold his breath for a really long time."

"Did you touch anything?"

"No."

"Yes," corrected Sophie. "You picked up a stick from nearby on the ground and used it to turn him over."

Claire relayed this.

"Anything else?" Basher asked. "No? Okay. Please go and check that Alex is in their room, but do not let them leave."

"Okay, but I can't stress how much the body is, right now, in the water and—"

Basher held a hand up. "Eidy and I will deal with that and

contact the others in the hotel. You only have to check on Alex, all right?"

He spun on his heel and crossed directly to Eidy's flat.

"All right, we've got our marching orders, come on," said Sophie.

"Oh right, you're coming with me, are you? Not going to moon around after the captain for a bit?"

Sophie shrugged. "I like Alex."

Claire ran up the steps to Alex's room. She knocked on the door a few times but got no response. Sophie stuck her head through the wall.

"They're asleep," she said when she'd come out again. "Lying on their back, dead to the world. Better to not wake them."

This was probably true, Claire thought, although she also had a strong idea that Alex would, when eventually roused, be absolutely furious they hadn't been told about the surprise death and included in events as they unfolded. It might be best to let them wake naturally. She and Sophie returned to her room, but to feel like she was still doing as Basher said, she sat in the open doorway with a cup of tea, to make sure nobody could bad-murder Alex without her seeing. It was still quite cold and rainy, so Claire put on two jumpers and a scarf, and tried to role-play as a detective on a stakeout. She wished she hadn't technically quit smoking because fags were a great world-weary cop prop.

"There they go, look," said Sophie. They watched as Basher and Eidy trooped out of Eidy's flat, wearing big waterproof boots and gloves. Basher had a tarpaulin bundled in his arms. Eidy had loops of rope over one shoulder and was wearing waders, which were not really necessary, and Claire considered them to be a bit of a fishermanly performance.

It occurred to Claire that if Basher was going to tell everyone at the hotel, George wouldn't be included in that, and he was actually one of Crypto Dan's proper friends—unlike her, who could be described by the uncharitable as one of Crypto Dan's enemies. Here Claire experienced a vague tremor of disquiet, because she knew from many podcasts and lurid documentaries that the police often look with particular interest at whoever it is who discovers a body, and if they discovered that said woman had scratched the dead man across the face mere hours before, a whole episode would be devoted to her. There'd be a bit where the camera zoomed in on the illustration of facial scratches on the autopsy report, and it'd cut to one of The Others describing the incident where she'd scratched him (which did not paint her as entirely stable, and would therefore be the exact sort of grist the true crime mill loved), and then there would be a whole forty minutes on her weird life. And her weird life was unfortunately well-documented, what with Sophie's disappearance and, later, that ill-advised, ill-fated, and much-publicized attempt to help the police find a missing teenager who was already dead.

All these factors were not helpful to Claire's sudden catastrophizing, but she at least had enough self-awareness to realize that was what she was doing, so she shook it off and went over to George's room, on the end of the row.

"What are you doing?" said Sophie, who was, nevertheless, still following her.

"I think someone should tell George, and right now the only person who can is me."

"I think you should leave it. Bash probably has strong opinions about, like, controlling the flow of information, all that kind of cop shit," Soph replied. "He'll have taken account of George in his plans."

"Well, he might not have. He didn't *say* anything about George," said Claire. "I think it's the right thing to do."

"Bollocks, this is some real heart over head shit you're doing right now."

"Shut up now, please," said Claire. They were in front of George's door, and she knocked tentatively, keeping in mind that it was half six in the morning. He opened it quite quickly.

"Back so soon?" he said, with an unnecessarily lascivious grin that almost made Claire forget how serious her errand was. "Did I hear you talking to someone just now, by the way?"

"Yes. I mean no. Um. I mean, I was talking to Basher, a minute ago."

"Strange answer, but not abnormal for you," George replied. He glanced over his shoulder. "Come on in out of the cold."

"This dude really has you sized up, doesn't he?" said Soph. "'Abnormal,' 'strange.' Bang on."

George's room was neat enough that Claire instantly resolved to never let him see the bomb site that was her own. Another unfortunate mark against the viability of their imaginary long-term relationship potential. The only blemishes were a slightly unmade bed, where he had obviously been lying moments before, and a suitcase and a large hiker-style rucksack in one corner. He'd even hung up his towels where he was supposed to.

George, who was in boxers and a T-shirt, moved forward to give her a hug, and she started to relax into it, before realizing again that this was not an appropriate way to tell someone their friend was dead, so she suddenly stiffened up under his arms. George, being a normal human man, noticed this.

"What's up?"

"I, um. I actually have bad news. Very. It's very bad, George." She gently pushed him away.

"What is it? Is everyone okay?" He took a step back and held her by the shoulders. She could tell he was quite freaked out.

". . . No. They're not. Dan is dead. I'm really sorry. I just found him out there in the water. I'm sorry."

"Jesus. What? Claire, what the fuck?"

"I don't know! I just found him, I ran back here and told Basher, and now I'm telling you."

"Where . . . does anyone else know? Are you sure he was dead? Claire, is this some sort of joke?" George paced up and down as he spoke.

"I don't think so—or, they might do. Basher used to be a cop—"

"I know, he told us at dinner," interrupted George. He had stopped pacing and had opened the chest of drawers to source a pair of trousers. Claire was momentarily stunned by this, because unpacking all your clothes in a hotel room was a concept that had never occurred to her.

"Right, um. Well, he said he and Eidy would get the bod—would get Dan out of the water and tell everyone at the hotel. I thought I'd better tell you."

"Okay. Where is he?"

"Out by, like, the grass bit directly in front of us here? Out there. Eidy and Basher will have found him."

"I'm going out there. You should go back to your room. Or the hotel, maybe. I don't know. Fuck. Fucking hell." George had got fully dressed in short order, and was talking in a clipped, aggressive way that didn't suit him. He wasn't looking at her.

"I'm sorry," she said again. "I'm sorry!"

But the doorway was now empty. George was down the stairs and accelerating.

"What did you think?" she asked Sophie quietly, watching as

George ran across the square in the dim morning light. Sophie was better at reading people.

"I think he's bad for you," she said.

"Not what I meant."

"Still true. But I think he was genuinely surprised and upset. Whether that Dan is dead or that Dan was found is another question."

Claire paused, before asking: "Is he angry at me?"

"Ohmigod. No. Are you serious? You are severely emotionally underdeveloped."

Whose fault is that? Claire thought. She couldn't even whisper it to herself, because Sophie was close enough to Claire that she'd hear it. Maybe close enough that she'd hear the thought. That wasn't a ghost power, Claire had always worried that Soph could read her mind.

"Let's go and check on Alex," said Sophie. "Maybe they're awake now."

About a minute of industrious hammering on Alex's door yielded a groggy teenager much aggrieved that they'd been woken up so early. When Claire told them what had happened, they switched to being furious that Claire had not woken them sooner, as Claire had expected.

"I could have been murdered in my bed," they grumbled, pulling on an oversized cardigan—although the objection was a half-hearted one, and they sounded a bit upset that it hadn't happened. Being murdered would presumably make a good TikTok.

Alex hurried toward the beach, dragging Claire and Sophie like comets, but before they reached it Basher came out to meet them. The ghosts had all gone, but George was standing on the grass, running both hands through his hair.

"Please do not come closer," he said, using what Claire thought of as his grown-up voice. "Eidy and I will bring him inside the hotel, to keep the body safe for when the proper authorities arrive. George, could you please go and wake up Minnie and tell her what has happened so she can contact the mainland. We also need to tell the others what has happened, starting with Ashley. Everyone should wait in the living area, please—yes, including you two," he said this last looking hard at Claire and Alex.

Having marching orders helped, and they all followed their instructions. Claire and Sophie sat with Alex in one corner of the living area, trying to be inconspicuous, and watched as everyone gathered there at George's request. They saw the news explode in the group like a casually tossed grenade. Claire looked at Ashley. Your husband being found dead in the estuary first thing in the morning is not the sort of thing you can prepare for—or should, really, unless you were the one responsible, which Claire reminded herself could be the case. Rather than dissolving into tears, Ashley became strangely blank. Her face, in the sterile overhead lighting of the dining area, was like a piece of paper. Claire looked at her reflection in the glass of the huge windows, as the sun started to rise, and didn't even see Ashley blink.

It was still very early, at least in Claire's self-employed book, but nobody wanted to go anywhere, least of all back to bed. Once Crypto Dan's body was secured, they split, broadly, into two groups: Basher, Eidy, and Minnie went to do practical things like contact the police and check the island over; everyone else waited in the living area, in a strange limbo. The Others were in one tight group, bringing their heads close to ask each other the same questions over and over again: what, where, how? Caity was fussy at being awake, and they took turns bouncing her. Occasionally they would burst like a dandelion clock, each of them pacing tearfully. But they always came back together.

Claire wasn't sure how much time had passed, but eventually the door flung open and Eidy, Basher, and Minnie strode in, in a scene that reminded Claire so much of a trailer shot of the scene from an edutainment *Avengers* knock-off—Fisher-man! Captain Library! Ms. Yoga!—that she almost laughed. As if all given the same direction, everyone else got up and gathered in front of Basher.

"What's going on?" asked Flick.

For an answer, Basher tossed something black, and about the size of a paperback book, onto the table. It landed with a plasticky snap and crunch.

"That is the satellite router from Minnie's office," said Basher. "As you can see, it has been smashed."

"You said there was a radio in case—" started George, but Eidy cut him off.

"That too," grunted Eidy. "And the safety box with all you gang's phones has gone. And someone has been in the dinghy and tried to sink it. And when that didn't work, they took a hammer to the outboard motor. Flare gun is missing too." He glared at the people there assembled. "So someone is going to have to pay for that," he added, and narrowed his eyes at them all. Claire tried not to laugh at this perfect line delivery for the role of local curmudgeon.

"Do you not have a ph—" Alex started to ask.

"No," Eidy replied. "I did have, but I dropped it in the toilet last week and I haven't got a new one yet. So."

Claire found the timing of this suspicious.

"So you're saying we're cut off?" she said.

Ashley said "Oh my God" very softly. Ritchie whistled. Claire was shocked to feel George's hand on her shoulder, and a gentle squeeze. Caity picked up on the atmosphere, squirmed out of

Ritchie's arms, and ran to Mac, where she buried her face in her mother's leg and started to cry. Mac, to Claire's surprise, ignored her, and ran to a tote bag hanging on a chair behind the group. She dumped the contents on a table and started sorting through pieces of rusk, a thumbed paperback, a purse, a banana. "I have—" she started to say. And then "No, wait," and she frowned, and started rummaging with more urgency. Nobody else seemed to have noticed her, because they were all asking Basher questions at once.

Bash raised his hands to quiet everyone. "Well. Do you want," said Basher, a ghost of a smile playing around his lips, "the good news, or the bad news."

"There's more bad news?" said George.

"The good news is that an admittedly quick search suggests that there isn't anyone else here," said Basher. He looked out of the huge window, and took in the grainy yellow sky heralding the new dawn. It was close to 8:00 a.m. He rubbed the back of his head, and seemed to consider how much he should tell them all. Claire could see the cogs turning as he decided that there wasn't much point trying to sugarcoat it.

"The bad news is that we are trapped on this island with no way of contacting the police until we can figure out a way to signal the mainland, and one of us is quite a clever murderer."

8

The Call Is Coming from Inside the Island

Alex threw both hands onto their head like a football manager who'd just witnessed a missed penalty. "Fucking hell, Uncle B," they said. "That's a lot of bad fucking news! Can we really not make a break for it?"

"No," said Eidy. His tone made it clear it was not arguable. "Not unless you want to try swimming, and that's another way of asking if you want to drown. I've never been a fan of it myself, like."

There was a pause. It had the same quality as the moment of silence in a Looney Tunes, and was then broken by everyone doing a loud, simultaneous panic in different directions. Tiffany, in particular, had really grasped what it meant to not have any phones and was scream-interrogating Basher and Eidy about whether they had checked everywhere, and Basher was saying that technically no not *everywhere* but everywhere it was reasonable for the safety box of phones to be, at which point Ritchie began to demand they check everywhere *un*reasonable, using words like *darn* and *dang*. Caity started wailing, and her mothers had an argument over her head as they passed her back and forth, and Minnie, for some reason, was shouting at George, repeating "the scandal will ruin me!" over and over again. Alex was also shouting, trying to get Basher's attention as he spoke to Tiffany and Ritchie. Just about the only person not shouting, Claire realized, was her. It wasn't that she didn't feel like panicked shouting would help, but more that everyone to shout at seemed to already be occupied. Apart from Eidy, but social embarrassment prevented her from shouting at him. Even as she watched, Eidy brought two fingers to his mouth and whistled so loudly that Claire was sure her earwax melted.

"Shut up," he added, for good measure. "This isn't helping."

"Sorry, but I think in the circumstances it's reasonable to be freaking out. But fine! What now, then?" asked George. He planted his hands on his hips and glared at Eidy.

"Well, for starters, I think everyone should stay here until we can contact the mainland," said Basher, answering for him.

"Smart," said Soph. "Keep an eye on everyone. And look at her! This is her fucking hotel, and she's just falling to pieces." She walked over to Minnie and eyeballed her, and Claire noticed that she was correct. Minnie's usual rattling sentences had stilled. She seemed happy enough for someone else to take charge, but in fairness, Claire thought, she probably would be, too, if she were in the same situation.

"We should search everyone," said Mac, abruptly, like it had just occurred to her. "Everyone turn out their pockets."

"What? Why?" said Tiffany. She waved her hands at her own pajama-y body. "I don't even have pockets."

"Anything suspicious," said Mac, her mouth a line. "The innocent have nothing to fear."

"Yes, traditionally people have responded negatively to that sentiment," said Basher.

"I have a kid. I want to know if anyone is hiding a knife or something," Mac insisted.

"Oh for fuck's sake," muttered Tiffany.

Under Mac's Gorgon stare, nobody actually objected. With various sighs and grumbles everyone relinquished their personal items, and laid them on a table. It seemed to Claire a mostly pointless exercise. Since most people weren't really ready for the day it was mostly things like bits of wool, pen tops, and a couple of wallets, all of which was dwarfed by the entire contents of Alex's tote, which they carried at all times and made the scene resemble the finds table on an episode of *Time Team* where they'd accidentally excavated a craft fair in a sex dungeon. Phil Harding, in his mud-colored fedora, pointing with extreme excitement: "That crocheted penis is fairly typical and dates this area to the early twenty-first century!"

Mac surveyed it all, huffed, and turned away.

"She's lost something," observed Sophie lazily. "Or, actually, she thinks someone has taken something from her."

"All right. Nothing dangerous in this room, at any rate . . ." said Basher. He said it in a way that made Claire think he was contemplating what could be hiding in other rooms. "Eidy has suggested we set up a rota to take turns trying to signal the mainland from the pier. I also think it prudent that we perform a *very* cursory examination of Dan. With Ashley's permission. I would not ordinarily recommend this, but we have already had to move the body, and it seems prudent to definitively rule in or out variables—the extremely unlikely but still possible presence of a gun, for example."

There was another uproar, which was almost instantly curtailed by Ashley, who spoke quietly but was of course able to command everyone's attention just now. "I'd like that, I think," she said. "I'd like to know how he died."

To Claire's surprise, Mac volunteered to examine Dan instead of George, who was pale and tense. It made a sort of sense, because Dan and George had been close, while Dan and Mac had not, and maybe Mac wouldn't mind poking at Dan's dead body so much. Claire had an absurd thought that maybe all Scottish people just knew how to do it, like maybe First Aid was part of the curriculum in Scotland, and that also included being able to tell how long a body had been dead, or whatever. But then Alex reminded her that Mac was, in fact, a vet, so did have a relevant qualification, and was probably smart enough that she wouldn't diagnose him with a disease specific to a rabbit or a hairless cat.

Crypto Dan was in the walk-in fridge in the back of the kitchen. Claire was going to object to that, because she envisaged going to get some ham to make a nice sandwich and having to step over a body bag, plus it didn't seem very sanitary to store food near a corpse at all. Although, if you were putting a body in your fridge at home, technically it would probably go on the shelf with uncooked meats, like where you put your chicken, and Claire had a vague recollection that a cannibal had once said that humans taste like pork, so it maybe wasn't far off ham, if you took a broad enough view, but in either case you'd definitely want to keep it away from your dairy . . .

Anyway, these fears were irrelevant because, as Minnie explained, there weren't meant to be any guests, so the food for the week was in the other, normal-size fridge. Minnie had turned the walk-in on specifically for corpse storage. Sophie pointed out that they had to put Dan somewhere until the police arrived, which Claire was forced to agree with.

Mac and Basher put on rubber gloves, and some catering hair nets and plastic aprons (which were about the only concessions to evidence preservation they were able to make at this stage), and grabbed The Big Scissors from the first aid kit in case they needed to cut Dan's clothes off. As the two of them trooped into the kitchen, Claire thought they looked like they were about to guest-star on an episode of *Inside the Factory*. Greg Davies shouting to be heard over the roar of machinery: "So you're telling me! That this body was alive just a few hours ago! That's incredible!"

"Yes, Greg, and you'll never guess what this machine is for!"

Claire was aware that she was thinking of the body as "Dan" and "Dan's body"; both "he" and "it." It occurred to her, and not for the first time, that as a medium—a genuine actual medium who could actually see actual ghosts—she should probably have a much more concrete position on religion and the immortal soul than she did. Her current thought process on it was basically "iunno," a teenager being asked how their day at school was. The phrase "Dan's body" indicated that it was a thing that belonged to Dan; the essential Dan-ness was something separate. Dan's body was a large part of him, but it was also an "it" when he wasn't moving it around. And according to what Claire could observe, this was in some measure correct. People could carry on after their body had stopped. But Claire didn't have any evidence there was a heaven or hell or anything else after the after. People were either ghosts, or they weren't.

Lately she was developing a depressing but vaguely scientific theory, after Alex had told her about a video game where someone's whole personality was reincarnated into a robot years after he'd died, via a brain scan taken before his death. Maybe whatever arrangement of atoms that made a brain cell fire in all the combinations that made a person *themself* could be sort of repli-cated in a shadowy, almost-gone, almost-there version of them. Maybe Claire could see them because of some weird quirk of her DNA that meant she had an extra, mutated rod or cone or whatever in her eye. Maybe that was why ghosts could fade over time, because the atoms started to lose their bonds. Maybe there was nothing after that.

She hadn't shared these ideas with Sophie.

Basher and Mac weren't gone very long, and when they returned the groups separated naturally again, like so much cur-dled egg custard. Alex and Claire, along with Sophie, sat awk-wardly on the sofa—which smelled of cushions that had only just been freed from plastic bags containing sachets of silica gel—on one side of the living area and waited for Basher to tell them what was going on. The Others were still on the dining side, and gathered around Ashley to do vague things like giving her a pat on the back every so often, and talking in low and sympathetic murmurs. George and Ritchie were standing up, arms folded and feet slightly more than shoulder width apart, talking as seri-ously as only men who aren't actually that comfortable with each other can.

Eidy was alone. He leaned against the wall, stroking his beard and knotting his brow, and Claire remembered that she had seen him last night, she had seen him right there by the beach . . .

"What's the verdict then, Uncle B?" said Alex. "Layman's terms, please."

Basher clasped his hands together in front of him like a news-reader. "To put it as bluntly as possible, it is fairly obvious he was twatted around the head—a scientific term—and strangled, most likely with a cord or rope. We can tell that both were done from behind, but absent more specialized experts I can't tell you how tall the person was or whether he was still breathing when he went into the water." Basher said this calmly and without rushing. He could just as well have been talking about the weather.

"So, definitely wasn't an accident, then?" said Claire, who had been holding out some faint hope.

"Definitely not, I am afraid," said Bash.

They'd been sitting with their heads close together and keeping their voices low, but now they all sat up at once to look at The Others like a troupe of slapstick clowns responding to a slide-whistle cue. Claire's and George's eyes met and he smiled almost apologetically. This startled her and, as one, the gang leaned back into each other again.

"But," said Basher, "having said that, I don't think this was planned. Not very far in advance, anyway. There is no way to prove that yet, obviously, but I think they were hoping Dan's body would wash out to sea. Gut instinct."

"What'd be the point of smashing up the boat with the outboard, though?" said Sophie. "If there's no body then there's no problem?"

Bash scratched under his chin, which he did when he was thinking. "I think they tried to scuttle the boat entirely, but it didn't work. They weren't very good at it. But that being the case, it could be they wanted us to think a third party committed the crime and escaped on the boat. Water makes sense as a forensic countermeasure, either way. It would destroy a decent amount of evidence, and if you were worried that the police might get here soon then you'd assume cold water would throw off the time line a bit, and you would not be wrong. That would be another reason to throw him in the water in any case.

"So, someone killed him—or at least, thought they had, and

dumped him in the water afterward. And it seems like you found him quite quickly, Claire." He held his arms out in front of him, a bit like a zombie, elbows and wrists a little relaxed. "I have seen a couple of bodies from drownings that were recovered while the bodies were still in rigor mortis," he explained, "and they were all like this, with their arms pointing out, because they were floating face down when the rigor set in."

"Eurgh, Uncle B," said Alex. "You've seen some shit."

"Job description, et cetera," he said, and shrugged.

"What does that mean, though? The water was cold, right? So if he had been in there for ages he wouldn't have been so . . . loose, like he was when we found him?" said Claire. She was aware, from *Murder Profile*, that rigor mortis was a key factor in establishing time of death, but it had never been explained how it worked—just that it did.

"You think that because you know rigor mortis is the body going stiff, correct? So you assume it's because the body gets cold?"

". . . Is it not that?"

"No. It is due to a chemical process in the body, and it is actually slowed down by the cold, for similar reasons to why we keep food—and dead people—in fridges. Warmth speeds it up."

"Oh, so he can't have been in there for that long, because otherwise he'd be locked in that position? Like a plank?" said Sophie, quick to grasp a new concept.

"Yes," said Basher, after a pause for Claire to quietly repeat Sophie. "Unless he was in the water for a *lot* longer, because after a while bodies go through rigor mortis and out the other side, so to speak. But he wasn't."

"Yeah, like, I dunno how long you're talking about but you lot saw him at dinner, right? I woke up somewhere around one a.m., maybe, and saw torchlight outside," said Claire, who was pleased to make a meaningful contribution. "I found him in the morning because some ghosts—oh, I forgot to say, there are some ghosts doing a sort of shit *West Side Story* but without the girls."

"Gay *West Side Story* would be huge, though," interjected Alex.

"On topic," murmured Basher.

"Fine, but can we cycle back to the presumably homoerotic ghosts," said Alex.

"Well anyway, I don't know what time that was exactly either, but maybe, I dunno, six fifteen? Can't have been much after that, anyway. Definitely before half six."

"Remind me that we should talk about the importance of accurate timekeeping again," said Basher, who was still aggrieved from an instance when they were supposed to meet for lunch, and Claire had been late because she'd made a cup of tea at home and then felt like she had to finish it but didn't check the time, and then had been distracted on the way to the café by the display in the window of a secondhand kitsch shop.

"But I mean . . . It sounds like it could have been anyone, really," said Claire. "We can't trust The Others."

"2001's spellbinding psychological horror film starring Nicole Kidman?" said Alex.

"That's what I call the other group. Like, the ones we don't know."

"I am going hit the emergency stop on the thought processes I can see spinning up," said Basher. "We shouldn't get involved. We'll just wait this out, make contact with the mainland, and stay together, okay?"

Sophie narrowed her eyes at him. "I know he's depressed and everything, but that's no reason to not be proactive about stopping a murderer," she said.

"I think it might be," said Claire, not bothering to tell Basher that Sophie was insulting him again.

Basher sighed. "I hate it when you talk to her without telling me what she said in the first place," he said. "I am quite sure it means she was being rude about me."

"See!" said Sophie. "He's a great detective, he'd sort it out in no time!"

"The fact is that you have no compelling reason to investigate this," Bash hissed. "I know what you three are like."

"I can't believe this. Are we all really going to sit around not saying the obvious?"

The voice rang out suddenly from the other side of the room.

"Uh-oh . . ." said Sophie. Claire turned. Tiffany had pushed her chair back and was standing. She was not yet dressed, and the shirt on her pink satiny pajama set heaved as she breathed so fast she was in danger of hyperventilating. Ritchie stepped toward her and offered a "Pumpkin . . ." but she glared so hard at him he stepped right back again.

"Sorry, but we all know who did it," said Tiffany. She put both hands on the table in front of her so she could lean forward for emphasis, in the same attitude deployed by agents trying to break a perp in *Murder Profile*. Claire was wise to these kinds of tricks, and anyway the full effect was lessened not only by the satiny pjs, but also the fact that Claire was still standing several meters away.

Fortunately, no amount of any leaning, from any person in any situation, would have any effect on Alex apart from making them even more noncompliant. They got up and slouched over to Tiffany, sat in a vacant chair directly opposite her, and put their feet up on the table. Basher hurried over, following his honed instincts for when Alex was going to escalate a situation.

"Don't just stand here by yourself, you'll look weird," said Sophie—so Claire snuffled after them.

"What," said Alex, stressing the *haitch* and giving Claire flashbacks to their extremely horrible, extremely posh dad, "do you mean?"

"Alex . . ." said Basher in his most warningest of tones.

"I mean that it was obviously your friend here!" said Tiffany. "You attack him and hours later he's dead? I'm sorry, but that doesn't seem like a coincidence to me."

"Claire had only just met Dan, she had no reason to kill him," said Basher. Claire wanted to feel pleased that he was defending her, but part of her suspected he was stepping in before Alex could say something more inflammatory.

"And most of us have known Dan for years without any issues. If we wanted to kill him, why wait until we're on holiday in another country? Don't the police always reinterview whoever found the body?"

Basher inclined his head. "That depends on the circumstances, but we are not the police. We need to figure out how to contact the mainland and not do anything rash."

Mac snorted. "Horse has already bolted on that."

"Can we not in front of Ashley?" said Flick.

Claire's skin started to prickle. She realized that several of The Others were looking at her with a new kind of thoughtful frown.

"Hey, look, I didn't . . . It wasn't me, all right?" she said. She found herself looking appealingly at George. "I know this is awful for you but it wasn't—"

"You were out there last night, in fairness," said Eidy from his lone vigil by the door.

"You see!" said Tiffany. Her voice verged on a shriek. "It was obviously her. She's dangerous!"

Alex actually laughed at this. "Claire eats unbuttered bread from the bag!" they said. Claire cringed and wondered if Alex had somehow seen her that morning, before realizing that eating dry slices of bread was something she did often enough for Alex to just know she did it. The embarrassment felt worse than being accused of murder. "She gets winded walking up more than two flights of stairs! She's not a danger to anyone except herself—no offense, C. Look, Tiffany, you're stressed," they added. "Hot. Maybe you need a cold drink. I think you could do with some ice."

"On it," said Sophie. She stepped into where Tiffany was standing, and Tiffany instantly started shivering. Claire looked away; Sophie didn't stand in people often, and it was usually an accident, but when she occupied almost exactly the same space as a living person it was like looking at a Magic Eye painting that gave you a migraine if you solved it, and Claire already had a headache. Instead, she looked out of the corner of her eye at Alex, who was smiling. Tiffany broke from the table, unable to maintain composure, and stalked a few feet away. "This is all so horrible!" she exclaimed.

"Look, sorry. Um. I know I don't really have any answers. I can only tell you what happened," said Claire.

"Right, that's okay," said George. He spoke slowly and gently. He pulled a chair out and sat near her. He seemed so large even sitting down. She had a flashback to the feeling of his thumb on her collarbone, and curled her toes. "But you need to explain why you went outside," he went on. "Did you hear anything? Or see anyone else apart from Eidy?"

"Er, well . . . I just woke up," she said. "I woke up because I heard something, like someone moving something heavy around. When I looked outside I saw a torch."

"Good, this all sounds pretty plausible," said Sophie. "Try to avoid mentioning any ghosts if at all possible."

"I thought I should go and see who it was—I mean, we're the only people here so I wasn't scared or anything," she lied. "It's not exactly very far to walk to get out there, and it turned out it was Eidy. Just out the front there. But actually . . ." She paused, trying to remember. "I did . . . I did think I heard something, after that. When I was going back to my room from . . . Um . . ." She trailed off, and looked at George. "I thought I imagined it. Because of everything else that happened. You know, the fort stuff. But it sounded like, well, like someone crying out. Like a shout or something. But it was windy."

"That's okay. Could you tell who it was?" asked George.

"No," said Claire. She was earnestly trying to remember. "I reckon it was a man, though. Maybe it was Dan? To be honest, at the time, I heard it and then just started to think it had been like an animal, or something. Which . . . Um . . . Yeah, that does sound quite silly, doesn't it?"

"I'll say," said Sophie, just as George said, "No, I get it. You can think weird things in the middle of the night."

"Oh, I bet she does," said Alex. Claire stared resolutely at the tablecloth, but she could tell that Alex had turned their head to look at her and, judging by their tone, was wiggling their eyebrows. Claire was alarmed that the *thing*, whatever it was, between her and George was so obvious. If Alex had noticed, that opened up the possibility that many other people had noticed, which was untenable.

"Well now, I don't know. Where I'm from girls don't just walk out into the night alone," said Ritchie.

Claire could see Sophie fighting to not roll her eyes, which she did every time Ritchie spoke. "Didn't say 'ya'll,' zero out of ten," Soph said. "Are we sure he's not a Russian sleeper spy who's just really shit at his job? 'Hello, I am genuine American boy, top Fonz, yeehaw!'"

Listening to this meant Claire had paused too long to reply to Ritchie's question, which Claire thought maybe made her look suspicious. It got worse the longer she didn't say anything.

"Trying to think up a good lie?" Tiffany said, speed-shuffling back over to mount up on her bad-cop high horse again.

"Actually, long pauses are quite normal for her," said George. He smiled at her, in a genuine way that made Claire feel a bit better. "I think we will probably have to reveal your great and shameful secret, though. Under the circumstances."

Claire nodded and looked at the table again, concentrating on not turning red. She felt Alex lean forward in their chair.

"Claire also saw me last night. After she ran into Eidy," said George.

"Knew it. Fucking knew it," crowed Sophie. "You have to tell me all about it. We will have words."

They would, actually, since Claire hadn't had a chance to ask Sophie what she'd spent all night doing. From her excitement at the prospect of a murder investigation it didn't seem like Soph had actually seen anything to do with Dan's death, but Claire's concern was largely Cole-based anyway. You did not, as a thirty-something childless woman, expect to have to worry about the dead teenager following you around being led astray by an older man. And yet here she was.

Unfortunately, Alex was now looking at Claire with an expression of joy unconfined, and even as Claire looked back at them their features rearranged as they, in real time, realized they shouldn't shout a sentence including the word *shagging* in the wake of a sudden death. They had half-risen from their seat, but managed to contain themself and slump back into it. Claire wasn't sure she could stand a lengthy post-snog debrief with Alex, who was a zoomer and therefore had a healthy attitude toward relationships that didn't really include space for shame.

"Interesting," they said, after another brief internal struggle. "Most . . . interesting." They pressed their lips together and smized aggressively.

"You could have come back and found me if you got freaked out, you know," said George. And Claire knew that if she had, he probably would have been lovely and laid down with her on his bed and talked quietly and kept the lights on, and would not have made her feel bad about it at all. Which, paradoxically, made her feel worse. Claire felt her neck getting hot. "Or Basher or Alex, right?" he added quickly, noticing her discomfort.

"That doesn't change things," said Tiffany. "After George went to bed you could have done anything."

"Yeah mate, she could have gone out and randomly murdered a guy a foot taller than her," said Alex, their voice and face flipping instantly to scorn. "Be serious. I actually feel sorry for you." They sounded it, too, which was often key to how devastating Alex's insults were. Alex was the sort of person whose approval you wanted, even if—like everyone else currently on the island—you were somewhere between ten and fifteen years older than they were.

"LOL. This girl is a solid bronze prick. If her mate isn't giving you a full alibi, that means you aren't giving him one, doesn't it?" said Sophie. "What if Dr. George went out in the night for a spot of murdering?"

"I didn't do anything and neither did George," mumbled Claire.

This turned out to be a mistake, because George looked at

her with a slight frown when he heard that. "Tiffany didn't say I'd done anything."

"No, I mean, just . . . Like, if you're not my alibi I'm not yours either, right?"

"Attagirl," said Sophie.

"I didn't think either of us needed one," said George. He looked, for the first time, a bit hurt.

"She's not trying to be horrible, she's just saying, if Tiffany is accusing her, she should just as much be accusing you. Right, C?" said Alex, who was clearly trying to help.

"Yeah, I suppose so," said Claire. She looked at her hands. Things were getting away from her a bit. Although if she was being honest, they'd got away from her a lot earlier.

"But you were still alone for most of the night?" asked Tiffany.

"I mean. Yeah. Technically. Yes," she replied.

"What I don't understand," said Ritchie, with the slowness of molasses, "is why you went out there again this morning. Taking out the bins?"

"All right, keep your jeans on, Mancy Drew," Alex snapped.

"That's a good point, honey," said Tiffany, leaning over the table again. It seemed to be a pose that she felt gave her a sense of authority. "What were you doing? And why did you go and wake up your friend instead of getting Minnie or any of us?"

Ritchie pulled a chair out to sit down as well, and tugged at his open collar—which displayed a triangle of chest as smooth as an advert in a glossy magazine. Tiffany put a hand on his shoulder.

"Probably not the time to say you can see ghosts and a group of them woke you up to tell you there was a body on the beach."

"I . . . couldn't sleep. It wasn't raining that much so I went out to get some fresh air. And I woke up Basher because I know Basher. I don't know you," said Claire simply. "And he used to be a police detective, so I thought he'd know what to do better than anyone else." This was not entirely true; Claire thought Basher would know what to do because she'd needed a grown-up, and Basher was the grown-up. He was sort of the life police.

"Right, well . . ." said Tiffany, who seemed reluctant to admit this was sort of sensible. "The only person who had any run-ins with Dan is still you. And we all know how weird you are. We know what your so-called job is."

Claire turned to Alex. "You told them?" It felt like a betrayal.

"Yeah, why not? There's no need to be embarrassed about it, it's cool!"

"Except thinking you can see ghosts isn't the sign of a healthy mind, is it?" said Tiffany. Claire narrowed her eyes.

"If I'm being honest. I have seen her. Sort of, you know. Talking to herself," said Minnie, who had been silent for the entire conversation but apparently didn't want to miss the chance to put the boot in on Claire. "Out by the beach yesterday, actually."

"If you're implying what you're clearly implying, someone having a mental illness has no correlation with them being likely to commit a violent crime," said Mac. Claire sensed a potential ally.

"The opposite is true, in fact," said Basher—who Claire felt could have actually been doing a better bloody job of being her ally.

"The important thing is that we all just want to know what happened, right?" said George. He was clearly making a play for the middle ground. "Dan was our friend."

"Yes, you all seemed to like him a lot and were very close," said Alex, almost but not quite under their breath.

"What's that supposed to mean?" snapped Tiffany.

"Nothing," said Alex. "Just, you're very keen on pointing your badly manicured nails at Claire, but you lot don't seem that cut up about it yourselves, and if I watched the sort of TV shows Claire does then I'd find that interesting."

"Seriously, though, she's being . . . forthright, but Tiffany is telling the truth," George said. He was looking at Claire. "At least, in theory. I can't think of anyone here who'd have a reason to kill Dan."

"Except you lot," said Tiffany, with a look of some satisfaction. "We know each other, but we know fuck all about any of you."

"I kind of love people who feel no need to even pretend they don't have a nasty streak," said Sophie, squinting at Tiffany in interest.

Claire looked at George. He winced in a "technically, she's right" way.

"Stand up for yourself, weirdo!" prompted Soph. "The evidence is all circumstantial, and weak at that. You know how to challenge circumstantial evidence. It comes up in every episode of that stupid show you love."

Claire inhaled slowly. Sophie was right. There had been a whole two-season arc on *Murder Profile* where Special Agent Dustin had been framed for multiple murders and held in a Canadian prison while the team worked to get him out.

"Er, look, honestly, you'd have to do better than that when the police arrive," said Claire. She looked at George, who smiled at her in a way she chose to believe was encouraging. "I'll ignore that the proposed motive is that I'm a bit weird. Even so, your theory is, what? I lured Dan out to the beach after you'd all gone to bed? And then I suppose I went back to bed until I pretended to discover the body. Okay. But why would I do that? From the killer's point of view, the longer the body goes undiscovered the better. Or is your brilliant theory that I killed him somewhere else and dragged him over to the water, by myself, in the dark?"

"Wow, you're doing really well. Imagine the soundtrack has changed to something triumphant, yeah?" said Sophie.

"I'm not saying you did it alone, maybe you three could be in it together somehow," said Tiffany.

"Don't you think Claire would have put some effort into looking less suspicious?" said Alex. "And none of us met you before this week. You might not believe us, but the police aren't going to find any links whatsoever. I mean, us even being here is totally unplanned. I'm having trouble remembering your name, even as I am looking right into your face."

"And you all said that you wouldn't benefit from Dan's death, but we're just having to take your word for that," Claire pointed out.

"Oh for God's sake! Dan didn't leave anyone millions in his will or anything," exclaimed Tiffany.

"Didn't he?" Claire had enough sense to skirt around outright accusing Ashley. Pointing the finger at the grieving widow wouldn't do much for her PR right now, even if it was statistically the most likely outcome. "Have any of you seen his will? Right, I thought not. Any one of you could have needed money for something."

"'Cept me, begging your pardon," interrupted Ritchie.

"Ritchie is from an old-money oil family," George said. "So yeah, he's right. Independently wealthy and it doesn't intersect with Dan's work."

"Anyone who's happy profiting from destroying the planet wouldn't stop at one individual human, if you ask me," muttered Alex.

"Nobody did ask you," said Tiffany, getting nasty again. "And I don't think that's a fair assumption to make. There are a lot of rich people but they haven't all killed someone with their own two hands."

"I say again," said Alex, narrowing their eyes as they stared at the cowboy, "as *far as we know*."

"Whoa now," said Ritchie, as if he were talking to a skittish horse. "Let's not get ornery."

"Well, all that's only if we assume money was the motive. You told me yourself that you think there's been resentment building, George," said Claire. She was quite pleased she'd remember this. "It could have been a crime of passion—I mean, it sounds like it, doesn't it? We don't know how many motives you all have, so I'm not going to just roll over and let you pin it on me. Sorry."

"Get 'em!" whooped Sophie. Alex punched the air. Ritchie brought a hand up to his face and rubbed his stubble, making a sound like a cheese grater across Astroturf.

"See? Who sounds like they have more motive: someone who'd never met the guy before, or a bunch of losers about to lose their house, or whatever, I don't know what you people own. A life-time supply of Vaseline and a Costa Club Card," said Alex. Alex had a particularly good line in insulting millennials, for whom they had a deep well of generational contempt.

"I didn't kill him," said Claire. "But one of you did."

At this, Ashley finally looked up again. She stared at Claire, her face still blank and still, with full dark eyes, unblinking. It made Claire uncomfortable, which was maybe why she said what she said next.

"And I'm going to prove it."

She regretted saying this almost instantly.

9

Skellington Is More Correct

Claire was extremely embarrassed after her pronouncement, and she knew this was the correct reaction because everyone else was looking at her like a puppy that had just pissed on the lino. Everyone except Alex, naturally, who was always game for any laugh of any kind.

"That was a big swing, weirdo," said Sophie. "I kind of respect you for it. Only kind of, though. LOL."

Someone cleared their throat. Basher put an arm around Claire and led her with exaggerated care back to the sofas, like when someone's aunt has too much to drink at Christmas and almost reveals who cousin Sharon's real mother is.

"Sit there and get your breath back for a second," he said. Alex came over and went to give her a high five, but Claire left them hanging.

"Look, I realize even as I say it that full compliance is unlikely at this point, but we should all stay in one place. This room, probably," Bash said. He rubbed his eyes.

"Like . . . literally in this room, for however long it takes to contact the mainland?" said Claire.

"Yes, because then you won't get killed without me knowing. There's food and water and we can get as much bedding as we need. It won't take that long, and if nothing else, the next tourist boat will be on Friday."

"We should work on the rota," grunted Eidy. "We should have people signaling the mainland or any passing ships with torches. In pairs, or threes, for safety, as late into the night as we can."

"I'm not going out there at night," said Tiffany quickly.

"Ashley should be exempt," said Mac.

"That's the point of setting up a rota," said Eidy, with a patience that was almost exaggerated. "So it's organized properly, like."

"Whatever, everyone who can take a turn, will take a turn. What about the whole staying in here thing? What if I need a piss?" said Alex.

Sophie nodded. "You know as soon as they break the seal they're back and forth every hour," she said with utmost seriousness.

"Going to the toilet is allowed, obviously. We do not have to be locked in the entire time. That goes for everyone else too," he said, raising his voice as he turned to the room at large. "We should stay here, in each other's sight. And whoever did this is still here, remember, so if anyone thinks they saw anything last night—"

"They should tell the whole darn lot of us now?" completed Ritchie.

"No, exactly the opposite of that! You should not say anything. Keep it entirely to yourself. Anyone who the killer thinks might have actual evidence against them is in danger."

Claire raised a hand. "Er. So I shouldn't have told everyone that I heard a scream and was walking around the island last night?"

"Well for fuck's sake, don't say it again, C!" said Alex. They started laughing.

"You're not actually going to do as he says, though, right? I mean if anything, logic says you're better off getting as far away from this lot as possible, and I can watch your back," said Sophie.

Claire wanted to say "Fat lot of good you've been doing of that so far," and other things of an argumentative nature. It was pretty clear that Sophie's actual motivation was wanting to go moon after a pirate again. But if Claire was going to investigate the murder, then talking to the ghosts was a good place to start. It was in fact a step they'd skipped entirely during the incident at Basher and Alex's family home, and it turned out it could have saved quite a lot of trouble.

Claire stood up, which visibly alarmed Basher. "I'm going for a walk," she said.

"Where?" asked Basher, which was a reasonable question because there weren't a lot of places to go.

"Look, I—my name has been, you know, besmirched," said Claire. Basher cocked an eyebrow at this, and tried unsuccessfully to stifle a smile. This did help Claire feel righteous and indignant, though, and she started to edge toward the door. "It has! I'm going to clear it. I'm going to look around the island. Anyway, you can't stop me short of tying me up or whatever. I'm an adult."

"This is technically if not substantively true," said Basher. "But please reconsider."

"Nah, come on, let's go," said Sophie. "No time like the present."

Alex opened their mouth but Basher cut them off. "I am absolutely putting my foot down with you for once," he said.

"G'wan, C, I'll give him the slip one way or the other," said Alex, with a twinkle. "I can't be contained!"

Claire half expected one of The Others to object, but Flick gave Tiffany's arm a restraining squeeze, and they merely watched her go with some suspicion. She glanced at Eidy, still standing by the door, and felt a sudden snake of anxiety writhe in her stomach as he stared her down, unblinking.

She scuttled out of the hotel as quickly as possible, and stood outside feeling indecisive. For a few precious minutes in the morning it had seemed like the weather would be clear and nice, but then a huge bank of fog had rolled over the cliffs of the mainland—they had watched it drop onto the water and advance in so gratuitously a dramatic manner that it looked like bad CGI. Now it lingered over the island and in the bay like an unwelcome guest: one who insists on keeping the curtains closed because the light is reflecting off the screen while they're trying to rewatch *Entourage*.

Standing in the courtyard, Claire almost couldn't see all the way across it. It was like being wrapped in cotton, and the fog seemed so solid it was surprising that you couldn't reach out and grab a handful of it. It must have been that thick out on the water, too, because they'd heard at least one ship sounding its horn repeatedly as it headed out to sea. Since then, they hadn't heard anything else to suggest the rest of the world existed, and even noises on Spike sounded odd and flat. It was like they were in a pocket universe, or an ironic afterlife punishment, which Claire did not like to contemplate too hard.

"You know," she said to Sophie, "if this was on TV it would be one of those, like, not a locked room mystery but like . . . a bottle episode, you know? We're all stuck here. Except there would be a group of weirdos who were there when they shouldn't have been, and everyone would think they did it. Like, they'd be the obvious murderers."

"Yeah? Exactly?" said Sophie.

"What do you mean?"

"Ohmigod. Claire. *We* are the extra group of weirdos. From their point of view, *we* shouldn't be here. *We* are the obvious murderers. Or, well, you, to be absolutely accurate. I swear you just sleepwalk through your own life."

This hadn't occurred to Claire, and she chewed it over. Going for a walk seemed like a much worse idea than it had sixty seconds ago.

"Which way should we go? The fort will probably be locked again, won't it?"

"We should find Cole," said Sophie, with a suspicious promptness. "He said they'd set a watch so the pirates are the most likely to have seen something. Let's follow the path round to where the other one—the Bones guy—is set up near the treasure."

"Is that where you went last night? Looking for pirates?"

"Maybe," said Sophie. There was no advance on this. Claire chewed her lip and worried about her friend, but quietly.

They went past the jetty they'd arrived at and carried on around the edge of the island. It was immediately disconcerting. Claire could hear the trees hissing in the wind, and everywhere were the remains of human structures from decades before, all covered with questing fingers of ivy that wheedled into the cracks and forced them open. The path wiggled a little, still hugging the waterline, and led away from the trees, past a single-story cottage so derelict there was a bush growing out of the chimney. An information board said it had been lodging for the schoolmaster when education had been provided for prisoners.

There followed a small gray concrete pillbox, which another

information board explained was one of three old gun nests on
the island. It looked over a sweep that might have counted as
a cove, with the remains of a wall tumbling into a slick of dark
seaweed on the tide line. It stank, a strange, salty, fecund odor
that was somehow almost pleasant. The cove also contained the
remains of a little boat, which would have carried maybe four
or five people if it hadn't had a hole in the side, and which had a
comprehensively smashed outboard motor. Whoever had tried
to sink it wasn't that smart, Claire thought—or at least, didn't
understand how the tide worked here, because even if it had
sunk entirely the boat would be visible again when the tide went
out—as it was now.

The path led away from the shore and up an incline. It became
bordered by a thicket of impenetrable brambles. Claire shivered.
The fog opened in front and closed up behind her as she walked.
There was, she could feel, a beautiful kind of bleakness in the
island, but it was hard to appreciate when you suspect someone
is about to garotte you from behind like in a Guy Ritchie movie.
The sun was properly out now, but it hadn't burned away any
of the fog; rather, the fog had taken on a too-bright luminosity
that made her squint into it. She hoped the graveyard didn't have
many deados hanging around, because graveyard deados were
the most annoying ones. They were the most desperate to have a
conversation, and also usually the most whiny.

She pulled her scarf higher around her ears and tailed Sophie,
who felt a kind of pull to graveyards—whether self-imposed or
not, Claire wasn't sure—along the gravel path, which petered
out into mown grass covered in clover, surrounded on either side
by unmown expanses of long grass and thistles. The prisoners'
graveyard had no graves. It was a walled-off plot of flat grass with

a single weathered monument. Claire hung back having spotted some ghosts wearing weird hoods that had a hanging flap over their faces with only small slits for eyes. Sophie walked among them a little, but they didn't seem to be able to see her—or much of anything, if it came to it, and Claire felt a stab of unidentifiable guilt.

After the graveyard, the path skirted a wide field, with some ancient football goal posts, which was open enough that Claire started to feel weird and exposed, even though the trees had run out long ago.

"Come on, hurry up," she muttered to Sophie, who had lingered in the graveyard.

"What's eating you?" said Sophie. "Only a bunch of ghosts. Not like they can do anything, right?"

Claire ignored her and hurried up the hill. "Fucking hell! You're no fun at all these days, you know!" Sophie called.

They'd gone in a sort of U shape from the hotel, around the edge of the island to face the fort again. Claire couldn't see it clearly, but she could feel it squatting there like a dormant animal. In front of them was the point of the star where Finny had been sitting the day before. Sophie suddenly squealed and ran right to the edge of the moat wall, which, on this side of the fort, was almost level with the top of the interior walls. Claire was surprised, until she saw that they'd found Cole. He was trading insults with one of the Opportunists, although the trade was very one-sided. Finny had been replaced by Mossie, who sat cross-legged on the grass, his cloak still hooded over his head, looking quite serene. He didn't seem to be as interested in shouting at pirates as either of his brothers.

"Knave!" bellowed Cole, shaking his fist.

"Mhmm. How are you, boy?" said Mossie. He didn't make a move to stand up, or raise any kind of alarm, but did briefly incline his head to Claire.

"Come, Miss Sophie, I would not have you disgraced by this grimy worm," said Cole. This passive-aggressive skirmish thus ticked off his to-do list, Cole took Sophie's arm and walked off the path and toward the southern edge of the island. This was much easier for a ghost to achieve than a human being, because there were more brambles and thistles and nettles to contend with, and Claire's progress after them was labored and punctuated by as many "fucksakes" and "shitting hells" as it was thorns from the local flora. Claire got the feeling she'd been tricked into taking Sophie to a date.

Cole and Sophie stopped at a lone squat, sturdy-looking tree almost directly in the middle of the coastline. It was a tree that had a bulldog aura, a tree that had withstood everything the elements could throw at it for many years, and wasn't about to give an inch now. This tree, Claire felt sure, could have done a ten-hour bouncer shift outside any pub in Essex you cared to name.

There appeared to be a Halloween decoration sitting underneath it.

Claire sighed. "Let me guess," she said, as the skeleton stood up. "This is Mister Bones, is it?"

"Well sussed!" said Cole. "Mister Bones is, as I intimated to you earlier, my first mate, and a finer man you couldn't ask for. A most steadfast colleague, aren't you, Mister Bones?"

Mister Bones gave a smart salute. It made a *clack!* noise. After her experience pulling a sticky, still-decomposing skeleton from the ground last Halloween, she had not been keen to see a skeleton again. But Mister Bones was such a friendly skeleton that she found she didn't mind. In fact, she felt some little weight lifting as she looked at him. He—presuming Cole's assessment of the gender of a skeleton was correct—was a very clean skeleton, with no trace of flesh hanging off him, though his bones were yellow with age. Mister Bones was further given a jaunty air by the addition of some large brown Cavalier boots with excessively floppy folded-down cuffs, and a brown leather tricorn hat, both of which were clearly, if you'll pardon the expression, very lived in.

Claire got the impression that Mister Bones was smiling. But then it was hard not to.

"For once I'm glad we ran into you, Cole," she said. "You didn't happen to see anything that went on last night, did you?"

"Alas, no!" said Cole. He did a quite lazy show of being disappointed that he hadn't witnessed the whole crime. "But Mister Bones did give an interesting report earlier this morning, so I shall leave you in his most excellent and capable hands," said Cole, which Claire mentally corrected to *phalanges*, a bone-specific term she had learned from another police procedural. "I needs must complete my own patrol of the island, for I'd not have Spraggs overrun on his watch. 'Twas most kind of you to walk with me, Miss Sophie. Perhaps we might chat more before I leave? I have matters of import to discuss."

Claire rolled her eyes at Cole's cosplayer-trying-to-sound-mysterious manner of speaking, and then narrowed them as he and Sophie walked farther away to talk in what Claire considered to be unnecessarily hushed tones. She made a mental note to ask Sophie what Cole's matters of import were, exactly. Cole reminded Claire of the captain of the boys' rugby team at school, a profligate underage drinker, fighter, and back-of-the-bike-sheds fingerer who was, nevertheless, a favorite among the teachers and parents because he did well on tests and remembered to say please and thank you very nicely when it counted.

Claire realized Mister Bones was looking at her. She looked back. Mister Bones waved again.

"Oh, can you not talk?"

Mister Bones shook his head, then gave her a thumbs-up.

"Do you know what all that's about?" she said, gesturing at Cole and Sophie.

Mister Bones gave an exaggerated shrug. Every time he made a significant movement it was like someone had dropped a xylophone, and Claire couldn't help but smile a little. Mister Bones was a fun person to be around.

Eventually Cole escorted Sophie back over. He bowed low to her, and then again to Claire.

"I regret that we have not talked properly, Miss Claire. I mean to make a friend of you, depend upon it!" he said.

"Yeah, sure. See you," she said.

Sophie tutted, and made an attempt at a faux curtsy, miming having skirts.

"Delightful!" said Cole. He turned and walked off, presumably to check on Spraggs, wherever he was.

"He's only being nice to me," said Sophie.

"Don't start. He isn't. But fine, sorry, all right? Fucksake. I'll be more polite to the big pompous historical theater kid." Sophie tutted again, but it wasn't entirely hostile.

"What's his deal, anyway? What was so important to talk to you about?"

"Nothing," said Sophie. Her face was carefully blank. "He says the pirates have a kind of secret hideout that he wants to show me. If it's actually where he says it is, it's pretty funny."

Claire noticed Mister Bones was watching them, with something of an air of expectation.

"Oh, sorry. I'm Claire, this is Sophie. Hello, Mister Bones," she said.

Mister Bones held up his right hand, finger and thumb together.

Claire was confused. "Er. Pinch? Tiny?"

Mister Bones shook his head, did the pinching sign again, and then did the "big fish, little fish" size indicator.

"Wait is this guy actually doing, fucking, charades?" said Sophie. Mister Bones nodded enthusiastically, and did the pinch again.

"Oh!" said Claire. "Shorter?"

Mister Bones nodded.

"What's shorter . . . You're shorter? No, okay. You don't have much time?"

"Fucking hell, it had better not be that or we'll have already run out," said Sophie.

Claire ignored her and continued pressing and guessing. "Small? We're small? Something is small . . . er . . . Backward. Go back? Go back small. People used to be shorter?"

"Get off the height thing, that's not it," said Sophie.

"Make something small. Oh! Yeah, right. Shorten 'Mister Bones'?" More enthusiastic nodding.

"So . . . you prefer just Bones?"

Bones clapped with a noise like a macabre wind chime, and gave a thumbs-up.

"Fucking hell," said Sophie. "That took so long that if I wasn't dead already I would have killed myself over it."

"Are you actually all right being called Bones?" Claire asked. "It seems a bit mean, given the circumstances."

Bones scratched his skull, which sounded like two pebbles rubbing together, and shrugged, as if to say, "Eh, you get used to it."

"I wonder if we could figure out your actual name . . ." said Claire, almost to herself. Bones flapped a hand, in an "eeh, don't worry about it" way, then pointed two fingers to his eye sockets and then out into the water, in the universal indicator to look at something. They moved a bit closer to the edge.

"How do you know how to do charades but not sign language?" grumbled Sophie.

"Probably much harder to learn modern sign language by watching someone do it than it is charades, isn't it?" said Claire. Bones pointed at the triangular black hole that represented where he used to have a nose with one hand, and at Claire with the other. It was quite unnerving looking Bones in the eye, because he didn't have any, so you just looked at the back of the eye sockets—which had little holes in where, Claire supposed, all the bits of body-string that connected the eyes to the brain were supposed to go. Still, he seemed to appreciate the effort.

Bones pointed at the water and down. Claire shielded her eyes.

"I can't see anything," she said, squinting. "Can you?"

Sophie leaned forward a bit. "LOL. Can't see fuck all."

Bones's shoulders moved in a way that suggested a sigh. He moved to stand just behind and to the side of Claire, and, being very careful not to actually touch her, put his unfortunately denuded head directly next to Claire's face in the way that potential lovers do when the heat is building in a romcom (Bones's head, of course, had the opposite effect of immediately making her left ear go numb with cold). He pointed again, this time almost directly on Claire's actual line of sight. Claire narrowed her eyes, peered through the fog, and made out something white bobbing about in the water. It was hard to spot, given that it was basically the same color as the fog.

"Is that . . . is that a fucking milk carton?"

Bones moved back and punched the air.

"Oh yeah!" said Sophie. "Ohmigod. Weird. Is that where the treasure is?"

Bones nodded, clackingly.

"Did you lot manage to put it there?" Claire asked, already knowing the answer. Bones shook his head. "It's new? So the person stealing the treasure has put it there?" Bones nodded.

"It must be weighted—attached to something so it doesn't just float away," said Claire.

"A genius deduction, Holmes," said Soph, and she rolled her eyes. "Doesn't actually help us, though, does it?"

Bones pointed urgently at the blasted tree that marked the area of his watch. Claire hesitated, and then bent to examine it. The ground around it was covered with thick, pillowy grass, shot through with blades of a taller, yellowy, more brittle kind.

"What, the bark? Oh, I see, there's a worn bit at the back here." It looked almost like the bark had been sandpapered away, in a little line. Claire stepped back and something hard clinked and slipped under her foot, in a decidedly non-grassy way. She bent down and picked up a loop of metal with a slightly irregular shape, like an oval that had been sat on. It had a little clip on one side. Claire flicked it.

"'That's one of those climbing things. Sounds like 'Ribena,'" said Sophie. "It's not rusted, must be fairly new." Claire slipped it into her pocket and regarded Bones thoughtfully.

"So, Bones," she said. "Did you hear about the dead guy? You were on watch still last night, weren't you? Cole said you had an interesting report, so did you see someone?"

Bones nodded enthusiastically.

"That's great! What did they look li— Oh, right, I see the problem."

Bones stroked his chin, and spread his hands.

"Well, like . . . was it a man?" asked Claire. Bones nodded, but then wavered his hand. "So, like, probably a man but maybe not, you can't be sure?" He nodded again.

"Ooh, okay, fun," said Sophie, brightening up a bit. "Tall or short?" Bones shrugged, and mimed looking at something, one hand on his forehead. "Oh, you were far away. And it was night too, right?"

Bones nodded and pointed down toward the playing field. Then he went into his most elaborate mime yet. First he mimed carrying something, then jumped to one side, tugged at an imaginary beard, and stomped around peering at things, holding one hand out in front of him.

"Er. No, I don't get it," said Claire. "You lost me."

"Ohmigod. You'd be thrown off the *Murder Profile* squad on your first day," said Sophie. "It's obvious! Bones was hanging out at the football pitch, because that's contested territory, right? And he saw someone carrying something. Then later on he saw Eidy, who came stomping along with his torch looking at things. Right, Bones?"

Bones applauded Sophie with the sound of clattering, snapping dry twigs.

"It was all in the performance," said Soph. Bones bowed.

"I thought you were guarding the treasure, though?" asked Claire. Bones pointed to the treasure and shrugged, and then mimed lolling his arms at his shoulders the way Conn did with his hurley.

"Riiiiight, so you saw the Wreckers," said Sophie, the Bones whisperer. "They drew you away." Bones gave a thumbs-up.

"The Opportunists," Claire corrected again. Bones looked at her, and tipped his head to one side.

"And the first person definitely wasn't Eidy?" said Claire. Bones shook his head. "Hmm. He was out and about in the middle of the night, though. I suppose maybe he has nothing to do with the theft."

"Or maybe it actually is him, and the first person Bones saw was just carrying something else. A coincidence," theorized Sophie.

"That'd be a massive coincidence, though," said Claire. "Like, if this was a TV show, Eidy would be the person we thought was the lead suspect at the first ad break, and then almost immediately we'd find evidence exonerating him."

"I've watched enough of those shows too," Soph replied, "and half the time, after the third ad break they find something that means it actually was the first suspect all along."

"That's true . . ." said Claire. Bones was watching them, skull turning back and forth like he was in the stands at a tennis match. "It would just be nice to definitively cross off a suspect, you know? There's fucking loads of them."

"True. What's Eidy like, Bones?" asked Soph. Bones put his hand, palm down, level with his knee, and then skipped about. Then put his hand up to head height and slumped. "Happy kid, sad adult? That tracks."

"Wait, you saw Eidy when he was a kid?" asked Claire. "How?" Bones seemed to consider how to mime an answer for a while. He did the arm motion that meant sea, and then drew a little square and pointed back toward the village, and then shrugged and gave up.

"Don't worry," said Sophie. "We'll figure it out."

"Will you be on watch here much longer, Bones?" asked Claire. Bones pointed down at the water and then did a rolling motion with both arms. That was clear enough: they changed watch when the tide turned.

"There'll be someone by this tree all night, though?" Sophie asked. Bones nodded.

"Oh, well, problem solved then, right? As soon as whoever it is comes back here for more loot, Bones or Spraggs will be able to ID them, and they won't even know!"

Bones gave a double thumbs-up: that was the plan.

"Fucking, bingo!" said Claire, and rubbed her hands together. If the pirates spotted whoever it was, that was surely case closed on the murder.

"LOL, stop doing that with your hands, weirdo. You look like some kind of eighties game show pervert," said Sophie. "You're just assuming whoever stole the treasure is also the murderer. That's not necessarily true, is it? What's the opposite of Bingo?"

"Unbingo?" said Claire. "Hm. Maybe you're right. This side of the island is really good if you want to secretly steal some stuff, because it's miles away from the hotel bit. If you were stealing the treasure, why would you end up killing someone back there?"

"What if Dan woke up like you did and went out to see what was going on, caught the thief in the act?"

"Nah, because he was fully dressed," Claire pointed out. "He was expecting to go outside; he didn't leap out of bed in surprise. I mean, I was fully dressed too, but that was an anomaly because I can't behave like an adult and go to bed normally."

"LOL. Let's not mark Dan down as a functional adult too

soon. Anyway, Eidy was out and fully dressed too, so he must have been up to something."

"It just seems like way too much of a coincidence to not be related, doesn't it? Someone trying to steal treasure and a guy getting murdered in the same week?"

"Stranger things have happened," said Sophie.

"Like a dead teenager trying to have a holiday romance?" said Claire, without thinking.

"Yeah, fuck you anyway," said Sophie after a pause. She started to stomp away back up the hill.

Claire was being unfair, and she knew it. But she was uneasy about what was brewing between Soph and Cole, even if she couldn't really put a finger on why. It wasn't as if Sophie could end up with a surprise pregnancy. There was a dead teenager called Elton, who had worked in the Brighton aquarium and who still did on a voluntary posthumous basis, with whom Sophie had been conducting the opening steps of a courtship dance, warily and at some distance. He was probably waiting, even now, for Soph to turn up and spend an afternoon not being interested in all his facts about jellyfish. Claire approved of Elton, with the weirdly maternal stance she sometimes took regarding Sophie. He seemed more age-appropriate. That was a hard thing to define, since Soph was seventeen but also approaching her midthirties, while Elton was simultaneously nineteen and well into his fifties. But Cole was in his thirties and also, like, five hundred, so on either count it felt weird and pervy. Especially because Soph hadn't had many experiences in that direction before she'd died. At least, Claire didn't think she had. There was a chance that she hadn't been honest about everything that happened at the house party for Luke's sixteenth, but Claire had told *her* what happened at the barbecue where they'd camped out on the college playing fields, so she'd be surprised if Sophie held anything back.

At no point before now had Sophie run around after men like a teenager. She didn't run around after anyone, in fact. When they were alive, Claire had run around after Sophie, because Sophie was the cool one.

"I'd better go after her," she said to Bones. "Kids today, eh?" Bones mimed doing a belly laugh, but Claire could not tell if he was being sarcastic or not. "You don't seem to much like Cole. I wonder what you really think of him."

Bones tipped his hat and held it over his face. It reminded Claire of when dogs on Instagram are filmed being ashamed after tipping a bin over. "Well, don't worry. Everyone has had an embarrassing boss at one time or another. All right well . . . see you later?"

Bones gave her another thumbs-up. She could feel him watching her as she scrambled after Sophie, and thus felt self-conscious about delicately picking her way between the thistles and brambles, trying not to touch anything. Her shoes were still a bit damp and were not all-terrain vehicles. She was also starting to get cold because she didn't have a proper coat.

Despite the increased length on the tether between them, Sophie still waited for Claire. They walked in uneasy silence for the rest of the way around the island, the path skirting the back of the fort and then along the side. The drop to the water was steeper here, though still covered in brambles and grass. Claire could feel the fort beside her, like she was being watched. Which, conceivably, she might be. She wanted to go inside the fort to ask the Opportunists if they'd seen anything, but they found the gate locked, so they doubled back a little way and took another path down the hill that brought them to the other side of the old village they were staying in. Claire disliked the area around the village more than the more barren side of the island, because here the whispering of the wind in the trees was always present. It was like someone was constantly trying to get her attention, or tell her a secret. She picked up a pebble and threw it into the trees, and a group of crows suddenly took off, cawing indignantly.

As they got closer to the trees, they heard screams—but playful ones, safe ones. Alex was playing tag with Flick, Mac, and Caity in the little town square, but it was going very poorly because of the mist. Claire sighed. Basher was right, it was unlikely anyone was going to agree to stay in the hotel. And she supposed a toddler would get fussy whether or not someone had been murdered.

"Wotcher, C," said Alex. "Have you cracked the case wide open yet?"

"No. Not even a bit, really."

"Probably because you haven't had lunch yet," said Flick.

"We've been hanging out all morning. Flick is teaching me loads about cooking and baking and stuff. I could probably make some blueberry cupcakes right now if you asked. Also, I was just telling them more about your job," said Alex quite cheerfully, as if they hadn't just detonated what Claire thought of as the social equivalent of a nuclear bomb. "They're interested. Did you see any more dead pirates?"

10

Lunch Break

"Er . . ." said Claire. She dragged it out, sounding like a computer that was thinking.

"It's not that embarrassing, you know," said Sophie. "What were you going to do? Pretend you're unemployed?"

"It's fine, don't worry," said Flick. She was pretty, pink cheeked and silvery with a slightly foxy face. She was like if Anne from The Famous Five grew up and disappointed her parents by getting a haircut, big boots, and a wife. "Mac thinks it's cool."

"Yeah, a lot of people say that but they don't actually mean it," said Claire, without thinking. To her surprise, Mac laughed.

"Well, I'm interested because you look quite, you know . . . I mean, you're not all eyeliner and silver raven skull jewelry."

"She was going to say you look normal and thought better of it," said Sophie, playing the role of Claire's horrible 3:00 a.m. paranoia.

Mac and Flick looked at each other and did some couple

telepathy. "We want you to have lunch with us," said Flick. She checked her watch. "Well, maybe brunch. I'm hungry, anyway."

"What, now?" said Alex. They paused in their gentle jog around the grass long enough for a small bear to clamp onto and subsequently maul their leg. Alex fell to the ground and rolled around in appropriate agony.

"I, um . . . I quite wanted to investigate the fort. And the crime scene," said Claire.

"Very official," said Mac. "By crime scene you mean sort of around here, where we are right now, I s'pose?"

Alex propped themself up on their elbows. "Yes, thinking about it, if Uncle B could see us now he'd be quite cross. But he's vanished somewhere with Eidy to try to make contact with the mainland. Fingers crossed he isn't dead, eh?"

"Well, let's reduce our own potential evidence ruining and go inside. I'll start cooking something and if you really want to, I don't know, look for a murder weapon, you can meet us inside in a bit," said Flick.

"Ooh, fun," said Alex. They got up and brushed down their big furry black coat. "Like a clandestine rendezvous in a spy movie."

Mac rolled her eyes. "Yeah, yeah. Give me the child, please." Alex handed over the giggling, apple-cheeked bear, and the family disappeared into the fog.

"It's like *Sile*—"

"Oh my God, C, don't say it's like *Silent Hill*. Everyone your age says any amount of fog or mist is like *Silent Hill*. You all only have about four cultural references between you. And I'm including all the animated kids' TV shows of the 1990s as one reference."

". . . It is like that, though," Claire said.

"Speaking of your generation doing embarrassing things," said Alex. "We must speak of Big George. At what point does withholding gossip from a friend become a form of abuse?"

"It's not gossip," mumbled Claire. "It's my life."

"Right, but when you tell me, then it becomes gossip. Oh, don't look at me like that, obviously I won't tell Uncle B. I'm pretty sure the closest he gets to sex is finding a first edition in a bookshop."

"There's not really anything to tell," Claire insisted. "We didn't actually have sex or anything, even."

"She's right, honestly," said Soph. "I mean, I wasn't actually there, but I bet it was boring as fuck. Go on, tell them I said that."

Claire did, mostly because she suspected Alex might put more weight in Sophie's opinions than her own. In any event, it did make Alex back off, albeit temporarily. "Fine, I'll leave it for now," they said. "But only because the tide is coming in and we won't have long to look for evidence. This is not a retreat. Merely a withdrawal. I'll be back. I'll flank you. Which is possibly something you could say about what the hot doctor did to yo—"

At this point Claire put her fingers in her ears and said "lalala not listening" until she felt it was safe, and turned toward the pond-colored beach. Apparently Basher hadn't thought it was worth establishing any kind of cordon, probably because there wasn't any way to maintain it—it's not like he was empowered to enforce it—but also because it was an estuary. The tide was coming in, as Alex had said, but there was enough beach left that they could walk around the area where they'd found Dan.

"Let's see if we can find anything," said Alex, and they hopped down onto the muddy sand—or possibly sandy mud, depending on from which direction you were approaching the estuary.

"Careful where you put your big physical feet," added Sophie.

They started to poke around. Dan's body hadn't left any kind of imprint. There was no chalk outline. Claire could maybe make out some marks where Eidy and Basher had walked around, but mostly the waterlogged sand had kind of melted back into itself, so the ground looked wiped clean like a giant Etch A Sketch. It was quite depressing, that people could just disappear. Even Dan's actual wife didn't seem that arsed. Claire wondered if he had parents, and then realized nobody would have been able to tell them yet if he did, making Dan a sort of Schrödinger's son. Like as far as Sophie's mother knew, Sophie was just missing. Missing presumed . . . missing. A technically open but very cold case. Claire very deliberately turned her eyes away, so she didn't glance at Sophie and get called a weirdo for her trouble.

This meant that her gaze instead fell on the ground by her feet, and she spotted an unexpectedly shiny something poking out of the sand, just next to her toes. It was bright silver in the weak, half-hearted light of the misty day, and almost offensively cold when Claire picked it up. She weighed it in her palm and rubbed off some of the wet sand clinging to it; it was a flat disk about the same diameter as one of the small rolls of sellotape you buy at the last minute from the card shop because you only just remembered it was your mum's birthday. There was something embellished on its face.

"Hey!" she called. "Check this out." She walked toward Alex, who was standing poking half-heartedly at things near the waterline. Alex and Sophie approached and peered at her find.

"What is that? A bird?"

"Yeah, think so. Hang on."

Claire, quite gingerly, went to the water and saw why Alex had been wandering about there so confidently. Because now that the wind had died down almost to nothing, the estuary was quite quiet again. There were no waves to speak of. The water lurked, with suspicious intent; the tide did not swell, it crept. But that was worse, almost, because it gave Claire the impression that it was waiting for you to turn your back. It was like being gaslit by geography. Claire bent and rinsed off the probably-a-bird in the silty sort-of-seawater. It definitely was a bird, seen from a, ho ho, bird's-eye view. The wings were stretched out and forward, and the tail was spread, so the shape it made fit roughly inside the circle.

"Weird. Is that a belt buckle?" said Alex. Claire handed it to them.

"I don't think so," she said, as Alex examined it. "There are two, kind of . . . I don't know, like loops on the back for it to attach to something, though, see? I wonder what it was. What is it, an owl?"

"It's probably a crow, the amount there are around here. This bay is where everyone in the town here had to dump their stuff when they were forced to leave the island, right?" said Sophie. She leaned over to look. "Maybe it's some fucking, I dunno, historical brooch or whatever."

"Oh, yeah, I found a bit of an old cup or something the other day," said Claire. "The storm must have thrown a bunch of stuff up. Ooh, hey, is it worth anything?"

Alex peered at it. "Probably not," they said. "It's not silver—at least I don't think so. It's weathered steel or aluminum, probably. Looks more expensive than it is. No idea what it's for, but clearly decorative." They flicked it back to Claire, who nearly dropped it. "Fill your boots."

"It looks familiar," said Sophie.

"Yeah, it's a bird. We've all seen those before," said Claire.

Sophie stuck her tongue out. "Did you find anything?" she asked Alex, via Claire repeating it again. Soph was, at least, less annoying when one of The Others wasn't around, because she could have mediated conversations with Alex and Basher and didn't get so frustrated.

"Nah. I mean, there's a heap of what I think is part of an old fishing net here, but I don't think you could kill someone with it. It's no smoking gun. Or, in this case, no . . . strangling rope? I guess?"

"I suppose it'd be hard to tell anyway," said Sophie.

"Uncle B would probably say we should bag literally everything, but we don't have any bags. I suppose in his hierarchy of needs, getting us off the island is the top of the, you know, food pyramid."

"How does he feel about mixing metaphors?" said Claire.

"Not great, smart-arse. Did you see anything else weird when you found Dan?"

"No," supplied Sophie. "There were a bunch of ghosts milling about to have a look, but ghosts are miserable fuckers and they always do stuff like that."

"Oh! What about the branch?" said Claire suddenly, thinking she might be able to do a clue. "Mac said Dan had been hit on the head, and the branch was basically next to Dan."

She scrambled back up onto the grass and looked around for the branch, which she'd dropped without thinking about it as she ran to get Bash. It was only a few feet away. They gathered to inspect it, and Alex rolled it over with a foot.

"I mean it doesn't have any brains on it or anything," Alex said.

"I don't think he was hit that hard. But this was definitely it," said Sophie.

"Sophie says they hit Dan with this," said Claire. "She can just tell sometimes. Like the ghost equivalent of intuition. Like last year she knew where a body had been stashed in your house."

"Thanks for bringing that up, it's such a lovely memory," said Alex—though mildly.

"It's way fucking better than intuition because it's right," protested Sophie. "I just know, for a fact, like how you can touch your finger to your nose with your eyes closed. I would have realized it this morning except all the other dead stuff in the vicinity was crowding it out."

After some discussion, they decided to not take back the heap of fishing net, but did decide to take the branch, which was about three feet long and would, Claire supposed, be roughly equivalent to walloping someone with a baseball bat. Alex picked it up around the middle—because after further discussion Sophie pointed out that was less likely than either end to have brains or fingerprints or whatever on it—and held it at arm's length all the way back to the hotel and into the cold room, while Claire dithered. Alex had an ability to hold their nerve in times of great stress. Either that or, as they pointed out, they suppressed feelings and used unhealthy avoidance tactics that would do damage to their psyche in the long term.

To deposit the branch/murder weapon, they had to walk through the kitchen, which was occupied by Flick, who was stirring a pot over one of the stove burners.

"I will not ask, because I have a feeling I don't want to know," she said as Alex closed the door to the cold room again. She wedged open the door to the living area with a doorstop, and heaved the pot off the heat. "C'mon then," she said. "There's still a lot of the olive bread left, and I warmed the leftover stew from last night."

They dutifully followed her and found a table laid with bowls and a breadboard. And a bear. Caity was standing in the middle laughing, and Mac appeared too tired to do anything about it, but Alex dutifully picked Caity up to make room for the reheated stew. Caity threw her arms up and said, "Alck!"

"Cheers for this, kindly lesbians," Alex said.

"You are welcome, genderless disaster," said Flick.

"Accuracy is important!" said Alex with a grin.

"You know, we're supposed to be on holiday," said Mac. "I don't want you to be chained to the kitchen the whole time."

"I think the holiday has really had the damper put on it, darling. And reheating doesn't count as cooking," said Flick. "Although honestly, I'd pick this over doing hot yoga and Ritchie asking us stuff like 'which one of you is the daddy?'"

"Ha! Knew it," said Sophie.

"Besides," Flick continued, "one of us has to hang out with Caity, so we might as well do it together in here, where it's warm."

"Go on then," said Sophie. "Do some investigating."

Claire hesitated. "Erm. Are you not really into the whole healthy lifestyle thing either? George said he wasn't that invested, really."

"My bakery isn't really a healthy cupcake kind of place. I don't reckon I'd be arsed to come to another one of these after this. Even if there hadn't been . . . you know . . . a murder."

"Sheesh, they're your friends. I didn't even want to come," said Mac. "I wanted to go on at least one walk, and look at the fort. It's the only thing on the island, so avoiding it seems daft."

"Er. I don't want to get in the middle of anything," said Claire.

"Ah, you're fine," said Mac.

"She's right, honestly. You know when you hang out with friends way longer than you should?"

"Uh, maybe," said Claire, not looking at Sophie. "I'm not in touch with any of my uni friends anymore."

"Hey, don't put yourself down, weirdo," said Sophie. "I'm not in touch with any school friends either, for fuck's sake."

"I think the older you get the more you weed out friends," said Alex, with the gravity and wisdom of someone who was almost not a teenager. "Like, at what point is maintaining a relationship with someone you don't like not just damaging for you both?"

"Well, it really has sort of got to the point that I don't have anything in common with this lot anymore," said Flick. She sighed, and wiped Caity's nose.

"George's all right," said Mac. "Maybe Tiffany, on her good days . . ."

". . . but she's a package deal these days," finished Flick. "Have some stew, come on."

"Where is everyone, anyway?" said Alex. "I've not seen any of the rest of you lot, and Uncle B said he was going to contact the mainland but I have no idea where the fu—"

"Ahem," said Mac.

"The funky gentleman actually is," finished Alex. They gave Caity a thumbs-up.

Alex ladled out bowlfuls for everyone. This began to make Claire uncomfortable, as the track record of events following her and Alex interrogating people over chicken-based soup and soup-adjacent dishes wasn't great (i.e., the one time they'd done it, most of Alex's family had ended up arrested within about a week). But nobody knew this was an interrogation this time, so it was probably not as cursed.

"Are we interrogating these two, then?" said Alex. Their mouth was full. Claire choked on a bit of chicken.

"Oh yes, please do," said Flick. "We were talking about it, and we're fairly sure you didn't do it. It wouldn't really make sense."

"Um," said Claire. Sophie started laughing. Claire tried to pull herself together, but she couldn't shake the feeling that it must be some kind of trap. "Okay, where were you between around one and two a.m. last night?"

"In bed," said Flick promptly. "Asleep. No witnesses except each other, technically, and no we didn't see anyone."

"Even Caity slept right through, it was great," said Mac.

"Okay. That's simple enough. And, um, did you have a reason to kill Dan?"

"Probably," said Mac. "He was a prick. I didn't like him at all. He did bung us some money for Flick's bakery, though."

"And that's going well, is it?"

"It's going all right, yeah. Almost finished paying him back, actually," said Flick. "Only owe him about three grand, now. Owed."

"Yeah, but that's exactly what you would say," Claire pointed out.

"Okay, well, I can't exactly show you my accounts right now," said Flick. "So you trust us on that, and we'll trust you when you say you're not delusional in a way that's harmful to others."

"Cheers, ta very much," said Claire. She, nevertheless, slurped down the stew. Really, she thought, she should have been more suspicious that it might be poisoned, but then Flick and Mac were both eating it as well. Mac produced a large-piece jigsaw puzzle of some superheroes and dumped it on the table for Caity.

"Get back on that Tiffany and Ritchie thread," prompted Sophie, as she leaned over the extra serving Alex had put down for her, examining the olive bread with some skepticism. "People always get chatty with strangers when they think there's an opportunity to bitch about their friends."

"So, er. You were saying, about Ritchie and Tiff. They're just always together now?"

"Inseparable," said Flick. "Like they've been in a honeymoon phase for a year."

"They're going to get married, I just know it," said Mac. "And they'll be weird about inviting me because I can't pretend I like him."

"I'll wear a big skirt and smuggle you in," replied Flick. She turned over a couple of jigsaw pieces for Caity.

"He is very . . ." started Alex.

". . . American," finished everyone at once.

"Which in some Americans is lovely," said Flick. "And in others is quite intense."

"It's like, when you're that enthusiastic it's hard to read as anything except disingenuous," said Claire.

"Good observation, Claire," said Sophie. "But Ritchie seems extra intense. He's probably just waiting for an opportunity to carry Tiffany off and brand her like a steer." She was drumming her fingers on the table. It was the sort of conversation where Sophie got bored quickly, because nothing interesting was happening, and Claire couldn't repeat what she said because Flick and Mac didn't know she was sitting there. "Ask how they met."

"How did they meet, anyway?" asked Alex, before Claire could open her mouth. "Was Tiffany blogging about, I dunno, cattle ranching or something?"

"Ha! No, they met at dinner? Or something? Help me out, Flick," said Mac.

"It was lunch. When she's working a full day Tiffany usually gets lunch in the same café, and he was there every day for like a week. I guess it's hard to *not* notice Ritchie if you're in the same room as him a lot," Flick said. "Eventually they had lunch in the café together."

"Sorry, but Ritchie is weird as fuck," Sophie chimed in. "In a slightly different time line this would be an article in one of those reader's stories magazines. 'Help, my cowboy boyfriend is clearly a stalker.'"

"What a nice, um, whatchacallit—meet-cute, though," said Claire, ostensibly talking to the others but maintaining eye contact with Sophie. "It's sweet that people can still meet in real life with harmless coincidences like that."

"Isn't he in oil?" asked Alex. "What does that mean?"

"Hell if any of us know," said Flick. "He says his family found some on their farmland years back, but for our purposes he just splashes money around. I don't think Dan liked not being the only rich guy in the group anymore."

Mac snorted. "You ask me—which nobody does, by the way—the oil business isn't going as well as he'd like."

"What d'you mean?" asked Claire, her mouth full. She had encountered a surprisingly big chunk of chicken in the stew.

Flick looked at Mac and widened her eyes while keeping her eyebrows flat, and Mac responded with a small frown as she jerked her head back an inch, a silent communication that was easily interpreted: we shouldn't be talking about this/oh who cares, it's not that important.

"*Weeeell*," said Mac, waving one of her hands as if the gossip was wrapped around it, and she needed to unspool it gradually. "Ritchie came in and it seemed like he had a lot of money, like Dan, but he doesn't really. Tiffany has decided she likes living dangerously, though, and I happen to know that Ritchie, like many of us, borrowed money from the lad who's actually financially solvent."

"Oh!" said Claire. "He owed Dan as well? How d'you know?"

"I overheard them talking at, oh, I think it was Ashley's birthday party last year. Ritchie said it would cost him less to borrow from Dan than it would to transfer money from America, because of the bank fees, but you could just tell he was lying."

"George was saying that Dan basically invested all his money in you lot," said Claire.

"Huh. I guess you can actually gather useful information without me," said Sophie.

"Well I s'pose George doesn't mind bringing that up since he'd just about paid Dan back," said Flick, rolling her eyes. "And like I said, I wasn't planning on coming to another of these. We're not really mates anymore."

"Yeah. He, er, said that too."

"Ncl Jerj!" said Caity.

"Yeeees, George visits us sometimes, doesn't he?" said Flick. She turned over some more jigsaw pieces for her daughter. "Where does this one go, d'you think?" Caity took the proffered piece and looked at the puzzle with pursed lips, diverted once again. It was sort of like how Bash wrangled Alex by presenting new, fun things to think about.

"But doesn't that mean that you basically all have a motive?" said Alex.

"Well that's the thing," said Flick. "That's partly why we wanted to be frank with you, because we can't work it out. Dan was always happy to just let us pay him back whenever. It was Ashley who kept on at us to pay back any money we owed. Now that it'll all revert to her—or, I assume it will—she's much more likely to call the debts in."

"I don't think it was all altruism. Dan bankrolled everyone's dreams, sure, but he had the money because he hit it big with all that NFT stuff," Mac explained. "He got into crypto while the getting was good, and splashing the cash around was a way of lording it over us, you know? But I'll take the lording if it comes with interest-free loans." She shrugged.

"We should figure out how that works," said Sophie. "Isn't cryptocurrency super volatile? Up and down like a fucking yo-yo."

"Yeah, do you know anything about that? The NFT stuff? I don't understand how it's saving the world or whatever. Eco NFTs?" Claire asked.

"Not really," said Flick. "It's something to do with planting trees? I'm not sure. They're animal-themed ones, aren't they? Lizards I think."

"Wait, NFTs of lizards?" Alex asked. They sat upright suddenly. "What kind of lizards exactly?"

"Um. I think George said chameleons to me," said Claire. She looked at Soph. She regretted offloading so much of her external memory to Sophie over the years.

"Definitely chameleons," said Sophie.

Alex made an instinctual motion that was them reaching for their phone, which wasn't there. "Ugh, I keep doing that," they said. "I can't show you to prove it, but I saw people posting about it on TikTok when we were on the train over here. The Sticky Tongue Corp rescue got rugged."

"Sorry, I think I might have just had a stroke for a second there," said Flick. "Is that sentence meant to make sense?"

"In very specific circumstances, yeah," said Alex.

Sophie frowned. "I have no idea about this either, and I'm the smart one. Please explain."

"Okay, see, Sticky Tongue Corp was the NFT collective doing

the chameleons. I say 'was' because the creators took all the money and ran, leaving the NFTs without real value—basically bankrupt, or whatever their digital fucking fake money version of that is—about a month ago," Alex went on. They got out their tobacco and papers and started skinning up a cigarette. Claire tried to ignore the siren call of nicotine. "Extra unlucky because they were part of the five percent of NFTs that were still worth anything at all. Anyway, then some other guys popped up saying they would rescue the project, hence that particular verb appearing in the headline of events here. But you had to invest more money in the rescue for it to work, right? Surprise surprise, once they'd milked as many chameleon cucks as they could, the supposed rescue rug-pulled—meaning they just took the money and ran too."

"Ah," said Mac. "So, you put it all together and you get Sticky Tongue Corp rescue got rugged."

"Correctamundo," replied Alex.

"So, by this point, anyone with a load of chameleons is shit out of luck?" clarified Claire. One needed to be thorough when one was an imaginary detective working for free.

"Luck and arbitrarily inflated value," said Alex. They waved their unlit cigarette in what was a vague, sort of sympathetic-if-you-squinted way. "So if most of dear Dan's digi-cash was in them lizards then he just kind of doesn't have it anymore. He was not, in fact, a rich man. Can't say my heart would have bled for him, but then neither does his anymore so . . ."

"How do you know this anyway?" asked Claire.

"Yes, same question," said Flick.

Alex shrugged. "I follow an account that tracks crypto Ls. As a sort-of artist I had a vested interest in how NFT shit was 'disrupting' art for a while there."

"Ah yes," said Sophie, nodding sagely. "Isn't that code for a dude with stock in Facebook fucking up some perfectly good analog thing?"

"But that's . . . I mean, come on, that's *bananas*," said Mac. "I knew this stuff was volatile, I suppose, but you can really just lose all your money that fast?"

"Yeah, overnight, basically," said Alex. "Although in fairness I think the same could be said for regular money. At what point must we not recognize the experiment of capitalism is a failed one? But I mean I don't understand it beyond the amount I need to know to thrive on the schadenfreude of tech bros losing all their savings on shitty mass-produced jpegs. I think it's kind of like a Ponzi scheme crossed with a multilevel marketing scheme, except instead of terrible makeup, you're selling functionally indistinguishable pictures that people rightly mock you for buying. If you don't cash out while there's enough money in the pot, you're left with an empty pot. One that you can't even piss in, because it's not a real pot."

Alex took a deep breath and blew it out again all in one go. "Sorry," they added. "I'm not good with extended metaphors."

"Oh," said Claire, remembering how Dan had been so desperate to get George to invest in something. "I think Dan was trying to pass the pot to George."

"Nice," said Alex. "Why ask your pal for help when you can make it his problem instead?"

"So it probably wasn't Ash, then," said Flick. "She's only going to inherit debt."

"Er. Unless she didn't know? That happens a lot, right?" If Claire had learned anything from *Murder Profile* (debatable), it was that wives had an infinite capacity to not notice their husbands were in enough debt to cover the GDP of a small town.

"'That's a big unless," said Sophie. She rolled her eyes. "'It turns out my rich husband isn't actually rich and now can't keep me in the manner to which I'm accustomed, i.e., shit hair dye and expensive dresses that don't suit me. How am I going to afford my Lululemon yoga leggings, sob sob sob, kill kill kill.' That's a likely scenario, right? Right? I'm right."

Claire ignored this. "Hmm," she said. "That's something to think about. I can't make it fit, but . . ."

"Maybe we should tell Ashley," said Flick. "It doesn't seem right to keep this secret if she doesn't know."

"Ah fuck it," said Mac. She clapped a hand guiltily over her mouth, but Caity didn't seem to have noticed. "What I mean is, what difference will it make telling her now? Anyway, I don't trust any of them." She jammed a neatly trimmed nail into the table for emphasis. "But I think we can trust you lot. Because of my phone."

"Wait, you have a phone?" said Alex.

"Flick warned me in advance. Not handing my phone over to that dafty cow, am I? Face like a bulldog licking—" She checked Caity was still absorbed in chewing bread and staring at her jigsaw. "Licking piss off a nettle. I have a kid, I want to be able to call emergency services if I need to."

"And you don't want to miss time on *Clash of Cla*—" started Flick.

"Yeah, all right, and I don't want to miss time on *Clash of Clans*. I gave Minnie an old dead handset. Christ, am I really the only person who thought to do that?"

"Oh my God. It's a shame you're already married," said Alex, in awed tones, "because I think I'm in love with you."

11

Behind Closed Doors

"This is amazing. Can I check my socials?" said Alex. They caught Claire's expression. "Oh, and we can ring the cops now right? And get out of here."

"Well, this is it, you see," said Flick. "Mac was *so* very impressed with her idea that she told me about it in here at dinner, before any of your lot had come in, and now she thinks one of our friends must have overheard and taken it."

"I don't *think*, I know. It was in my bag during the big murder meeting this morning, and it bloody isn't now, is it?"

"That's why you got everyone to turn their pockets out, then," said Claire.

"Told you," said Sophie.

"Right. Should have strip-searched them. One of them probably smuggled it out up their tight arse. But that's why I trust you bunch more than our lot. Because you didn't know about my phone, and there's only one reason someone would want rid of it. I'm keeping quiet about it, though. Whoever will know I've noticed it's missing, but there's no sense making more of a fuss about it and drawing their attention."

Mac was, Claire thought, quite right. The only person who wouldn't want the police to get to this island as quickly as possible would, logically, be someone who had done at least one crime. Thus, Claire resolved to try to locate and steal back the phone if the opportunity arose and it hadn't been chucked in the sea with everything else. She hoped the murderer hadn't kept it on them. Claire had never tried to pickpocket anyone, and was not especially dexterous at normal things like, for example, tying shoelaces or not falling over on a flat bit of pavement, but it didn't seem like nicking a phone would be that hard. Someone had basically gotten away with murder less than twelve hours ago, so light theft seemed like it would go entirely unnoticed. But probably not by the person she thefted it from, who, again, was probably a murderer . . .

"If you try to nick the phone back your chances of survival are about on par with a chocolate dildo at a Swiss orgy," said Sophie, demonstrating her ability to read Claire's thoughts as if they were hovering over her head.

"Well anyway, if you think it was one of your gang, but it wasn't one of you two, then who was it?" said Alex.

Mac and Flick exchanged glances. "Opinion is divided," said Flick. "Until you revealed all this NFT stuff, I thought Ashley. Mac is withholding final judgment. Which is weird because she's not usually shy about judging the group. Or anyone."

Mac shot her wife a look, but decided not to pick a fight. She shrugged. "Dan was a prick, so it could've been any of them."

"I thought you'd be gunning for Ritchie," said Claire.

"Aye, well he's a prick too," said Mac reflectively. "But I don't think he'd have the stomach for it. Anyway, from what I've heard, Tiffany has had worse boyfriends."

Flick frowned. "I mean, not many. Who d'you mean?"

"That wee freak who you kicked out of the group?"

"*Andy?* Oof, he wasn't her boyfriend. He was a stalker, basically."

"That's the guy who was scribbled out of that picture Tiffany showed you," said Sophie.

"Oh yeah!" said Claire. "Tiffany showed me a picture he was in. She said he had a thing for her."

Flick stared into her bowl, lost in a memory. "That's putting it mildly. He seemed harmless, you know—fun even. I liked him! He wore sleeveless wool vests and bow ties and things, trying to have a *thing*, and hung out with some of the performing arts kids. I remember he was quite ill for a bit, he missed a couple of seminars because he had to have brain scans and stuff. So he just didn't seem like the sort of person who would be dangerous. But then I suppose they don't, do they?"

"I never met him," said Mac. "Didn't he get kicked out in your final year?"

"Yeah, he'd always liked Tiffany and he just got weirder and weirder with it," said Flick. "I think in third year he felt like it was his last shot. Things kept turning up in her flat—flowers and cheap chocolates on her pillow, weird poems about her, and her housemates said they didn't know anything about it. George was visiting Andy one day and he needed to borrow something— walking shoes or something, I dunno—and he found all this *stuff*. Loads of Tiffany's underwear, even a lock of her hair he must have cut off without her knowing. Proper horrible creep stuff. He got kicked out before exams."

"That's pretty good of the university," said Alex.

"Yeah well," said Flick. "He was also doing terribly in all his coursework and would have dragged down the year's honors average. That probably helped. Gotta think about those university rankings."

"Heavy," said Mac. "I had it in my head they actually dated, dunno why."

"Maybe Randy Andy is lurking in the tunnels at the fort," said Alex.

"Unlikely. Found out he won the lottery years ago. Proper jackpot. Another uni friend sent me a little local news clipping to point out that life is unfair and the guilty are not punished for their crimes—although because the university basically did the whole hushing-up thing I didn't expect he ever would be," said Flick. "He's probably living it up in the Costa del Cockhead now." She shivered.

"How did you two meet? Did you steal Mac's underwear?" said Alex, ever able to read when they should change the subject.

Mac snorted. "Flick brought her pet cat to the practice where I was training."

"God bless Catmilla Purrker Bowles for getting me laid, may she rest in peace," added Flick.

"Ah, so you're not a very *good* vet . . ." said Alex. This made Flick roar with laughter.

"George stayed in Edinburgh while he finished his doctorate, so we were all best pals for a while," said Mac. "Then the turncoat bastard went down to London. Anyway, now you've given us the third degree, I get to grill you two." She pointed at Alex.

"I am an open book," said Alex. They opened their arms. "Although I warn you: the pages are mostly covered with rude cartoons."

"What's with the two bowls thing? You did it last night at dinner too. I know it's rude to talk about someone's eating habits, but you don't look like you're, I dunno, carb-loading for a marathon or anything."

Alex looked down. They had indeed set an extra bowl of stew in front of an empty chair for Sophie again, and had, in the middle of the conversation, hoicked it over and started horfing it up once they'd finished their own portion.

"Oh! Yeah, sorry. I do it automatically now. I could lie . . ." they said.

"Yeah, you *could* do that," said Claire, starting to panic a bit. She thought Mac had forgotten about the whole "Claire can see ghosts" thing that Alex had raised, and was hoping to get away without talking about it.

"Ohmigod, shut up weirdo. People can know I exist!" said Soph. "We only just got done with a fight, are you really going to be a bitch again straight away?"

"So, you know I said Claire is a medium?" Alex started. They kept their tone very unbothered.

"Oh yeah, we were going to ask about that. Do you have a spirit guide or something?" said Flick, in a tone of voice that indicated she was making a joke about it, because nobody would actually have a spirit guide.

"Haha, no, of course not," said Claire, looking at her bowl. It came out more bitter than she'd intended, and Sophie stood up with the sort of pre-thunderous expression she wore when she was getting ready to shout at Claire, or storm off, or both. Alex coughed on their mouthful of stew.

"Alex, um, they are just hungry all the time. They're growing fast," she said. It sounded stupid even to herself. Alex was glaring at her.

Claire felt the back of her neck go hot. She chewed the inside of her lip. The whole ghost thing was all new and exciting for Alex, and, having grown up under the crushing weight of a family that had expectations, they'd somehow slipped out of the side with an absolute determination to do whatever they wanted and not really care about what people thought. Claire had been caring what people thought for her entire life. If she leaned into it more—thick eyeliner, a lot of drapey scarves and incense—then she'd probably be a better medium, but it's easy to pretend to see ghosts when you can't. Seeing them all the time was pretty horrible. Sophie's mere existence was, to Claire, a reminder every day that her best friend had been murdered, and the killer had never been caught.

"Fucking hell, weirdo! Say something! Acknowledge me!" said Sophie. "Why are you like this?"

"Since you're a medium, though, does that mean, you know, God, and heaven and hell, is all real? That there's an afterlife?" Flick asked.

Claire shrugged with one arm and gave the honest answer: "Dunno." Then, aware that she must look like a giant sulking child, she rubbed her nose and looked up. "Like. Um. Any ghost hanging around has, by definition, not gone anywhere else. You can't talk to a ghost who isn't on earth in front of you. So I have no idea, and neither do they."

This wasn't the answer she gave most people, especially if they weren't regular clients, because most people wanted to hear about how their grandmother was happy in heaven. Regulars, like the elderly woman who wanted to continue arguing with her dead sister in the way they had when they were alive, were thrilled to know that she was, say, still standing around the kitchen in their old council house, yelling about not liking egg mayonnaise, but those people were few and far between.

Flick was smiling, in the way that people did when Claire was forced to tell people she talked to ghosts—as she had to, to do séances and make a living. It was indulgent and condescending. Mac and Flick weren't going to be mean about it, Claire could tell, but they regarded this as a kind of shared fantasy. Maybe she should have just admitted Sophie was real. But it was too late now.

"Well, that's a relief, I suppose," said Mac. "Peter Pan did say it would be an awfully big adventure, so it's good to know there aren't spoilers."

"Dying isn't a fucking Marvel movie," Sophie snapped. "I've had enough of this. I'm going to find Cole again."

She walked out. Claire couldn't respond.

"It's funny, though, you're not all dramatic and dressed in black lace and stuff," said Mac. "Like I said. I didn't expect a medium to be so sort of . . . average."

"Dressing in black lace is a lot of effort," Claire mumbled. "Thanks for lunch, anyway. I'm going to . . . I should go and look around more."

Alex was still looking at her weirdly. In the absence of something to do, she took the empty bowls back into the kitchen and washed them up, mechanically, with hot clumsy fingers. She felt the twanging on the tether to Sophie; at one point it jerked so hard that she nearly dropped one of the bowls.

After a while Alex walked into the kitchen, and Claire felt sure they'd been talking about her in the other room. "You going back out for a bit, C?" they said.

"I dunno," she said. "Not sure, really."

"Well, let me know if you run into Uncle B," said Alex. "In a bit, yeah?"

"Yeah, in a bit," said Claire, imagining that actually it would be a while, and that Alex was probably going to decide that they preferred hanging out with Mac and Flick, learning to make bread, than hanging around with the uninteresting relay for a dead girl they couldn't see or hear. At least probably couldn't. Claire suspected Alex was starting to pick something up when Soph spoke, even if just a vibe. If they could talk to Sophie without needing Claire's input, she'd basically be surplus to requirements.

So. What to do? She assumed Eidy and Basher had worked up their rota for signaling the mainland, but nobody had asked her about it and she assumed that meant her time was her own still. She could go to find Soph—she could still feel the occasional twinge from the pull of the tether, like when the small of your back protests if you bend the wrong way, but without actually hurting. She should also interview other suspects, and look for more clues, because at the moment they didn't have any physical evidence at all, apart from (possibly) a branch, and (possibly) a (possibly) belt buckle with (possibly) an owl on it. It also seemed important to open the fort and talk to the Opportunists at some point. She decided to interview suspects, because that was the first thing you always did in *Murder Profile*. They might be variably compliant, but George, for example, would probably be quite nice.

She was deep in thought about this when she walked past the door to Minnie's office, and noticed it was open. This hadn't been the case earlier, she was fairly sure, which told her honed investigator brain two things. One: Minnie was or had recently been in the building; two: she could go in and see if there was any evidence lying around.

Claire leaned back to check that the hallways were definitely empty, then, before she had a chance to think about it too much, stepped inside. She started to open drawers in the hope there would be some giant keys labeled *FOR THE FORT GATE XO*, or a sheaf of papers with a title page reading "Why I Killed Dan: A Memoir." Unfortunately this was not the case, no matter how many printouts of financials she rifled through.

The rifling did reveal a very interesting document in the folder marked, in extremely precise block capital letters, MORTGAGE, where Minnie had stored a sheet of lined paper covered with some quick Biro calculations. It looked like she was trying to work out how large a second mortgage on the hotel she'd have to take out to pay back a sum of almost half a million quid marked "D Loan."

Claire—who wrote her own financial data on the back of napkins and receipts stored in a binder that was right now, probably, under her bed—thought that it was obviously stupid to keep this kind of evidence in a clearly marked folder, and that the hosts of all the podcasts she listened to would find it hilarious. But in the end, it was useful that Minnie had done it, because although Claire wasn't numerically gifted (she and Soph both having passed GCSE maths by the skin of their teeth, and largely by copying homework answers from Zoe Graham), it looked like if Minnie were forced to return the loan Crypto Dan had given her, she would be—to use a technical term—double fucked with a thorny dildo. Claire couldn't take a picture of the document with her phone, because her phone was currently probably in the sea, but she felt that it was within the abilities of even her erratic brain to remember the basic inference that Dan had asked Minnie to return her loan, and she could not afford to give it back. Claire wondered if he'd been calling in *all*

the loans, because that was definitely motive. Although if Claire
was feeling nasty, which, as the day progressed, she increasingly
was, she would have said that Mac was right and anyone who
met Crypto Dan and spoke to him for more than about ninety
seconds would have a motive to murder him.

After she'd finished the rifling, Claire realized she should have
rifled more carefully, because the state of the office would reveal
it had been rifled and naturally suspicion would be cast on the
rifler. So, she spent some time trying to un-rifle before someone
found her, and panicked a bit about how open the door had been
when she'd first entered. She stood listening, trying to breathe
as quietly as possible, to make sure nobody had seen—because
she was self-aware enough to know that getting caught looking
through someone's stuff doesn't make you look like a *less* suspicious person—when she heard a weird sort of snuffling noise.
And then a sort of cough.

She looked around to try to identify where it was coming
from, and saw that one of the studio rooms was also unlocked,
the door slightly ajar. Steeling herself with what she imagined
was the bravery of a seasoned detective, she looked through the
crack and saw a medium-size room with a wood panel floor and
a mirrored back wall. In one corner Minnie was on her knees in
front of some built-in cupboards, sorting through a spaghetti of
bungee cords. Claire watched as she rolled up a yoga mat, held
it between her thighs, and wound a bungee cord around it until
she could pull the cord tight and connect the two hooked ends.
Then she gave the cord a snap to check the tension and stacked
the yoga mat in the cupboard in front of her, in a row of different
colored ones—sea green, amethyst, light blue. Claire held her
breath and watched as Minnie repeated the same process several

times, pulling the cord tight and snapping it with satisfaction every time, without seeming to get tired.

But she was also crying. This was, Claire knew, a normal reaction to a friend dying. But was it also a sign of guilt? She leaned a bit closer, and her nose nudged the door, which creaked. In a split-second decision she opened the door as if she'd only just come up to it, although Minnie was already turning around to look.

Had she managed to style it out? It seemed unlikely. Claire hadn't managed to style anything out since she was three years old and had Laura Ashley dungarees. The early noughties trend toward long, tiered boho skirts had not been kind to her. She had looked like a novelty toilet roll cover.

"Ah! Hello. Thought I heard something," said Minnie. She turned away to wipe her face, and Claire pretended not to notice. She heard Minnie's knees crackle as she stood up.

"Um. Sorry, didn't mean to startle you. I just thought I'd see how you are."

"Of course. Sorry. About earlier, I mean," she said. "I think we overreacted a bit. It's all just horrible. And unexpected. Obviously." Claire noticed Minnie's lips were chapped. She licked them every so often. It was like when Claire saw Gareth Southgate on the telly. He always looked a bit like he needed ChapStick.

"That's okay. I know it's a hard time. I um . . ." Claire paused, and realized Minnie was trying to be kind. She took a breath. "I—I mean, we, us three—we saw a dead body last year. Someone had been killed at Basher's parents' house and it was horrible. Since then I've been imagining bad stuff happening. Not, like, seeing things, but just thinking, 'What if the cathedral collapsed on the town?' or putting a chair in front of my bedroom door in case someone comes in . . ." She trailed off, because she realized this would make her seem more aggressively weird than The Others already thought she was, and mentioning another murder would, to an outside observer, probably constitute a suspicious coincidence.

"I see what you mean. Well, yes, that's certainly traumatic," said Minnie. Claire was not sure she believed Minnie could, in fact, see what she meant. "It's a shame. We probably won't be doing yoga. Or anything else now."

Claire eyed the coils of bungee cord and decided now was not the moment to ask Minnie about her mortgage.

"Oh, yeah, the yoga. Er. George said you were certified?"

"Yes. Took years, you know. Quite proud of it. Although I studied history at uni."

"Me too!" said Claire, suddenly more enthused.

"Oh, cool! Did you specialize? I miss it. I wanted to become a genealogist at one stage. Still do it. As a side hobby. I was going to do a bit of it about this island. Trace the old families. It has a really fascinating history. I was talking to some of my friends on the forums. A few of them think there really is pirate treasure."

"Oh, right?" Claire thought about this. It might be a way to get information on The Case of the Annoying Ghosts and Their Treasure without Minnie even knowing that's what she was doing. "I might have heard something that could be helpful actually."

"Oh, really?" Minnie lit up, which made Claire feel bad. Ritchie had been hamming up his introductions enough to fill the sandwiches of every non-vegetarian child on the island of Ireland, but it seemed like Minnie really did like genealogy and historical research more than running a hotel. Maybe it would be nice to hang out with her. Claire hardly thought about her degree these days.

"Yeah, er. When we were waiting for Eidy we ended up chatting to a local . . ." Claire said, inventing furiously and wishing Sophie would appear to help her out. "Um. Anyway, he told this story—well, um, more of a legend, really—but it was about a pirate who was shipwrecked here, Captain Cole Tovey, and um, the man who lived near this island who stole some of the cargo from the wreck . . . Fionnbharr, I think. And his brothers Conn and Mossie. I'm not sure. I thought it would help."

"Oh, I know about the captain. He has some descendants in Cornwall or Gloucestershire or something. They have a website and say they'll contest any treasure trove found here."

"Could they do that?" Claire asked. She wasn't exactly sure how treasure troves worked. Or treasure in general. What made something a trove versus being just regular treasure?

"Well, it depends. I don't think they could. Not really. But they could be a pain in the arse. And if there are descendants of a local family maybe they'd contest too, which would be interesting. Not that I expect the treasure is real, in truth. Fun project, though. Is there a last name? For the locals?"

Claire shook her head, but if anything, Minnie seemed to relish the challenge this presented. "Well, never mind, I'm sure we can come up with something," she said. "There were records left here, although not that old, probably. Nobody was really interested, but I kept all of it." Minnie went to turn back to her yoga mats, and then hesitated. "Do you think you could check on Ashley? She's upstairs. I've been looking in on her. To make sure she's all right. But if you go up, I can finish these."

She made brief, embarrassed eye contact with Claire, and Claire realized it was a sort of trust offering. A weird olive branch.

"Sure, no problem," she said, and swallowed. She backed out of the room and watched Minnie, reflected in the giant mirror, pull another bungee cord tight.

On the one hand, Minnie's request sort of played into her hands, because she did want to talk to the other suspects. But on the other, it meant going upstairs in the hotel, crossing a threshold that was hitherto uncrossed. She wished that Sophie was there, because she would shout at Claire until Claire was embarrassed and/or annoyed into taking action.

Nevertheless, she approached the bottom of the staircase and started to climb it, imagining it as a scene in a dramatic documentary about extreme sports, intercut with her doing a talking head about all the preparation you have to do to go up hotel stairs. *You've got to practice. Every. Single. Day of the week. You want a family? Forget about your family. The stairs are your life now. If the weather closes in when you're up there, you're dead.*

The sense of danger was significantly lessened when Claire made it around the bend in the staircase and did not see a murderer running at her waving a fire axe. There was a part of her that had been expecting it. Reaching the top of the stairs was similarly uneventful, and she envisioned the triumphant final episode of the series detailing her summiting in record time.

The upstairs hallway was almost identical to the one downstairs, although with fewer doors leading off it. Minnie hadn't said which room Ashley was in, so Claire went up to the first door on her left. It didn't have a number, but there was a spray of long, thin leaves painted on it. She was not sure what this was supposed to mean, so she put her ear up against it and heard someone moving around, and decided against checking that one for the moment. The next door had a different illustration of dark leaves with rounded blobby edges. She couldn't hear anything on the other side, so she tried to open it, and was surprised when it gave without any resistance.

It turned out to be the right one. Claire deduced this by noting that Ashley was sitting on the bed, in leggings and socks, hugging her knees. She didn't look shocked to see Claire. In fact, she looked sort of sleepy, and reacted slowly, blinking like a sundrunk lizard.

"Er . . ." said Claire.

"Hello," said Ashley. "What are you doing here?" She sounded sleepy, too, but had an air of calm about her that was only produced by medication.

"Um. I was actually looking for you," she said. "Minnie asked me to check on you. I wasn't sure which number room you were in, though."

"Oh, they all have names instead of numbers," Ashley explained. "This is the Oak room. Named after the leaves."

"What if you don't know which leaves are which?" said Claire, a born-and-raised city kid.

"Well then you're fucked I s'pose," said Ashley. She burst out laughing. Her neat blond hair was flat on one side, and her face was pink on that side, too, as if she'd only recently been napping. "Most of the rooms are empty still. Minnie's flat is on the end somewhere. Tiffany and Ritchie are in Willow; Mac and Flick are in Chestnut. At least, I think they are. Maybe it's the other way around . . ."

"Oh. Thank you. I'll try to remember," said Claire, who still did not have any idea what the leaves of said species looked like. "Um. Are you all right here, on your own, you know?"

"D'you know, it's quite funny—I mean, I find it funny probably because Flick poured a few diazepam down my throat, I think I'd be quite upset otherwise—but after you left everyone was talking about hunkering down as couples. Well, I think they just sort of forgot that I'm not in one anymore." Ashley giggle-snorted. "I suppose it's quite a recent development," she added.

"Er, yeah, s'pose so," said Claire. It was quite hard for her to get a read on the situation. She'd never spoken to someone whose husband had been murdered less than twenty-four hours previously, let alone someone whose husband had been murdered less than twenty-four hours previously and who was on an anecdotally large dose of antianxiety drugs. There was no blueprint on how either person in this dialogue should be acting or reacting. "Did you . . . Have you had some sleep, at least?"

"Oh yes, loads. Now I'm just sitting. I'm not sure where anyone else is. The murderer is going to have a lot of targets to choose from. Fucking Hungry Hungry Hippos out there. The lot of them. All taking money off Dan," said Ashley.

Claire could tell that Ashley's mind was bouncing between parallel lines of thought. It was a feeling she was familiar with herself.

"Yeah, I actually went out as well, with Alex," she admitted. "We wanted to . . . well, maybe we found a clue, but we're not sure." She fished in her pocket and pulled out the maybe-a-belt-buckle. "Do you recognize it?"

Ashley leaned forward to peer at the bird decoration, and then shook her head. She waved a hand. "I wouldn't worry about clues. They'll all finish each other off anyway."

"Oh yeah?" said Claire, as she tried to edge backward toward the door again.

"I know none of them like Dan. *Liked* him," she corrected herself, still dreamy and remote. "And because they thought they were better than us, they'd tell me all their secrets, you see. Because they felt safe telling me. 'Oh poor little thing, married to

Dan, that's a much worse problem than my weird personal life shit.' I heard Mac and Flick arguing the other night. They argue loads, you know, even though they pretend to be all perfect. Flick tells me all the time. She caught a PI following her once—can't have been very good, can he? But he was taking pictures. He wouldn't say who hired him, but she said, well, it has to be Mac. Thinks Mac thinks she's cheating, and that makes Flick think Mac is cheating, of course. Guilty mind."

"Right, yeah. Nightmare," said Claire, wondering if this was what it was like to have conversations with her when she was drunk and/or high. Then her brain caught up with her ears. "Wait, what did you say about Mac and Flick? You heard them arguing?"

"Hm? Oh yes. All the time, like I said. None of them would give back the money, you know."

"Wait, what—no, put a pin in that. I mean, you heard Mac and Flick arguing this morning? What did they say?"

Ashley waved a hand again, this time impatiently. "No, the first night we were here, before you arrived. Oh, something stupid. I don't know. Mac had found something out and Flick was saying it was fine, but Mac didn't think it was fine at all. She said something about 'we owe him way more than you said,' and Flick started going on like 'oh, what do you mean, blah blah blah.' You know. Is it important?"

"I mean it sounds quite important? I think? Maybe. Yeah, definitely." Claire was strangely disappointed that Flick and Mac had been hiding something from her, but then this was, she reminded herself, par for the course with many investigations.

"Oh, well. You should ask them about it."

"I might, thanks. Er." Claire approached the bed, like an Australian vet approaching a restrained crocodile, which was how she approached anyone having visible emotions. Except, Ashley wasn't having visible emotions, which made it more disconcerting. "Are you . . . are you okay? I mean, um, like, obviously no, you're not, but I mean in a less general . . . like . . . right now, are you okay?"

"Right now, yes. Because I'm quite high, you know. And in general . . . I'm sad about Dan, of course I am, but I'm thinking so much about what I have to do next that I'm not thinking about him. Does that make sense?"

"You mean like . . ." Claire clutched vaguely. ". . . Like canceling his Netflix, that kind of thing?"

"Netflix was in my name. No, it's the money stuff. The Sticky Tongue crash."

"Oh, I know about that," said Claire.

"You *do?*" said Ashley "Hmm. Come and sit here." She patted the bedspread next to her, and Claire climbed on a bit awkwardly, trying to keep her shoes off the side because you're not supposed to get your shoes on the bed, are you?

"The chameleons losing value meant we lost everything. All the money Dan had loaned everyone? That was from liquidating some crypto. But the fuckers wouldn't give it back. So he said he'd find a way to make them pay. Said he had information. But I don't know what it was, so now I don't have anything."

This, in fairness, was quite a big break in the case. Claire had been right that almost everyone had a motive.

"What about your own, er, portfolio?" asked Claire. That was a thing, wasn't it? Rich people had portfolios.

"I moved most of mine over. It's not just the pricking bastard chameleons, all of that stuff is going tits up. We were supposed to be able to cash out, but not enough people were cashing *in*." Ashley sighed heavily. "So that's mostly what I'm thinking about.

Being broke. Although, actually, he had a very good life insurance policy. A very good one, now that I think about it. Hmm."

Ashley flung an arm around Claire's shoulder, and she caught the sour tang of an unwashed pit. Which was understandable, in the circumstances. Claire left the arm there, though, because while she didn't know the correct length of time she'd have to wait before shrugging it off, *immediately* definitely seemed like it would be too soon. Being broke was probably a relative state for people like Dan and Ashley, Claire thought.

"This place is fucked up, isn't it?" said Ashley suddenly. "I've had a horrible feeling about it this whole time. Maybe I'm only imagining I have, because now my husband has been killed. But I swear I spent the whole first day we were here just waiting for something to happen. Something bad. You know what I mean?"

"Um, I sort of do, actually."

The room faced away from the water so that all that was visible through the window were the crowns of some evergreen trees, all soft and candy-flossed in the mist; the glass was mostly a dark square that was quite stark against the white wall. Claire looked away from it, because it made her feel like they were inside a tiny, clean, excessively linen-y pocket universe away from everything else going on outside, and she wasn't sure if she was okay with that feeling right now. Ashley was looking at her, and that made her feel worse.

"Who do you think did it?" Claire asked.

Ashely ignored this. "Your friend Alex said you talk to ghosts. Is that true?"

Claire blinked. "Yes. No. Well, sort of," she said. "In séances, you know. It's like a . . . a freelance thing."

"I don't suppose you've—"

"No," said Claire quickly, keen to pull the emergency brakes on that particular train of thought. "Sorry. Doesn't work like that."

"Of course. It wouldn't, would it?"

They sat in silence for an uncomfortable couple of seconds.

"Not that I believe—" said Ashley.

"No, it's fine, most people don't."

"I think it was Minnie," Ashley added, still following the free-wheeling, skimming, skipping path of her thoughts and looping back around to an earlier point of solid ground.

"Really?" Claire asked. "Um. Why?"

"I heard them arguing too. I said I hear everything, right? It was yesterday morning, before you all arrived. Dan hadn't told me how much money we'd lost—he hadn't told me we'd lost any, in fact, and I found out because I heard him and Minnie shouting at each other in the yoga room downstairs. He needed to call in the loan he gave her to open this place, and she said she didn't have it—that she'd lose the retreat before it even opened. It was the largest amount of money he gave anyone."

"That makes sense," said Claire.

"Yeah. And the thing is, I think he'd found a way to make her pay. That night he told me he'd found a way to get a lot of our money back, so we'd be okay—at least in the short term."

"Do you know what time he went out last night?"

Ashley shook her head. "Normally I wake up if Dan so much as rolls over, but we had a nightcap with Ritchie and I had a bit too much bourbon. He's always going on about bourbon. Anyway. I was out of it. Out. Of. It."

She paused, and seemed to think, and then Ashley looked straight at Claire and held eye contact, unblinkingly, for longer than Claire felt was normal or comfortable. "I used to think these people were so nice. Who knows what might make someone snap in the end?" she said dreamily.

This made Claire realize that while an old friend could snap when asked to suddenly return a huge loan with no warning, it would be entirely possible that a wife could snap on finding out that her previously luxurious lifestyle was about to take a serious turn toward Tesco's end-of-day discount shelf, especially in light of an admittedly "very good" life insurance payout in the event of his death . . .

Claire got up, noting that her shoes had in fact left a tiny streak of dirt on the perfect white duvet cover, and subtly tried to brush it off. There was no way to make it look natural, and Ashley just watched while Claire gently stroked the bed as one would calm an angry terrier.

"Er. Sorry. There was something . . ."

Claire had a startling epiphany then, that it would have been fine—indeed better, and less weird—if she'd just said that she had accidentally got some dry mud from her shoes on the bedspread and briskly brushed it off. It was a realization that she felt sure would change her life, but in fact she'd had it several times before, and every time she forgot it. And she would this time as well.

"I'm going to try to find, um, that is, I think I'm probably going to go now," she said.

"Yes, of course. Let me know if I can answer any other questions," said Ashley, who was wearing an expression of helpfulness on her face that was akin to a toddler who had just told you they wanted a chocolate chip cookie and was now guilelessly pointing toward where the biscuit tin was kept.

Claire slid toward the door. "Uh. Thanks. Hope you're doing okay. And eating and sleeping enough, and stuff like that."

"Drinking enough water, getting enough exercise," said Ashley, with a wan smile. As Claire slipped back out into the corridor, she peeked back over her shoulder and saw Ashley flop back onto the bed, her arms akimbo. Claire closed the door quietly.

In the spirit of in for a penny, Claire decided to check some of the other doors. She went to the first one, knocked after a mere minute or so of hesitation, and found that it, too, was unlocked. "Fucking hell, it's like these people want to get whacked," she muttered to herself.

The room she entered was empty, and almost a mirror of Ashley's room, except it was facing the sea and there was a doe-colored cowboy hat, evidently a spare for the trip, perched jauntily on the chairback. Claire picked it up and tried it on, but it was much too big for her head, and fell in front of her eyes. She giggled, because she felt like a child dressing up, and took it off to look at the size. A little label that said 7½ was attached to the bottom of a slightly larger label that had a Union Jack embroidered next to script that read *Montgomery's Hatters—Made in London* in such an excessively fancy font that Claire had to squint to determine that it was, in fact, from a hatter in London. Claire very carefully replaced the hat, and then panicked about whether it was in exactly the position it had been before, or at least close enough that nobody would really notice—but in *Murder Profile* people always seemed to be able to tell their room had been searched as soon as they walked into it, stopping and posing like a mouse who's spotted a cat, whiskers twitching. Although Ritchie—for this was surely Ritchie and Tiffany's room, unless one of the other couples was into a weird meta role-play, the likes of which Claire did not want to speculate about—was less of a mouse and more of a big, weird coyote.

She looked around and opened a few drawers, but found

nothing as interesting as the large cowboy hat. It turned out that Tiffany and Ritchie were also the sort of people who unpacked all their clothes from their respective cases, and Claire wondered if that was just a sign of a functional person. She remembered to look in the bathroom cabinet, because that's what they always did on TV. She didn't find mountains of pill bottles for antidepressants—always a sure-fire sign of a murderer on TV shows, and something that Basher, an avowed antidepressant taker of some long-standing, protested about at volume whenever Claire put on an episode in which it happened—but there was a blister pack of pills, the foil stamped with VALPROATE (a medicine Claire did not recognize, immediately exposing the flaw in searching medicine cabinets if your suspects didn't have easily identifiable brand medicine), a number of sleeping pills, and diazepam. Otherwise, there were just some cotton pads and moisturizer made of oats, both of which were disappointingly mundane.

She left, still moving cautiously and stopping every few minutes in case she heard something or had imagined hearing something, and put her ear to the next room along, which was marked by a five-pointed leaf that looked like a chubbier version of weed. Her experience with trees was mostly limited to binaries like leaves/no leaves (sub: orange leaves/green leaves). But she could recognize a conker from the times that she had lost playing the extremely violent and, if the more lurid tabloids were to be believed, latterly extremely banned, playground game wherein children whirl conkers on strings into each other with great force, and dangerously close to their tiny child knuckles. Sophie had always been extremely good at playing conkers, because she had no fear, and was always excited every September to collect new specimens, rolling the spiked green casings under her patent leather school shoes to split them, and peeling apart creamy flesh to reveal the impossibly shiny and still-damp nut inside. She carefully noted all the rumors she heard about how to make the hardest conkers, and the kitchen at her house came to be a sort of seasonal My First Frankenstein's Lab, with test conkers pickling in vinegar or vodka, while others were baked at various temperatures and for varying times. Claire was pressed into helping find new conkers for the weird science—in fact, it was one of the first things they did together, after Sophie declared they were friends on the first day of big school. So, although Sophie decided she was too cool and grown-up to play conkers by the time she turned thirteen, Claire could, at least, reliably identify a chestnut leaf.

All of which meant that she was probably in front of Mac and Flick's room. She knocked in case they'd come back upstairs while she was talking to Ashley, but it was quiet inside—and when Claire tried the doorknob it turned out to be locked. Claire was sort of proud that her new friends-ish knew to lock their door, but it was a bit annoying for carrying out a comprehensive investigation.

The four other doors were locked as well, and a fifth, right on the end, confused her. It had a little plaque saying "STAFF ONLY," and was probably Minnie's apartment, except on that side was also Ashley's room, two locked doors that Claire theorized were unfurnished rooms, and then this door. So either Minnie lived in a cupboard or a TARDIS.

. . . Or, Claire realized, as she opened the door and saw a set of steep, narrow stairs, the secret third option, which was that Minnie lived in the converted attic that nobody had explicitly told her existed. It was a good idea, because it gave Minnie a much larger floor plan—albeit a lower roof, but Minnie was quite small anyway, so she probably didn't notice. Claire crept up the stairs, which were uncarpeted pine and very new, wincing at how loud the creaks were. She wondered how long it would take Minnie to reroll and store all her yoga mats.

It was one long, low room, with an open kitchen area in one corner, and in contrast to the rest of the place, it was dark and cluttered. Minnie's external zen minimalism was balanced by private maximalism. Claire walked forward and instantly lost any semblance of stealth because she slammed into a coffee table she hadn't seen in the gloom and swore at full volume because her shins felt like they had been smashed by a huge comedy mallet.

Claire surveyed what she could make out of the room. She wasn't really in a place to judge. But still. She frowned as she looked at the coffee table that had so recently attacked her, unprovoked. It was probably a psychology thing. Maybe it was easier to have an extremely itemized filing cabinet in your office if in your house you've left out a used coffee cup for so long that it was sustaining a mold colony that looked advanced enough to have discovered fire and be on the way to domesticating wolves into chihuahuas. Claire gave up hope of finding anything at all in here, apart from, probably, a brochure from a garden center Minnie had been to three years before, and a birthday card from an undisclosed year. It was kind of a marvel that Minnie had managed to make it as messy as it was in such a short space of time; in fact, it reminded her quite a lot of Alex's room back in Brighton, where Alex operated on a "all the floor is potential floordrobe space" basis.

She turned to leave and saw, on the wall by the top of the staircase, a little key rack, from which hung exactly one set of keys. They were unlabeled, but extremely large, so Claire took them before she had time to think about how she shouldn't have taken them. She decided that the fact she'd seen them at all was serendipitous, possibly the result of a higher power, the patron saint of citizen detectives, and therefore it was all okay.

When she got back down into the hallway she realized that, possibly excluding the indeterminate number of hours Sophie had gone out last night while Claire was sleeping, it was the longest she'd been alone since she'd been seventeen years old. And it was the longest she'd gone without thinking about what Sophie would say to her if she could see her. She wondered what Sophie was doing. She wondered what Alex and Basher were doing.

The descent back down to the ground floor was less triumphant and heroic than the ascent had been. The weather was closing in. They'd lost one of the team. The documentary's voice-over was taking on a reproachful tone.

But! Claire thought. *It wasn't all in vain! We have several clues and physical items that could be of interest. If we can work out which ones are actually clues.*

This didn't sound like a very compelling hook for the next episode of *Landing: Stair Climbers*, even to her.

12

You Made a Believer Out of Me

Technically she should probably have taken statements from the other witness-suspects, but Claire didn't fancy another walk around an island covered in enough mist to be a Prince music video without Sophie to watch her back. It was like finding out your burglar alarm didn't work. And also that your burglar alarm could walk around by itself. Instead, Claire convinced herself that going back to her bedroom and locking the door was the best thing to do, as long as she used the time to write some notes because talking to people was exhausting, even when there wasn't a statistically significant chance they were a murderer.

This did, however, make her feel like the squad on *Murder Profile* would be disappointed, so she decided to make an effort and check out the jetty first, in case Basher and Eidy really were there. That seemed close enough to the hotel that she couldn't get in any real trouble, and would, if push came to stab, be within chest-bursting panicked sprint of at least one other person, even if Basher and Eidy turned out to be somewhere else.

She walked with a little caution along to the jetty, and kept turning to look behind her in case she was being followed. The pull on the tether to Sophie increased, and Claire deduced that meant Sophie had been still—or, still-ish—and Claire had dragged her a bit by moving farther away.

At the end of the jetty she found a toolbox and the sort of industrial-size torch that was only used by road workers or grizzled deputies looking for bodies and/or crocodiles in Floridian swamps, but no angry boatmen or depressive ex-cops. She was about to panic and then realized they probably weren't far, because they wouldn't have just left an open toolbox in the middle of nowhere, so she walked back and started calling Basher's name self-consciously. Despite the fact she was looking for him, she was still surprised when he appeared from a small, ruined building near the end of the jetty. She was so surprised she went "ah!"

"Sorry," he said. He was still wearing his orange waterproof cape thing. "What are you doing? Is Alex all right?"

"They're fine, they're back at the hotel. What are *you* doing?"

"We've been trying to signal in Morse code through the mist, but it's sort of impossible to tell if anyone has seen us. If nobody comes, we'll rota for another pair to keep doing it when it gets dark, as well. More chance someone will see it then."

"No, what are you doing in the weird little house . . . shed . . . thing?"

"Oh. Well, we heard someone coming and it struck me that this outfit is not very tactical if one is keen on avoiding an ambush by a murderer, so we hid in here until they went past."

"Er. Right, okay. That might have been me I suppose. Isn't that why there are two of you, though? To avoid ambush?" And, she added silently, as Eidy's head appeared in the glassless window frame like an angry moon, maybe Eidy was the murderer, which seemed an obvious flaw in Basher's plan that he had not identified.

"I suppose so. It has been quite a tiring morning," said Basher with a small smile. He looked a bit embarrassed.

"What d'you want, anyway?" said Eidy, in what Claire thought was an unnecessarily hostile tone.

"Nothing, I just wanted to make sure Basher was okay," said Claire. She was going to ask Eidy where he was at the time of the murder, except she already knew he was up and about, and he always looked so angry that even with Basher there she was a bit afraid. So she told them that there was reheated stew at the hotel if they wanted anything to eat. Basher said that was probably a good idea, but they'd pack up the tools and things first, and while she waited for them, hopping from foot to foot amid the ceaseless whispering of the trees, she heard a herd of homicidal elephants coming down the path that looped around the island.

This turned out to be the rest of The Others—George, Tiffany, and Ritchie. Ritchie was wearing a double-breasted sheepskin coat and consequently looked quite a lot like a big *Brokeback Mountain* fan.

"Hello," said George with a heart-stopping smile. "What are you up to?"

"Oh. Er. Hello. I'm waiting for Eidy and Basher. Flick reheated some stew so they're coming in to get something to eat."

"Hmm," said Tiffany, making a show of looking her up and down like a former queen bitch of the playground whose life had peaked at age seventeen. She had at least changed out of her satiny pajamas. "I am pretty hungry," she said.

"My Tiffany wanted to stretch her legs, and darned if I wasn't feeling as cooped up as a bullfrog in a jerry can myself," said Ritchie.

"We decided to go in a three," said George. "Because then if one of us is the murderer there are still two non-murderers to deal with them." He smiled at Claire again and she presumed he had forgiven her for obliquely accusing him earlier.

"Did you find anything interesting?"

"Just seaweed and birds," said Tiffany. "Not that it's any of your business. I expect you've been skulking around, have you?"

"Tiffy, there's nothing wrong with someone getting out and about, now is there?" asked Ritchie. He spoke very lightly, but there was a slight tension. Maybe he wasn't as oblivious as he seemed.

"Me and Alex looked at the . . . well, I suppose it's the crime scene," said Claire, thinking as she spoke. "But we only found a branch. Although it might have been used to hit Dan—oh, sorry. I keep forgetting you were all close. He paid for your bakery, didn't he?"

"No, that was Mac and Flick," said Tiffany, who could not resist correcting Claire. "Dan lent us a load of money when Ritchie's UK bank couldn't advance—"

But Ritchie quickly cut her off. "Now, now, Tiffany, you know I think it's unseemly to talk about that kind of thing in polite company," he said, and put a hand to Tiff's elbow.

If Claire had been able to, she would have punched the air. She'd got independent corroboration of the motive! And there wasn't even anyone there to show off to!

"You find anything else?" asked Tiff, very obviously trying to steer the conversation in a different direction to the one that was making Ritchie a bit mardy with her.

"Not really. There's a milk bottle floating in the water out the other side of the island, though. Like a marker."

"Oh, well, I guess that about salts the chowder," Ritchie said. "Sounds like a crab pot to me." A lazy smile crept back onto his face and he seemed more relaxed. "Y'all have crabs here?"

"Yes," said Claire very seriously, because she could not tell if he was joking. "We do have crabs."

Ritchie laughed uproariously, as was his fashion. "Boy this weather really is colder'n a salmon's ass!" he said. "I just can't get used to it. Can barely see my own hand in front of my face."

"Are salmon asses known to be particularly cold?" asked George, in a tone of polite inquiry.

"Not if you slap that sumbitch on the barbecue!" said Ritchie. Claire wondered if he knew when people were making fun of him, or if, being a very cheerful American, he assumed everyone was as sincere as he was, all of the time. It seemed exhausting. She stole a look at Tiffany, who seemed unfazed. Possibly you built up a tolerance over time with enough exposure. And then later in life if a small shrill Sicilian tried to poison you by putting American into your wine, it would have no effect.

Eidy and Basher had by now retrieved the toolbox, and they started to walk back to the hotel as a group.

"How is your investigation going?" George asked Claire.

"Um. Well, it hasn't been long. But there have been some developments," she said. Tiffany snorted.

"Oh yes," she said. "Would you like to know our movements on the night in question?"

"Well I mean . . . It wouldn't hurt," said Claire, looking at her shoes.

"We were tucked up in bed!" said Ritchie promptly. "Snug as two prairie dogs."

Sophie was right, Claire thought. It got a bit much sometimes, the Texanisms. Apart from anything else she had no frame of reference for how snug prairie dogs are supposed to be.

George lowered his voice a little. "I'm sorry about earlier. Friends?" he said.

"Oh yeah, of course," said Claire. "Friends. I just felt, um, a bit attacked, you know?"

"All right, good," he said. "Let's put it behind us. Are you having stew?"

"Oh, I already had some. I'm going to lock myself in my room and lie down for a bit. I'm actually quite tired," she said. Which was in fact true. But she could also feel the weight of the keys to the fort in her pocket, and sneaking off to talk to the Opportunists didn't seem like an activity to do with any of The Others. She looked up the path toward the fort as they passed it, and saw Sophie walking down it toward her. She fell into step next to Claire, who was luckily well practiced at not turning to look at Sophie in front of other people.

"That makes sense. We're all knackered," said George, who of course had no idea that a sullen and betracksuited dead adolescent was next to him. "Hopefully someone will rescue us soon, though. Although if we're still here later, can I sit at your table at dinner?"

"Oh. Um. Yeah," said Claire. She felt herself blushing so hard that she was surprised that the mist in the air wasn't evaporating off her face like steam. "It's, like, a date?"

"Worst first date ever," said George.

Claire's worst first date until that moment had involved a mis-understanding with a man whose profile she thought had indicated he really liked Francis Ford Coppola's *Dracula* movie (a sound film to like), but who had in fact wanted to actually bite her neck in the alley by a Wetherspoons that used to be a cinema. Sophie had naturally found this very funny.

"You're thinking about your actual worst first date, aren't you?" said George.

"Yeah. It'd take some beating to be honest."

"Well, you can tell me the story later," he said. The group had reached the hotel, and Claire and Sophie peeled off as the rest of them went inside. Basher told her to be careful, and she just about stopped herself rolling her eyes. Everyone else was, as far as she could tell, presently in the hotel, which made her very safe.

"What's actually going on with you and the dreamboat doctor?" said Sophie as they made it back to their room. She was clearly too curious to maintain her strop.

"Dunno," said Claire. "We kissed. And he keeps talking to me. Like, voluntarily and everything." Somewhere in the back of her mind Claire was dimly aware that if she had said this kind of thing in front of Alex, they would tell her to accept that there were reasons someone might want to spend time with her. But Alex was not here, Alex was probably making onion and chive muffins or whatever with their newfound family.

"Yeah, I saw," said Sophie, confirming Claire's suspicion she'd been skulking about last night. "Wonder what's wrong with him, LOL."

"You've got Cole hanging around you," said Claire. She switched the kettle on to make tea. It was very quiet compared to the one in Basher's kitchen in Brighton. It was probably some kind of low-impact energy-saving kettle powered by wind, while Basher's used the same amount of electricity as a small town. Claire realized she was starting to feel quite maudlin. "What has he been saying to you anyway? He said to think about what he told you, right?"

"Eh, it's nothing," said Sophie. "Just standard boring spook stuff. Hasn't spoken to anyone in years. You know how it is."

This struck Claire as an overexplanation and an underexplanation at the same time, but there was no point pressing Soph on it now.

"Let's make some notes on The Case," she said instead, getting out her notebook and sitting on the end of the bed.

Sophie whistled. "Ohmigod! Organization! As I live and breathe!"

"I know," said Claire, who, despite herself, felt pleased, like a child with their first-ever school workbook. "I thought I should keep one on me for working on case notes, like a proper investigator, in case anything happened again. Basher said keeping your case notes on the backs of old water bill envelopes and rail tickets wasn't standard operating procedure."

"He'd know. That man *is* a standard operating procedure," said Soph.

"Okay so," said Claire, ignoring her. "I've already got the ghosts and the suspects . . ."

She thumbed to the pages she'd written earlier, and felt cold prickles on her neck as Sophie leaned closer, but did not look around. She first updated the entry on Bones so it read *skellington* instead of *theoretical*. She also updated the list of other ghosts on the island to include *men in graveyard* and *monk???* Then she looked at the facing page and wrote *MOTIVES* very carefully, and then another list below it.

•*Minnie: owed Dan money, could lose hotel before it opens*

•*Ashley: lost everything because of chameleons, needed Dan's life insurance*

・Ritchie: *also owed Dan money*

・Flick: *also owed Dan money and lied about how much*

・Mac: *thinks Dan ~~is~~ was a prick*

・Eidy: *treasure??*

"Huh, did you find all that out when I was gone?" said Sophie.

"Yes," said Claire, secretly very proud of herself for developing into a seasoned detective. "This is quite hard, isn't it?" she said, staring at the page. She tapped her chin with the Biro. "Nobody is really ruled out."

"Mmm. Well, I think it's probably one of the lads," said Sophie. "I know we technically can't confirm it is, but strangling someone to death takes some doing, and the women aren't beef-cake types."

"I don't think we should cross off Minnie. The way she was dealing with the yoga mats was intense. And of the men . . . I think Eidy is a likely suspect, and we saw him with rope that could fit the murder weapon. I'm just not sure what motive he'd have, because he didn't know Dan personally—I think he might be a bet for the one who's stealing the treasure. Bones said he saw Eidy after whoever was legging it away with the treasure, but he didn't say that definitely wasn't Eidy as well. And we saw him near the beach where Dan died. He just seems shady."

"Shady as fuck," agreed Sophie. "You know, if we're saying the treasure could be involved, we should be looking for the equipment whoever the culprit is uses as well," said Sophie.

"What d'you mean?" asked Claire. "You don't need special equipment for carrying boxes."

"No, dipshit, but you do need it for getting boxes out of the sea and up a small cliff, don't you?"

"Oh, right. Yeah." This was a good point, and reminded Claire of the Ribena thing she'd found near the tree. Possibly somewhere on the island there was a scuba suit stashed under a rock or something. Wherever you stashed scuba suits. Proper James Bond job.

"I should have told Cole to keep an eye out for something like that," said Sophie. "That lot probably only just about know that diving flippers are a thing. They're doing a grid search of the island for the treasure, you know? But they haven't found anything yet."

"I suppose the problem is that you'd only need to be keeping your stolen box of goods inside another, larger box, or your detailed confession inside an envelope, and a bunch of ghosts wouldn't really be able to find it."

"Yeah, dying does increase your ability to walk through doors, but limits your ability to open them," Soph said.

"Oh, fucksake!" said Claire. "I forgot to ask the others about the bird-broach-belt thing." She emptied her pockets and put the Ribena thing, the shard of cup from the beach, and the probably-a-bird-buckle on the side table. Then she got out the fort key, and lined them all up in a neat row, like suspects. Being a detective was a good deal less about following your gut and a good deal more about being organized than Claire was happy about.

"I'm going to go up to the fort," she said. *And figure out what you've been doing up there, if it comes to it*, she added silently, glancing sideways at Sophie. She was starting to suspect the pirates had some sort of secret project going on inside it, on the basis that Cole would think it was very funny to do something

piratical right under Finny's nose, but she couldn't figure out
how they'd get in and out without the Opportunists realizing.

She downed the end of her tea just as the window was rattled
by a sudden attack of rain. Claire jumped up and went over to
look, peering out through glass that was now running with a
sheet of water that distorted the little town square in front of
them. "The fuck did this come from?" she moaned. "I haven't got
a properly waterproof coat."

"Maybe Minnie will timetable some indoor netball."

"Har har," said Claire, who had never been good at any school
sports (although Sophie had been on the gymnastics team, and,
when she vanished, had been in the process of starting a cheer-
leading squad, which was fiercely resisted by the faculty on the
basis of being an unnecessary Americanization of cricket).

"You don't have to go out or do any of this, you know," Sophie
added.

"I can't crack the case without clues, or case the suspects without spending time around them," she said.

"Stop saying 'case.' Do detectives case suspects? I thought
criminals cased joints?"

". . . Maybe. Whatever. I'm going to go."

Claire layered up her big scarf, then a hoodie, then a black
denim jacket on top of the hoodie. "I've got fuck all else to do
now, haven't I? Everyone else has gone off doing whatever without me."

Sophie surveyed Claire who, with her hood up, the scarf
wound around her neck, and stuffed under her layers, had the
same range of motion as if she were in a neck brace. She had
to turn her entire torso to look around. "You look like the very
hungry caterpillar," Sophie said.

"Piss off," said Claire.

Someone knocked on the door, surprising them both. It was Basher.

"Hello," he said, and shouldered inside. "I have brought you an umbrella, because you are not an all-weather packing sort of person. Are you all right? I realize this morning was stressful for you." He proffered the named portable canopy, and Claire took it, but he didn't leave. He was still wearing the rain poncho. It was quite hard to look directly at him.

"I'm fine," she said, adding, somewhat defiantly, "I've actually been making good progress."

"Mhmm. Well, I would like to impress upon you how important I think it is that you just leave everything well alone. Please consider doing that."

"It's all right for you to say, you've not been accused of anything," said Claire.

"Well, I presume you did not actually kill anyone, and therefore I have no concern that you'll be arrested or put in prison," he said. Claire remembered that Basher, despite having quit the police force almost two years before, still maintained a belief that the justice system was fundamentally able to punish the guilty and protect the innocent.

"In any case. I have been sent to ask you if you want to go screaming."

"Pardon?"

The screaming, Bash explained, was a guided therapy session led by Minnie, who was not only a trained yoga instructor, but had done courses on all manner of wellness and wellness-adjacent things. Claire was sort of jealous of people who are multitalented, but also suspected that one could get a degree in special shouting without too much effort. Minnie had suggested it as a stress reliever for the group. Claire agreed, thinking it would be a good opportunity to observe the psychology of the suspects, like on *Murder Profile*, and also hoping it might take place inside.

This hope turned out to be an empty one. Minnie's concession to the sudden turn toward the inclement that the weather had taken was to have the screaming take place in front of the hotel, looking at the town and the water, rather than on the football pitch halfway around the island where she usually did it. It seemed the class would be fairly well attended, despite the weather, and everyone waiting was standing around sort of bouncing from foot to foot and cradling their arms in an effort to, if not stay warm, at least not totally freeze. There were a couple of umbrellas, under which people were huddling in groups. Bash sloped over with Claire and Sophie, and joined Alex. Claire did her best to hold the umbrella high enough to cover all of them, but she didn't have particularly good arm strength.

"Say he looks like someone murdered a tangerine. No, say he looks like Casper the Friendly Ghost fucked a tangerine," said Sophie. Claire did not respond to this, because she couldn't think of a joke about an unfriendly ghost to return to Sophie in time.

"Probably not going to go back to signaling after this I s'pose?" she said to Basher instead.

"Flick and Mac agreed to cover for a while, although I suspect they will regret it in this weather, and given they have a toddler, we should get someone to relieve them as soon as possible. If we can do that, I might go for a walk to check the island again, actually. The weather is quite bracing." He smoothed down the front of his rain poncho, giving it great attention. Claire glared at him. She considered this evasive behavior. Apparently, Sophie did, too.

"He's up to something," she said.

"Mmm . . ." said Claire. It was hard to imagine what someone like Basher could get up to, though. Wanton putting down of mugs on wooden surfaces without coasters. Getting books wet. Not opening monthly bank statements, with extreme prejudice. As ex-detectives went, he was pretty boring.

"You look like a depressed satsuma, Uncle B," said Alex. In a typical display of Alex's own personal magic powers, they had conjured a stylish alternative coat from the deep reaches of their bag: a tan-colored swallow-tailed raincoat, showing flashes of a shocking aquamarine lining when it flapped in the wind.

"I'm sure I do," he said. "But we will see which of us is more dry in half an hour."

Bash didn't strike Claire as a screaming man, but then she wasn't very enthused about it herself. George broke away from the other umbrella group and came over to her. He had changed into jogging bottoms and trainers, but had a proper waterproof coat buttoned up. Rain was collecting on his pale eyelashes, but he looked very cheerful. Claire could feel the water soaking through the cloth hood of her hoodie already.

"Hello. How's things?" said George.

"Er. This isn't going to be a physical activity, is it?"

"Hm?" He looked down at his joggers, while Claire tried not to. "Oh. Honestly I don't know, I just thought I should change for the look of the thing. Although I'm regretting the choice, given the rain. Excited to scream?"

"I am," said Alex. "Is it like heavy metal screaming, d'you think? I had a mate who was in a metal band and he did loads of it, but it always sounded like he was shouting the name 'Roy.' You know, like, 'Roooooooooyyyyy!'" George started to laugh.

"Christ, I hope it's not that," he said.

"Ohmigod, I hope it is," said Soph, looking at Claire. "I'd like to see if you have that in you, weirdo."

Claire looked at her still-soggy toes and tried to retract farther into her scarf. She realized her shoulders were up, constant tension, and tried to force herself to relax. She looked around and saw that the other screamers included almost everyone, saving Eidy, Mac, and Flick, which was a boon for her investigation. Minnie, who was supposed to be leading the whole thing, still hadn't arrived. Ashley caught Claire looking, and gave her the upward nod hello of people who recognize, but do not really know, one another. The group formed into a larger natural huddle, as if they were a rugby team, and were now hanging outside the cover of the umbrella.

"Hello," said Ashley, still vague and a bit Bambi-on-ice wobbly. Claire wondered if it wasn't a pretty bad idea to have her out here, so near to where her husband had been found. "Bit brass monkeys, isn't it?"

"I wonder where that phrase comes from," said George, half to himself.

"It is from old ships, I believe," said Basher. "Cannonballs used to be stored in triangles made of brass that—"

"You believe wrong," interrupted Claire, unable to stop herself. "Historians—of which I technically am one, you'll remember—can find no basis for that." Basher looked a bit put out. He loved facts.

"So where does it come from?" asked Alex.

"You know the Three Wise Monkeys? See no evil, hear no evil, speak no evil? Brass models of them were a really popular cheap souvenir from a hundred and some years ago. It's probably that," she explained.

"Which are you three, then?" said George, grinning. "No, let me guess . . ." He waved his finger between Alex, Claire, and Basher. "Basher is probably speak no evil . . ."

Basher inclined his head. "I would like to think so."

". . . Alex seems like a see-no-evil sort of person . . ."

"Too right, Doctor G!" said Alex. "I'm no narc. You steal bread from Sainsbury's, I didn't see anything."

". . . and that leaves hear no evil. Claire no evil."

"I wish," said Claire, looking at Soph. "And that doesn't even rhyme. Terrible nickname."

"I'm okay being excluded from the three, because I'm none of them," said Sophie. "I speak, see, and hear evil. And do it. The anti-monkey. Rawr. Anyway, I thought you wanted to do some detecting. Have at it."

Minnie spared her this by slamming the door of the hotel shut against the wind and coming over.

"Right. Good. Hello. Oh, Claire—thank you for the tip. I was looking through some of the old papers, left in my office—found during the renovation. I think there's some useful stuff. Combined with the names of those brothers. Might be able to trace their family right down to the current generation, with some work."

"What's this about, now?" asked George.

"Yeah, what *is* this about?" Alex echoed.

"Claire told me about that local legend, you know, of the pirates and wreckers on the island," explained Minnie, radiating helpfulness.

"Did she, now?" said Alex, eyeing Claire. Bash looked at her, too, and smiled his most infuriating, knowing smile.

"Um, yeah, like, you remember that woman in the shop I was talking to?" said Claire, hoping that Alex wasn't cruel enough to openly laugh at her lies. But they weren't, of course they weren't.

"I dabble in genealogy. I told Claire about it earlier, actually. I've been looking into the island's history a bit," Minnie went on. She looked genuinely enthused. "I'd already traced the pirate's family in England. Claire gave me the names of some Irish brothers connected with that story. I found out their last name is probably Ó Liatháin. It's tricky because Irish names got anglicized and changed a bit. Fascinating stuff."

"Ah yes, very exciting," said Alex, who sounded like they did not in fact find it at all interesting. Presumably the treasure hunting prospect had been eclipsed by the excitement of a murder.

"Yes! Because this Fionnbharr and his family. If there are any existing relatives, they could challenge the right to anything found. Slim chance, obviously, even if treasure exists. Maybe Eidy is descended from him."

"What?" said Basher, looking startled. "What does Eidy have to do with it?"

"Oh, didn't you know? Eidy's family used to live here, a generation or so ago. His grandad worked at the prison. All the families left in the eighties and nineties," said Minnie. "Eidy's dad was a fisherman, and then when he retired from that he drove the tourist boat out here to Spike."

"Is that what you meant when you said he came with the place?" asked Claire. "Like, pay extra to keep the furnishings, and the angry man." George laughed.

"Well remembered, weirdo," said Sophie.

"He made a bit of a fuss, said that this development was building over the island's heritage, his family's heritage. He said it should have been preserved or rebuilt as it was." Minnie lowered her voice, in case Eidy was lurking nearby somehow, but Claire could barely hear her. "I felt a bit of an obligation. Also, locals kicking up a fuss can be bad for business."

"Maybe it really was Eidy," said Sophie. Her dark eyes were alight. "He'd know the secrets of the island, and all about the tides. The treasure could be a family secret. Passed down generation unto generation, until he was caught moving it by a smug Web3 pyramid scheme salesman, who tried to blackmail him!"

"Has this got anything to do with fucking shouting?" said Tiffany, who was clearly having second thoughts.

"Right. Shall we?" said Minnie.

The group shuffled into a sort of ragged squad formation, with those not holding umbrellas extremely reluctant to move away from them. It reminded Claire of the reality TV shows where quantity surveyors and Parkrun enthusiasts volunteer to spend three weeks having mud thrown at them by bearded pit bulls who claim to have worked in the special forces. Minnie—nervous, staccato—explained a bit about the popular history of yelling for your health. Proponents apparently included Yoko Ono and John Lennon.

"And yet," muttered Alex, out of the corner of their mouth, "you will not endorse me staying in bed all day."

"Shut up," Basher replied, equally quietly. Sophie snorted.

The actual substance of the screaming seemed to be just . . . yelling. Minnie made a point of giving it more weight: think of something that is frustrating you; imagine the energy in the Earth's core, swirling around as molten rock. Imagine that power coming up through the ground and entering your toes, traveling up your legs and exploding out of you. Breathe deeply. Shout from your belly not your throat. That kind of thing. But at the end of the day, Claire thought, it sounded like regular yelling to her. She looked sideways and caught George's eye. He winked at her. She looked away.

Minnie demonstrated with an abrupt scream, with her little fists balled in concentration.

"Right, yes. So that's the idea. Releases endorphins, and eases tension. Let's all give it a try," said Minnie.

Everyone looked around a little sheepishly. To Claire's supreme surprise, Basher was the first to go. He unleashed a surprisingly guttural roar. Alex turned round to him in astonishment.

"Fucking hell, Uncle B," they said. "I'm glad the walls in the flat are thick."

This broke the dam a bit. Alex screamed away quite happily, and then started having a go at doing death metal Roys. Tiffany screamed like the final girl in a horror film. Ritchie was giving it socks in a Javert-esque baritone that Claire found extremely surprising, and George, after trying to get away with doing the Alan Partridge "Ah-HA!," received a withering look from Minnie and entered into the spirit of things with a few war cries. Minnie walked around and said "very good" or slightly corrected people's postures, like yoga teachers are wont to do, although Claire thought this was basically for show. Claire found it quite difficult to tell if any of this indicated a propensity toward whacking your mate on the head and then strangling him to death and throwing him in the sea.

The only people who weren't yelling were Claire and apparently Ashley, who was holding her umbrella straight above her head with slightly trembling hands. Claire just felt too awkward about it.

"Come on, girls," said Minnie, casting herself as a brisk PE teacher type. "Everyone else is giving it a go."

"Think of it this way, C," said Alex. "Right now you're in the minority of non-screamers, which in context makes you more weird than if you were screaming, right?"

"I think it should be allowed for people to not scream," mumbled Claire.

"Then why did you fucking come here at all, weirdo?" said Sophie.

Sophie started screaming, too, loud and cheerful. She jogged around the group a bit and went to yell right in Tiffany's face. It was all right for Sophie, Claire thought. Nobody could see or hear her doing it.

Claire now wished people hadn't been saying the word *screaming* so much because it just made her think of the girl she'd been in student halls with in first year. The girl had brought a guy back to her room during freshers week and hadn't closed her door properly, and then the other lad in their flat had told his mates in the other block over, and then they'd told all their friends in lectures, and then everyone had called her Screamer for the rest of her time at university. Eventually she just accepted it, even changed her Facebook profile. Claire could no longer remember what the girl's actual name had been. This reminded her of the one good bit of advice that she'd been given before going to university, delivered by the outwardly matronly but covertly hardcore school librarian, which was to avoid being the one to throw up all over the communal lounge, and to as far as possible avoid doing anything else that could otherwise be remarked upon, during the first couple of weeks of term. Claire had mostly managed this by not talking about Sophie to people—which had, of course, made Soph furious.

"Come on mate, give it the old college try," said Alex again, this time employing a startlingly good impression of the nasal accent of other, posher, more murdery members of their family.

Claire opened her mouth to protest again that maybe screaming wasn't for everyone, and was interrupted by a long, agonized shriek.

Everyone else stopped. It was Ashley. She had found the scream within her. She had dropped the umbrella and had turned toward the rest of the group. As she screamed, she advanced slowly, but so aggressively—veins in her neck tensed, head forward as if she was about to charge—that they all took several steps back. Her shrieks became louder and shorter, until Ritchie grabbed her wrist. Ashley slapped him across the face with her other hand. She smiled. Then she giggled. Then she could not stop giggling, and eventually bent over double at the waist, laughing. She collapsed onto her hands and knees. In *Murder Profile* this would have been viewed as deeply suspicious behavior, because anything other than a dramatic wail upon being informed of a loved one's death, and constant dignified tearfulness (with a single folded white handkerchief to dab at tears) was the behavior of a potential murderer—unless you cried too much, or in the wrong way, which was also suspicious. But Claire had been told by Alex, many times, that people processed traumatic events in different ways.

It's just, Ashley's way was quite unsettling.

13

Receiving Guests

For a full minute Ashley stayed on the ground, digging her fingers into the mud, and nobody dared approach or touch her, perhaps out of fear she would break entirely. Abruptly she clambered to her feet, and ran toward the hotel. It broke the spell, and The Others all ran after her at once. Claire wished she had her case notes with her, so she could add some supplemental thoughts. She was about to follow the group, because it seemed important to observe what happened, but Basher interrupted her.

"You should probably dry off, Strange," he said. He was obviously unsatisfied at her efforts with the umbrella. At the conclusion of their last case she'd caught the flu—although she still insisted it had just been a bad cold—after being out in the rain most of the night, and since then Basher had been convinced that she was of a particularly weak constitution that suffered intensely when exposed to too much rain (an arbitrary threshold determined by Basher himself).

In this case, though, he was right. The whole of her hood was soaked through and clinging to the back of her head. Her ears were getting quite cold, even for someone who was used to being quite cold, quite a lot of the time. The weather had escalated, too. It seemed the puny humans shouting into it had only made it angry, and so it had responded by showing that it could, if it felt like it, fuck all of them into the sea with a moment's notice— without any notice in fact; it wouldn't even be aiming for the little matchstick people that happened to get in the way. The rain was coming down in stinging sheets and the water in the estuary was churning, the color of dark metal, but molten and spitting up waves that were alarmingly close to the buildings on the island's shore. The hotel proper was closer, but all of Claire's dry socks were in her room, so she decided to run back there, change, and then return to the hotel for dinner.

"That's where Eidy's flat thing is, isn't it?" said Sophie, as they walked through the entrance to the little square. "On the right, there?"

Claire remembered that Minnie had told them Eidy lived in what was the old church. It was a single-story building sort of like a tiny bungalow, and like everything else was built to proportions appropriate to people in the 1930s, when apparently everyone was four feet tall. There was a small door set in the middle of it, with tiny windows on either side. On an impulse, Claire staggered up to it, one hand hanging on to her umbrella, and one still holding up her sopping wet hood to stop the wind from blowing it off her head, more out of habit than for any real protection from the weather. She knocked on the door. There was no answer. She hammered on it, and then turned and raised her eyebrows at Sophie.

"Oh, right, yeah. Fucksake. Sorry," said Sophie. Claire watched her friend's big bouncy ponytail, still to all appearances voluminous and dry, disappear through the wall as Sophie walked straight into Eidy's house. She often forgot this was a thing she could do, partly out of habit from not being able to do it when she was alive, and partly because she was so used to having to wait for Claire to open newspapers or put on *Bargain Hunt* for her, that it just sort of didn't compute that she didn't need a door to be opened in order to pass through.

Claire hopped from one foot to the other until Sophie came back out.

"Pretty sure he's not in there," she said. "But, like, obviously enough I can't turn on any bastard lights, so . . ."

"What's it like?"

"Seems like an open-plan kitchen and living bit, and a separate bedroom and bathroom down the end there. So . . ."

"So, nicer than our flat back home?"

"Correct."

"Bollocks to this, anyway," said Claire. She hurried across the square and up the stairs to her room, slipping a bit on the steps. She wondered if Minnie had accounted for them being slippery when wet. It seemed like the sort of thing one should account for.

When she got inside, she cranked the heating, had a shower, and changed into dry clothes, but this presented a problem because most of the ones she had were either already damp or had noodle residue on them. So what she actually did was put on the complimentary terry-cloth dressing gown. She hung her jeans, scarf, and hoodie on the radiator and wondered if it would be dangerous to keep them there overnight. Like, was there a chance the hoodie would spontaneously combust? The scarf was definitely made of something cheap and synthetic-y rather than actual wool, but did that make it more or less flammable? She remembered seeing a public information film by the fire service that warned against falling asleep while smoking because it would immolate your baby almost instantly. You might as well have put a doll-shaped lump of paraffin wax in a crib.

"Why are you staring at the radiator, weirdo?" asked Sophie.

Claire abruptly snatched the clothes off the radiator. There was a heated towel rail in the bathroom, which seemed safer, because that was where you were supposed to put damp materials. Potential fire-starting would surely be accounted for during the design process.

"I swear, you're going completely off your fucking rocker these days," said Sophie. She offered a half-hearted "LOL."

"Sure. Where do you keep disappearing to, anyway? I never know if you're going to be there when I turn around or not," Claire said. "You weren't there after I kissed George last night, you were gone after lunch. What's going on with you?"

"Nothing."

"You can't have done nothing for hours, you get bored in about two-point-five seconds. You're like the opposite of a goldfish. Every experience is instantly old to you."

"I hung out with Cole, okay?"

"And what, pray tell, does 'hung out with' mean?"

"Christ, back off! Are you afraid I'm going to get pregnant or something?"

"Well *are* you going to get pregnant?"

"I don't know, do ghosts get pregnant?"

"I don't know!"

"I don't know either! Just be cool about stuff, okay? I'm not having imaginary ghost sex and getting ectoplasm in my fucking hair, or whatever. Unlike you, who is definitely having factual alive person sex," said Sophie.

"I bloody am not."

"LOL, yeah, sure."

"Oh my God, fine, I'll be cool if you be cool? Okay?" replied Claire. She threw one of her pillows through Sophie.

"As long as you know I don't like that guy," said Soph.

"Yeah, well I don't like your guy either."

"Fine."

"*Fine.*"

They looked away from each other in moody silence for a minute.

Claire sat up suddenly. She thought she heard a creak outside the door. She got up and walked over, put her ear to it, but she couldn't hear anything else, so she went and sat down again.

"Okay I was kind of joking before, but now I actually think you are going properly off your rocker," said Sophie.

"No! I just keep thinking I can hear people following me or moving stuff or something. You keep fucking off and I'm not used to having to watch my own back."

"Ohmigod, stop being so paranoid."

"Someone has literally been murdered. I'm not being paranoid, I'm being sensible. Someone's going to snap. Can you not see how weird and tense this all is? Even if Ashley didn't kill her husband, she's going to kill the next person that touches her. And Basher and Alex aren't really helping. I'm supposed to be clearing my name or whatever and they're not even arsed."

There was a tentative knock on the door. It was Alex, trying to rearrange their face into the expression of someone who had definitely not just been listening, hunkered down under their umbrella. Claire started to blush out of social embarrassment.

"Uncle Basher predicted that you would already have run out of clean dry clothes," they said. Claire made a face, because the prediction was correct but she didn't really want to concede the point to Bash. Alex came in out of the rain, and handed over a Lidl bag containing some joggers, a T-shirt, and their black furry hellcoat, none of which had been folded or ironed at any point in their lifespan. "Don't get too adventurous. The coat is dry-clean only."

"I'll look like a charity case," said Claire.

"You do anyway," said Sophie.

"Nothing wrong with needing charity," said Alex automatically. "I'm going to stay here while you get changed to make sure you aren't murdered. Nothing can go wrong with me here, right?"

Claire thought that actually when you were with Alex plenty of things could go wrong, usually at Alex's instigation, including trying white wine with a tequila shot mixed in your glass because they'd read online that "you basically can't taste it and it fortifies the wine" and things of that nature. On the other hand, a wellness retreat didn't seem likely to have a liquor cabinet. Alex was still intermittently complaining that a hotel specifically for neo-hippie types didn't have a weed bar.

Alex got up and examined Claire's side table of odd items and possible clues. "Where did you find a carabiner?"

Alex had never mentioned any interest in climbing before, but Claire shouldn't have been surprised. Though they were very clear on who they were, Alex wasn't clear on what job they wanted to do beyond making cool stuff (mostly embroidery hoops featuring chicken nuggets, or robots sixty-nining). As such, they had an ongoing or passing generalist interest in most available hobbies, usually via someone they knew from fabricating a staff for a Sailor Moon cosplay or some kind of knitting club that met in the library every other Wednesday to make jumpers.

"I knew it was something like that!" crowed Sophie, as Alex picked up the little metal loop.

"Oh yeah, we found that by a tree on the far side of the island. I think it has something to do with the treasure. The tree looked like it might have a rope mark on it."

"Aha," said Alex. "I believe this is what those secret agent fuckers on your shows would call an actual clue? I bet he—or, whoever—used it as an anchor for the rope. You wouldn't expect rope burn, necessarily, but if he was hauling something quite heavy up, and the tree was quite thin . . . That's some good proof, right? A climbing rope would be a good strangling device."

"Oh yeah, I s'pose so. I hadn't thought of that," Claire said.

Claire changed in the bathroom, and found the T-shirt and joggers were quite comfortable (Alex's clothes operating at either end of a scale going from the extremes of "suitable for nap" and "suitable for couture drag ball") and since she hadn't had a lot of sleep still, she immediately lay down on the bed.

"No, come on, wake up," said Alex. "I'm going to reveal that my motives here are extremely ulterior. Apparently we need to take a turn on the end of the pier so the fragile mothers can come inside. Which is fair enough. And hey, it proves Uncle B thinks you're adult enough to not get me killed! So, a thumbs-up there."

"Nyawwwwwidonwanna," she said, and pulled the duvet over her head.

Alex pulled it off and started clapping at her like a parent making their child get up for school. "Come on, spit-spot!" they said. "Helping out will strengthen your case that you're not a murderer. Plus, if you fall asleep now you'll be up until two a.m. later, and then you'll be cross tomorrow as well."

"God, when did you become a grown-up?" said Claire.

They walked down to the end of the pier-thing together, Alex and Claire standing close under the umbrella since the rain, though much lighter than during the screaming session, was spit-spottering. Sophie just seemed pleased enough to hang out with Alex. They found Flick and Mac standing in the little concrete shelter occasionally flashing a big torch out to sea as a subtask to entertaining their daughter, who was in enough layers of winter-wear that she looked like a small beach ball. They were only too eager to switch out.

Alex agreed to hold the umbrella if Claire flashed the SOS, and after a brief pause for Sophie to explain the Morse code for SOS, they settled in.

"So, you think the murder is to do with the treasure stuff? Someone actually is in league, except it's with the ghosts?" Alex asked. Claire felt like they were only asking because they'd overheard what she'd said about them and Basher not really helping—in fact, Basher had probably specifically told them to come and make conversation with her. It was like your mum not turning up to watch you in the school's production of *Grease* but being really enthusiastic about picking you up afterward.

"No. Well. Maybe. Like, generally people can't be in league with ghosts," said Claire.

"Except you!"

"I'm not in league with fuck all, my whole situation is very inconvenient."

"Oh yeah, sorry, just looking for the bow for the world's tiniest fucking violin over here," said Sophie.

"I think it's more likely Dan saw someone moving some treasure, and that treasure also happens to be something some annoying old ghosts are obsessing over," said Claire. "Because I think it would be a pretty big fucking coincidence if Dan came to this island and got killed over something else."

"And at what point do enough coincidences stack up before we entertain the idea that they're, you know, not that?"

"Right. I've been thinking maybe someone here is descended from either the ghost pirate captain or the ghost Irish locals."

"Sure, that makes sense," said Alex. "What other clues do you have? You've got proof someone tied a rope around that tree, right? Because of the carabiner."

"Well, we've got proof someone dropped a carabiner and *probably* attached a rope to the tree," said Claire, simultaneously not wanting Alex (the wild card) to ruin The Case by misinterpreting evidence, and realizing she was thinking of this as The Case now. "We don't know what they did with it."

"Ah yes, guv'nor. Sorry for improper police work. I'll hand in my badge and gun. Can we at least adopt it as a working hypothesis? I thought you were supposed to be the ideas woman. The imaginative one."

Claire made a face. "I'm trying to imagine things less, just at the moment."

"Right, yeah. Are you feeling okay?"

"Mostly."

"And getting enough sleep."

"Probably not."

"And the early morning sex with the big hot doctor was how good?"

Sophie burst out laughing.

"You'll have to do better than that," Claire replied. Claire was quite proud of herself for that, because only a few months ago she would probably have immediately frozen, if not performed a full stop, drop, and, if not roll, pretend she was looking industriously for a lost earring.

"You know your silence about the Hot Doc speaks volumes, right?"

"An omission is not a confession. We didn't have sex, we just kissed. Maybe I just don't want to talk about it? You wouldn't even have guessed if he hadn't had to tell everyone."

"Oh, I *so* would have guessed, there were charged looks straight away. You can't hide that sort of thing when everyone is trapped on a small island. Give it time. The day is young." Claire shot them a sour look. "What, I thought you'd enjoy this! This is like an interrogation scene from one of the shows you watch."

"It's mainly one show," mumbled Claire.

"Well, I only wanted to say 'good for you,' anyway," they said, and nudged her. "It's good to have hobbies."

Claire grimaced. "I wouldn't call it a hobby, exactly."

"Oh, you know what I mean! You never seem to have any fun. It's okay to let your hair down. I imagine he did as well . . ."

"Yeah, well. There's a one in eight chance he's a murderer."

"That means basically a ninety percent chance he isn't!" said Alex, completing the strange echo of the argument Claire and Sophie had at the fort when she'd had her freak-out at footsteps. "Cheer up. And thanks for not counting me and Uncle B in your statistic."

"Should I have?" said Claire. She always belatedly remembered that good detectives should be suspicious of everyone but it was a lot of effort doing that—and in any case, it only seemed to actually be important to do so if the murderer turned out to be a corrupt cop.

"Wouldn't have thought so . . ." said Alex. "You never know with me, though. Wouldn't put anything past me. Anyway, the point is, if you enjoyed yourself, then where's the harm?"

"I'm not really sure I did, to be honest," said Claire. "Although I never really do."

"Oh, well. Maybe you're ace?"

"Thanks, you're cool too," said Claire a bit absentmindedly.

"Ha! God, you and Uncle B do seem old sometimes. Remind me to bring it up to you again in a less murdery situation. Just don't overthink things."

"Fat fucking chance of you ever managing that," said Sophie.

"That lot are right, you know, you're very cheerful given the situation," said Claire.

"Don't be shitty, C. Not much point being anything else but cheerful at a time like this. Choose life, choose a job, choose to assume that you won't be murdered."

Their interest in the murder apparently exhausted for the time being, Alex spent some more time questioning Claire about the specifics of the interpersonal relationships of the various ghosts on the island, and then even more specifically about what was going on between Sophie and Cole, to which Claire could only respond, "Honestly I have no idea, but I don't like it," which made Sophie hoot with rage.

"I suppose if we're thinking a ghost's descendent is involved, it's probably not Ritchie. I mean I know there was a lot of emigration but not a lot of them settled in Texas. I think I just find him weird. I asked Tiffany about how they met," said Alex. "Because, like, it's usually friends of friends or internet dating now. Lot of apps."

"I believe dying alone is quite popular with mine and Claire's generation," said Sophie.

"Well, quite. She said it was a total coincidence. Ritchie came into the café she worked at, because she was living and working in South London at the time."

"Oh, like Brixton?" said Claire. She and Claire had lived in South London for basically all of their lives before moving to Brighton.

"That's the weird thing!" said Alex with a grimace. "It wasn't even a little bit more central, it was fucking Croydon."

"Wow. Nobody likes visiting Croydon, not even people who already live in Croydon," said Sophie. "And Croydon's miles from anywhere except more Croydon."

Alex shrugged. "Everyone's gotta live somewhere. Just seems unusually lucky for her that a rich Texan decided to get his tourist on out there I suppose," they said. "Anyway. Will you actually hang out once our shift is over? Flick and Mac are going to teach me to make pasta sauce from scratch."

"Yeah, that's great for you," said Claire. If Mac had been accused of murder, Alex would probably have been all over the effort to prove her innocence.

Alex looked at her and raised an eyebrow. "Uhuh. Weird little mood we're in, is it?"

"I want to go," said Sophie.

"I'm tired," said Claire.

"Suit yourself, I suppose. You shouldn't spend the whole night alone. Uncle B will be worried."

"He doesn't seem it."

Alex sighed, and stopped talking. Claire continued to silently flick the torch on and off. It was just lighting up the fog in front of them like fake snow in a shop window. She was pretty sure no passing ships would see it unless they were literally ten feet away. She wondered how long they had to stay out there. She made a mental note to buy an actual watch, in case she ever went to a tech-free retreat again and needed to tell the time while on the go.

"You know, dickhead, if you treat everyone like they're horrible and just waiting to drop you, then it becomes a self-fulfilling prophecy," said Sophie, eventually, in a strangled voice. She was trying to do a handstand. She had been on the verge of figuring it out when she'd died, and now it was always just out of reach.

Claire ignored her. She felt Sophie was offering the sort of psychological analysis you could get from *Good Morning* or an episode of *Peppa Pig*, and she was not in the mood. She glanced at Alex, and tried to figure out how she could answer Sophie in a neutral way. Even if they hadn't been there, it would have been hard to explain to Sophie the feelings of social isolation and jealousy because she had never really had them when she was alive. Sophie was the teenage girl you were jealous *of*. She was chewing this over when she heard footsteps approaching from behind them, appearing from nowhere because of the noise-dampening effect of the mist. She swung the torch 'round on instinct.

"Halt! Who goes there?" she said. This made Alex and Sophie laugh, which did feel quite normal.

"In the name of the king, be ye friend or be ye foe!" added Alex.

"I think they're quite proud of not having to do anything in the name of the king in this country," said George's voice. He came into view, with a smaller shape beside him that resolved into Flick.

"You've been out here a while now, as it happens, and Eidy said there's no point anyone keeping at it until it gets properly dark," said Flick. "So we came to tell you you're relieved."

"Oh, fun," said Alex. "Are you sure?"

"Yes, and I come bearing you a sandwich," said Flick. She withdrew a tinfoil package from her pocket. "I wasn't sure if you were coming in for dinner, or if you wanted to have a shower and warm up, but I thought you might be hungry. It's chicken salad. Oh, sorry, Claire. I didn't think you'd want one—"

"It's fine, don't worry about it," said Claire. Her tone of voice did not indicate that it was fine. It was actually quite upsetting.

"Well, I'm definitely coming to dinner," said Alex. "C, if you're not going to come in again you can have the sandwich." They offered it to her, and Claire snatched it in a graceless way she immediately felt bad about.

"God, you're such a child," said Sophie.

"Thanks. Um. Thanks, Flick."

"Can I walk you back to your room, then?" George asked, smiling at Claire. "We're all moving in herds. Or, well, pairs," said George with a smile. "I was going to say it's like *Jurassic Park*, but it's actually like the *Cluedo* movie, isn't it?"

"Um, yeah, okay. Thank you." Claire knew she should probably be suspicious of George and not walk around alone with people she didn't trust, but she did trust George because he was the only person being nice to her, as far as she could tell. For a moment Claire thought Sophie was going to peel off and follow Alex, but in the end she trailed after Claire.

George leaned easily against the doorframe when they got to her room, almost as if he wanted to be invited in. Claire blushed because the room was chaos. She saw him looking toward the side table, which had a bra hanging off the bedside lamp for reasons of Claire throwing it there accidentally when she got changed, and then forgetting it needed to be put away whenever she was not directly looking at it.

"Um. Mine's a bit messier than yours," she said.

"Yeah, if the state of this room doesn't put him off I don't know what will," said Sophie.

"I'm terrifically anal about packing," he said. "Yours is charmingly cluttered. Would you come over to the hotel, though? Strength in numbers."

Claire nodded, but in her experience it was safer by herself, because people were either disappointed or disappointing, and she'd managed so far with just her and Sophie. "Maybe," she said.

George sighed. "That means you won't, doesn't it? Careful out here by yourself."

"Thanks, I think?" Claire mumbled. "See you later." She shut the door and watched George leave the square from the window. The rain started coming down hard again, and he started to jog. Claire was feeling quite emotionally confused, and she was glad she'd left the heating on. She could be emotionally confused and at least have warm fingers.

"What are we going to do, then? I thought you were set on cracking the case or whatever the fuck?" said Sophie. "If we're not going to have dinner, can we at least not hang around here the whole time?" She was visibly frustrated, standing with her hands bunched and fizzing in a way that suggested she was close to stamping her foot.

"I'm going to wait until they're all having dinner and then go up to the fort," said Claire decisively. "And we can set up there to watch the treasure from the walls. That way we can catch the person in the act, but they won't even know we're there."

"Okay, that's too far the other way toward adventure. It'll be pitch black and there are no lights there, you'll wet yourself and fall over. You're not strong or brave enough to perform a citizen's arrest."

"I won't be trying to; we're just going to watch from where the Opportunists sit."

"That's stupid, as soon as you leave the walls you'll lose sight of whoever it is, if there's even anyone there, so you won't really know who it is or where they go."

"I'll work it out," she snapped.

"Ohmigod, take the exit ramp, abandon your stupid plan to die in a storm. You don't even have a real coat, you're wearing Alex's fluffy nightmare!"

"We'll busk the details!" said Claire. "I'm going to figure this out, without anyone else's help if I have to. Which apparently I do," she added bitterly.

"Fucking hell, all right, John McClane, I hope the fort has some ducts for you to fall out of."

Sophie was adept at deflating Claire's attempts to be heroic, or at the very least feel heroic.

"Well, whatever. Stage one of the plan is still to wait for them to be at dinner without me." Claire checked the clock on the bedside table and completely failed to work out how to set an alarm. "Wake me up in like an hour and a half, okay?"

14

Rumble

Claire felt an awful crick in her neck, and sat up to roll it. The muscles in her shoulders crackled like Rice Krispies as she flexed them. It took her a moment to realize that Sophie had gone again, and she pulled herself up to check the time. The clock by the bed was showing just after midnight, and she realized that Sophie had not, in fact, woken her up when she'd asked her to.

The storm, which she'd hoped would ease up slightly, had eased on with a vengeance. Claire could hear the wind screaming outside, and the rain was falling so fast that it became one continuous wall of noise, like ball bearings rolling down sheet metal rather than drops of water.

She next noticed that she was very hungry, and located the sandwich she'd neglected to eat earlier. This made her feel a bit better, but she could feel the tether pulling and plucking at her . . . what? Her insides? Her soul? Whatever it was, she could feel Sophie pulling against it again, and she frowned. How far was too far? When did it stop being safe? If Soph could just leave would she . . . not come back again?

A piece of chicken was dangling half out of her mouth when she realized having the lights on in your room isn't good for espionage, so she scrambled for the light switch. What seemed like only seconds later, a light from outside flickered across the ceiling. She twitched the curtain, cautiously, to peer out into the darkness. There it was again! The flash of a torch near the entrance to the village square.

Right, she thought. *I'm going to fucking have you, you prick.* She would have been more scared of going out into the night to accost a random probable murderer, except she was very angry at everyone, especially Basher and Alex for not trying harder to make her have dinner, but especially Sophie for deserting her again. She felt pretty confident if she took Basher's advice and kicked whoever it was in the crotch hard enough, they would go and stay down.

The weather was much more of a deterrent. Luckily her jeans, which seemed a more robust choice for late-night stakeouts than Alex's borrowed joggers, were basically dry, although they were still uncomfortably damp around the pockets. It was like being touched up by a snowman, although Claire reasoned it probably wouldn't matter because she'd be soaked almost as soon as she got outside. She should have brought a big oilskin like proper sailors have—although she did silently thank Basher for making Alex give her the umbrella and their black hellcoat. She would not, obviously, thank him to his stupid face.

Claire opened the umbrella before opening the door, and then remembered that was supposed to be bad luck—although she didn't know why, and it didn't make sense. Maybe there had been a spate of Victorians opening their umbrellas inside and then stepping outside to immediately get smashed in the face with a brick thrown by a disgruntled poor person.

Then she discovered that the real reason you don't open an umbrella inside is that it's pretty fucking hard to walk out of the door holding it.

Once she got outside, she began to regret the decision, because it really was a horrible night, but she held the umbrella high up the handle, so the canopy bit was resting on her head, and it formed a turtle shell of protection that kept the wind and rain off a large part of her upper torso, as well as making it harder for the wind to lift it. The disadvantage was that it was very hard to see, so she advanced quite slowly. She did very quickly regret not having a torch, though, because it was also quite dark.

She shuffled along the edge of the square, out of the entrance, and then lifted the umbrella briefly. She was hoping to be rewarded by a glimpse of a moving light, but what she got was a slap in the face by more rain. In fairness, there might actually have been a light in the distance, but it was so dark and rainy that it was hard to really tell. She turned and squinted at the town across the water, and found she couldn't properly make out the lights there, either. Still, if someone was out to steal treasure tonight there was basically only one place they'd be going.

There was one light visible, though. A light upstairs in the hotel was on. But even as she looked, it winked out, and then she couldn't remember which window it was or might have been. It took any semblance of night vision she'd managed to scrape up with it, and she swore under her breath and carried on, shuffling her feet to make sure she wasn't moving off the path and onto the grass. The sound of water on her right was violent, and if the tide hadn't been low she knew she would have felt spray hit her. It seemed like a risky move, to go for treasure tonight.

It was around then that she realized she couldn't feel Sophie. She didn't know where she was. She couldn't feel a pull in any direction. Was she close, or had she run off somewhere? That she had disappeared entirely was unthinkable.

This, more than anything, made Claire panic, and she started to walk faster, her breath becoming ragged. Her desperate inhalations made her swallow her own spit, so she started coughing, and she tried to stop and calm down. Though she had often (secretly, guiltily) imagined what her life would be like if Sophie didn't exist, and all the things she'd do if she was alone, now that Sophie had actually, properly left her, she was completely nonplussed. Like finding you have a free afternoon and then spending four hours sucking the chocolate off Maltesers and watching videos of a Canadian icing cookies in the shape of Luigi Mario, rather than reading the self-improvement book you meant to. Except also you are suddenly, acutely aware of your mortality.

Inhale for two. Out for three. Technically nothing could really happen to Sophie. The storm was worse than she'd thought, and she should probably turn back. On the other hand, a mutinous part of her suggested, it would be very good to prove Basher and Alex and Sophie wrong. Not that they'd specifically said she was useless, but it definitely, actually, really felt like if she managed to catch a thief by herself she would be proving them wrong about *something*, anyway.

She kept her head down and leaned forward, angling the umbrella slightly to the right because it felt like that's where the wind was mostly coming from. In this way she made it to the path up to the fort much drier than she'd expected—

although she could tell she was soaked from the thighs down, so if the thief turned his torch on her he'd think he'd been caught by the Dip-Dye Denim Avenger, 2012's most fashionable hero. There was another light, she noticed, but it was at the end of the pier, presumably to stop any ships from crashing into it— although she couldn't imagine there were any out and about. Higher up were some flashing white lights in the sky, which threw her off until she realized they marked the top of the wind turbines on the mainland, and flashed as the blades passed in front of them.

She'd only just started up the hill when she heard an eerie, high-pitched whistle. The wind eased off because of the tree cover, but hit twice as hard once she got to the open grassy slopes around the fort itself. She powered up and heard the whistle again: shrill, unnatural. She'd reached the gates of the fort before she peeked out from under the umbrella again, and despite the cold and the weather and the everything, she found herself stopping dead, with her mouth hanging open and staring at the sight on the other side of the gates.

The two gangs of ghosts appeared to be having a prison yard rumble.

She'd never actually seen ghosts having a fight before, because they were all too apathetic to really give enough of a shit, but given that just about the only thing ghosts could touch was other ghosts, it made sense. She'd never seen it, but for all Claire knew, ghosts were at it like rabbits, which is why she was so suspicious of what Sophie was getting up to with Cole.

The noise that had attracted Claire turned out to be Finny, who was struggling manfully against the scrappy headlock that Captain Cole had him in; Finny was continuously elbowing Cole in the stomach and every so often he paused to stick the fingers of his other hand in his mouth to loose off another ear-splitting whistle. Mossie was wrestling on the ground with Spraggs, and Mossie would have had the better of him, Claire thought, except Bones was dancing around somewhat nervously, trying to grab hold of Mossie's legs, and having to kick Bones away was putting Mossie at a bit of a disadvantage.

Sophie was leaning against the gate, on the other side from Claire, which Claire found alarming because it meant she'd walked at least four hundred meters from the hotel room without Claire. That was much farther than she'd expected. She appeared to be quite disinterested, and eventually came through the bars of the gate to stand under the umbrella, the top of her ponytail clipping through it slightly like a glitching video game character. It was the peculiarity of ghosts being more visible at night that meant Claire could see the ridiculous theatrics playing out in front of her better than she could see anything surrounding it.

"Fuck's all this then?" she said evenly.

"Pirates decided to try to take the fort," Soph replied.

"Nice night for it."

Moments later Finny's whistling paid dividends, as a raggedy man-shaped bullet, which Claire was just about able to recognize as Conn, shot out from the gates, apparently having been patrolling some distant region of the fort, and tackled Bones around the waist. They went down together and rolled through the gate, just missing Claire's feet, and tumbled some way down the hill. Conn, who was obviously more practiced at this sort of thing, jumped up first, and waited for Bones to do the same, swinging his hurley to and fro, laughing.

"Took you long enough, boy!" yelled Finny.

As soon as Bones was on his feet, Conn took a huge swing at

his shoulders with his sports-equipment-cum-deadly-weapon and hit his target so hard that Bones's head actually flew off. Bones's body, suddenly stripped of one of its most critical assets, dropped to its (his? Was the skull the him bit and the body just the body?) knees and started feeling around for the skull, as Conn, having tipped the odds at least temporarily in his family's favor, ran back over to Mossie and set about battering Spraggs.

Claire had never seen a ghost's head come off before. She hadn't known they could do that, and it was sort of impressive. It looked like Bones's skull had rolled a bit down the hill, then come to rest on a leveled-out section a little farther down. The body was making its way over. It was like watching a very convincing local theater troupe perform an episode of *Scooby Doo*.

Something occurred to Claire. "Were you with them?" she asked.

"What?"

"Were you with the pirates when they attacked the fort?"

"I mean, like. No, in the sense that I was not with them when they *attacked* the fort," said Soph. "But sort of yes, in the sense that I was with them, and then they attacked the fort. And I was still with them."

Claire sighed. She and Sophie watched as Finny managed to get a foot behind one of Cole's legs and kick it out from under him so that they both went over backward. Mossie and Conn had subdued Spraggs, and Mossie was sitting on Spraggs's chest. But Bones had found his skull—although he was making a great show of dusting off his leather hat, and did not seem particularly disposed to returning to the fray. He struck Claire as an odd choice for a first mate. Needs must, she supposed. Cole's whole crew was a shit found family, and it didn't seem to function quite as well as Finny's actual family did.

"Is anything going to happen?" said Claire.

"I don't think so, really," said Sophie. "I think this is just what they do."

Claire opened her mouth to reply, and explain that she thought the thief and/or murderer was abroad—as in not on a two-week break in the Canary Islands but out and about in very much the local vicinity tonight—but a well-timed gust of wind dumped a sharp spray of rain right into her open mouth. She put her hands in her pocket to find the fort keys, and realized she'd left them in her room, so the entire project had been doomed from the start. She made an executive decision.

"Fuck this, then," she said, and walked back down the hill. She didn't wait to see if Sophie was following her. It was one in the fucking morning. That was a problem she could put a pin in until the morning. The real morning; this didn't count. Tomorrow happened at breakfast; everyone knew that.

Going back down the hill was much harder than going up, and she was trying to keep her head down and follow the snaky path without tripping on the decline when she was startled by another ghost poking their head under the umbrella. It was Mossie.

"How's the form?" he said, and smiled. He was holding one side of his hood, as if the wind could really blow his cloak away. "I've come to show you the shortcut, just here, see?"

He laid a hand on her arm unthinkingly, as if to guide her, and they both jerked away at the same moment.

"Oh! Sorry, girl. I . . . Hm. Well, it's this way, so," he said, and pointed straight down. "I s'pose you can't see, but there's a dirt road down here, that leads straight to the village. I'll walk ahead and you can follow me. No sense you getting even more wet."

Claire followed Mossie cautiously, and as they walked he

cheerfully explained that most of the structures now on the island were built with stone quarried from the island itself, and this path had led up from two of the quarries where they forced prisoners to work—but in his own day, you know, 'twas a rugged and beautiful little island, a grand place, not so tamed and flattened off as it was now.

"Its proper name is Inis Píc, and that's how I still think of it really," he said. "If ye gang were staying I could teach you to speak—ah, well, you're not, anyway. So here we are, and your rooms are there on the right, I believe."

They were. Mossie had deposited her just outside the entrance to the square. Claire was faintly surprised. "Thanks," she said.

"No bother," said Mossie. "I've not been down here for a while you know, because the pirates have it, but they're fairly distracted just now, anyway. Nice to see the place . . ." He looked around a little, then shrugged. Claire realized that Mossie had watched his home be colonized and decolonized over hundreds of years, and now she was here with a bunch of English people, staying in a hotel that another English person had built on the ruins of yet more local history. She could see why Eidy had been upset at the hotel's existence. Maybe that upset was still bubbling away.

"Oh wait," Claire said suddenly. She was shouting over the wind. "You didn't happen to see who murdered the guy here last night, did you?"

"Not me. I'd tell you, if I had," he said. Claire believed him, although if she'd been asked by a superintendent or a special agent, she wouldn't have a good reason why. "That's me away, so. Mind yourself!"

He took off at a jog, the tail of his cape whipping behind him in a way that made Claire think of Robin Hood. He was, she noticed, heading to the east, around the side of the island rather than back toward the fort entrance. She wondered whether he was doing something on his brother's orders, or if he was subtly rebelling, like Bones's deliberate delay to rejoin the fight.

Claire turtled down under her umbrella again and turned into the square. Despite scuffing her feet every few steps to make sure she was staying on the gravelly path round the outside she accidentally wandered a little way off it and onto the grass. This was slick in the rain—almost, she discovered when she next scuffed her feet, as slippery as ice. Thus, she promptly fell onto her arse, jarring her tailbone and dropping the umbrella. She had enough presence of mind to grab for it before it blew away.

"This is the worst fucking holiday ever," she groaned. Maybe she could get up early, make sure she had the keys, and go to the fort before anyone was awake, although this didn't seem like the sort of thing she'd do. When she got to her room and turned the light on, she found that she'd been in such a hurry to identify her suspect that she hadn't remembered to lock the door. And when she got in, she found that the TV shows were actually quite accurate.

"Someone's been in my room," she said out loud.

The piece of cup, the carabiner, and the metal owl ornament were where she'd left them. But the fort keys were gone.

15

Ominous Second Morning

Claire's instinct was to believe she'd made a mistake, because a lifetime of experience had taught her that was quite likely. But she could very clearly remember the four things lined up next to each other, all neatly—which was why she could remember it, because neatly lining things up wasn't something she did very often.

She then had a brief panic attack about the prospect of someone still being in her room—perhaps crouched next to the toilet holding a silenced pistol or something. Probably not a pistol, actually. Ireland was quite agrarian so it was more likely the imaginary assailant had sourced a shotgun. She jumped forward and slammed the bathroom door open, finding it empty. Then she worried that now she was in the bathroom whoever it was had come back through the front door, so she ran back and turned the latch. Then she double-checked that the window was definitely locked, and then closed the curtains to within an inch of their cloth lives.

After about a minute she remembered to check under the bed, but there wasn't even any dust under there.

Claire's normal impulse at this point would have been to find Alex and Basher, but she didn't want to leave the room while it was still dark. She was also very wet and cold, but did not want to lose sight of the door. She compromised by hanging the hellcoat—which now resembled an animal from an early noughties appeal for cormorants caught in oil spills—over the back of the desk chair and stripping off her resoaked jeans, and then forming a kind of nest in front of the door by cocooning herself in the duvet. She rubbed her cold legs, which were simultaneously numb and stinging, and were as pink as shelled prawns.

She sat that way until the storm lessened and a grimy light started to filter through the curtains and clash with the bedroom light like tea spilled into a washing-up bowl. Claire couldn't be sure that she hadn't fallen asleep at some point; she had itchy eyes and felt so tired it was verging on hallucinogenic, like her eyeballs were moving a few seconds after the rest of her head did. Every time she heard a tree creak in the wind she was wide-awake again. At one point she'd thought she heard a sudden thump, like someone had punched the wall, and she'd strained to hear, feeling her heart rate spike in sudden panic. But she'd heard nothing else apart from the rain and the wind.

She was also still totally alone. Sophie couldn't get any more murdered than she already was, but some habits are hard to kick, and she didn't like wandering around in the dark any more than Claire did. So Claire was worried about her.

Claire considered again how unrestful this holiday had turned out to be. Her usual habit was to wake up and eat a bowl of Aldi-brand Ricicles for brunch at around eleven thirty. Today, as yesterday, she was awake to see the dawn, and she couldn't see what the fuss was about. Dawn was fucking rubbish.

She tested the door and found it still locked and apparently unmolested, so she felt safe enough to army crawl over the floor in her duvet burrito, and thence into the shower. It did not help, despite everyone at various stages of her life claiming that having a shower always made you feel better.

What she really wanted to do was to text Basher and Alex to see if they were awake and alive, but she could not do this, and she did not feel safe enough to leave the room yet. She made a cup of tea with her hotel kettle, and worried about how she'd read once that people (sociopaths) cleaned their pants in hotels by boiling them in the kettles. But then she remembered that Minnie said they were the first people to use all this stuff, so she felt better about the tea.

Sophie walked through the wall at about eight o'clock. Claire was vibrating with so much anxiety at this point that she compared favorably to a washing machine mid spin cycle.

"Where the Sam fuck have you been? Did you spend the whole rest of the night with the pirates? What happened?"

"Nothing." Sophie looked at her with sulky defiance.

"Fine," said Claire, narrowing her eyes. "I'm too tired to argue right now. Someone was in my room last night. This would never have happened if you were with me."

"That's a stupid thing to say and you fucking know it. Me following you around wouldn't have stopped anyone getting in your boring empty stupid room, all right? How do you know, anyway?"

"The keys to the fort are gone. I put them on the table there, and they're gone."

"Are you sure you didn't lose them?"

"I didn't, all right? Christ. Don't be such a dickhead."

"You first. You probably just need to eat something, weirdo," said Sophie. She rolled her eyes.

Claire was actually quite hungry, although her hierarchy of needs had become less a pyramid and more of a kaleidoscope of shifting impulses.

". . . Can you at least check there's nobody, like, lying in wait out there?" she said.

"Ohmigod. Fine. You big baby."

Sophie stomped through the door in a huff. After repeated assurances that the coast was, in fact, clear, Claire scurried down the steps and tapped fervently at the door to Basher's room, and then Alex's. There was no answer from either of them.

"They're probably having breakfast, idiot," said Sophie. She sighed and rolled her eyes again when Claire did not move. "I promise I will tell you if someone is about to swing a pickaxe at the back of your head or whatever."

It had turned into a lovely day, which was a shock after yesterday's milk-white fog. The sky was a perfect watercolor blue, and the water was rippling in a light breeze so that it sparkled in the sun like a lake of sequins. Claire started sweating almost as soon as she began walking, but it would probably do the hellcoat some good to get aired out in the sunshine. She awkwardly run-walked 'round to the hotel, zigzagging slightly in case the murderer was actually in a sniper's nest somewhere. The building was, once again, as quiet as the grave. She stepped more confidently inside the main living area where she found George, slightly unexpectedly. He was getting up from behind one of the sofas, where he had apparently been lying on the floor. He quickly swooped on her and wrapped her into a big hug, picking her up as she was stood on the higher level and was, therefore, about the same height as him. (In the stair documentary, she thought, this would be the turning point at the end of the third episode where a billionaire who was also an expert in dangerous stair climbing would take a lofty interest in the project at random because he saw a Tweet about it on a day he was bored, so decided to come and save everyone on a whim.)

"Hello, you," he said. He was talking into her hair so it vibrated through her head. "Are you okay?" The hug felt unusually desperate, like a drowning person clinging to driftwood.

"Yes," she said, into his shoulder, after considering the wisdom of saying that she was not. He smelled of the outside, and she breathed in slowly. "Um. Why were you on the floor?"

"I decided to sleep in the hotel, like your friend Basher suggested, so we were all in here." He gestured vaguely behind him, where Claire could see some of the fluffy sofas were set up as makeshift beds with pillows and duvets. "I woke up very early and was going to go for a walk, but when I got out there, to the beachy bit, I had to come straight back. I don't know what it was, I went past it a bunch yesterday. I think it's only hitting me now, somehow. I came back in and had a lie down on the floor."

Claire nodded. This made perfect sense to her. Sometimes you really did just need to lie on the floor. But she was quite hurt at the same time. Nobody had bothered to check where she was, or ask her if she wanted to sleep in the big house with everyone else. It would serve them all right if she had been flayed and had all her organs removed or something.

George stroked the back of her head—or at least tried to, but then his fingers got stuck in a tangle. He laughed, and pulled back a bit to look at her.

"God, you're a mess," he said, but he was smiling very nicely, so Claire didn't feel bad about it. He gave her a kiss—which surprised Claire until she remembered he had form on wanting to kiss her—and swung her around and put her on the floor by the sofa. Sophie pretended to be sick.

"Maybe you should sit here by the fake fire, you're frozen. How do you not notice? Is it a ghost thing?" He was still smiling, Claire noted.

"Um. I mean a bit, maybe," she said. "Where's everyone else? Or anyone else?"

"I'm not sure. A few people are upstairs. Some others are in the kitchen. Do you want to sit down?"

Claire's tummy rumbled very loudly. She gave an apologetic smile and backed away. "I think I need something to eat, actually. Sorry."

"Yeah, men hate it when women have bodily functions," said Sophie.

The kitchen smelled strongly of bacon. Flick was scrambling eggs and Alex was sitting to the side.

"Good morning," said Flick.

"Jesus, C," Alex said with a frown. "What did I say about dry-clean only?"

"Oh," said Claire. She looked down at the hellcoat. It was now merely damp instead of rain-soaked, but it was still looking quite matted. "I'm sorry. I'll pay for . . . for whatever, I don't know."

"You look beat," they said. "Have some toast."

"Or crumpets," added Flick. "Nearly everyone else is still asleep, so you get first dibs on the bacon. Minnie should have got back from her run a while ago."

"Where's Basher?" Claire asked, with some urgency.

"Dunno. You all right?"

Claire still felt stung that nobody had actually come to check on her after dinner. "I'd quite like to talk to him, that's all."

"Wow, are we not telling Alex when you're having a nervy b now?"

"I think I saw him out of the window when I got up," said Flick. "Looked like he was going out to your rooms."

Claire nodded, and tore into a buttered crumpet like a hippo eating a whole pumpkin. She strode out of the kitchen, imagining herself in an Aaron Sorkin walk-and-talk scene. *The West Wing* would, she thought, only have been improved by Martin Sheen having his mouth constantly full of dough. It would've made the president more relatable.

"Whoa, slow down, for fuck's sake," said Sophie.

"We're no closer to figuring anything out and nobody is helping and I'm narked off."

"Alex loaned you their coat," Sophie pointed out.

"That's not the same," said Claire. "Nobody has a real alibi, and we know of at least three things that could have been the murder weapon, and someone is fucking about in the middle of the night still. I'm not fucking having it. It's not on. Basher needs to take some responsibility."

"'It's not on'? All right, someone's dad getting annoyed about an umpire call in the final of the county over-fifty cricket tournament."

"Talking to yourself again, I see," said Tiffany. Claire spun round. Tiffany, Ritchie, and Mac were coming down the stairs. Mac was holding Caity on her hip.

"Do they not have any other clothes for that child, or do they have multiples of the same bear onesie?" said Sophie.

Claire colored. "It. Um. Helps me think," she told Tiffany. "I need to talk to Basher."

"Is Minnie back yet?" said Mac. "She said last night she was going to leave at seven."

"Um, no, I don't think so."

George came down the hallway behind Claire. "We could go and look for her. She can't have actually gone anywhere, after all," he said.

Ritchie nodded. "Better safe than sorry," he said. "That's what my meemaw always used to say," he added, almost as an afterthought.

"Something's up," said Sophie. Claire chewed the inside of her cheek. She remembered George had told her that Minnie went for a run in the mornings and opened up the fort gates on her way around, but she couldn't have done that this morning because someone else had her keys. Unless it was Minnie who'd been in Claire's room the night before . . . It did not, however, seem like a good time to share this information, as it meant also confessing to having snatched Minnie's keys in the first place.

It was then that Basher and Eidy walked into the hotel. Basher had shed his poncho now that the weather had perked up, which was one positive development.

"Good morning," he said quite cheerfully. "We are not too sure the torch will work as a signal this morning, what with all the glare from the water, but Eidy thinks there may be some old signal flags in the museum."

"Proper old school. Spraggs will wet himself in naval excitement, I shouldn't wonder," said Sophie.

Claire met eyes with Mac, and she shook her head very slightly. Claire had forgotten to look for it, but it looked like Mac's spare phone hadn't turned up by itself.

"Up in the fort?" Claire asked.

"Yes," grunted Eidy. This appeared, once again, to be his limit.

Claire frowned. The pieces of the morning weren't fitting together quite right, but she couldn't tell how or why.

She pulled Basher aside, glancing at George. "Oh, okay. Can I . . . I need to talk to you," she said.

"Can it wait?"

"Not really." Claire shuffled her feet and felt awkward. She didn't really want everyone to know what happened, but it was important Basher knew. "I think someone was in my room last night," she said eventually.

"When you were sleeping?"

Ah. She glanced at Eidy. His face was unreadable. "No I . . . went out. In the storm. I saw lights again. Or at least I thought I did."

"What time?" Eidy asked.

"Um. After midnight?"

Eidy tucked his chin to his chest, which made it look like he was trying to swallow his own beard. "Near high tide again," he said, almost to himself.

"I don't think it was him, you know," said Sophie suddenly. "Definitely not the murder, anyway." Claire glanced at her quickly. Sophie liked to announce she'd had a revelation but not explain why, so she could lord it over Claire about being the smarter one of them.

"What's going on?" asked George.

"We'll come back to that soon," said Basher quietly. Claire sighed.

"What are you fine folks up to, then?" called Ritchie.

"God, him and his noughties nose job face are very off-putting," said Sophie with a wince.

"Museum," said Eidy. This was all the explanation he offered, and Ritchie blinked, his smile frozen for half a second too long at the prospect of a conversation with someone on the opposite end of the enthusiasm spectrum to himself.

"Something's wrong," Sophie said again. "You can tell, right?" It took about forty minutes to do a loop of the island, and if you were an absurdly fit person doing a run Claire suspected it would take you a lot less than that. So it *was* odd that Minnie wasn't back yet, unless she was doing multiple loops—but that would still take her past the hotel again at least once. Basher and Eidy decided to head up to the fort, and George, Tiffany, and Ritchie said they'd do a loop of the island and look for Minnie— just in case something had happened. Claire tried not to get too doomy about it, but she elected to return to the living room and eat another crumpet to settle her nerves.

"Do you reckon anyone has just . . . knocked on her door?" said Sophie, while Claire stared, unseeing, at the table in front of her. "Maybe the murder of her friend meant she took a day off running. I bloody would."

"Hm. Okay," said Claire out loud. "I'm going to see if Minnie is in her flat upstairs."

Flick, who was now both eating and trying to get her daughter to eat, looked up from her scrambled eggs on toast. "I think someone already tried knocking, but can't hurt."

"Mamamama," said Caity. "Eg!"

Claire summited the stairs again (*She's done it! She's beaten her own record!*) and paused to see if there was any movement on the floor above her.

"She lives in the attic," she explained to Sophie, whispering in case Ashley was awake.

"Duh, I saw it the first time I snooped around this place," Sophie replied.

Claire knocked on the door to Minnie's flat, and then tried it. It swung open, and she looked up the narrow stairs to the gloom beyond.

"Claire," said Sophie. There was a warning note in her voice. A drop of lead. The air felt very cold. Claire breathed out and saw it mist in front of her.

She took the stairs slowly, hearing each one creak as it took her weight. At the top she looked at the key rack and saw the fort keys hanging there. She reached out a finger and touched the metal, then snapped her hand back. The keys were rimy with a delicate layer of frost, and the dark spot left by the heat from Claire's finger was closing over even as she looked at it.

"Oh no," she said. The words crystallized in front of her.

It must be, Claire thought, upsetting for most people to only find out that ghosts are real when they become one. Claire had never asked Sophie about what it was like, and from the expression on Minnie's face as she looked down at her own body, she never would.

Minnie's corpse was lying in her kitchen area, in a shaft of bright sunlight from a skylight that illuminated the dust in the air and her mint green shorts. They were such a contrast to her normal black-on-black clothes that Claire felt a hot lump rise in her throat. Minnie's ghost was wearing them as well.

A few other ghosts from the island had congregated like before, which was why the small space was so cold. Claire took a tentative step into the room and they noticed her. She looked down at her feet quickly—but the ghosts didn't really seem interested in pestering her. It was as if they had been waiting for someone to find Minnie, and now they could go. They began to troop past Claire and leave, down the stairs.

A monk paused next to her. "She'll be gone soon," he said quietly, in a voice like dust and old cobwebs.

Sophie walked closer to Minnie's ghost, which made Minnie look up and catch sight of Claire.

"Help," she said. A tear rolled down her cheek.

"Oh. Um. I will. I'm sorry. It'll be okay," said Claire. She felt foolish because there wasn't much that she could do for Minnie now.

Minnie raised a hand and pointed at the fridge. "There." Staccato in life, in death she seemed even more abbreviated. It reminded Claire of Eidy.

"Okay. I'll look. I'll do . . . whatever. With the fridge," she said.

Sophie nodded. "We'll figure it out, Minnie, don't worry," she said, gentle as a cat with a kitten.

"Who was it, Minnie?" said Claire.

"He lied," said Minnie. She looked utterly betrayed. She began to disappear, dissolving into the dust in the sunbeam. "Don't trust him. He's not who he is."

16

Her Becomes Death

Claire breathed in slowly. She was trying not to look too closely, but the broad strokes definitely included Minnie's face—the physical one, that is—locked in a look of quite cod-like open-mouthed surprise, splayed limbs, and her hair having a matted, sticky quality. This latter point was why Claire was going for broad picture stuff rather than details.

Right. Don't panic, but panic a little bit because you don't have long to look around before you plausibly have to tell someone you've found her up here. She crossed quickly to the fridge and opened it. It was full of milk, carrot batons, hummus, and a block of cheddar wrapped in clingfilm. It was not full of murder weapons. She closed it again, and scanned a magnetized to-do list pad on the door. It was not an itemized list of how Minnie had been killed. There were several pictures stuck up as well—one of what was clearly Minnie as a child with her parents, another as a twentysomething in a cap and gown at university graduation, one of a dog. Normal life event photos. One in particular caught Claire's eye: it was the same one that Tiffany had showed Claire on her phone on the boat trip over, except this one didn't have the weirdo scribbled out. Claire studied him, and agreed with the group consensus from The Others that he looked largely passive and unremarkable. He had a thin, eggy face, both because it was a pale oval and because it was a bit flabby and boneless. The most remarkable thing about him was that he, at age eighteen or so, had been able to grow a pretty full beard. But more than that, Andy was one of those natural Etch A Sketch sort of people. If you weren't looking directly at him, you forgot what he looked like.

"Like Armie Hammer," she said out loud to herself.

"What are you on about now?" said Soph, behind her.

"Like, if I'd been poisoned and getting the antidote depended on picking either Armie Hammer or this guy Andy out of a lineup, I'd have to draft my will. He doesn't look like Armie Hammer, but if you had to describe Armie Hammer right now, you couldn't."

"Stop saying 'Armie Hammer' so much," Sophie replied. "I heard he ate three women and buried them in the desert."

"You can't eat three people *and* bury them," said Claire. "Don't believe everything Alex says to you." She turned back to Sophie, who was bent over Minnie's head, her face about an inch from the wound.

"Stop that," said Claire, who was still avoiding looking directly at it.

"What, I've never seen one before."

"You've seen loads of weird, fucked-up dead people, what are you talking about? You saw one like a day ago."

"Yeah, but not like this," Soph said. "Not like . . . gooey in the flesh. It's interesting. Do you reckon this happened to me?"

This was a morbid line of questioning that Claire hadn't expected, but that Sophie sometimes returned to as she got sort-of older.

"We don't know what happened to you," said Claire. "Anything could have, really."

"Yeah, s'pose." Sophie stood up, staring into the distance, her face alarmingly blank. Sometimes it was like she went somewhere else. "What d'you reckon did it? To Minnie, I mean."

"I haven't had time to do a fingertip search of the area or anything," said Claire. "She's definitely been walloped, though, right?"

"Mhmm." Sophie moved back and started to scan the floor farther out from the body, in a gradually widening circle. "There's not a lot of blood . . ."

Claire looked back at the fridge. Had Minnie been pointing at the photos? She stepped back and pursed her lips, then relaxed her eyes like she was doing a Magic Eye picture, trying to take in the whole fridge. There was a box file on top of it, she realized, and she stood on tiptoe to check the contents.

"She was doing research on everyone's families. Which is a bit invasive . . . Well, most people, I think there are some people missing . . ." Claire leafed through the files a bit, but was conscious she shouldn't spend much more time alone in the flat with Minnie's body. "Fucking hell! Eidy's name is *Poseidon!*" Sophie came and stood beside her.

"What, really?" She burst out laughing. "That's amazing. That's some Boy Named Sue shit from his parents, LOL."

"I assumed Eidy was, you know, an Irish name. Like Eoin or something. But I suppose it's better than going by Posey."

"Hmm. There's a bit of paper sticking out from under the fridge. Idiot. Get it out then? I can't do fuck all."

"Basher will—" Claire started to say, except Sophie immediately cut her off with: "*Ohmigod* so just don't tell Basher then?" and a roll of her eyes.

It looked like it had slipped in the little gap between the fridge and the kitchen counter, and then fallen half to the floor so a tiny corner was poking out from the bottom of the fridge. Claire carefully tugged it out, hoping it wouldn't tear—but actually it came free quite easily. It was a sheet of lined A4 notepaper, perforated along the side from where someone had pulled it out of a ring binder, and covered with a web of scribbly handwritten notes.

"This is great. It's, like, one step below Minnie having a torn note clutched in her fist," said Claire, scanning the writing. "It's a family tree. Oh, shit. It's part of Finny's family tree, look!"

Finny, Conn, and Mossie were all on there, near the top, where a link between their parents showed that Conn and Mossie were Finny's brothers by the same father, but they had a different mother. Other family members were marked, including a half sister and multiple other cousins. Toward the bottom of the page, the surname morphed into the more anglicized "Lehane." Sophie leaned over her shoulder to read it.

"She must have traced the family, like she said she would. I'm amazed she found the time," muttered Claire. She pulled at her lip.

Sophie pointed to the bottom of the page. "It says 'cont' in brackets in the corner there," she said. "There must have been other pages. I wonder where they are? Maybe when she figured out who those lads' descendants are, it led to someone here, and they wanted to shut her up about it."

"Oh shit, you could be right. She said 'he's not who he is,' so maybe someone is using a fake name. And it's not Eidy either, because we just saw his family tree and Finny wasn't on it."

"I mean, most of The Others have known each other since uni, though," said Sophie. "That's a pretty long con. Plus Eidy's family tree didn't go back that far, and he does have family ties to the island. Even if he isn't related to Finny, he could still have ancestral grievances, maybe?"

"Well, whatever. But it means whoever killed Dan really is the same person stealing the treasure, right?" said Claire. "That's a massive coincidence otherwise."

"I dunno," said Sophie. She sounded thoughtful. "I think Eidy figured out the same thing just now. It doesn't make sense if it's the same person because of the time."

"What? What do you mean the time?"

But Sophie was already thinking about something else. Claire exhaled sharply and swallowed her frustration; she could try to redirect Sophie later, but there wasn't time to get into a big argument with her now.

"Does this look off to you?" Sophie said. She waved her arm to encompass the whole scene of Minnie's sad string-cut-puppet body.

"I don't know," said Claire. "It looks like a scene from a TV show." Which, Claire realized, was the point. She looked again. The body was lying face down, but with the head tilted on one side. The right arm was crooked at the elbow and reaching slightly forward, and the left was lying straight down. The right leg was crooked as well. Claire stepped closer. Minnie's trainers were in the corner, but she had gym socks on and, in addition to her running shorts, was wearing a loose running vest over a regular black bra.

Claire scratched the back of her head. She listened for a moment, but couldn't hear anyone coming, so she went quickly into Minnie's bedroom which was, unhelpfully, as chaotic as the living area, with an overflowing laundry basket. She tried to lift the lid on it with a pen, like on TV, but that was very difficult, so she just opened it. There was nothing overtly suspicious. The window was open, letting a nice breeze in.

"Found anything?" Sophie called.

"No. I don't think so," said Claire. She stared at the window, and then shook herself. "Come on, let's get out of here."

Claire tried to estimate how long they'd been gone, as she walked slowly back down the stairs. It felt like about two hours, but really it must have been minutes.

"This isn't going to look good for you, you know," said Sophie quite conversationally.

"Fuck off, it looks fine," Claire replied, although she undercut her nonchalance by immediately following up with, "What do you mean?"

"A pattern has emerged, weirdo," said Sophie. "One of their friends dies, and you're the one to find the body. They're not going to like this."

"Nah, I only got to the hotel this morning, and I talked to like three people just before this," she said, trying to sound more confident than she felt. "Anyway, fuck off," she snapped, after a moment's thought, which was enough to make her feel aggrieved that everyone had been deserting her in her hour(s) of need. "It's not like you've been much help this entire time."

She started to run downstairs, as a normal person would if they had just found a dead body.

"Whoa! What are you talking about? What's with the sudden hostility, weirdo?" said Sophie, jogging alongside her.

"Because you keep going! You keep leaving, everyone keeps fucking leaving me and stuff like this keeps happening and I'm fucking freaking out!"

"Calm down, Jesus Christ, nothing has actually happened to you," said Sophie. She laughed at Claire, and it felt like being laughed at in school again.

"Shut up, that's not the point. You know that's not what I mean. And I've found two bodies in as many days! That counts as something happening to me."

She slammed open the door to the living area and was faintly shocked that people were in it still. She tried to arrange her features into an expression approximating urgency and horror (and sort of worried she looked like a toddler with a full nappy as a result). Eidy and Basher had come back from the fort and had apparently had a successful trip, because one table was covered in multicolored flags. Mac and Flick were taking it in turns to hold Caity while she got toast all over her face, and Alex was eating scrambled eggs with great enthusiasm. For narrative purposes Claire would have liked it most if she'd been alone with the body and everyone had come *to her* from different directions. Claire was left to once again consider how annoying real life was when compared to TV and movies.

"Um," she said.

"Are you all right?" said Basher.

"Er. Minnie's dead."

Flick nearly dropped her daughter. "What? Are you sure?"

"Um. Yeeeeeup. Pretty. Pretty sure. Sorry."

"You must have made a mistake." Flick stood up. Mac took Caity, but put a hand on her wife's shoulder. Alex's mouth dropped open in shock, and they looked automatically at their uncle, who had already moved toward the door.

"Show me," he said softly.

They all thundered back up to the landing, with Basher almost running to keep ahead of Flick. Claire stayed out of Minnie's flat, but Flick was fighting to get up there. Caity started crying, and Mac handed her off to Alex, then wrapped her arms around her wife.

"You mustn't go up there, love. Have to let her be. Just for now. I'm sorry," she said. She was gentle but unyielding, her long fingers wrapped around Flick's shoulders like the grasping toes of a lizard hanging on a branch, and the whole thing started to make Claire feel a bit queasy. She took a step away, and half turned her back in what she hoped was a respectful way.

Flick started making a choking noise, sort of like the last of the water going down the plughole after you've had a bath.

It wasn't that Claire minded people having strong emotions—she had them, after all—but why couldn't everyone just suppress everything and do it quietly? People had been emotioning everywhere recently, including herself, and she wasn't comfortable with it. Alex had given her several lectures about the need to allow oneself to experience all emotions honestly and openly, because suppressing everything eventually resulted in it squeezing out the sides in the form of, say, bad digestion and, most disastrously, bad skin. But although Alex had already had to deal with a lot in their comparatively short life, Claire still thought they weren't at the "seeing mangled dead people every day of existence" level. She felt like if she wanted to suppress things, she should be allowed to.

Eidy came down the stairs in front of Basher. His expression was as grim and unmoving as it normally was.

"I think Eidy would be acting exactly the same if a fucking sheep had dropped dead," remarked Sophie. "Or, actually, he'd probably see a sheep as having more measurable value, so he'd be like, tutting about the loss of a decent sheep, y'know?"

Basher hurried over to Claire. "Okay, can you tell me everything that happened, please? As many details as you can remember," he said. He was not literally flipping open an official police notebook, but spiritually that was the vibe.

"There isn't much to tell, really. Like, nothing you don't really already know . . ." She explained that she had come upstairs shortly after eating a second crumpet, because it had occurred to her that maybe someone should have just checked to see if Minnie was in her flat. "Sorry, but I don't know the timings better, because, like, obviously, I don't have a clock without my phone—" She paused for Basher to pinch the bridge of his nose, which he did, and then showed him the piece of paper. He clicked his tongue at her and told her she'd got too close to the body. Nevertheless, Basher looked at the paper carefully. "Hmm. It looks like she went for her run this morning as usual and was killed when she came back. But . . . Something is not quite adding up here," he said, almost to himself. He looked up at the ceiling.

"I'd say the woman with her head smashed in is a bit out of the ordinary," snorted Sophie.

Basher asked Mac if she'd be able to establish a time of death, and she looked at him as if he'd just asked her if she could pull an elephant out of her arse. "Not for nothing," she said, "but dammit, Bash, I'm a vet, not a doctor. We've been through this. We throwing her in the fridge? Sorry, hen," she added, when Flick looked alarmed at this dispassionate attitude, "but I'm being practical here."

Basher explained that, because Minnie's flat was much more of a preservable crime scene than the beach outside, his post-professional opinion was that they should leave Minnie where she was and make sure nothing near her was disturbed.

Flick nodded, coughed, and spat on the floor like a twenty-eight-year-old lad in skinny chinos leaving a Wetherspoons, without any apparent embarrassment. Then she looked up and narrowed her eyes at Claire.

"This is the second time you've found a friend of mine dead," she said.

"Oop, told ya," said Sophie.

"Whoa, hang on," said Claire. "We've been through this already with Dan."

Flick pushed herself upward with a kind of cold horror blooming on her face. "It could have been any of you." She shoved Mac away and took a couple of steps backward.

"Flicker, come on, I was with you!" said Mac.

"You've always hated them all, I know you have!" Flick cried. She backed into the door to Ashley's room just as Ashley opened it at the commotion, and jumped in surprise. Flick was, as Claire's mother would have said, going off on one. And in fairness Claire couldn't blame her. She felt close to it herself. Caity started wailing again, and Alex tried to bounce her into submission.

"Oh, okay," said Sophie. "This is actually an interesting twist I wasn't expecting. She doesn't suspect you, she suspects *everyone*. LOL. Good for her. Smart woman. Brains of the operation, her."

"Killer at small," murmured Claire without thinking. It wasn't really a big enough island, she thought, for it to be a killer at large.

"And you! We've all seen you, you know!" Claire jumped because Flick had turned to point at her again. "Walking around talking to yourself all the time! Freaking out! What the hell is wrong with you?"

"We suspect unresolved and unacknowledged trauma," said Basher, who was still looking up at the ceiling.

"Oooh, they've been talking about you, weirdo," said Sophie. Claire frowned. Sophie was inarguably correct.

Flick tried to snatch Caity from Alex, but Mac got between

them. "Flick, you need to calm down. I know it's fucked up, but we've got a baby to think about. You know it wasn't me."

Flick started to breathe with deliberation, and paced across a small patch of floor. "Okay, okay. I just need . . . I don't know. I don't know, nothing makes sense!"

"Blimey," said Ashley, who seemed to still be aloft on lovely chemical clouds. This gave Claire an idea, and she dashed next door into Tiffany and Ritchie's room, which they had mercifully left open again, and swept up the entire contents of the medicine cabinet, returning to dump it on the floor.

"Erm, something in here might calm her down. If she'll take it," she said. Ashley nodded in agreement.

Mac bent over and sorted through them. "I didn't know Tiffany had epilepsy," she said, briefly considering the blister pack of pills with the name Claire hadn't recognized before.

Claire realized at this point that sharing Tiffany and Ritchie's medicine with everyone was probably some sort of breach of privacy, but it was an emergency, and she was pretty sure that, as a civilian, she wasn't subject to the Hippocratic oath.

Mac and Flick started talking quietly, and Claire moved away, slightly embarrassed.

"What happened?" said Ashley.

Claire paused. "She looks the most equipped to deal with the news, honestly," said Sophie. But that was not what was making Claire pause. Ashley had been alone in her room, basically unwatched, for hours, mere feet from where Minnie had been killed.

"Minnie's dead," she said eventually.

"Oh," said Ashley. She shrugged. "I suppose I own this place now, then, do I? As the beneficiary of the principal investor."

Bash was conferring quietly with Eidy, which concerned

Claire, because he still seemed like quite a good suspect, no matter what Sophie said. Minnie had said "*he* lied," and if Minnie had been researching Finny's family tree then Eidy could be a candidate for whoever appeared on the missing pages—or at least, it seemed more likely he would than, for example, a big Texan, given his family was a local one that had lived on the island for generations.

Basher locked the door to Minnie's flat, and requested everyone go downstairs, where they would wait for the group walking around the island to return—at which point Basher and Eidy could resume signaling for help with the naval flags. Everyone but Flick complied with this request, asking instead that she be allowed to lie down in bed with the door locked—which, given the strength of the sleeping pills Mac had just administered, was probably a good idea.

Downstairs, Mac paced fretfully, jiggling Caity on her hip and placating her with biscuits from the kitchen. Eidy and Basher were at the other side of the room, entirely absorbed in sorting through what were, to Claire, functionally indistinguishable flags.

"Fucking hell," said Mac. She was so worried she didn't even guiltily look at Caity when she swore. "God, if only we had that fucking phone."

"What phone?" asked Ashley.

"Mac, a genius, managed to hold onto her phone, but someone took it the morning Claire found Da—the morning Mac got us to turn our pockets out," explained Alex.

Ashley actually rolled her eyes at the mangled near-mention of her husband. "So do they still have it?"

"Well . . . I mean, no, probably not. It wasn't found on anyone, but they probably smuggled it out of here and threw it in the sea or something," said Claire.

"Well, you know what they say about assumptions," Ashley chirruped.

"I hadn't actually used the word," said Claire, faintly disgruntled.

"Occam's razor and so on," said Ashley. She was still a touch floaty, but was growing less so every minute as her pharmaceutical helpers wore off.

"I suppose . . ." said Sophie slowly, ". . . if you were about to be searched in this room, you'd hide whatever it was you weren't supposed to have in this room."

"Like how drug dealers always throw their bags of cocaine under the nearest bin if they're being chased by the cops," said Claire, thinking about *Murder Profile*, as she so often did.

"What?" said Alex.

Claire closed her eyes. You'd hide it as soon as you knew you were going to be searched, but since then nobody has really been by themselves, so you wouldn't be able to come back to get it. Was it really that stupid? Had it been here the whole time?

She tried to picture the room as it had been that morning. A pressure cooker of sadness and fear. Mac's bag had been on *that* chair. The table where they'd turned out their pockets and bags was *there*. If you needed to hide something quickly, where would you put it? They'd all been looking at the table . . .

She opened her eyes and walked over to the sideboard and opened the drawers. But that was too obvious because somebody might open a drawer at any time—plus opening them made a noise. She felt around the back, and peered into a vase and then, with growing resignation and annoyance, got onto her knees and looked underneath the sideboard. And yes, just visible in the shadow was a slim black smartphone. Claire lay down and spider-walked her hand up to it—it was almost out of reach—

and pulled it out by her fingertips. The group gathered around in excited awe. Mac snatched her phone and squealed.

"Eight percent battery left. Right," she said, face set. She handed Caity to Alex.

"This bitch is going rogue," said Sophie.

"I really hope I'm not going to regret this but . . . Alex, I trust you. Look after Caity for half an hour, because I'm going up to the fort, to get signal and call the police. Alex, give Caity to Flick as soon as she wakes up. Caity-Bear, you stay here with Alex, okay? Mum's going for a wee walk."

"That's a terrible play," said Sophie, as Mac left.

"I mean, logically what she is doing is very silly. *I* know I'm trustworthy, but in her situation I wouldn't have given me her entire child," said Alex. "Anyway— Wait, where are you going?"

Claire had her hand on the door, too. "I want to check something," said Claire. "I won't be long."

She went outside, not bothering to shut the door because, if all went to plan, she would be back in a couple of minutes. Mac was already quite far down the path from the hotel, moving at a decent clip.

"Where are we going?" said Sophie. "Also, shouldn't we have mentioned the surprise phone to Basher?"

"Probably, actually," Claire said. "Don't worry. I bet Alex is telling him right now. He'll go spare."

"You're a terrible lead detective," said Sophie. Claire ignored her and walked around to the side of the building, alternating looking upward to find her place with swearing as she tried not to get caught on brambles.

"That's the window from Minnie's bedroom, right?" she said, pointing. "I just have a feeling . . ."

She poked around in the dense undergrowth until she found

a Tesco shopping bag. It was farther from the house than she expected, so it took her quite a long time to find it. The bag was very heavy. This turned out to be because it contained an old brick from one of the still-ruined buildings on the town square. It also contained what appeared to be women's clothes covered in blood. Sophie tried not to look impressed. "How did you—" she started to say.

"I can figure things out myself, you know," said Claire. She chewed her lip reflectively. She found a stick to slip through the handles of the bag, so she could take it inside without touching it.

Inside, Basher and Alex were having a flaming row. "—a phone this *entire time*," Claire heard Basher say, as she walked back in. "Unbelievable! You should have told me. And now Mac could be in danger."

"It's not like I'm in control of what all these other people do, for Christ's sake!" replied Alex.

"Er," said Claire. She said this a lot around Alex and Bash, so it didn't make a dent in their shouting.

"You put all of us in danger as well, not to mention yourself!"

Eidy backed out of the kitchen holding a tray with a steaming teapot. He had, Claire noticed, arranged some biscuits on a plate.

"I think someone is missing from this scene, you know . . ." said Sophie. Claire dropped the bag she was holding.

"Oh fuck. Um. I left the front door open. Has anyone seen Caity?"

17

Curse Your Sudden but Inevitable Betrayal

Suddenly everyone was yelling, but about a new thing, forming a chorus in the key of "She was just here a second ago" and "Seriously, just wide open," harmonizing with "You were supposed to be looking after her."

"Are you three," interrupted Eidy, his voice starting off loud to get their attention but swiftly dropping back to his normal, almost lazy monotone, "going to stand around shouting, or are we going to look for her?"

They stared at him. He put down the tea tray.

"That's what I thought. We can work quickly. There's no traffic, and no strangers who'll run off with her, like."

"I mean, um. Not to be that guy," said Claire, "but there's a double murderer also."

"Grand so, we won't bother trying then," said Eidy tartly. Claire flushed, despite herself. "Whoever it was killed the other two has no business with a kid. The fort has the most dangerous parts, but she won't have been able to get that far. Alex, double-check that Caity isn't here at the hotel still, and see if the other two upstairs are in a state to help. The rest of us should stay within earshot of each other and search the village buildings as quick as we can just to rule them out, and then start moving along the path. She'll be looking for her mum, and the rest of the group will be coming back around the island soon anyway, so she'll run into someone sooner or later. The thing to worry about is the water, so make that a priority as we move."

Basher was staring at Eidy with a weird light in his eyes; he must be jealous, Claire thought, that someone else was taking charge and being all practical, when that was usually his job.

Being so clearly directed, they got going quickly. Flick was asleep still, but Ashley was awake enough to help, or at least to insist she wanted to help and, no tiny bear-toddler being evident in the hotel, they began to go through the village buildings around the square. The restored buildings, where Claire and the others had been sleeping, were mostly locked, but Claire rattled the doors and sent Sophie in to check them anyway.

"Empty as well," she said, coming back out of the room underneath George's. "Looks like a storage room. There are boxes under a tarp, but no rogue child."

Claire cupped her hands to the window and tried to peer through a crack in the closed curtains, but the light in the room was very dim, and she could barely make anything out. She sighed.

"Well, that's not good," she said.

She could hear the others occasionally shouting out Caity's name; they sounded like strange echoing birdsong. She crossed the courtyard to the corner opposite Eidy's flat, where Basher was checking one of the still-derelict, undeveloped buildings.

She was trying to keep a lid on her panic but it was getting difficult.

"That side is clear," she said.

"How are you feeling?" said Basher. He was talking calmly but his movements were frantic as he pulled foliage aside to check corners.

"I could be worse. Of course, there's my unresolved trauma," said Claire, putting some heavy sauce on the final two words.

They ran to the next building, still talking absurdly normally despite how they were stumbling over their own feet to move as quickly as they could. It helped. If they didn't find Caity safe then it would be awful, so Claire's brain was treating finding Caity safe as the only viable possibility.

They'd cleared all the buildings in the village in a few minutes and began striding along the path, which Claire had now traipsed down so many times that the whole thing felt like a very wet and upsetting Groundhog Day. When you're looking for a missing toddler minutes slow down until they can be measured in the longest unit Claire could imagine, which, after an ill-advised attempt at a Tinder date two months previously, was "tabletop role-playing fan explaining a really funny anecdote that happened in their last Dungeons & Dragons session, insisting on describing all the characters and their dynamic in the game thus far, even though you yourself have never met any of the people involved."

Eidy pointed to the rain-soft mud beside the path. There was a trail of determined little footprints visible. "That looks like a child-size seven to me," he said. "The tide's out, and she's keeping away from the water side of the path. Let's go."

They sped up, although there was a sense of a shared exhalation of some relief.

"It would, of course, be normal for you to not be fine because you have just found two bodies in as many days," said Basher, who was at least relieved enough to resume his gentle interrogation.

"See dead people all the time, don't I?" mumbled Claire.

"Ah yes. Is she gracing us with her presence?"

"Who's 'she,' the cat's mother?" said Sophie.

"Yeah, she is," said Claire. Soph tutted.

"I suppose she would hardly be anywhere else," said Basher.

"You say that, but she's becoming more independent lately," said Claire.

"They grow up so fast," said Bash.

"Yes, and I disapprove of her boyfriends," muttered Claire.

"Oh, fuck off," said Sophie automatically.

"I hope you do not fall out over boys. Always very tedious when that happens," said Bash. "Anyway, is the cold one willing to help at all?"

"I'm helping," said Sophie. "You should ask him." She pointed to the trees alongside the path and Claire saw, in the under-growth, the cloaked figure of Mossie, watching them and looking very grave. No pun intended. As Claire looked he turned away and disappeared literally through the bushes, stepping backward so that he looked almost exactly like that clip of Homer Simpson melting into a hedge. Claire involuntarily barked a laugh— and then hoped nobody had noticed, because it wasn't the time or place.

"What did you see?" said Basher.

"It's too late, he's gone. Was one of the Opportunists."

"The what?"

Claire sighed very heavily. "It's what I call the Irish gang of ghosts who've gone fully Jets and Sharks at each other over this stupid fucking island."

"Oh yes, I remember. And one of them is a skeleton, I think Alex said?"

"That's one of the pirates."

"Goodness me. You've been busy. Getting on all right, aren't you?"

"I fucking wish," said Claire bitterly. She kicked a pebble.

"You've figured something out, haven't you? What are you thinking?" Soph asked. "Independent thought isn't like you. I'm gravely concerned."

"Where the fuck is everyone else, that's what I want to know," said Claire. "The island isn't that big. If they were doing a loop and going up to the fort they should have been back ages ago."

"I have started to wonder that myself," said Basher. "Most people are unaccounted for during the time that Dan was killed— the time we believe he was killed, anyway. But basically everyone *is* accounted for this morning, when Minnie was killed."

"Ashley told me she thinks it was"—Claire glanced behind them to where Ashley trailed them, occasionally peering over the wall into the trees, mouthed the name—"*Minnie* who killed Dan. But recent events suggest . . . probably not, right? I think Ashley herself might have killed him, honestly. She was acting weird. But also was on drugs."

"LOL. You did that the wrong way 'round," said Sophie. "You should have said 'Minnie' out loud and 'Ashley' quietly."

"But anyway," said Claire, ignoring her. "I spoke to Minnie's ghost and she said 'he lied,' not 'she lied,' so it must have been a man who killed her, right?"

"As I'm sure you considered, a man could have lied to her and a woman could have killed her for reasons separate or related to said liar," said Basher. "And either way, 'a ghost told me' would be circumstantial evidence at best, I'm afraid. But we will put a pin in all that for now. Missing toddler takes priority for the time being."

"She can't actually have gone far, though, really," said Sophie. "Literally, because it is an island, and also because she has tiny idiot legs."

"You would be surprised," said Basher. "When Alex was a toddler they could work up a fair turn of speed. I was babysitting one afternoon and the little rat-bastard had run into the kitchen, pulled a chair to the counter, and climbed up to get the chocolate chip cookies out of the top cabinet in the time it took me to turn around and notice they had gone."

The teenager in question now came up behind them.

"Don't worry, C, we'll find Caity. Small C, I suppose."

"I wasn't worried," said Claire. "Why would I be worried?"

"Well, you know. You left the door open."

Claire balked at this. "Yeah, and you just put down a child and looked away. I left the door open because I was trying to figure out who's been killing people, and you two haven't helped at all. Maybe if I wasn't alone the whole time none of this would be happening. You're just going off with your new friends and showing off about Sophie, but you don't have to deal with her the whole time. Beats me why she likes you."

"That's quite a reaction," said Basher.

"Don't you start," Claire snapped, surprised at her own sudden frustration. Sophie was staying quiet, watching her with unreadable dark eyes. "You've been AWOL this entire time, and you're supposed to be, like, in charge."

"Uncle Bash isn't supposed to be in charge of anything. You're a grown-up. Don't be mean, C. And Soph likes me because I like her," said Alex. They sped up. "Because I'm not embarrassed of her like you are," they muttered, almost but not quite under their breath.

Claire was hurt and angry and wasn't sure how the conversation had suddenly escalated to the point that Alex was cross with her, because she'd been doing her best this week. And when Alex was angry they were usually angry, very loudly so, so it was particularly galling that they'd resorted to mutinous teenagery passive-aggression.

Rather than heading up to the fort, Alex stormed along the path around the island that Claire had taken the day before. They were soon out of sight around the corner.

"Oh, for goodness' sake! What on earth is the matter?" said Basher eventually. "Are you really going to throw a tantrum and pick fights now? When we're looking for a missing child?"

"I've just been alone most of the last few days, that's all."

"Why do I always have to be on call for everyone? Did it not occur to you that I had other things to do, which were important for your well-being in the long term? As Alex said, you are, notionally, an adult."

This struck Claire as monstrously unfair. "Literally the only reason I'm here is because you didn't think Alex is adult enough to go on holiday by themself!" she shot back. "And a fat lot of fucking guardianing you've been doing so far."

"Being concerned for someone I care about is not the same as thinking I shouldn't be able to leave you alone for twelve hours without you imagining some slight against you because of my very absence," he said, in his most infuriatingly reasonable voice. "Can't you find other things to do?"

"No! I mean, yes, maybe, but that's not the point."

"And what is?" said Basher, still wearing a faint half-smile like a very smug sort of therapist asking you leading questions that they already know the answer to. Because surely it was obvious that Claire had assumed that being invited on holiday would mean her friends would want to spend time with her, when, now that they were all literally trapped on an island together, they seemed to be avoiding her.

"It is not a trick question, Strange, believe it or not," said Basher. "We see each other all the time at home. Just because you and I have not seen each other for a little bit, that does not mean we've stopped being friends."

Claire didn't know what to say about that, because her suspicion was that it did. At least, in her experience, that was always how it started. They stop hanging out with you, then they stop responding to your texts, and then you're back to watching a repeat of the fifteenth season of *Murder Profile* (the worst season) with a dead teenager.

Claire was now extremely hot in the black hellcoat, which was greedily absorbing the sun's rays, and she also kept catching a scent like a wet dog in a microwave that she suspected was coming from the coat itself. But taking the coat off would mean she was carrying the coat, and she was lazy enough to just continue to sweat until such time as she passed out from heat stroke.

They came around the bend, past the falling-down old schoolhouse covered in ivy and bushes, and then toward the gray pillbox that overlooked the beach covered in seaweed, and Sophie grabbed Claire's arm without thinking. Claire shook her off before the energy drain properly caught her.

"Did you hear that?" said Sophie.

"No?"

"Stop. Someone's crying."

Claire stood still, and put a hand out to stop Basher as well, so she couldn't hear the crunch of his feet on the gravelly path. A thin, high-pitched sob was coming from somewhere, but it was echoing off something, and it took Claire a moment to discover the origin was inside the pillbox. There was a small bear facing into one gray, dank corner, covering its eyes.

"Oh," she said. "Hello."

There followed a short period of excitement, wherein everyone was pleased, and Caity was persuaded to allow Ashley to pick her up, because she knew Ashley.

"Well done," said Ashley. "Did your ghost help? Alex said you had one."

"Er." Claire was thrown by this. She didn't know how to respond.

"I thought she might have been using her sixth sense or something?" said Ashley, still quite relaxed over what was now a siren wail emanating from Caity, who was going so red in the face Claire feared she might actually pass out.

"I used my fucking earholes like a normal person," said Soph. "Tell her that."

Claire was paralyzed by embarrassment.

"Fucking hell, weirdo! Even now, you won't acknowledge me? Cole was right."

Something strange broke in Sophie's face, and Claire looked at her feet and felt tears threatening to gather in her eyes, so she swallowed it all down.

"Well, anyway, no harm done," said Ashley. "I just wondered because Alex mentioned to me yesterday that—"

"Where *is* Alex?" said Eidy quietly. "They surely didn't go past without hearing Caity."

Caity's wailing took on form. "Ah! Ah! Ah-leeeeeeeeek!" she said, and then hurled her face back into Ashley's neck.

For the second time that morning Claire got a horrible cold feeling in the pit of her stomach. She ran round to the other side of the pillbox.

Alex was lying there, crumpled up like a crushed paper doll.

Claire felt dizzy and half collapsed on the wall, tried to breathe in the way Alex had taught her to calm down, and then immediately freaked out again. Basher ran past her, fell onto his knees, and started to shake Alex, all calm self-control evaporated. Eidy pried him away and checked for a pulse, before gently moving Alex into the recovery position.

"They're alive then," said Sophie with a quiet sigh of relief. Claire slid down the rough concrete of the pillbox, feeling it scrape her palm.

"Goose egg on the back of their head," grunted Eidy. "Can't have happened long ago." He pinched Alex's earlobe using his nails and their eyes fluttered open.

"Fkoff," they said. And then: "Ow."

"Oh, thank God," said Basher. He turned his face away and put a hand to his eyes briefly.

Eidy moved Basher around, still directing everyone with firm, gentle touches, and sat Basher down so he was kneeling by Alex's head. He grasped Claire's shoulders and helped her upright, and then started to pull off the hellcoat.

"Oh, right," said Claire. She began to fold it up, and all her clues fell out of one of the pockets. Eventually, Alex was lying on their back with their head on their uncle's knees, pillowed by their own coat and wincing at the sunlight. "Ow," they said again.

Claire began to stuff her clues into the pockets of her jeans, where there was scarcely any room, and went to pick up the owl maybe-a-belt-buckle from where it lay on the grass near Alex's head. Alex's hand shot out and they grabbed Claire by the wrist.

Alex frowned. They said something that Claire couldn't hear properly.

"Shirt? Did you say shirt, Alex?" she asked. They were probably swearing, she thought.

"That is not a priority right now," said Basher. People started talking at once, each putting forward a different priority:

"But whoever did it is—"

"Caity needs something to drink, she's dehydrated."

"We need to make contact with—"

"Weirdo. Hey. Fucking concentrate. You won't help Alex by having a panic attack," said Sophie. Claire blinked. Sophie was and had been the lodestar of her existence since she was seventeen. She felt her brain snapping to attention without any conscious input from her.

"Okay. Erm. What should I do?"

Sophie snorted. "You shouldn't try to think without me, you know. You'll hurt yourself. It's a fucking liability. Come on, follow me. The murderer must have gone this way."

"Okay. Um. Sure."

"Hey. Where are you going?" said Basher. He looked astonished. "Alex is hurt. I need your help."

"Hey! We don't have loads of time! Come on!" shouted Sophie—actually shouted, with an emphasis that had a physical chill behind it. Even in the bright sunshine Claire saw Ashley shiver and hold Caity closer.

"I . . . I have to go . . . I'm sorry . . ." She trailed off in pure shame and turned away, began walking forward toward Sophie. So she didn't see Basher's face when he shouted after her:

"*You're* leaving *us!*"

Claire wrapped her arms around herself and did not look back. It was easier going now she didn't have the coat on, and

Sophie chivvied her along, toward the other side of the island, at a brisk pace. In the bright light of day Claire could see the strange, ragged beauty of the place—the gorse bushes and the waving grasses. Somewhere she heard a crow calling again. Sophie looked fixedly ahead.

"Come on, keep moving up the hill," she said as they passed the playing field and the graveyard. "You'll warm up. It'll be better if you're warmer when we get up there," said Sophie.

"Where are we going?" Claire asked. "Are we going to catch up with the killer? Because if that's the plan, honestly, I don't think coming alone was a good idea."

Sophie looked over at Claire. "You're not alone," she said, and smiled quickly, before returning to look ahead again. She seemed certain of what they should do, and that made Claire feel better. Sophie had always been certain of most things, and it was one of the things Claire relied on her for. She'd been too mean these past few days. She should tell Soph that. After they were out of immediate danger. She did quite want to find whoever had hurt Alex and poke them in the eye, at a minimum.

"Imagine if Alex were a ghost," said Claire. "They'd be more annoying than you."

"If Alex were a ghost I'd have literally zero fucking reason to talk to you ever again, you giant loser," said Sophie. "Come on, don't slow down."

After ten minutes of industrious striding and wheezing, they'd made it to the back of the fort, where the gun placements were looking out. There wasn't an Opportunist on watch, which made Claire feel a bit sad.

"They look like . . . You know. The toasters. Robot toasters," she said to Sophie, pointing at the dark slit in the gray wall of the fort bastion.

"What? Oh! You mean *Battlestar Galactica*? They're called Cylons." She seemed distracted.

"Yeah, but they call them toasters, right?"

Sophie ignored her, and pointed down toward the tree where Bones had been on guard. "There," she said. "Let's go."

Claire clambered obediently onto the rough slope and made her way through the dense grass. Sophie gave Claire a little dig in the small of her back, like pressing an ice cube into her spine, and it made her stumble.

"Don't do that," she whined. "It's steep."

"We don't have loads of time, though. I told you already. Keep going. Bit farther down here."

After the tree, the undergrowth became thicker and even less welcoming. Claire forced her way through the gnarled fingers of brambles that tugged at her ankles, and then down onto the rocks that ringed the island—it was steeper here, too, and she nearly fell. The tide was out, and the seaweed in the hot sun smelled of rot.

"Here, see?" said Sophie. She was pointing to a hole in the side of the island.

Or, Claire realized, as she looked at it properly, the entrance to a tunnel.

"The murderer came in here?" she asked. "It's really dark."

"Come on, there's a torch just inside the entrance for staff," said Sophie. She walked into the darkness, and only seemed more solid, more real, the further she went.

Wearily, and with a great sense of impending doom, Claire complied. She felt around by the floor and found a storage box containing not just some torches, but hard hats and high-vis vests, too. "Oh," she said to herself, remembering something George had told her. "VIP tunnel tours . . ."

The torch didn't really make her feel better. It illuminated a short, squat tunnel with a dirt floor and an arched brick roof, which was dotted with tiny icicles of sediment that didn't deserve the name stalactite. Sophie had been waiting for the light, and began walking down the tunnel, which seemed to go on for miles. Claire felt wrong and on edge again. It was dark and damp, and she was still only in a T-shirt. She started shivering, but whether out of fear or cold she wasn't sure.

"Basher's going to be livid," she mumbled, mostly to make herself feel better.

"Hurry up, fucking idiot," said Soph. She was glancing nervously around. Claire frowned.

"Are you okay?"

"Ohmigod, obviously not."

Eventually, Claire nearly walked into a stone spiral staircase, which was even more narrow and claustrophobic than the tunnel, and crept up it, trying not to touch anything. Her whole mouth and throat were full of the taste of mold and damp. There was another tunnel at the top, and she found herself dropping to a squat to crawl out into a much larger tunnel. This was painted, although the paint was peeling away, hanging down in long curling strips like rolls of parchment.

"Soph, where the fuck are we? I thought we were tracking down the murderer or whatever," she said. She turned. Sophie wasn't in front of her. She wasn't behind her, either. "Soph?"

Claire felt panic rising, not slow like the tide but fast, like a flood. She picked a direction at random and started walking. These tunnels were deathly cold, and she regretted leaving the coat.

Something flew in front of the beam of the torch and Claire nearly dropped it in panic. There was a small bird trapped there with her, hopping around on stick-thin legs that didn't look strong enough to hold its body up, and flying at the walls and floor and light. *If the bird got in,* Claire thought, *then I can get out . . .*

She kept walking, listening to the sound of her own heartbeat as it increased. She heard a whisper, she was certain, and spun around suddenly. She felt a breath on her neck.

Claire didn't know how long she'd been down there in the dark when she heard the footsteps again. The ones that had chased her at the fort before. She tried to breathe but it wouldn't come. Her legs tingled pins and needles as she sped up, turning to look over her shoulder as she went. The torch picked out a wobbling circle of plaster as she ran. Empty. Empty. But still the footsteps echoed in the silence.

Suddenly she came upon a wide alcove in the tunnel—a room without a fourth wall, really. Sophie was sitting against the back wall.

"Soph," she whispered. "Can you hear it?"

"Yeah," said Sophie. "Sorry."

"What's happening? I don't know what's going on." Claire turned and trained the torchlight back at the tunnel. Still empty.

"Look again, madam," said Cole. Claire spun around in shock. The pirate captain was there next to Sophie, grinning nastily with all of his shiny gold teeth. Claire frowned. She took a couple of steps back to look down the tunnel again, and now it wasn't empty. Spraggs, his uniform forever perfect, crisp, with polished buttons and nothing out of place, was walking toward her at his leisure. The light from the torch washed him out, but even so Claire could see that as he walked the sound of footsteps rang in time with his very shiny black shoes.

She turned back, with a sudden lump in her throat. She'd run from murderers before, and been cold and afraid and hidden thinking that if she got caught she might die. But now what she'd thought was a fundamental truth in her life had been obliterated.

"You tricked me," she whispered.

"Yes," said Cole. "She did."

And then Cole grabbed Claire by the throat.

18

The Ladykillers

Claire sank to her knees, and then fell backward against the floor. The torch skittered away, only half-lighting the room—which at least made the ghosts easier to see. Claire's shadow stretched into a grotesque, long-limbed spider of a thing. If she'd been able to pull Cole's hand away as soon as he'd grabbed her, she might have been able to make a break for it. But she was already so cold and tired and scared, and her fingers so numb, that she'd only been able to grab hold of his wrist—which had been a stupid idea anyway, because touching him with her skin only strengthened the connection he'd made, and she felt more of her energy pouring into him like light dissolving into a black hole. The pirates' secret hideout had been inside the fort the whole time. Right under Finny's nose.

Cole clamped his other hand to the side of her head, and it burned cold. She felt the *zip* double up again, the little almost-electric feeling that she got whenever Sophie touched her during a séance. Sophie borrowed Claire's energy to move small objects. She must have told Cole how it worked.

"What are you going to do?" she asked, her voice weak like a sick child. "You won't be able to lift the treasure."

"Ah, but I shan't know unless I try, shall I?" said Cole. His voice was as light and airy as ever—friendly, even—but his grip didn't lessen at all. The side of Claire's face was going numb. She wondered if ghosts could give you ice burn like when you left chicken in the freezer too long. But the discomfort was becoming more and more remote, and the numbness was spreading to her whole body, and she could feel herself disappearing into it. The hollow feeling of not sleeping, the stress that had been a knot in her stomach for hours, was just a buzzing now. Such a little thing. She wasn't even cold, really. This was what Sophie used to do when she couldn't sleep. They'd hold hands for a while until Claire drifted off—passed out, really.

Sophie always let go. She didn't think Cole was going to.

"Let go," she said weakly. "Let go. I'll die." And she heard someone else echoing her. It was Sophie. Her voice sounded very far away, like through a pocket call.

"You can't take it all. You said you wouldn't. I don't want her to die."

"That's what people do, my sweetheart," said Cole. "That's what happened to us—and why should it have? She'll die anyway one day," said Cole. "Why shouldn't I live again?"

He kept one hand on the side of Claire's face and reached up to the damp, peeling wall. Claire tried to see but she couldn't turn her head. Cole laughed like a child and brought his hand back, and in it he was holding a little strip of peeling paint that coiled in his fingers like a girl's ringlet. He held it out to Sophie and she opened her hand automatically, and watched as the coil fell through it and onto the dirty floor.

"It doesn't work like that. You'll have lost it all again before you can walk out of the fort," whispered Claire. "You'll always be dead, you stupid self-aggrandizing cunt."

Cole slipped his hand from her face to her neck, and used the other to slap her sharply across the cheek. It stung, and he laughed again with genuine joy, rich and warm and oh, *so* likable.

"Ohmigod, that's enough, come on," said Sophie. She tried to push Cole—but her arm went through him.

"Help," croaked Claire, looking at Sophie. There was a horrible weight in her chest. She felt tears slip from her eyes, but they froze on her cheek.

"Her? She can't help you!" cried Cole in elation. "Why, she's as useless and lackwitted as you!"

"Hey, get fucked," mumbled Soph. "You . . . fuck off. Fuck off!"

"Yes, very erudite. All I had to do was say you were pretty once or twice and you near fell over yourself to do whatever I asked."

"Go . . . get . . . f—" said Claire, but she couldn't finish the sentence. She saw through the heavy lids of her eyes that Sophie was backing away. Claire realized she was completely alone— not just by herself, but *alone*. Nobody was coming to help her. She had no friends left. She stopped trying to sit up, and felt her shoulders slump against the floor. Something pointy was digging into her hip and she tried to focus on it to clear her head, but it was as if a big sad mist had descended on her.

"Stop Sophie," said Cole lazily, gesturing toward Spraggs, who had until then been silent, but was drawing closer to Claire with an expression of powerful curiosity on his face.

"What for?" said Spraggs, staring at Claire. "I want some. You said we could share it."

"She's mine," snapped Cole. "She may not have enough energy for two of us. Only one of us should drain her."

"And why should it be you?" said Spraggs.

"Because I'm your captain, Spraggs!" shouted Cole.

Mistake to shout, he won't respond well to the shouting, Claire thought.

"And why should it be that you're the captain?" said Spraggs. Cole turned to look at him, with the same expression of annoyance, incredulity, and the small but increasing bit of fear that Claire imagined every dictator had worn when someone knocked at the door of their palace to explain very politely that they and the rest of the mob had been reading a very interesting book, actually, and so there were two ways that the rest of the conversation could go, and one involved significantly more beheading than the other . . .

"Mutiny, is it, Mister Spraggs?" said Cole.

Spraggs saluted. "Aye, sir," he said, and punched Cole in the face. Or at least, tried to. If it had connected, it would have been quite a vicious and effective right hook, but his fist passed right through his captain's temple. Cole, though, still tried to dodge the blow.

At the same moment, Claire felt a jerk on the line between her and Sophie—a sharp pull that made her gasp and twitch like a fish. Then came another. She fell back and felt one of the ghosts grab her wrist again, and gritted her teeth. There was another tug on the invisible thread and then, without warning, a great rending, tearing feeling, like her rib cage was being pulled out of her chest without any regard for the fact it was still attached to her. She screamed, but it was a ragged, feeble sound, and the pain was so acute that it sharpened to a point in her mind until there was nothing else, until she was trapped in it, until it was the only thing she could see.

Dimly, she realized Cole wasn't touching her anymore. The pain had made her convulse, extending her limbs and back like a gymnast, and she'd writhed away from Cole's arm without even meaning to. Claire was so drained that all she could do was try to drag herself sideways, in the direction most away from Cole. Spraggs put his hand out as if to help her up, and she took it without thinking, and then said "Ah, fuuuuuuuu—" when she realized what she'd done, and fell back again. Spraggs grinned, pupils dilated, as he got a hit of the living, but in the next moment Cole had grabbed one of Spraggs's ankles and pulled *up*, so the rest of Spraggs went toward the floor. Cole lunged back at Claire and took her hand, but then again he was yanked off her as Spraggs grabbed him around the waist. Claire pulled herself forward a few inches while they scuffled, flickering and phasing in and out of solidity, until Cole got the better of Spraggs long enough to grab Claire's bare ankle. But then Spraggs headbutted his former captain and pulled him back.

It went like that, the pair of them fighting and giving Claire moments of space to crawl by her fingertips, making progress by centimeters but still being drained of everything in her in flickering fits and starts like a badly connected light bulb. The ghosts, too, were flickering in and out of an increased solidity that made their fight erratic and unpredictable. Claire had just about reached the wall, and had pulled herself up to sitting in a corner away from the direct beam of the torch. Whatever was digging into her hip was still there. She reached down to swat it away and realized it was the broken piece of teacup in her pocket, the fragment of the island's history. She thought about how many people had died here, and felt the fort like a great weight around her neck, pulling her toward them.

On the edge of her darkening vision, she saw Cole come at her again. He knotted his fingers into her hair, so he was cradling her head, almost like a lover. She looked into his handsome smiling face, and heard the drumbeat of her heart slowing.

"That's right," he said. "It'll be easier. I don't think you even like being alive, really, do you?"

Claire blinked slowly. Her heart felt bruised. When she breathed she was aware of the mechanics of it; she felt her lungs as a pair of bellows that had to be operated manually, and it was hard work to do it. It wasn't like she achieved much with living. Sophie pointed that out quite often. Maybe he was right. This was easier.

She blinked again, and frowned. A foot had gone through Cole's head.

Someone was shouting, but she heard it from very far away, or as if she was lying underwater in the bath. An ice bath.

"HithimhithimClaire hit him!"

She heard it like the Doppler effect of a race car going past, quiet and then suddenly loud and at full speed. Someone was here. Someone was trying to help.

She looked at Cole again and thought: *What if I become a ghost? What if I'm trapped on this island with him?*

And she watched with some interest as her arm came up and she sliced down his cheek with the razor-sharp piece of porcelain still in her fist.

Cole screamed and reflexively clutched his face with both hands.

Claire blacked out for a second. It was only a moment or two, but when she opened her eyes again she screamed, too, because she still saw nothing but darkness. The darkness pulled back a couple of inches and Claire realized that Bones had been looking at her very up close. Satisfied of Claire's consciousness by the scream, he gave her a thumbs-up and stepped back even farther.

"I . . . give me a second . . ." Claire mumbled, but Bones responded by putting his hands on his hips in quite a sarcastic fashion, as if to point out that she did not have the luxury of all the time in the world. Claire blinked and took in that the small room was suddenly much more crowded than it had been moments before. Spraggs came toward Bones, who was standing in front of Claire like a guardian warrior, legs apart and knees slightly bent to lower his center of gravity. Bones deflected Spraggs's wide swing and casually delivered his own roundhouse blow that was strong enough that it spun Spraggs around before he fell to the floor. Bones did bring his own knuckle dusters with him, Claire supposed.

Sophie stood away from it all in the tunnel, nervously picking at her hangnails again and watching Cole, who was pinned against the wall by a now-familiar hooded figure. Mossie had a hold of the front of Cole's shirt and held him back with his full weight pushing forward, his other hand balled in a fist at his side. His body vibrated with the same energy you see in a furious terrier before it tries to tear the throat out of a much bigger dog.

Bones snapped his fingers in front of her face—or at least, did the motion, and produced a noise like two pebbles being hit together—and pointed again, more emphatically, down the tunnel nearest to her. Claire moaned and pulled herself to her hands and knees. She felt like her entire body was bruised.

"She needs energy. I know how to give her some if I touch her," said Sophie.

"Don't you fucking touch me," Claire hissed. "I can do it."

"Do you need me, Claire?" asked Mossie. Cole laughed nastily and imitated him, and Mossie pressed his forearm against Cole's throat.

"What're you going to do?" Cole said. "I can't die *again*." There was a long, ragged wound down the side of his face and over his top lip, twisting his smile. It looked like it was bleeding, even. Claire was fascinated.

"You'll fucking wish you could," Mossie replied. "Get out of here, Claire. They won't follow you."

"You're a damned traitor, Mister Bones!" yelled Cole. Bones stuck the Vs up at Cole, and then flapped his hands at Claire to get her moving again. She pushed herself to her feet by leaning heavily on the wall and walking forward until she was vaguely upright, like a pisshead navigating the tunnels on the Circle Line. The torch, when she picked it up, was about a million times heavier than it had been before, and the light roamed drunkenly as she walked. Bones kept pace a little ahead of her, cheerfully guiding her through the moldering labyrinth.

Gunna find Alex, she told herself. *Gunna find Alex and Basher. Then it'll be all right.*

She staggered along, feeling dizzy and hot and cold all at once, until she nearly walked into a plain door—or at least, some sort of board with a Yale lock on it that she was, thank Christ, able to open from this side without a key—and considered how this was the second time this kind of near-death experience had happened to her in less than a year, and she was not a fan. That was too much near-death-experience-because-of-ghosts for anyone in real life. The tunnels vomited her up onto the courtyard of the fort, and although it wasn't as sunny as before, the light contrast was bright enough that Claire was immediately sick herself, on her hands and knees. She was aware that Sophie was hovering around behind her, just on her periphery, but wasn't getting too close. Good. Bones gave her another thumbs-up and headed back through the now-closed door, presumably to help Mossie.

The sun had become a low-level shower. Claire added this to the growing list of things she felt were deeply unfair. But Claire was so cold that even the rain felt like a heated shower. She raised her head and saw Conn and Finny were sauntering up to her. She rolled onto her side and wiped the frozen tears from her face, and sniffed like a snotty child. Sophie stepped around her and retreated a few more paces.

"Fuck have you been?" croaked Claire, eyeing the Opportunists.

"Fuck have *you* been?" said Finny. "You look awful, girl."

"Cole tried to kill me," she said.

"Ah, well. That sounds like him, in fairness," said Conn, nodding sagely.

"Well, you'll want to be getting on, anyway," said Finny happily. "Some of your lot are on top of number three bastion. Some sort of standoff happening there, I believe."

He pointed. Claire turned, and saw that she had come out underneath the lookout spot she and Sophie had stood at on the first morning, and only a few hundred yards from where she'd freaked out and attacked Dan. She could hear raised voices coming from the top of the fort, where she and Sophie had looked out at the sea.

"Right. Brilliant. Fuck off, then," said Claire.

"Grand, so," said Conn, with a megawatt smile. He and Finny started to walk up the zigzagged slope to the top.

"God, they're really all just a bunch of dickheads, aren't they," said Sophie, as if she had not, mere minutes ago, nearly got Claire killed because she'd been played by a hot man. It was weird the lengths people would go to if they thought there was a chance they'd get laid. Not even laid; get a nice word from someone they thought was cute.

This thought made several things about the weekend suddenly make sense. "Oh," she said. She stared through Sophie for a second, as other thoughts lined up neatly. "Yeah, I mean. That sort of makes sense, doesn't it?"

She was feeling better, but also had a definite awareness that the current ceiling on how good she'd feel as a totality was as extremely low as one of the island's impractical historical cottages. That kind of low. She was grateful that she could feel things and was alive, but on the other hand that appeared to come with a migraine.

"Right," she said. "Fuck it. Let's get this over with, then." She slapped her hands on her thighs like a keen PE teacher, which did actually help trick her into getting up. "I don't think this is going to go well," she added, almost speaking out loud.

"Why?" said Soph. They started walking.

"I just figured out who the murderer is."

19

The Fall

It seemed that basically everyone on the entire island was already standing around in a group, on the triangle of gravel that made a lookout point for tourists—including Conn and Finny, who clearly viewed the whole situation as entertainment. Claire was relieved. In TV shows and books the great detective had someone to round up the suspects for them. He could just say "gather everyone in the library, would you?" and lo, they would be gathered. But Claire didn't have a sidekick who'd do that, and she was in no mood to do it herself. And though she was battling an absolute brain-melter of a headache, Claire was quite sure her head hurt less than Alex's. She was incredibly relieved to see that they were there, on their feet, and shouting hoarsely.

"This is a fucking disaster! This is a farce! I am going to kill at least one person and quite possibly everyone, you're obviously the fucking murderer! You attacked me!"

Basher, who clearly thought this was too much exertion for someone who was only recently unconscious, was keeping a firm hold of Alex's arm. Eidy was on Alex's other side, and they were facing George, Ritchie, and Tiffany, while Mac, holding her daughter, was standing close to George. Ashley was a little off to the side, and seemed to have relieved herself of Caity expressly so she could shotgun hotel mini-bar bottles of booze. She looked rather like she was enjoying herself. There were already a couple of empty miniatures at her feet, and Claire watched her take one of those single-glass-size bottles of red wine out of her pocket and see it off. Claire was quite jealous, and wondered where Ashley had got hold of them, because her hotel mini-bar had held no such things.

Nobody seemed to have noticed Claire, and she sat down heavily on one of the benches provided. Everyone was standing quite close to the thin wire fence, about thigh height, that had been erected to stop them going dangerously close to the edge of the fort's inner wall. The outer wall was a few meters away, and the gap between them yawned open.

"It sounds like it might have been an accident," said George, in a very "I'm a reasonable man trying to keep everyone calm" voice that he couldn't have calculated to infuriate Alex more if he had tried. "I mean, you hit your head when you were pushed, right?"

"Oh, give me a fucking break!" they said.

"I'm with Alex," said Mac. "I mean, the only person who'd want to stop me phoning the police is someone with something to hide. And by the way, you can pay for a new iPhone."

"Oh for God's sake, it's probably fine! It didn't fall very far," said Tiffany. Without warning she stepped over the wire fence and walked over the grassy point of the star to the edge. She was looking down into the dry moat between the fort's walls, standing on the edge of the inner wall. Ritchie followed her without hesitation, and put a hand on her waist protectively, quietly exhorting her to be careful.

"I can see it from here, look! We'll just get down there and collect it," said Tiffany.

Claire got up to move closer, and George noticed her and came over. "Oh, thank God," he muttered. "I was worried something had happened to you."

"Were you really?"

"Of course. Well, it looks like something has, anyway. Fucking hell, you're freezing. You've no coat on. Here." George stripped off his big black wool coat and wrapped it around Claire's shoulders. She put her arms into the sleeves and her hands didn't reach the end. It was gloriously warm from George's body heat, and she leaned into him in spite of herself.

"If you're finished with your love-in," snapped Sophie. Which was a bold tone for her to take, Claire thought.

"What's going on?" she asked, even though she had a pretty good idea.

"Tiffany, Ritchie, and I walked 'round the island and then decided to check the fort, in case Minnie was in here. As we were leaving, Mac came up and told us what had happened, and that she was going to find signal to call the police. I waited with her, but Tiffany said she wanted to walk the long way back around to the hotel to clear her head."

"Sus," said Alex grimly.

"Mac managed to find signal and put a call through, but then Ritchie and Tiffany came haring back," George said.

"And then the wee Texan prick grabbed my phone and threw it off the side here! Said we mustn't call the cops."

"You've missed out that in the interval, the almighty fuckhead knocked me out and I went down like a sack of extremely sexy shit!"

"Look," said Tiffany. She flapped her arms in frustration. "You've got no evidence of anything, let's all just stop being silly."

"Can we speed things up?" said Claire wearily. "Like, obviously Ritchie did it."

"Excellent," said Conn. Claire hoped the ghosts weren't going to provide commentary the whole time.

"Exactly! The necktie! That's my point!" said Alex. "The stupid cowboy bolo tie. He's wearing another one today, and the ornament on it is about the same shape as the one we got on the beach." Claire obligingly got it out of her pocket. Alex pointed at it. "Yeah, exactly. I recognized it and tried to grab it, and he shoved me."

Ritchie was being uncharacteristically silent in his own defense, but here he piped up. "That was an accident," he said, without any of his usual bluster. He stepped closer to Tiffany, and Claire thought that she should probably have waited until they were back on the other side of the minimal safety fence before she'd started dropping revelations.

"And that clasp could have fallen off any old time," Ritchie went on. "Matter of fact, I don't even think it's mine."

"And Ritchie was with me the whole morning, so he can't have killed Minnie."

"Minnie was killed last night," said Claire. She paused, and was rewarded with gasps. "He hit her with a brick from one of the ruined houses when her back was turned, then changed her out of her regular clothes and into her running gear to make it seem like it happened this morning. Except she wasn't in her sports bra. Er. I dunno, maybe he got embarrassed, or it was hard to get on? But no one goes running in a normal bra. He threw all the evidence out of the window, and he opened the gates of the fort to make it seem like she'd been on her normal run to open them up this morning. He stole the keys from my room."

"Why on earth did you have the keys?" said Basher.

"I stole them from Minnie's room," said Claire.

"That is all total and complete bullhickey. I never did anything like that in my life, swear on my mama's grave," said Ritchie. He laughed. "If anything, you just made yourself sound guilty!" His confidence shook Claire's.

"Right," said Tiffany. She walked a few steps away from the edge of the wall, which made everyone slightly less tense. "And why would Ritchie have a reason to kill Minnie, anyway?"

Claire took a deep breath. She knew what she said next would be a hard sell.

"Because that isn't Ritchie," she said.

There was a silence. Then Tiffany started laughing.

"Is that really the best you have?"

"I can prove it." *At least, I hope I can.* "Minnie was doing gene-alogical research to see who might be related to the Irish locals who lived here hundreds of years ago. I think she might have found out the same thing Dan did. Ritchie Walker doesn't exist."

"Claire, he's standing right there. If it's not Ritchie, then who is it?" said George.

"That's Tiffany's old stalker. That's Andy."

"Ohhh, fucking what? That's great!" said Alex. They lowered their voice guiltily. "I mean, I knew it was him who hit me on the head, and obviously none of this is *actually* great, but like, narratively it's a good twist."

"Ohmigod, by the way, I totally knew that guy wasn't a real

Texan. Right from the start I knew, I called it," said Sophie. Claire ignored her.

Andy had frozen, and Tiffany gasped.

"Wh . . . what?" she said, voice cracking. "Andy . . . Andy from uni, Andy?"

This triggered something in Andy, but it wasn't a good or rational thing. He jerked into motion and threw an arm around Tiffany's shoulders from behind, dragging her close to him. She screamed, and nearly fell down, trying to pull his arm off her, but also suddenly disgusted by his touch. All of the others ran toward the safety fence, but Andy motioned as if he were going to throw Tiffany off the wall, and they all stopped. The pair were standing almost in the tip of the pointed part of the bastion, and as Claire watched a gust of wind took the cowboy hat off Andy's head and flipped it into the dry moat below.

"What's the plan, Andy?" Mac called. "I told you, the call went through. The police are already on the way, in a helicopter or a boat or something. There's nowhere for you to go."

"Just come in, mate, you don't want to hurt Tiff, do you?" George added. Claire noticed how people never really called someone "mate" when they meant it.

It was still raining, giving the scene a little background score of splats and pops where it hit the grass and gravel, like Rice Krispies.

"He's definitely not going to hurt her going over that wall," said Finny's voice. Finny and Conn had been watching quietly, but now moved through the group to stand very close to Andy and Tiffany. Finny looked over the drop, and tutted like a builder pricing up lengths of wood. "Not hurt her much, anyway," he added.

"'Tis only about thirty feet high, like," said Conn. "And on to grass. That fall won't kill you."

Claire thought back to hostage negotiations on *Murder Profile*, which were many and varied. You had to either confuse the perp or do everything he said or do nothing he said or build trust, depending on the whims of the writers. She took a deep breath.

"When you won the lottery, you remembered what Tiffany had said, didn't you?" said Claire. "About how you'd have to change everything about yourself. And, like, you did. You went away for a bit and you came back as someone else. You shaved, dyed your hair, spray tanned, but you went further than that. George mentioned the other day that Dan had been looking up extreme plastic surgery options—he made a joke about it, really, but I think it was because Dan was suspicious of you, not because he wanted any surgery himself. Cheeks, brow, jaw—you got a whole new face. My friend even said you have a noughties plastic surgery nose, which . . . well, that was mean, but then she is kind of mean, to be honest. That's okay, I get that. I'd probably do that if I could, you know?"

Andy jerked his chin up as if trying not to cry. Out of the corner of her eye, Claire saw Eidy step slowly over what for him was a knee-high fence.

"You found out where she worked and went to the same place she got lunch every day, and made it seem like a coincidence. But it wasn't."

"What the fuck! What the *fuck*," screamed Tiffany. She wriggled and tried to break way. "Get your fucking hands off me, you *lunatic*."

"And I don't think you did that much research on actual Texans, did you? You just guessed most people have never met one, and you *knew* this group of friends hadn't. The one thing you couldn't do was cure having epilepsy, but the medication you have now keeps it way more under control than when you were at uni. So, you figured it didn't matter. Um. It wasn't stalking, right? It was love."

Andy swallowed. "I knew . . . if she could get to know me . . . she'd see that we're right for each other."

Eidy took another step toward Andy. Claire moved to the right as she kept talking, so that Andy was looking at her instead.

"You're doing really good," said Sophie.

"She's right. Keep going," said Finny with approval.

"But you started to run out of money, didn't you? Because you're not *really* an oil-rich Texan, and Tiffany had become accustomed to a certain way of living. So you borrowed some off Dan. But then he called the debt in, and you couldn't pay. And then he found out who you were. Because he was digging up dirt on everyone, or at least trying to. He had Flick followed by a private investigator—she assumed Mac thought she was cheating."

"I hadn't hidden everything well enough," said Andy, whose accent was sloughing off him like a snakeskin to expose a soft Midlands underbelly. "Accounts in my own name. One of the surgeons had before and after photos of my face . . . Stupid."

"He tried to blackmail you. And you panicked. You asked him to meet you late at night so nobody would see—maybe you told him you were embarrassed, I don't know—and you knew Ashley was a light sleeper, so when you went over to their room with a nightcap, you'd put some of Tiffany's sleeping pills in Ashley's drink. That way, Ashley wouldn't wake up when Dan left the room."

"And when he didn't stay down from being hit on the head,

Cosplay Texas Ranger here used the string bit on his bolo tie," said Sophie. "I knew I'd seen that bird thing before."

"I couldn't let him . . . I didn't have the money, but Tiffany could never know."

"I fucking do now, you head case," she shouted. "Let go of me right now."

Andy's face twisted into an expression of complete misery and despair, and he turned to look at his other yet living victim as she writhed in his grasp. It was all the brief window needed for Eidy to say "Fuck this," and insta-sprint the few feet separating them, grab Andy by his current, non–murder weapon bolo tie, and headbutt him. Andy was taller than Eidy, so he had to really jump into it, and if he'd hit him square on, Andy would probably have been properly taken out. At least he let go of Tiffany, who immediately ran to Ashley and burst into tears.

Andy took half a step back, blood pouring from his nose, and only just managed to *not* fall over the edge.

"Come on, mate," said George again. "There's nothing you can do."

For a second it looked like Andy might walk toward them— he took half a step—but as he did Tiffany cringed, and burrowed her face into Ashley's shoulder, looking almost identical to Caity. He stopped.

"You could try flying for it, you grim fuckwit!" said Ashley suddenly. She laughed. She looked joyful.

"Not helping," Basher shot at her.

"Not trying to, dickhead," said Ashley.

"You know, I like her a lot more now," mused Soph.

Andy pulled his hands through his hair, until his normally neatly greased cowlick was standing on end in two horns either side of his head. He was sobbing.

"I wouldn't have hurt her!" he said. "I wouldn't have hurt her!"

"Piss off, you pathetic little wanker," shouted Ashley. "You killed my fucking husband, and my best friend. You ruined all our fucking lives!"

She lobbed the wine bottle at him. It hit him square in the chest, and, light as it was, Andy took another step back automatically.

Onto nothing. It almost happened in slow motion. He half tripped over thin air and threw his hands back, tipping all the way over. Ashley laughed with wine-gray teeth into the growing fury of the wind and the rain.

"Oh, headfirst," said Conn. He looked over the side, and then turned back to Claire, with another big smile. "I stand corrected."

20

Secret Secrets Are No Fun

Claire was sitting underneath the tree near the treasure marker, tented under the umbrella Bash had given her. It was quite soothing, really: the sound of the rain softly hitting the canvas. It had eased up a bit. Sophie was sitting a couple of feet away, but outside the umbrella. She seemed to understand that she wasn't allowed in yet.

"So," said Claire. "You broke the tether. Did it hurt you?"

"Yes. Obviously. It had stretched a lot, but I'd still been meeting Co . . . I mean, that wanker, in the village and the slopes of the fort. I hadn't actually been in those tunnels before, he just coached me on where to go. When I ran to find help, I ended up going all the way back to the village to find Mossie and Bones. It was twice as far as I'd managed to stretch. Felt like I might pass out."

"Thanks, I guess. Does that mean you can fuck off forever now?"

"LOL. No, sorry. Look." Sophie stood and walked a few

meters, until suddenly Claire felt a pain in her chest and she gasped involuntarily. It didn't used to hurt. And now the length of it was shorter than ever.

"You know you said it was like stretching a tendon? Now I think it's like, when you fuck a tendon or whatever," said Sophie, coming back. "It's still there, but now it's painful and you have to start from scratch again once it heals."

"Great. Brilliant."

"I wouldn't have hurt her," said another ghost on her left.

"Shut the fuck up, Andy."

He'd appeared soon after he'd died, except he wasn't sure which version of him he was. He tuned in and out like a bad radio, so sometimes he was a weak-chinned but basically inoffensive nerd in a sweater vest, and sometimes he was Ritchie the cowboy, with the accent and swagger to go with it. Sometimes the change would happen mid-sentence, which had so far invariably been the same sentence. He was very insistent he wouldn't have hurt Tiff. Although Claire wasn't sure he actually knew who Tiffany was anymore.

Basher had said it was better that he'd died, in a sense, because there probably wasn't a lot of hard evidence linking him to either murder. If it had gone to trial, he might have got off. Alex had punched their uncle in the shoulder and called him an "awful fucking ghoul" for saying that. Looking at him, Claire did not think it was better for Andy that he'd died.

The Opportunists and Bones were also gathered around her. There were so many ghosts in the vicinity that the rain was in danger of turning into localized sleet in the cold, but Claire was still snuggled down in George's coat. It was ironic that she had started off the trip bargaining with Cole to be left alone by ghosts, and the deal had resulted in her being surrounded by a lot of them.

"Sorry we weren't on our normal watch," said Finny. "Cole had yer man causing a ruckus on the other side of the village." He gestured to Bones. "Seemed like a normal enough day. But after a spell your girl got to us. Was like she was running into a wall there for a while. Our Mossie and the dry bones fella couldn't wait to help you out."

Mossie scratched his nose. "Truth be told, we were getting bored of Cole running around in those tunnels, anyway."

"Wait, you knew?" said Sophie. "You fucking knew the pirates were inside the fort the whole time?"

"Ah here, of course we did! Cole's not as clever as he thinks, and he wasn't doing any harm. Kept him entertained, like," said Conn very amiably. "We were going to wait until he decided to ambush us from inside our own walls to let him know we'd been watching him the whole time, but here it seems he found a new idea."

"We were planning a sort of peace treaty anyway," said Mossie. Bones reached out to him for a fist bump, and he obliged.

"Ruins the fun, in my opinion," said Finny, although he was still very placid about the whole thing.

"Yeah, well if you lot hadn't been busy having playground fights with each other, you might have actually seen the murders and saved everyone a lot of trouble," Claire pointed out. It was the inverse problem to the last death they'd investigated, when a ghost had seen the whole thing and they just hadn't bothered to ask him.

"God, you're such a bunch of fucking losers," spat Soph.

"Ah, well," said Finny. He tugged at his beard, and looked at

Sophie with a twinkle in his eye. "We didn't get tricked by him, did we? And it depends on how you see things. From where we're looking, it never gets old."

"I suppose from where you're looking England is still in mid-conquest of your country," said Claire, thinking back to how much genuine fun Finny had appeared to be having during the ghost scrap in the middle of the night.

"Ah, we're not as bitter as all that, although I'll allow that being a Brit doesn't make Cole any less punchable than his nature makes him already. But we're not so behind. We hear the main news that happens," said Finny. "In dribbles, like."

"Independence was good, but 'twas a grand day when we heard about that singing contest," said Mossie. "We were happy enough with that, all right."

"Fucking hell, he's talking about Eurovision isn't he?" said Sophie. "If I wasn't dead this conversation would make me want to die. I don't know how you cope."

"It is a daily struggle," said Claire, eyeing her. "You bitch," she added, for good measure. Soph's mouth became a line.

"Well, this has been the most eventful few days we've had in a while, anyway," said Conn.

"Better than Eurovision?" asked Sophie. She was almost being nice enough that you wouldn't catch the edge of nasty sarcasm in her voice. Unless you knew her really well.

"Cole's had a bloody nose, so he'll be trying to get back at us," said Finny, "so that'll be fun. Well, he got a bloody face, thanks to you, which was interesting to see. Did you know it hadn't healed yet? He might be stuck that way forever. We didn't know that could happen."

"Neither did we," admitted Claire.

"Maybe in another fifty years another one of you will turn up who'll be able to break his nose," said Conn. "Or maybe he'll convince a medium to attack me! I think I'd be awful good-looking with a scar."

"Plus, we're a man up now, due to yer man Bones, and he's two men down what with falling out with Spraggs too," added Finny. "Maybe one of us will change sides again in another few hundred years. An exciting thought, no?"

"You really are just in it for the fun, aren't you?" said Claire.

"I don't know any other way to be, in fairness," said Finny. "Especially now I'm dead, d'you know?"

"Would you not want to finish some unfinished business and fuck off?"

"Not at all, not. At. All," said Finny. "I reckon we could go whenever we wanted."

"Just not of a mind to yet," added Conn. "Besides. I've a new toy to play with now." He grinned in a vindictive way and prodded Andy.

"Come on, let's be away. The guards will come to collect you soon, I'd say, so we'll say goodbye now," said Finny. He was probably right. A few local gardaí had come over on a boat, and once they had assessed that the situation involved three dead bodies they got quite excited, and had called for loads more guards, of different types. Claire had managed to slip away, but someone would come to find her soon. Finny and Conn stood up, and made a show of dusting themselves off.

"Don't write," said Claire.

"Don't know how," replied Conn with good cheer.

"See you again, Claire. Sophie," said Finny.

"I fucking hope not," said Soph, which made Finny laugh.

"Grand, so. Good luck and thanks."

Finny waved, and walked away, master of all he surveyed. *We must imagine*, thought Claire, *Sisyphus happy*. And he really was. It was comforting, in a way.

"Grand. That's me away. Ye go safe, girls," said Conn, making his own move to go.

"I wouldn't have hurt her," said Andy.

Conn turned to him with a suddenly venomous expression, his lip curled in contempt, his eyes cold.

"Yes," he said. "You fucking would." Andy shrank back from him, and began to walk away, much to Claire's relief. "You coming, Moss?" said Conn.

Mossie waved him away. "I'll be along," he said. He was looking out to sea contemplatively.

Bones shrugged, and stood up, too. He made a great show of sweeping his hat off and bowing low to Claire, like Cole would have done. It made Claire laugh.

"Thanks for helping save me, Bones. You're a decent sort." Bones gave her the double thumbs-up like the Fonz, and shook Soph's hand, before he, too, walked away.

"It's like the last episode of a sitcom," muttered Sophie. Mossie hadn't moved. Claire looked at him and thought, suddenly, of the bird trapped in the tunnels under the fort, and that life really was monstrously unfair. But Mossie seemed quite content. He stretched his legs out and looked at the sea—a magnificent horizon of bright gray sky and choppy water kissed with white spray—with great satisfaction.

After a while they heard human footsteps. George bent over and poked his head under the umbrella.

"Room for one more? I brought your coat. I thought we could swap. Are you okay? There's loads more gardaí coming ashore and being told about everything, so you'll have to go back soon, I'm afraid."

"Okay."

"What happened to you earlier?"

"Pirate ghost tried to kill me," said Claire, too emotionally and physically exhausted to say anything else.

"Well. Shit. That must have been rubbish."

"Really? That's it?"

"Well. Yeah. What else would there be? I do like you, you know," he said.

"He might be an actual keeper," said Sophie. "I take back when I was mean about him." Claire sighed quite heavily.

"What are you a doctor of?" she asked. "I assumed medical, but it's not, is it?"

"Everyone assumes medical. I'm sure my parents would rather it was that," he said with a grin. "My PhD is in history."

"Ah, thought it might be that. You and Minnie must have been close."

"Yeah, we took some of the same modules, back in the day." He shook his head sadly, and tried to smile. "So, great detective. When did you figure out it was Ritchie—Andy?"

"Really late. Eleventh-hour kind of stuff," said Claire. "I thought it was Minnie for a while, but she just seemed too by the book. Like, she'd just restructure her mortgage or something like that. And I thought it was Eidy for a bit, because he was never around and then also always up at night. He pretended that we were stuck here the first day, and then it just happens to be that his phone broke last week? But then I realized that he and Basher have just spent most of the time shagging, and it didn't leave him much room to do any murdering. Like, whenever I saw Basher at a weird time he was always sneaking off to Eidy's flat or whatever."

Soph whistled. "Okay, didn't catch that one. Alex'll be livid they didn't either. And you realize this means you and Basher have the same type, right? Gingery tough boys. Don't think about *that* too hard. Absolutely grim."

This had not occurred to Claire, so she continued her current policy of studiously ignoring Sophie.

"With Ritchie—Andy, whatever—I knew he was creepy, and I knew he wasn't *right*. Like, he said very English-y words sometimes, and he had a fake tan, when if you're actually working outdoors a lot you have a real one, like Eidy. But I just thought he was, you know, a fake sort of person, I guess." Claire scuffed the grass with her foot. She didn't look at George, but he made an encouraging noise.

"I couldn't figure out why he would bother to kill Dan, though," she went on. "TV shows make it seem like everyone is two inches from murder all the time. You drop your toast butterside down and you'll kill your postman. One moment of slight financial pressure and you're gutting people left and right. Alex and Basher make fun of me for liking shows like that, but I know most people wouldn't actually do that in real life. Like, we live in a society, right? But I was thinking about what people do when they like someone. Or think they love them, I guess. And that made more sense. I had to make some lucky guesses. Flick remembered Andy having a brain-related illness at uni, and then I found what turned out to be epilepsy meds in his bedside cabinet. The real stumbling block, I suppose, was that he does look very different, but then I thought maybe it's not that hard to change how you look these days if you have the money and time and a willing team of plastic surgeons. Especially if the last time someone saw you was like twenty years ago, and you had a beard before."

"Blimey. Glad you figured it out before he worked his way through all of us," said George. "Well done, Claire-Bear."

"It was strange," said Claire, still not looking at him. "I was convinced that whoever killed Dan was the one trying to steal the treasure. But Sophie said something about why she didn't think it was Eidy."

"The tides, right?" said Sophie, eager to prove she'd been right about something. "Basher said whoever killed Dan must have expected him to be taken out on the tide, and that meant it had to have been someone who didn't understand the tides around here."

"Right. And that meant Dan's killer couldn't have been the treasure thief, because they had sunk a marker on the treasure, and were going out at night to get it when the tide was highest. So they did understand the tide," summarized Claire. George looked slightly confused, probably because there had been a pause and then Claire had replied to that silence. Her conversations with Sophie were discombobulating to everyone else.

"I'm just relieved we can all get off this island for now. There's going to be a lot of grieving to do later," said George. "I guess it was just an annoying coincidence."

"Yeah," said Claire. "I thought that too." She took a deep, shuddering breath and stared out at the horizon. "And then about twenty minutes ago I put my hand in your coat pocket."

She drew it out again, and held up a few leaves of notepaper that completed Finny's family tree. One of the more modern branches of the family name had become Lyons. And there was George Lyons, written right at the bottom in Minnie's handwriting.

"*Most* people won't kill over money. But some people will," she said.

There was a pause. "Claire, I swear—"

"Don't. I wasn't even surprised. Little things add up, you know? Like you having a scuba qualification, and climbing. You needed more milk, even though Minnie said you'd already had a carton." She pointed out at the water. "That's where the first one went, right? Then there was the water and mud in the room next to mine. That's where you'd put all of the stuff you brought up, and you'd moved it so I wouldn't hear you bring more boxes in and open them up. Except I still did! That's why you were so keen to take one of the rooms outside with us, and that's why you came into the empty room so fast when you heard me the night we . . . that night. You were just trying to distract me, and it worked! And your hair was wet because you'd been out in the storm, not because you'd had a shower at one a.m. Stupid. Stupid!"

"It wasn't like that. She . . . I was just going to talk to her, but she thought I was the one who killed Dan. I swear, it was an accident," said George. He was talking slowly and calmly, as if he had decided to tell the truth, or at least something that could be true.

"You made me your alibi this morning," said Claire. She felt gray. She was crying, but she only knew she was crying because she could feel the tears on her chin.

"I didn't plan to. I'm so sorry. I really do like you, Claire. You weren't a contingency plan!"

Claire shrugged off his coat and wordlessly took back her own hoodie and jacket combo. She didn't look at him, but took several deep, ragged breaths, and a little hiccup-gasp of sadness, like a child crying too hard to breathe.

"You're okay," said Sophie quietly. "You're okay. You've got this."

"Claire?" George said. "Please, can we talk about this? It was an accident."

"Did you find anything?" she asked finally.

"No. That's the stupidest fucking part. It's all gone, if there was ever anything there." His voice became muffled as he put his head in his hands. "Just boxes of mud, basically. I'm never going to be okay with what I did, Claire, but I didn't mean it—but nobody will believe me if I say it wasn't on purpose. Please, Claire."

"But you're lying," she said at last. "You took a lump of brick with you. You stole the keys from my room, and you tried to get away with it. You planned it. You're lying. You're lying!"

He didn't try to take the papers from her yet, but she could feel him looking at her, the weight of his gaze as heavy as lead. "Nobody would believe you anyway," he said suddenly. "You've been walking around talking to yourself this whole time. All my friends will agree you're fucking mental."

"I take back my taking back," said Sophie.

"Mind yourself, Claire," Mossie said. Claire had almost forgotten he was there.

Claire's feet were bunched under her, so when George did snatch for the notepaper, she pushed forward like a spring. She pushed the umbrella into his face and half-fell a few feet down the slope, while considering that she had been incredibly stupid. In a split second she realized that down was easier, but up was more sensible, so she used the thin trunk of the tree to swing around and pull herself up, Gene Kelly style—but as if Gene Kelly were in fear of his life for the second time in a morning. George, who had longer limbs to get under control, took longer to stand, but she felt his fingers graze an ankle as she scrambled past.

"Use your hands too, let's go," said Soph. "Scratches are temporary but death is forever. Fucking trust me on that one." Mossie ran alongside, too, directing her around hidden rocks and the worst of the gorse bushes.

She was going too slowly, she knew, and she was so tired,

and she didn't know what he'd do if George caught her, but she couldn't let him get the notepaper . . .

Claire, lungs on fire, vision going worryingly white, had almost reached the path again when she tripped over a leggy strand of a bramble that tangled in her laces, and it was enough of a slowdown that George was able to grab the hood on her top and yank her head back.

"You fucking—" he started to growl, but he never completed the sentence, because there came a loud sort of war yodel, and a streak of red flashed in front of Claire's eyes, and something slammed into George's side.

It was Alex, going for a low tackle. But George was strong enough, big enough, that he managed to keep his footing, and his grip on Claire, even as Alex started pulling at his legs and threatening to bite him. With his free hand, he grabbed hold of their hair, and they yowled and let go. George roared, like a colossus swatting away mosquitoes.

It probably wouldn't have gone well for Claire and Alex if Basher had not arrived within seconds and, with only a little hesitation, kicked George extremely hard in the nuts.

Claire experienced it as very much like the moment the Riders of Rohan came over the hill in *The Lord of the Rings*. The effect was only slightly lessened by the fact he had the orange rain poncho on again. But it was still very heroic.

"Oh dear," he said. "Please don't tell anyone I did that . . ." He helped Claire and Alex up, as George rolled over in the fetal position and made a noise exactly the same as an unoiled door hinge. Some guards, in the high vis and bulky black that said "police" in any visual language, arrived soon afterward and were initially unsure who to handcuff until Claire explained some things.

"Should you have done that with a head injury?" Sophie asked Alex.

They grinned. "Paramedic said I should avoid going to sleep. She was nonspecific about tackling massive lads. Anyway. He was trying to hurt Claire, and we can't allow that. A small bit of concussion is no barrier."

"You're lucky we were worried and came looking for you, Strange," said Basher. "I did say you should have waited for a boat back with us, did I not? Flick says she is relieved she slept through it all, although she is quite angry with Mac. The guards are still bagging evidence, but we will have to give lots of interviews and things. Come on."

Basher and Alex started to follow the police, who were walking a cuffed George down the path. Bash was fussing with Alex's head, and they kept flicking his hands away, and eventually gave him a playful shove. She heard Alex's laugh floating back toward her, over the sound of the rain.

Mossie chuckled to himself, watching as Basher pulled his orange hood back up.

"What?"

"Nothing. Ignore me." He paused again, and appeared to be thinking. Still waters running deep. He cleared his throat. "You know, Claire," he said. "I'd consider it a great favor to me, if you ever get real sick, like, if you'd come out here to die."

Claire leaned forward to look at him in surprise. He was looking back at her, a shy little grin on his face. "I've unfinished business with you."

Claire chewed it over. "Probably not. I don't want to give you false hope, you know."

"I'm dead. It's the only kind of hope I have," he replied. "You'll at least think about it? I was party to saving your life after all."

"All right. I will. I promise I'll think about it."

"That's good enough for me. I'll be here, anyway," he said. "I won't say goodbye, for I'm confident I'll see you again."

Claire rolled her eyes, but she smiled. "Thanks," she said.

"Anytime." He walked away, whistling through his teeth, and went back down the hill to sit under the tree again. Claire was slightly humiliated by how short her desperate run had actually been. She stuck her hands in her pockets and looked sideways at Sophie.

"You did some good detective work," said Sophie. "Like, actually good."

"Thanks. I guess we were both pretty stupid about boys," said Claire.

"LOL. Yeah. Sorry. Let's not bother with them again," Soph replied. She sounded incredibly relieved.

"Well, not for a while, at least," she added. She turned and looked down the slope at Mossie, who was sitting quite still, hooded, beatific, gloriously serene as the world raged around him. "He's quite hot, in a sort of ye olde grubby barefoot bit of rough way. You could do worse. You *have* done worse."

"Uh, like *who?*" said Claire, affronted.

"That guy from Hungerford. He was like a country eight but a city five. Weird hair. You should have known *way* better."

"He was really nice, though."

"Yeah, I bet your mum would have loved him. Ohmigod, and that one from the drama club who played a munchkin in year eight."

"Oh okay, if we're talking ancient history then what about—"

"Oi!" shouted Alex, cutting short the argument. They were waiting with Basher in the rain, and were exasperated. "Are you coming? We're not going anywhere without you two."

AUTHOR'S NOTE

Spike Island is a real and very interesting place in the mouth of the port of Cork, Ireland, and I recommend you visit it for yourself. In the course of pinching it for this book I have taken a few liberties. One is that, in real life, it is very close to the naval base at Haulbowline Island, and it seems unlikely you'd be stranded on Spike without being able to get attention and help for even a few hours. Likewise, there is a tunnel that runs from the outside into the middle of the fort, but I have moved the exit a bit (and also you can't tour it, but I thought Claire could do with a torch). There is a rumor about pirate treasure off the side of the island, but in a different place to what I describe in this book, and it is unrelated to the Armada. It's true that some boats of the Spanish Armada did make landfall along the west coast of Ireland, but as noted by Claire, none of them made it to County Cork. Cole and his crew are entirely made up, as are Finny, Conn, and Mossie—and their names are probably slightly more anglicized than what their parents would have called them, but then they've been hanging around for a few hundred years, so maybe they moved with the times. I hope you, the reader, will forgive these sleights of hand, especially if you're local. I reiterate my suggestion to visit Spike for yourself, where you can explore the fort and the ruined village (sans hotel). If you're particularly interested, I also recommend the work of local author John Crotty, who has done a lot of work documenting the history and context of Spike Island.

ACKNOWLEDGMENTS

To all of my wonderful family and loved ones: still love you, see last year's acknowledgments for further. Special mention to Colm, who had to live with me while I was writing this and was extremely tolerant.

Much love and thanks due to people who have been endlessly supportive, including but not limited to Aisling, Graham, Chris (who still texts me when I'm busy), the WAP who got a dedication this time and therefore don't get mentioned by name, Darren and the *Blades in the Dark* cult, the book club at Costigans, and Jamie for visiting and talking about Kenneth Branagh's directorial choices. Thanks to Richy Craven for being sound and also congrats for having his own debut book out right now!!!

Stevie Finegan at Zeno remains a wonderful person and agent, although I got fewer pictures of dogs this year, but I did get very prompt replies to all my inane emails.

Thank you again to Sarah Hodgson at Atlantic and Anna Kaufman at PRH for being extremely patient when the first draft I handed in was a bucket of shit and had to be basically entirely rewritten (and for not themselves using the term "bucket of shit," because they're very clever and professional).

Many hands at both publishing houses were kind enough to touch this book. On the US side I am indebted to production editor Kayla Overbey, copy editor Lyn Rosen, Hayley Jozwiak and Robin Witkin for proofreading, interior designer Nicholas Alguire, cover designer Mark Abrams and cover illustrator Matt Saunders, publicist Kelsey Curtis, and marketer Stevie Pannenberg. Of all of these, I'd like to particularly highlight the copy editor and the proofreaders, who all put in heroic efforts in pointing out how much I still say *actually* and write *alright* instead of *all right*.

Shout-out to the developers of *PowerWash Simulator* and *Immortals Fenyx Rising*, both games that I put many hours into in 2023 in the pursuit of calm. Similarly, I read a lot of fantastic books in 2023, and you're all great.

Mega shout-out to the collegiate and lovely Irish crime authors and to the Spike Island Literary Festival (organized by Michelle Dunne, a neighbor of mine).

Biggest thanks of all for anyone who bought my first book. You're my favorite.

ALSO BY

ALICE BELL

GRAVE EXPECTATIONS

Almost-authentic medium Claire and her best friend,
Sophie, agree to take on a seemingly simple job at a crum-
bling old manor in the English countryside: performing a
séance for the family matriarch's eightieth birthday. The
pair have been friends since before Sophie went missing when they were seventeen. Everyone else is convinced
Sophie simply ran away, but Claire knows the truth. Claire
knows Sophie was murdered because Sophie has been
haunting her ever since. Despite this traumatic past, Claire
and Sophie are still unprepared for what they encoun-
ter when they arrive at the manor: a ghost, tragic and
unrecognizable, and clearly the spirit of someone killed
in a rage at the previous year's party. Given her obsession
with crime shows, Claire decides they're the best people to
solve the case. And with the help of the only obviously not-
guilty members of their host family—sexy ex-policeman
Sebastian and far-too-cool nonbinary teen Alex—they
launch an investigation into which of last year's guests
never escaped the manor's grounds. As Claire desperately
tries to keep a lid on the shameful secret that would definitely alienate her new friends, the gang must race against
their own incompetence to find the murderer before the
murderer finds them.

Fiction